WHERE YOU
Belong

New York Times and *USA Today* Bestselling Author
KRISTEN PROBY

&
AMPERSAND
PUBLISHING, INC.

Where You Belong

THE BLACKWELLS OF MONTANA

KRISTEN PROBY

&
AMPERSAND
PUBLISHING, INC.

WHERE YOU BELONG

A Blackwells of Montana Novel

Kristen Proby

Copyright © 2025 by Kristen Proby

Content Warning

Your mental health is always the most important thing. Please be advised that there is mention of suicide of a parent, not on page, and suicide of a spouse and/or friend, also not on page.

For a full list of triggers, please go to my website.

https://www.kristenprobyauthor.com/potential-trigger-content-warnings

Dedication

This is for anyone who feels like they can't catch a break. I see you.
It's going to get better.

Dear Reader,

I can't believe it's time to say goodbye to another amazing family. I have to tell you, spending the past year with the Blackwells has changed my life. This family made me a better person. They absolutely made me a better writer. Saying farewell and good luck to them is bittersweet. Spending the past two years in Bitterroot Valley, Montana, has been an absolute joy. What an amazing group of people that I got to introduce us all to! From the minute Erin Montgomery set foot in town and decided to stay way back in the beginning, until the epilogue of this book, I've been absolutely in love with every single character. They made me laugh and cry. They definitely challenged me every single day. And they will always be with me. Don't worry, this isn't goodbye for good. We'll catch glimpses of these families in the series to come, and I'm excited for that.

But in the meantime, grab yourself something delicious to drink and find a cozy spot, and let me introduce you to Brooks and Juliet...

Love,

Kristen

Spicy Girls Book Club

TBR

Sinful King by Natalie Kane
War by Brittanée Nicole
Be With Me by Gabrielle Sands
Over the Moon by Laura Pavlov
His Tesoro by Emilia Rossi
At the Edge of Surrender by AL Jackson
Play Along by Liz Tomforde
The Empress by Michelle Heard
Handsome Devil by LJ Shen
Chasing Forever by Piper Rayne

Prologue

BROOKS

Fifteen Years Ago

"So they're delivering the flowers?" I ask Mom while I tap my pocket for the fortieth time in the past five minutes.

The ring's still there.

"Yes. In thirty minutes. Sweetheart, we have this handled." She pats my cheek, and her eyes fill with tears.

"Don't do that."

"You're my baby, and you're about to ask that girl to marry you, so I'm allowed to shed a tear or two. Are you sure this is what you want? You're both so young, Brooks."

I've never been more positive about anything in my life.

I've loved Juliet, my wildfire, since I was sixteen.

More than five years. She's it for me. The beginning and the end, and I want to marry her.

I need to marry her.

"Yes, I'm sure."

"She's not even out of college yet. You have so much time ahead of you. Let her graduate, come home, and then propose. That's only a few months away."

"Mom." I kiss her on the head, and she wraps her arms around my middle, giving me a hug. "I know you worry. But everything's fine. We'll get engaged now, and with everyone's help, I can get the house fixed up by the time she gets home from college."

"I'm glad you seem to have it all figured out." She pats my chest and steps away. "Everything will be ready by the time you get here. Flowers, the food, everything is ready."

I smile at her. "Thanks, Mom."

"Of course. You're my baby." She winks at me, and I step outside, where my brothers toss around a football and Dad cleans the grill.

After I take Jules to the spot I have planned and propose, we'll come back here for a celebratory dinner with my family. Her mom can't come because she's working the night shift at the hospital, but she said she'd try to get off work early to stop by.

It'll be a small party for now, and that's fine. I'll give her a big wedding later.

"I ordered the lumber for that bathroom," Dad says. He's excited to help me renovate the little house I bought.

Thank God. Because no way could I afford to hire it

out, and I want it mostly done by the time she comes home for good in a few months. The house isn't *that* bad. Nothing a new bathroom, flooring, paint, and elbow grease can't fix up.

"Thanks." I pat Dad on the shoulder, then check the time. "I have to go."

"Good luck, buddy." He grins at me, and I saunter down the steps, wave at my siblings, then hop on my Harley after making sure I have her helmet and leathers with me.

My wildfire loves the bike.

When I pull up to Juliet's mom's house and cut the engine, I frown when she doesn't come bounding out of the house with a big smile for me. Shit, I haven't seen her since Christmas, and even that trip was cut short. I'm anxious to get my hands on her.

I'm going to kiss the fuck out of her.

And if she doesn't get her fine ass out here, I'll push her back to her bedroom and fuck her six ways to Sunday, and while that'll definitely be happening at some point today, I have a plan to execute first.

Shit, I've been working my ass off at Old Man Hanson's garage for the past two years to make today happen. Saved every dime, worked overtime, and took side jobs. I need to get this ring out of my pocket and on her finger.

I pat the pocket again, then knock on the door.

No one answers.

The fuck?

I knock again, and this time the door swings open, and Jules is there, but instead of a big smile, she's crying.

"Whoa. Baby, what's wrong?"

She's got her phone to her ear, but I don't care. I immediately pull her against me, rubbing my hand up and down her back.

"No, don't let him do that."

Fuck. Me. Sideways.

I know exactly who she's talking about.

If this motherfucker ruins this for me, I'll hunt him down and kill him myself.

"I don't care how you have to get in there, break down the fucking door," she yells as she pulls out of my arms and stomps into her bedroom. I'm right behind her.

And to my complete horror, she starts to pack her suitcase.

"You're not going back today," I tell her, but she's shaking her head, ignoring me. "Juliet. JULIET."

Her head snaps in my direction, and her face crumples. "I'm so sorry."

"Hang up the phone, Jules."

But she ignores me and keeps talking into the device, and my blood starts to fucking boil.

"What was that noise? Did you break down the door? Good. What's he ... oh, shit. Fuck! Call the ambulance. I'm on my way."

"No. You're not."

She's tossing things into the suitcase, not even glancing my way, and it pisses me the fuck off.

Taking her phone from her hand, I end the call, toss the phone on the bed, and take her by the shoulders, turning her to me.

"Why did you do that?" she demands.

4

"You just got here, baby. You're not going to turn around and go back to Seattle."

"Brooks, I'm so sorry." She leans her forehead against my chest and fists her hands into the fabric at my sides. "I miss you so much, and I needed to see you. But Justin tried to kill himself this morning, so I need to get home—"

Shit. Not this again.

"You *are* home."

"You know what I mean."

Shaking my head, I pace to the other side of the room and turn to glare at my girlfriend. The love of my fucking life. The one person in this world who knows me inside out and loves me anyway.

"Eight people live in that house, Jules. He has people to help him."

Justin has been one of her roommates for the past two years, and I hate the fucker. He manipulates the hell out of my girl, and she refuses to see it.

He's the reason she went back to college early at Christmas.

He's the reason she ends our evening calls before either of us is ready.

He's the reason for every fucking fight we have.

"I know, but they can't get through to him like I can. Brooks, I don't want to hurt you, but he could *die*, and that would be on my conscience. I have to go calm down the situation, and then I can come back."

"I need you here." I cross to her and cup her face. "Baby, *I* need you here. I haven't seen you in months. Haven't touched you, held you, kissed you.

5

Christ, we haven't had sex in more than nine months—"

"A man's life is a little more important than sex, Brooks."

I let go of her completely and step away, my heart hammering.

"He manipulates you. That son of a bitch controls you, Juliet."

She shakes her head and pushes her hands through her blond curls. "I can't have this conversation with you again. It always comes back to your jealousy."

"I'm not the jealous one. Isn't it convenient that he pulls this stunt the day you're coming home to *me*, Jules? He did it at Christmas, too."

"He's sick, and—"

"I. Don't. Fucking. Give a shit." My voice is hard and a little mean now, but I can't help it. Christ, my heart is being ripped out of my chest. "I care about *you*, and I see you being used and controlled, and it pisses me off. If you leave here today and go back to him in Seattle, we're done."

Fuck! How did we get here?

Her face goes white.

"Brooks."

"I'm serious. I'm not bluffing. He's bullying you, and I won't just stand by and let it happen. I won't sit here and be second place anymore. I've talked to you about this until I'm blue in the face, but you won't fucking listen, so now I'm telling you that I need you to stay here for the week like we planned. If you choose to go to him, I won't be here anymore."

I swallow hard, feeling like I might throw up. Jesus. *Jesus.*

What is even happening?

My wildfire takes a long, shaky breath, and just when I think she's going to come to her senses, she shakes her head.

"What you're asking isn't fair."

And that's my answer.

"Goodbye, Juliet."

With my heart bleeding outside of my chest, I leave her bedroom and head for the door.

"Brooks!"

"You've made your choice. Better go take care of a man who doesn't need your help."

"That's *not fair.*"

I spin and take her face in my hands. "You want to know what isn't fair? The fact that I was literally minutes away from giving you *everything*, and you just threw it all back in my fucking face. Have a good life, Jules."

I slam my mouth onto hers one last time, then push her away and walk out the door.

Christ.

Jesus fucking Christ.

Now I have to find a way to tell my family that not only aren't we engaged, but she's gone. She's gone, and she's never coming back to me.

Chapter One

JULIET

Present Day

Afterr making sure the deadbolt on my apartment is engaged, I turn to walk down the steps but then spin back around to check that the door is locked again.

I do that three more times before I finally feel confident enough to descend the stairs to the alley behind my restaurant, Sage & Citrus, to start my morning walk.

I never have anything in my ears during my walks. I don't own earbuds or headphones. I never listen to podcasts or audiobooks or music when I take walks. I know that Bitterroot Valley is safe, and that the odds of being mugged during the early morning hours here in town are very low, but that habit has been ingrained in me for years.

I don't like surprises.

I don't do well with being startled.

Besides, this way I can hear the birds waking up, the

tick-tick-tick of the lawn sprinklers, and the occasional car drive by. I like the way my town sounds so early in the day.

I know this town like the back of my hand, yet it's still so foreign to me. I had been away for almost two decades before I finally made my way home. And that's what this tiny town in Montana is.

Home.

But I don't really belong here anymore. I definitely don't fit in. I'm an outsider, a move-in, despite being born here and coming from three generations of Bitterroot Valley citizens. The friendships I had as a child are all gone. I don't have family since Mom passed away about ten years ago, and Dad ... well, Dad's been gone for a long time.

So it doesn't necessarily make sense that when I finally found my freedom and could go anywhere to start over, I chose to come back to the place where I was born, where there seems to be nothing but ghosts of the past that haunt me.

Taunt me.

Remind me that I was stupid and made choices that destroyed me.

However, I knew, deep in my soul, that Bitterroot Valley was the one place on this godforsaken rock hurling through space that could heal me. I need the mountains, the fresh air, and even if they don't want to have anything to do with me, the people who live here, whether they're familiar to me or not. Just knowing that they're nearby soothes me.

Making my way down the block and into the oldest

residential neighborhood in town, I take a deep breath. Fall is fast approaching, but summer is holding on by its fingernails. There's a slight nip in the air this morning, but flowers still bloom, and none of the trees have started to turn quite yet.

I slow my stride just a bit when I get to the corner where my favorite house in town sits. It's funny how when you're a kid, things look bigger. Or, maybe, it's just the memory that's skewed. If you'd have asked me when I was sixteen about this house, I would have told you it's a mansion.

But I've lived in a mansion three times this size, and this house is so much better in every way. So much more of a home than the cold fortress I spent my entire marriage in.

In reality, the house before me is a large older home, white with a red roof and black trim, and it sits on a huge corner lot. Whoever owns it now doesn't seem to like flowers, as there's no landscaping to speak of, but the lawn is cut religiously every Sunday.

This house needs rose bushes and hydrangeas. Maybe lilacs on that one side. A pretty mixed garden in that corner. And in the back, I'd plant a garden with herbs and veggies.

Brooks and I used to talk about this place all the time. We took a lot of walks or went for rides through town, and we often came this way.

"How many bedrooms do you think it has?" I ask as I lean on the open passenger window, letting the cool wind blow through my hair.

"I dunno," Brooks says. "Maybe four? Five?"

"That's a lot of bedrooms. We'd have to have a lot of kids to fill it up."

"Not really. There are five of us kids at my house, so four bedrooms wouldn't be enough. Why, how many kids do you want, Wildfire?"

I grin back at him, see him watching me with those gorgeous hazel eyes. "The right amount to fill up that house."

I shake my head and keep walking. It seems like every corner of this town has memories. But that's the price I have to pay to be here.

To feel safe.

So I'll gladly pay it.

Pulling myself out of *that* funk, I start making a mental list of all of the food I need to order for the restaurant today. It's ordering day, and because my place has become so popular this summer, it will be a big one.

That makes me almost giddy.

I've wanted to open a restaurant like this for as long as I can remember. I have gluten sensitivities. I suspect I have celiac disease, but I've never been diagnosed. However, since I've been working in and using a clean kitchen, I've had minimal issues.

Feeling good is a luxury I'll never take for granted again.

On my way back through downtown, I come across Jackie, the owner of the Sugar Studio, as she sets her chalkboard on the sidewalk.

"Good morning," she says with a big smile. Jackie and my mom were good friends, and she's been one of the few people who's been sincerely excited to have me back home. "How are you, beautiful girl?"

I let her hug me close even though touch is something I'm still getting used to again, and I give her a smile when I pull away.

"I'm doing well, thanks. How are you, Jackie? How's your knee?"

"Meh." Jackie shrugs. "It hurts like a bitch most days, but who has time for knee replacement surgery?"

"Um, *you* need to make time. You're on your feet every day, remember?"

"Oh, trust me, this knee doesn't let me forget it. But I'm okay, sweetie. It's nothing a little ibuprofen can't help with. I have a new gluten-free scone recipe for you. Or, if you want, I can come by one evening, and we can make them in your kitchen."

I love this woman. I know she'd make it for me in *her* kitchen—Jackie makes the best pastries in the state—but her facility isn't gluten-free, so it might make me sick.

Instead, we've spent plenty of time in my restaurant, and her recipes never miss.

"I'd love that. Anytime works for me. I've decided to start closing at four on Sundays."

She tilts her head to the side. "Why's that?"

"Well, working from seven in the morning until nine at night makes for a long-ass week." I chuckle and brush some hair behind my ear.

"You have girls who work for you," she reminds me. "Let them handle a day by themselves so you can take it off."

I wrinkle my nose. "I don't need a whole day. What

would I do with myself? But half a day would be great. Plus, I'd get to see you. I can't wait to try those scones."

She grins at me, but I see the worry in her eyes. "You work too hard, baby girl. Your mama would tell me to make you slow down."

"My mama worked two jobs all my life," I remind her and turn to leave. "So she'd have no room to talk. I'll see you later."

When I get down the block to my place, and before I can walk around to the alley that holds the stairwell that leads to my apartment, movement across the street catches my eye. I see Brooks Blackwell walk out of Bitterroot Valley Coffee Co. with a cup in hand. He doesn't see me at first, so I'm able to take him in.

God, he's beautiful.

Taller and more muscular than he was when I was in college, Brooks grew up very well. Okay, that's the understatement of the year. He's the sexiest man I've ever seen in my life. His jawline is firm and chiseled, and his dark hair a little too long and tousled, as if he just rolled out of bed.

Or had sex.

Fuck, don't think about that.

His deep red T-shirt is tucked into his jeans, showcasing a narrow waist and sculpted abs. But it's always been his arms that make me weak in the knees. That shirt looks like it's a second skin around his biceps.

I know how it feels to have those arms wrapped around me, and there's nothing like it in the whole world.

Suddenly, his eyes come up to mine, and his stride slows, just a smidge. His eyes harden. His jaw clenches.

And then he turns the other way and walks to his garage, as if I don't even exist.

That's the part that tears my heart out.

"You're nothing." His eyes bore into mine, so much anger shooting through him, and landing right on me.

I was invited to his brother Blake's engagement party by Harper, Blake's fiancée. She's a sweetheart and a loyal customer of mine. I love her to death.

She's my friend, and I don't have many of those.

But it's shitty luck that she's marrying Blake because that means that I'll have to be very careful to pick and choose which invitations I accept from her. I don't wish to be anywhere I'm not wanted.

"Holy shit, this salad is *so good*," Harper says with a moan. She sits back and closes her eyes, enjoying her mouthful of salad, and it makes me smile.

My friend is pregnant, and she's been craving this particular meal every day.

I finally stopped charging her for them. They don't cost me much to make, and I didn't want her to go broke.

"So good," Ava, Harper's best friend, echoes. "Like smack-my-ass-and-call-me-Sally good."

I snort out a laugh and shake my head. "I'm glad you

like them. I'm thinking about adding artichoke hearts to that one. What do you think?"

"Yes." Harper nods enthusiastically.

"No." Ava wrinkles her nose. "It's the texture for me. I can't do it."

"Maybe I'll offer it as an add-on." I wink at them and leave them to their lunch. I clear off a table and wipe it down, then head back behind the counter.

My full-service restaurant offers breakfast, lunch, and dinner. Everything is gluten-free, including the bread and pastries, and it's safe for anyone with celiac disease to eat here.

Including me.

The food is pretty good, if I do say so myself.

And I try to rotate things through with the seasons. Now that summer is ending, I'm starting to come up with ideas for fall, but clearly, that salad that Harper's in love with will have to stay forever.

My phone pings in my pocket with a text, making me scowl. Only one person ever texts me these days, and I only keep my phone on me for emergencies.

Pulling it out, I sigh at the message.

Unknown Number: I need two grand.

I keep blocking her number, but she just gets a new one. It's constant. And exhausting. She knows she's only supposed to email me, but she doesn't care.

She's not good with boundaries.

Without replying, I block this one, too, then shove the phone back in my pocket.

"You okay?" Christy asks with a frown.

"I'm great. Just a spam text." I shrug and get to work filling an order for the shrimp tacos that came in through the take-out app. "Hazel's coming in at noon today, and Tandy said she'd be in at four to help with dinner."

"Actually, Tandy just called." Christy winces. "She was doing cartwheels with her niece and sprained her ankle."

I close my eyes and sigh in resignation. "I'll call Erica in."

"Erica is at Yellowstone with her boyfriend," Christy reminds me. "Don't worry about it. I'll stay."

"You've been working doubles all week."

"So have you, boss lady." She winks. "It's fine, I can use the overtime. I have my eye on a pair of shoes that will most likely maim me and make me bleed, but they're *so pretty*."

"Then it sounds like you need them." I pat her on the shoulder. "Thanks for staying. I'll stay, too, and the three of us will be good to go. I have three new hires coming in throughout the month, as long as they don't back out on me. They all want different hours, so I can stagger them throughout the week. I don't think we'll have much of a shoulder season, but I'm not complaining about that."

"This is exactly what this town needed," Christy says. "It's different and fresh, and the food is amazing. So it doesn't surprise me that we're busy. Tandy feels so bad since she knows Erica's gone."

"We'll be fine."

I will never complain about having to put in extra hours or being exhausted from running this place.

17

It's something I never thought I'd have, and it's all mine. I bought the building, free and clear, and I own everything inside it.

No one can take any of it away from me.

And the fact that I'm already doing so well just boosts my confidence and reminds me that despite having moments of doubt, this really is where I'm supposed to be.

Chapter Two

BROOKS

"Uncle Brooks!"

I can't help my grin as my sweet seven-year-old niece, Birdie, comes running into my garage and throws her arms around my legs, hugging me.

"I have oil on my hands, peanut, or I'd pick you up."

"I know." She smiles up at me, and my heart lifts. It always does when she's around. She's the light of my life, and now she has a little brother I love just as much.

Additionally, Blake and Billie are both expecting.

It's about time we had a bunch of babies to spoil around here.

"What are you up to? Are you by yourself? Did you steal your dad's fire truck again?"

Birdie giggles and shakes her head. "I'm not old enough to drive."

"What? You're seventeen, right?"

"I'm seven." She rolls her eyes. "Dad! Uncle Brooks is trying to be funny again."

"Ouch." I chuckle and wash my hands real quick so I can pick my girl up and kiss her soft cheek. "It's good I have you to be honest, Birdie girl."

"You're not too busy today," Bridger observes as he walks in, wearing a baby strapped to his chest. My nephew is fast asleep, sucking his little blue binkie.

"It's just been steady." I shrug. "Not too crazy. What are you all doing? Where's your wife?"

Bridger married Dani almost two years ago. We've all known her pretty much all our lives, and I've never seen my brother happier.

"She's having lunch with the girls." He presses a kiss on the baby's head. "The kids and I took a walk, and we decided to come see you."

"I missed you." Birdie bats her pretty dark eyelashes at me.

"You did?"

She nods and kisses my cheek.

"I just saw you at Sunday dinner last week."

"That was *days ago*."

"You're right. I always miss you, too." I blow a raspberry on her cheek, making her giggle. "I love it when you come see me."

"Did you know there's a restaurant here that's safe for my tummy?"

My eyes move to Bridger, and he watches me with sober eyes.

I fucking hate this.

"Is that right?"

Birdie nods. "I can have *anything* there. Mommy

doesn't have to study the menu and worry that there was cross contamimem."

"Cross contamination?" I ask her, and she nods.

"Well, that's good news. I bet you've missed eating out, haven't you, baby?"

She nods but then shrugs. "It's okay. At least I feel better."

"That's the most important thing."

"Maybe we can go there on a date. Just you and me. Daddy takes Mommy on dates. You should take me on one."

Bridger grins from ear to ear, and I can't help but chuckle at her. "You're my best girl. Of course, I'll take you out."

But I might have to get takeout from the one safe restaurant in town for my peanut.

The baby starts to squirm and fuss, and Bridger sways side to side.

"Someone's about to wake up, need a diaper change, and a bottle. We'd better head home, baby bird."

"Okay." Birdie sighs as if it's the saddest thing ever, then gives me a hug. "Don't work too hard, Uncle Brooks."

"I'll do my best, baby girl."

I set her on her feet, then walk to Bridger so I can kiss the baby.

"Thanks for stopping by."

"Come for dinner tomorrow night. I'm grilling steaks."

"I'll be there."

He nods. Birdie slips her hand in his, and the three of them walk out of my garage.

I'm alone in here today. I have three guys who work for me. My other master mechanic, Gabe, is on vacation with his husband and wife. Mitch took the afternoon off to take his wife to the doctor.

Jake Wild, who just graduated from high school in the spring, worked his ass off for me all summer, but now he's off to college. He'll put hours in for me whenever he's home. I was sorry to see him go.

The kid has one hell of a work ethic.

He had to get it from his dad. Ryan Wild is a billionaire several times over and one of the best men I know. He and Polly are raising one hell of a kid.

I grab a cold bottle of water and drink half of it down before I turn on some music—some Aerosmith today—and get back to the truck I'm working on. I'd like to have it done by the end of the day.

Birdie looked good today. For too long, she was a tiny thing, and she was *so sick*. We couldn't figure out what in the hell was going on, and it really upset Blake, the doctor in the family, that he didn't have answers.

But finally, Birdie was diagnosed with celiac, and now that we know what foods aren't safe for her, we can keep her healthy.

I both love and hate that there is a clean kitchen in our town. I didn't even know what *clean kitchen* meant until everyone in the family had a sit-down with Blake to talk about what Birdie's diagnosis meant, and how we all could protect her.

So yeah, I love that there's a place here where Birdie

can walk in, carefree, and order anything she wants, just like any other kid without food sensitivities.

But I fucking *hate* that it's Juliet who brought it here.

I never spoke to her again after the day she chose to go back to that asshole. Not once. She tried to call me, but I ignored it, and after a while, she gave up. I told my family she was gone, and that was the end of it.

I've never told a soul what actually happened on the day I was supposed to propose to her and start my life with her.

I've done a good job of keeping it all in the past. It took a while, but I eventually dug myself out of the grief and started to feel, to live again. I fixed up the house and still live there. Bought this business from Old Man Hanson, and I've done quite well with it.

I don't date. I'll never be in a committed relationship again.

I do, however, fuck. Usually tourists.

Although, since *someone* moved back to town, I've been in a dry spell. Because I can't stand the thought of touching someone else when she's *right here*.

And that's stupid as fuck because she hasn't been mine in more than fifteen motherfucking years. A lifetime. I don't even know her anymore.

But I can't bring myself to want anyone else, and that's what really pisses me off.

I see her everywhere, and the pull is still there. For the first six months or so that she was back, I never saw her. I don't know how, but I never ran into her at all.

It was fucking bliss.

Now, my wildfire seems to be everywhere I fucking turn.

Jesus, she was even at my brother's engagement party because she and Harper have become friends.

I see her coming out of the grocery store. This morning, she was across the street when I exited the coffee shop.

Everywhere.

Am I being punished for something? And if so, what? Because I did everything right by that woman. I was faithful. I was going to marry her, provide for her, and have a family with her. Fuck, I loved her more than anything.

So why am I being ambushed by her *now*?

I send a text to my customer and let him know that he can pick his truck up tomorrow morning, then I wash my hands and close the shop for the day. I take a quick shower in my shop bathroom. Installing this shower was the best thing I ever did. I don't have to go home covered in grime and grease.

Then I decide to grab dinner at Kay's Diner by myself.

After a short drive across town, I park my truck and walk inside, wave at the server, and take a seat at the bar.

Kay's is an old-fashioned 1950s-style diner. The booths and seats are covered in red vinyl, the floors are black-and-white tile, and old rock-and-roll paraphernalia hangs all over the walls. The jukebox in the corner is pumping out an old Fleetwood Mac tune.

It's a great spot.

"Hey, there," Shirley, one of the servers, says. "Your usual?"

"Please."

I don't have to see the menu. I get the same thing every time. Mushroom burger with fries and a Coke.

"You must be a regular."

I turn to my left and find a pretty little redhead smiling up at me. She's a tiny thing with deep dimples in her cheeks and bright blue eyes.

She's beautiful.

And not at all what I want.

"Might be," I reply.

"I'm Layla," she says.

I just nod and pull my phone out of my pocket to check my email.

"What's your name?" she asks, not giving up.

"Why do you want to know?" I set the phone down and turn back to her.

"I'm obviously really bad at this, but I think you're handsome, and I thought I'd make conversation. That's all." She lifts a shoulder and tucks her hair behind her ear, obviously flirting with me.

"Do you live here?" I ask her.

"No." She shakes her head and smiles again. "I'm visiting from back East. I came to see an old college roommate, but she's busy."

"Do I know the roommate?"

She tips her head to the side. "Probably not. I don't know, actually. Margie Smith?"

I don't know her.

Shaking my head, I take a sip of the cola that was just set in front of me. "Never heard of her."

"Is that good or bad?"

"For the purposes of this conversation?" I tilt my head back and forth. "It's probably good."

"Would you still be talking to me if I told you I lived here?"

"No, ma'am. It's nothing personal."

That makes her laugh, and it's the kind of laugh that grates on my nerves.

"At least you're honest. I'm staying—"

"No." I shake my head, and her face loses the smile. "I'm sure you're nice and probably a great fuck. But I'm not interested."

"Gay?"

I snort, and Shirley sets my basket of food in front of me, then gives me a wink.

"Not that it matters, but no."

"Married? I don't see a ring."

"Sometimes the answer's just no, Layla."

"Huh." Her shoulders slump. "I'm not used to that."

I'm sure you're not, sweetheart.

I have to respect her for not changing seats. She also doesn't try to drag me into any other conversations, and we eat side by side in a comfortable silence. She gets up to leave, but pauses.

"Do you want my number, just in case you change your mind?"

Jesus.

"I won't change my mind. Safe travels, Layla."

She nods and then walks away. Shirley crosses over to hand me my bill.

"You're just breaking hearts all over town, Brooks."

"I didn't break her heart. That's not what she was interested in."

Shirley laughs and takes my credit card.

And now, I really want a glimpse of my wildfire.

Which is stupid as fuck.

Because she's not mine, and I can't have her, and seeing her, even for a second, is not healthy.

But that doesn't mean I don't want it.

So to torture myself after dinner, I drive back into downtown and park in front of Sage & Citrus. I can admit, it's a cute place. It's classy. It looks like something from one of those farmhouse home improvement shows.

And moving back and forth behind the long counter at the back is Juliet.

She's wearing a white T-shirt with a red apron over it. Her blond curls are teased up into a bun, and she has little ringlets that have sprung free that hang around her face.

I want to touch them. My fingertips rub against my thumb involuntarily because all I can think about is touching that soft hair.

Does she still smell like jasmine? Or has she changed her shampoo?

Is anything still the same?

Jules laughs at something someone says, and it makes my heart physically ache. Rubbing my hand over my chest, I start the truck and pull out of the parking spot.

I need to stop this shit. Go back to avoiding her.

Stay away from her.

Because now it'll be weeks before I'll feel like I can breathe again.

Chapter Three

JULIET

"Six hundred dollars?" I stare at the asshole across from me and wish with all my might that I were a violent woman.

Because I'd slap his smug, condescending face.

"Yep," he says and leans his greasy hands on his counter. "Part was a hundred and twenty, and the rest is labor. Had to practically take the engine out to get to it. I know, it's tough."

He shakes his head and presses his lips together, as if he's being sympathetic, but I see the gleam in his eye. He's fucking mocking me.

I look up at the ceiling and wish I hadn't told Christy to go ahead and leave me here. She dropped me off to pick up my piece-of-crap car, but I didn't plan on the repairs costing this much money.

This guy, *Barry*, owns this mechanic shop in Silver Springs, which is roughly thirty minutes from Bitterroot Valley. It's the only auto-repair shop near me that isn't Brooks's place.

Because Brooks made it very clear to me that my car and I are not welcome there.

So this is my only option. And I'm pretty sure Barry has been dicking me around, but I'm not a mechanic. I watched Brooks work on cars most of my teenage years, but I didn't pay attention. I was too busy ogling his muscles.

With my heart in my throat, I pay with my credit card, and then I'm finally on my way home. I'm now about five grand in on repairs on this heap. It's probably not worth it, but I can't afford to buy something new.

I mean, I *could* afford it, but I refuse to touch any of the money left in the trust from my dead husband.

Fuck that shit. I don't want anything from him.

"It'll be fine," I mutter to myself as I turn onto the highway and head back to Bitterroot Valley. "I just can't renovate the upstairs bathroom for a few more months. No big deal. Maybe I should just join the gym and take showers there."

But the idea of packing a bag and going to the other side of town to shower doesn't excite me. It's not that the shower I have isn't usable, but it's so tiny, and as much as I've scrubbed it, it never feels clean.

I also need to insulate and drywall the apartment upstairs. The summer was brutal in the heat, but at least I spent most of my time downstairs in the nicely air-conditioned restaurant. I even slept down there a few nights when the upstairs was sweltering.

Now, though, the weather is calming down, and there's a nice breeze that blows through in the evenings. This morning, it was even a little chilly up there when I woke up, and it felt great. However, this winter could pose a problem if I don't complete the walls.

The last owners used the upstairs for storage. It's been framed in as an apartment, but no one ever needed to finish it.

Until now.

I've never been a DIY kind of girl, but I'm about to be. I can watch YouTube and figure it out. I bet I can even rent some tools somewhere. I'm going to make it work because I sank all of the money I was comfortable taking from Justin into my business. I need to live above the restaurant.

And once it's all fixed up, it'll be so amazing.

It's just going to be a process, and that's okay. I've lived in far, far worse.

My car gets me home without any trouble, and I park it in the alley, in my spot behind the restaurant, then cross to the stairs to my place so I can change for work. It's been raining pretty much constantly since last night, so the metal steps are a little slick. I slip, and my shin scrapes along the teeth on the metal steps, making me cry out in pain.

"Oh shit, that hurt." I turn and sit my butt on the steps, not caring at all that I'm getting wet, so I can catch my breath and breathe through the pain.

When I pull up my jeans, I see blood running down my leg.

"Fuck."

Do I have bandages? Probably not.

So rather than climb up the rest of the way, I return to my car and drive the few blocks over to the pharmacy.

I'm sure I'm a mess. Wet hair, wet ass, and the blood is soaking through the front of my jeans, which makes me panic a little.

I love these jeans. I don't want to ruin them. There's a little hole from my fall, but I can patch that.

I limp inside, make my way to the bandage aisle, grab the supplies I need, and take them to the checkout counter.

Just as I turn to walk out to my car, I see Brooks stride in, and my heart sinks.

Really? He has to see me today? When I'm all bloody and limping and look like a drowned rat?

His eyes narrow and sweep down my body, and when he sees the blood, his hands fist, and he stomps over to me.

"What happened?"

He's talking to me? Voluntarily?

My mouth falls open, but no noise comes out. He hasn't started a conversation with me in more than fifteen years. My heart thumps, sending blood roaring through my ears.

"Juliet, what happened?"

His voice is hard. Deeper than it was all those years ago.

"I swear to God, Jules—"

"I just fell on my stairs. They were slick. It's fine." I lick my lips and move to step around him, needing to get home to clean myself up and get to work. Plus, being near him makes me ... sad.

But when I get to my car, I startle because he's standing behind me.

"Uh, what—"

"Let me see it."

Shaking my head, I unlock the door and open it, toss the bag of bandages and antiseptic cream onto the passenger seat, and turn to face the man who broke my heart all those years ago. We're standing in the rain, but neither of us seems to notice that we're getting soaked to the bone.

Or care.

"I'll be fine. Thanks for asking, though."

He frowns and swallows hard, then looks back down at my leg. "You're limping."

"Yeah, I cut my leg." I tilt my head to the side, watching him. If I didn't know better, I'd say he cares. That he's worried.

But I know that's not the case.

"I need to clean this up, try to salvage these jeans, then I have to get to work. But really. Thanks for asking."

His jaw clenches, and then he nods once and walks away.

Aside from when I made him talk to me at Harper and Blake's engagement party, that's the most he's said to me in *years*.

After he disappears inside, I drive back to my place and carefully climb the stairs to the apartment, where I have to rush to change and get ready for work. After a quick internet search, it appears that soaking the bloodied jeans in ice water may help with the stains. So I go downstairs to grab a bucket of ice, then return upstairs to soak the denim before I go to work.

Tandy's ankle is doing better, and she's with me this morning, serving breakfast. Hazel will be here in an hour.

And it's a good thing because it's a busy morning.

But by the time lunch is over, things calm down considerably, and I decide that after the shit morning I had, I deserve a trip to the bookstore. I've finished everything I previously bought, and I think there's a new book club read to buy.

I don't actually attend book club meetings. I don't want to make things weird for Billie, the youngest of the Blackwell siblings, and the only girl. I always thought of Billie as a younger sister, and I'm so fucking proud of the badass woman she's become. Not only is she absolutely gorgeous, with curves for days, beautiful long dark hair, and a fashion sense that would make any woman just a little jealous but she has also opened this brick-and-mortar bookstore, which specializes in romance and women's fiction, and it's thriving.

The store itself is gorgeous inside, with rows of pretty bookshelves and tables set with fun accessories, such as candles, bookmarks, and water bottles. The inviting chairs situated by the windows almost always have someone curled up in them, reading or working on a laptop.

She's brought a lot of joy to this town.

I walk across the street, hardly limping at all now, and push inside.

"Hey, you," Bee calls out with a wave. "I'll be right there."

"I'm just browsing," I assure her, and immediately pick up this month's Spicy Girls Book Club read. *Over the Moon* by Laura Pavlov. I do enjoy small-town romance, so this will be a fun one.

Then I proceed to make my way around the entire store, checking out everything new, and then approach the checkout with about a half dozen new finds.

"Oh, this one by Maggie Rawdon is *so good*," Bee says. "You'll love it. How are you, Jules?"

"I'm doing just fine. How are you, Bug?" I've called her that since she was little. Because she *is* as cute as a bug.

Although I don't know why anyone thought up that expression.

"Aside from super pregnant and ready to be done with swollen ankles? I can't complain." She glows as she smiles over at me.

"You're feeling okay?"

Bee nods and pulls a bag out from under the counter for my books. "Yeah, I'm okay. Pregnancy is rough, but at least I'm not throwing up every ten minutes anymore. Connor's making me cut my hours down to part-time in the store starting next month, and then I'll do admin from home with my feet up."

Billie's married to a literal billionaire. A sexy, Irish, obsessed-with-her billionaire.

She's living in a romance novel.

"I think that's the sweetest thing I've ever heard."

"He's kind of swoony," she admits. "So you bought the book club book. Does this mean you're actually coming to the meeting this time?"

The smile falls from my face.

"Bug, you know that I don't want to step on any toes."

That's code for, *I know your family hates me, and I don't want to make things horrible for you.*

"Number one, you're a paying customer, Jules. Two, my brother never comes in here. It's not like you'll be sitting next to him or something. Three, I love you and want you to come. It's so much fun. You're right across the street, so if you drink too much wine, you can just walk home."

I chuckle and wrinkle my nose. I want to come. I want to so badly. I know that Harper and Ava attend, and I know some of the other girls, too, from back in the day.

"It's Friday night at seven," Billie continues. "And you're more than welcome to join us. It's fun. You already know most of the people. Even Jackie comes."

I didn't know that.

"She does?"

"Yep, and she brings treats with her."

"I could bring some gluten-free options, if you want."

"Oh, that would be awesome! Perhaps you and Jackie could alternate bringing the snacks. Or you each bring one. Honestly, you don't have to bring anything, just come. Chat about sexy books and laugh with us for a while."

I don't remember the last time I truly laughed.

"Okay."

Billie's eyes go wide. "I'm sorry, what did you just say?"

"If you know for sure that your brother won't be here, and it's okay with the others if I come, then yes. I'd like to join you."

Just thinking about it makes me sweaty. Justin would be *so pissed*. There's no way he'd allow it.

He's dead, Juliet. He doesn't have a say. You don't have to ask permission.

"Holy shit, this is the best day of my life." Billie claps her hands. "I promise you'll have so much fun."

"I know I will. Thanks, Bug. I'd better get back over there."

With a bag full of new books and a little bit of hope that book club might work out after all, I walk back across the street and around to the staircase to carry these upstairs before heading back down to get ready for the dinner rush.

But when I reach the stairs, I pause.

Because on each step, the metal has been covered with anti-slip stair treads.

Blinking back tears, I reach down to touch them. They're real. I'm not hallucinating.

Brooks.

He's the only one who knew I fell this morning. He's the only one who knew it was because my stairs were slick.

He fixed them.

He made sure that I'm as safe from that particular injury as I can be, and he did it all without being asked.

Oh God.

What does this mean? Does it mean anything at all? He's so angry with me, there's no way he would do something for me out of the goodness of his heart. He's made it clear that I'm nothing to him. I don't exist in his world.

But then why did he do this? It's so damn confusing. I loved him with all my heart. He was everything to me, and I did everything wrong. I let someone else manipulate me, lie to me, and ruin the best thing in my life.

I was supposed to marry Brooks. Have a family with him. Grow old with him.

Instead, I lost him because I believed a liar who convinced me that if he didn't have my attention, he'd end his own life.

And Justin knew that he could do that to me because suicide is my trigger. That'll happen to someone after they find their own father hanging in their garage at the tender age of twelve.

Brooks saw it as me choosing Justin over him, but that's not what it was at all. I truly thought I was saving a man's life.

But I lost the one person who's ever truly loved me instead. Not just lost him but made him *hate* me with every fiber of his being.

And now, after all this time, he's helped me, and I don't know why. I should march myself right over to his garage and ask him.

I won't do that, though. Because being on the receiving end of Brooks's harsh words is almost worse than anything Justin did to me.

Okay, maybe not.

But it hurts all the same.

So I send out a silent thank-you to the universe and

climb the stairs to my apartment, where I tuck my new books away and get back to work.

Chapter Four

BROOKS

Buying a second house was a dumb fucking idea.

Even if they are right across the street from each other.

When the big corner house came up for sale last year, I bought it without really considering the consequences. It's Juliet's dream home, and I couldn't stand the thought of anyone else buying it.

She didn't even live here when I made the offer. I just *did it.* I blame it on temporary insanity because that's the only explanation for a spur-of-the-moment property purchase.

Now, Jules is back, and every time I walk inside this house, it's just another reminder of her. I've never lived in it. I still live in the house across the street that I bought all those years ago.

It's time I fixed up this big home and sold it. I don't need it. I don't want to be a landlord. I have no idea what I was thinking when I purchased it.

Again, temporary insanity.

And maybe a moment of feeling sentimental over a girl who didn't choose me in the end.

I'm a fucking sucker.

Up before dawn, I'm standing on the porch of the big house with a can of red paint, brushing it on the door. Next, I'll repair and paint the porch. Because when you buy a house that was built a hundred years ago, you buy all the problems that come with it. It's pretty, with good bones, but it needs a lot of work. Work I don't have time for.

After applying the second coat, I walk home to let it dry, pour myself a cup of coffee, and stare out the window.

You're turning into a motherfucking stalker. Shaking my head, I sip the coffee. I might be disgusted with myself, but that doesn't mean I'll walk away from this window. Just like the other night, I want to catch a glimpse of her. I don't like her. I don't want to have anything to do with her, but dammit, she's like a freaking drug.

It's ridiculous.

Sure enough, not five minutes later, Jules comes walking down the block. She takes this walk every morning at this time. Sometimes she looks sad. Other times, it looks like she's talking to herself. But every single time, she slows down to look at the house across the street, and I know that she strolls into the past every time, thinking about the conversations we had when we were kids about the place.

She's wearing green shorts, and I can see where she tore the flesh on her shin. It's scabbed up, bruised and looks like it hurt like a bitch. Seeing her with blood on her made my own blood boil. I may not trust her, but my wildfire being hurt is not a fucking option.

So I fixed her steps. I shouldn't have. She's not my problem, but the thought of her hurting herself like that again doesn't sit well with me.

Today, she comes to a complete stop and turns her back to me, facing the freshly painted door, her hands on her hips. She's on my side of the street, right in front of my house.

What was supposed to be our house.

I have the window open, so I can hear her breath coming fast from the exercise. Her ass looks damn fucking irresistible in those green shorts, and I want to lean in and kiss her cheek.

Press my face to her neck.

Pull her against me.

For fuck's sake. I don't like her, can't have her, yet it's like every molecule in my body is a magnet and she's the only thing it seeks.

"Something's different," she whispers, and the rasp of her voice goes right to my cock.

Christ Jesus.

"The door. They painted the door." She swallows and leans forward, like she's trying to see it better, and in doing so, she pushes her ass out farther. Her long, lean legs stretch, showing me muscle and smooth skin, and I have to adjust my cock in my pants. "I like the red. Jazzes it up."

Why am I suddenly proud of myself for choosing a fucking paint color?

"Needs flowers," she mutters to herself, then shrugs a shoulder, as if she's pushing that thought aside. Jules always did talk to herself. I always found it endearing. "I wonder what's behind that window on the second floor."

My eyes follow her gaze, and I take a sip of my coffee.

It's a bathroom. Needs to be gutted.

Suddenly, her phone rings, and Juliet jumps into the air and lets out a little squeak. She's shifted so I can see her profile, and her brows pull together as she looks at the screen.

Who the fuck is calling her at six in the morning?

"What." Her voice is devoid of any emotion as she answers the call. I tilt my head to the side, intrigued.

I've never heard that tone from her before.

"No. You're not allowed to call or text me. Email only. You know the conditions. I'm not sending you any more money this month. Figure it out for yourself."

She hangs up and starts walking again, but after she slips the phone in her back pocket, she wipes a tear from her cheek, and that pisses me off.

Who the fuck just made my wildfire cry?

"How much money do you think I have?" Birdie asks me. She's perched on my lap in the backyard of Bridger and Dani's house, eating a hot dog, having a conversation like she's thirty.

43

"About ten thousand," I reply and take a bite of my steak. "Give or take."

"Not that much," she says and bites her hot dog. "I could buy a house with that much."

My lips twitch, and I lean in to kiss her cheek. "Okay, I give. How much do you have?"

"Eight dollars and twenty-seven cents. I'm saving."

"What are you saving for?"

She scrunches up her nose and looks around to see if anyone is listening.

This should be good.

"A puppy."

I lift an eyebrow. "You're just gonna go out and buy a puppy without your parents knowing about it?"

"I can hide her in my room."

I nod slowly, as if I'm thinking it over. "How are you going to feed her? Take her out to go potty and exercise?"

"When they aren't looking."

I continue nodding. "Are you gonna steal your mom's car to go get it?"

"No, I was hoping *you* would give me a ride."

"You want me to be an accomplice to Puppygate?" I shake my head. "I don't think I can do that, baby bird. Your mama would be mad at me, and I do my best to keep the women in my life happy."

"*I'm* a woman in your life," she says, so perfectly calmly, you'd think we were negotiating the price of a used car. "And it would make me happy to help me get my puppy. Her name is Tabitha."

Jesus, she's too smart for her own good.

"You've already named her?"

"Of course. She's a rottweiler."

I blink down at her. "Baby, you know those dogs are *huge*, right? There's no hiding that from anyone."

"She'll be quiet."

I chuckle and kiss the top of her head. "I love you."

"Is that a yes?"

"That's a heck no."

"Aw, come on! I bet Uncle Blake would do it."

"Then you should go charm Uncle Blake."

She narrows her pretty eyes at me, then hops off my lap and goes in search of a different uncle she can manipulate. Bridger said he was throwing a couple of steaks on the grill the other day, but it turned into a full family dinner, and I'm not complaining.

I love my family.

"She try to get you to help her with the dog?" Bridger asks as he sits next to me.

"Oh, so it's *not* the secret she thinks it is."

"She's already tried with Dad and Beckett." He shakes his head, and I snort out a laugh.

"Here I thought I was special. Are you going to get her the puppy?"

My brother's eyes sober, and he looks over at his wife, who's rocking the baby back and forth while she chats with the other girls. "No. Dani's finally okay with the cat that adopted us. I don't think I could get her comfortable with a dog. Especially not the big one that Birdie wants."

I fucking hate the asshole father of Dani and her siblings that abused them to the point where they're afraid of common household pets. He deserved a far worse death than what he got.

"I think Mom and Dad might get a mid-sized dog this winter, and they'll call it Birdie's dog. That might pacify her." Bridger takes a drink of his water. "How are you?"

"Never better."

His eyes narrow. "We don't lie to each other around here."

Shaking my head, I push my empty plate away and sit back in the chair, watching my brother across the table.

"I'm fine."

"Oh my God, I forgot to tell you," Billie says, catching my attention, although she's not talking to me. She's with Dani, Skyla, and Harper. "Jules is coming to book club on Friday! I finally talked her into it."

I feel my jaw tighten and Bridger's eyes on me.

"Still fine?" he asks.

"I don't attend book club," I remind him. "So it makes no difference to me where she goes."

Bridger nods and watches Birdie flit around, talking to everyone.

"It has to fucking suck," he says at last.

"What?" I might pretend I don't know what he's talking about, but I do.

And yeah, it fucking sucks.

"Having her here again."

"It was a long time ago." *It feels like it was fucking yesterday.* "What she does isn't any of my business."

"We've had takeout from her place a few times. Birdie loves it."

"Good. I'm a fan of anything safe for our peanut."

"Jules told me that she thinks she might have celiac,

too, but she's not sure. She started the restaurant because of her own sensitivities."

Is she sick? I don't remember her having stomach issues when we were younger.

"Sounds like it was the right thing for her to do then."

"You know—"

"Why are we talking about this?" I ask him. "I don't want to discuss my ex any more than you want to talk about yours."

"Point taken," he says, holding up his hands in surrender. Dani walks over to us, and she looks a little tired as she kisses the top of the baby's head.

"He's getting heavy," she says, and I stand before my brother can.

"I'll take him."

Dani carefully maneuvers the sleeping infant into my arms, then kisses my cheek.

"Thanks, Uncle Brooks." She grins, then walks back to talk to the women.

The baby doesn't even stir as I sit back down and get him comfy against my chest.

"You look good with a baby," Bridger says. "You should have a few."

"Sure. I'll just go make that happen."

He smirks. "There are ways."

Shaking my head, I drag my fingertip down Bryce's round cheek. The one person I could see myself having a family with is out of the question.

I would have had a dozen babies with her. That was one more thing I mourned after I lost her.

Bryce sighs and fists my T-shirt in his little hand.

"You guys are all having babies, and I get to love on them, spoil the shit out of them, and then give them back." Bryce makes a little sound, and I rub my hand over his back to calm him. "How many more are you going to have?"

"I think this is enough," Bridger says with a laugh. "Two's plenty. But Billie and Harper are adding to the clan soon."

"Me too," Beck says as he and Blake join us. "Skyla's pregnant."

"Holy shit." Bridger stands to hug Beckett, and I shake his hand.

"Congrats," I tell him.

I'm happy for all of my siblings. They've all found people to love. To spend their lives with. And they all chose well.

"That's a whole lot of hormones in the family at one time," Blake says with a cringe. "A *lot*."

"At least they're a little staggered," Bridger says. "Hey, where's Connor?"

"Ireland," Blake says. "Until Saturday."

We all glance over at Billie, who's sitting with her feet up and snuggling Birdie. And all of us brothers are wondering the same thing: Does that mean she's not sleeping well?

Billie's always been a night owl, but it's more than that. She doesn't sleep much at all. Or, she didn't, until Connor.

And I don't even want to think about what happens in their bed. I'm the oldest, and Billie is my baby sister.

Nope, not thinking about it.

Two hours later, I swing through the plant nursery on the way home. They're a few minutes from closing, and Mr. Dugan, the owner, meets me by the hanging baskets.

"Summer's almost over," he says as he props his hands on his hips.

I don't even know what the fuck I'm doing here.

"Yeah, I know. Any of these hardy enough to make it through fall? I want to add some color to my porch."

He nods and points out one with orange and yellow blooms. "Mums should last you into October, especially on a porch or something like that."

"I'll take three of those," I say with a nod, and stow them in the back of my truck before heading home.

Rather than pull into my driveway, I stop in across the street at the big house. First, I have to walk over to my garage and find some hooks and a drill. Then I cross back over, climb the steps of the porch, and install three hooks above the railing, eyeballing the spacing. Returning to the truck bed, I pull out all three baskets, then hang them on the hooks.

Stepping off the porch, I back away to examine my handiwork. They seem to be pretty evenly spaced, and the yellow and orange look nice with the red door.

She wanted flowers.

She got fucking flowers.

I drive right across into my own driveway and cut the engine. Then, with anger simmering in my veins, I walk inside.

What the fuck am I doing?

49

She's not my problem. If she wants flowers, she can buy herself fucking flowers. They don't need to hang on a house I'm trying to fix up so I can sell.

But dammit, ever since I heard her say it this morning, I couldn't stop thinking about it. It's as if I'm on autopilot, and whatever Juliet wants, she gets. Like my brain hasn't read the *we don't give a shit about Juliet* memo.

And it's pissing me the fuck off.

First, the steps, and now goddamn flowers.

What's next?

Shaking my head, I head to my bathroom to shower. I don't want to do things that I think will make her happy. I don't want to feel bad for her, or help her, or *care* about her.

Fuck, I don't trust her.

But dammit. *Dammit.*

Her eyes are still so fucking kind, and she looked so lost when she hurt her leg.

I turn on the water, and when it's hot enough, I step under the spray and let it pound on my head and stream down my face.

And here, in this three-by-six-foot box with the water hammering down on me, I can admit that she's still beautiful. Fuck, that curly blond hair should be wrapped around my fist. Her lips, so full and pouty, should be on my cock.

"Jesus."

I fist the base of my dick and give it a tug with thoughts of my wildfire front and center.

The way her eyes light up and she smiles when she's being particularly sarcastic.

The way she bit her lip when I spoke to her at the pharmacy.

The way she looks wearing those shorts with her long legs on display.

And I grunt out her name as I come against the tile.

Fuck.

I need to stop this. Nothing good can come of it. She chose, and it wasn't me.

But goddammit, a part of me still wants her.

It's fucking torture.

Chapter Five

JULIET

"Thanks for the ride, you guys."

Ava grins at me through the rearview mirror. When they heard I had to take my car to get fixed—*again*—Harper and Ava offered to pick me up on their way to book club, which was so kind, and I was not about to pass it up. There aren't exactly a lot of rideshares around here. I usually have one of the girls from work do it and pay them an hour's wage for it, but this way, I didn't have to bother them.

"Why do you take it all the way to Silver Springs?" Ava asks. "Even my brothers won't go to that shop. They use Brooks. He's right down the street from you."

"Yeah, well, I'm not exactly welcome there."

Ava frowns. "Why?"

"History." I shrug, and Harper sighs. I don't know how much either of these girls knows about my history with Brooks. I assume that Blake has told Harper all about what went down and why we broke up. "I wish I could afford to replace that stupid car. It would have been cheaper than all of these damn repairs."

"I bought my car from Brooks," Harper says. "It's not pretty, but it runs great."

"Well, hopefully, this will be the last repair for a while."

"I hope so, too," Harper replies. "Your dress is adorable, by the way."

I glance down at the red sundress that I splurged on earlier this summer. We're having some warm late summer days, and I decided to break this out for book club since I don't get to wear it to work and haven't had any other occasions to get a little dressed up.

"Thanks. You guys ... I'm a nervous wreck."

"Why?" Ava frowns at me in the mirror. "Didn't you read the book?"

That makes me laugh. "I read it. I loved it. Thanks to Billie's recommendations, I really enjoy Laura Pavlov's stories. No, that's not it."

"Then what?" Harper asks as Ava turns down the main street to the bookstore.

"I'm not good around people," I finally admit, and even that makes me nervous. Boy, I was conditioned more than I realized. "I was in a relationship with someone who restricted who I could talk to and interact with. I haven't had friends since college. So being social isn't easy for me anymore."

Ava parks, but none of us gets out of the car for a minute. Damn, what are they thinking? Did I say too much?

"I'm so sorry that happened to you," Harper finally says. "What a dick."

You have no idea.

"So he'd be pretty pissed if he knew you were doing this, I assume?" Ava asks.

"Oh, beyond pissed. Actually, I wouldn't go in the first place."

"But you're no longer together," Harper clarifies.

I shake my head.

"Then you have nothing to be nervous about." Ava reaches back to lay her hand on my arm. I don't even flinch at the touch. Not that Justin ever physically hurt me, but he rarely touched me, either. "You know most of these people, and we have a great time."

"Okay." My response is quiet, and with their pep talk in the front of my mind, we get out of the car and walk into the store.

Billie has arranged the chairs in a circle. There's a folding table set up nearby that has wine, soda, and water, along with platters of some chocolate goodness from Jackie.

"This is the *best* book club ever," Billie says as she immediately throws her arms around me and hugs me close. My nervous system comes down a notch, taking me from fight or flight to simple butterflies. "I'm so happy you're here, Jules."

I'm still damn nervous. But this welcome has helped considerably. I take a deep breath and grab a bottle of water from the table before I find a seat.

Harper immediately sits to my right, and Ava sits on the other side of her.

"What are you reading right now?" Harper asks me.

"I just finished a Mafia romance called *His Tesoro* by Emilia Rossi. I loved it so much, I might read it again."

"Holy shit, I need that," Ava says, pulling her phone out. "There. Just downloaded it. Mafia is my jam."

"It's a marriage of convenience story, and the heroine has medical challenges that made me love her even more. And the hero? Holy shit, I swooned."

"Sold," Harper agrees.

"Billie carries it," I tell them.

"I heard my name," Billie says as she sits to my left. "What did I do?"

"*His Tesoro*," I tell her, and she immediately nods.

"Yes, everyone needs to read that one. Highly recommend."

And that's how the evening goes. We discuss books, specifically the Laura Pavlov novel we all read, but it segues into other books as well. I love that I've read many of the books talked about and added others to my list.

I recognize so many of the people here, and no one looks at me weird. No one tells me I don't belong.

"I'm happy you came tonight," Skyla says later when people have broken up into little groups, just naturally forming little conversation groups as the meeting winds to a close. "And I love your restaurant."

"Oh, thanks." Skyla's gorgeous red hair is braided, and I could listen to her speak with her Irish accent all day long. "It's a relief that it's going well."

"I'm sure it is," she replies with a soft smile. "But you're an excellent chef, and the restaurant is cute as a button. Will you have the fajitas on the fall menu?"

"I think I'm going to switch it up," I tell her.

"Wait." Harper turns her head and glares at me. "You're not taking away my salad, right?"

I snort, and Skyla giggles next to me. "No, your salad is safe for all of eternity."

"Thank fuck." Harper sighs and rubs her tiny baby bump.

"Apparently, baby hormones are a thing."

"Oh, they are," Skyla agrees. "Beck and I just found out that I'm expecting as well."

"Oh my God, that's so wonderful." I take her hand and give it a squeeze. "Beckett is the *best*, Skyla. I'm so happy for you."

"He *is* the best," she agrees. "And thank you."

I loved all of the Blackwell siblings. Each one of them was like a brother or sister to me, and I still miss them. It helps that I get to see Billie here at the bookstore, but I rarely see the guys. That would be weird.

Beckett was always a little quiet and stoic. But he was a good listener.

And all of them are so dang handsome.

"So many new Blackwells and Gallaghers on the way," Dani says with a smile.

A lot of the girls have left. Jackie couldn't make it, but she dropped some goodies off beforehand. I'll have to check in with her later to see if she's feeling okay.

Just as I'm about to get up and head home, the door opens, and four *very* handsome men walk in.

Three of them I recognize as Blackwell brothers.

And the fourth is Billie's husband, Connor.

"I swear, you're a very tall gang." Ava shakes her head. "Why do you always crash book club?"

"Because we're here to get our girls," Blake tells her, then smiles at me. "Hey, Jules."

"Hi, Blake."

I clear my throat and breathe through my nose.

Do not cry.

I'm in a room with four out of the five Blackwell siblings, and that hasn't happened in a *really* long time.

Of course, there's no sign of Brooks. There wouldn't be. But I love every glimpse of him I get, even if it only makes me feel like shit and bruises my heart every single time.

Soon, with Harper gone with Blake, Ava loops her arm through mine as we walk outside.

"Is it weird that I want one of your salads right now?" She raises an eyebrow at me, practically *daring* me to say yes.

"Doesn't seem weird to me," I reply. "I have some in the grab-and-go cooler. Want to come in and have one?"

"Hell yes, I do," she declares with a nod. We walk across the street, where I unlock the door for us. Locking back up once we're inside, we move to the cooler and each of us grabs a salad, a fork, and we sit at a table by the front windows. "Mmm, this is so good."

"I'm glad everyone likes them." I take a bite and study Ava. "Are you from Silver Springs?"

"Born and raised," she says with a nod. "I have a big family, like Billie. And, like her, I'm the only biological girl. Except I just have three brothers. And Harper. We adopted her when we were in grade school."

"Officially adopted, or she just spent a lot of time at your house adopted?"

"Sort of in the middle?" She tips her head to the side. "Harper's parents died, and my dad took her in. Raised her with us from then on, so she's our sister."

"I love that."

"Me too," Ava says. "Okay, enough small talk. Tell me why everyone walks on eggshells around you. And why this is your first book club."

I blink at her in surprise. "You don't know the story?"

"No, no one talks about it. It's just this big secret drama. The *thing that shall not be named*. It's honestly annoying. We're all adults. So what happened? I get that you dated Brooks, but nothing else is ever said."

I push my mostly eaten salad away and quickly debate how much to tell her.

"Hey." Ava reaches over and lays her hand on my arm. "In all seriousness, we're in the cone of silence. I won't take anything you say anywhere else. It's not my story to tell. I just hate being in the dark."

I don't remember the last time I had a friend to tell secrets to. I like Ava so much, and I kind of wish Harper was here, too. I can trust them. And I want to open up to Ava.

So I do.

"Yeah, Brooks and I dated. We got together when we were sixteen and broke up when I was almost done with college."

"Did he go to college, too?"

"No, he stayed here. He attended auto mechanic

school and eventually bought the shop. We did the long-distance thing for all four years."

"And then you broke up right before you were finished?" Her eyebrows climb. "That sucks."

"Big time." I nod, thinking back to everything that went down, and feel my heart ache. "There was a guy, Justin, who was *just my friend*. But he was needy, and now I know he was manipulative, and he succeeded in breaking us up. I didn't know that was his goal. I was just trying to be a good friend, but Brooks saw it as me choosing Justin over him."

Ava's face falls. "Well, shit."

"Yeah. It really hurt Brooks. I mean, it hurt both of us. I don't think I've recovered from it even still. But I broke Brooks's heart, and I know he'll never forgive me. He's angry. He made it clear that he doesn't want me around, and I honestly can't blame him. But it makes it hard because this is a small town. I *want* to go to things like the book club and not worry about what will happen if I run into him."

"And you should be able to," she insists. "I get wanting to avoid an ex. We've all been there, but you have to be able to live your life, Jules. You can't hide away."

"I've spent the past fifteen years hiding away," I admit for the first time. "And it felt like prison."

"Then stop it. Live your life, and if Brooks doesn't like it, he can look the other way. What ever happened to Justin?"

"He died."

He did so much more than die.

"Wow."

59

"Yeah."

"You know what we need?"

I grin at her. "What?"

"One of those brownies you have over there."

"Let's do it."

I haven't had my car for five whole days, and although it doesn't normally bother me, I *really* need to go run errands.

"You okay, Jules?" Christy asks when I check my phone yet again to see if I missed a call from Barry.

Nope. Of course not. The man's going to keep my hanging forever and charge me another fortune.

"Yeah, just waiting to hear from the garage about when I can get my car."

"*Again*?" she asks, and all I can do is laugh.

Because yes. Again.

Harper and Ava are here, which is typical for them on a Tuesday. When their orders are ready, I load up their plates and deliver them to the table.

"So hungry," Harper says, wiggling in her seat. "Thank you."

"You're welcome." I let the tray fall to my side as the girls dig into their food. "I hope you like it."

Just then, my phone rings. I yank it out of my jeans and answer it.

"Hello."

"Hey, Juliet, this is Barry. Your car's finished and ready to go."

"Oh, great. What time do you close?"

"Five."

My heart sinks. It's already one, and I don't know if one of the girls can give me a ride.

"Okay, I'll figure it out. Thanks."

I hang up and scrunch up my nose.

"What's wrong?" Harper asks.

"My car is ready, but I don't know if I can grab it today."

"I'll take you," Ava offers. "I'm headed home that way anyway."

"Really?" I grin at her. "It's not too far out of the way?"

"It's literally on the way," she replies. "No worries. Can you go when I'm finished with lunch?"

"Yep, let me just let my girls know."

Thank God for Ava.

"Just call me if you need anything," Ava says as I climb out of her car.

"Thanks, and thanks for the ride." I grin at her and then wave before I walk into the garage.

Barry glances up and sees me, wipes his hands on a towel, and gives me that greasy smile that makes me extra uncomfortable as he approaches the counter.

"Hey, Barry," I say without much enthusiasm.

"Hey. Okay, she's all ready for you. Turned out to be a faulty oil filter."

"It took you five days to figure that out?"

He narrows his eyes at me. "We're busy around here, and you didn't have an appointment."

"It wasn't planned," I remind him. "What's the damage?"

"Four hundred and seventy-five dollars."

I feel the blood drain from my face.

"For an *oil filter*?"

"There were a few hours of labor while we figured out what the issue was."

Jesus Christ. I need a new car.

After paying, and without another word to Barry, who looks as happy as a clam, I get into my car and fight tears as I start it and leave the parking lot, on the highway headed back to Bitterroot Valley.

I no longer have any desire to run errands. I can't really afford the few things I wanted to pick up anyway, and I can live without them.

This is so fucked up.

I really have to find another mechanic. I can't keep going to that creep. I'm pretty sure he's raping me with the prices, and I can't afford him.

I wonder if I could get a loan for a decent used car?

Or perhaps I'll take some money out of my inheritance from Justin and buy a new car. It's *my* money, but I hate using it.

It seems that this time, I don't have a choice.

I've just turned the curve that marks the halfway

point between the two towns when suddenly, the car starts to grind and knock, then dies altogether. I barely manage to get it to the side of the road, out of the way of traffic.

Breathing hard, I stare straight ahead, both hands gripping the wheel.

Shit, I'm lucky I didn't get in a wreck.

But now, I let the tears come.

Because I can't afford another tow truck.

And I can't afford another goddamn bill from that fucker, Barry.

Fuck. What am I going to do?

Chapter Six

BROOKS

I t's a nice day, and with fall pretty much here, there won't be many days left to ride my motorcycle before it gets too cold and the snow flies. I've been putting in long hours at work, so I took the afternoon off and decided to ride around the valley. I took backroads from Bitterroot Valley over to Silver Springs, breathing in the fresh mountain air, feeling the bike beneath me, and letting the sun bake me a little.

I need to work on forgetting a certain blonde who's had my attention for more than two decades. I'm still pissed at myself for buying the flowers for the porch. It was stupid.

But the following morning, when she walked past, she smiled. Her whole gorgeous face just lit right up, as if it were fireworks at Disney World.

And dammit, I'd do it again.

Fuck.

There I go thinking about her again.

I drive through Silver Springs, slowing down as I pass

through the downtown area. It's a tiny town, even smaller than Bitterroot Valley, and within minutes, I'm out on the highway, headed for home.

Slowing to go around a tight corner in the road, I notice a car broken down on the shoulder, and when I narrow my eyes, I see that it's Jules sitting in the driver's seat.

Crying.

Motherfucker.

Checking my mirrors, I slow and make a U-turn, then circle back and come to a stop behind her. After setting the bike on the kickstand and removing my helmet, I make my way to the passenger door so I'm not close to traffic and tap on the glass.

Jules startles and screams, but when she sees it's me, she hits the mechanism to unlock the door, and I pull it open.

"Hey." I frown as it looks like she's fighting to catch her breath. "Are you okay?"

She shakes her head and wipes the tears from her cheeks. "Not good at being spooked. Fuck."

That's new.

"Whoa. It's okay, it's just me. Take a deep breath. Breathe with me, Jules."

She's not looking at me, but she follows my direction, pulling in a deep breath with me. After the third one, she's calmed down considerably.

"Thanks," she whispers.

"What happened?"

She bites her lip and won't look me in the face, and I fucking hate that. I realize that I don't just want to know what happened right now, to put her here at the side of the road, I want to know what happened to make her startle so bad, and every other moment from that day so long ago.

But for now, I'll settle for why she's sitting on the side of the road.

"My car sucks," she finally says, her breath shuddering. "I *just* picked it up from that asshole in Silver Springs, and it already broke down again."

Unease moves through me, followed quickly by anger.

"Pop the hood."

"Oh, you don't have to look. I'll call a tow—"

"Pop the fucking hood, Wildfire."

Her eyes widen at the use of the old nickname, and she reaches below the steering wheel to pull the lever. I walk around the front and push it up so I can see what's going on.

And what I see is a huge fucking mess.

This engine looks like it's being held together by duct tape and cotton swabs. Who the hell was the mechanic, MacGyver?

Knowing there's nothing I can do right now, I close the hood and return to the passenger side, resigned to taking her with me.

On my bike.

Pressed up against my back for miles, just like the old days.

"Who did the repairs?"

"Barry in Silver Springs did it every time."

I tilt my head. "How many times have you had it in to him, Jules?"

"Oh, geez, a half dozen? It always breaks down again. This time, I think it's really dead. The noises were horrible. I'm more than six grand into repairs—"

"You're fucking *what?*"

She jumps and then blinks at me. "Sorry. TMI. I'll call—"

"I've got this." Jesus, I'm going to be making a trip to Barry's garage, and I'm going to teach him a goddamn lesson. And get her money back. "I'll tow it to my garage and sort it out. And I want you to show me everything he did."

"Uh, how am I supposed to do that?"

"I assume you have receipts?"

"Sure."

"I want to see them. Come on, you're with me."

Her jaw drops, and for a moment, she just blinks at me.

"You're on your motorcycle."

Yeah, and you love it.

"Problem?"

"I don't have—"

"I have everything you need. Let's go, Juliet."

I close the door and walk back to the bike. Seconds later, she opens her door, checks for traffic, then joins me, with her purse in her arms.

I stow her purse in my saddlebag, and set my helmet on her head.

"I know it's too big, but it'll keep you safe the rest of the way into town."

67

"What about you?" She stares up at me as I adjust the chin strap. Christ, I haven't been this close to her in so fucking long. Her skin is warm and smooth where my fingers brush her chin as I adjust the strap, and it makes my dick twitch.

"I'll be fine."

She frowns, but she doesn't argue. Instead, she says, "Please drive safely. I don't want you to get hurt."

Fuck me.

"I always drive safely. I don't have a leather jacket on me, and I'd feel better if you were wearing one."

"I'm all out of leather jackets," she says with a half smile. I eye her T-shirt and jeans. At least she's not in shorts, but I'd rather she were wearing a coat of some sort to protect her arms.

Jesus, I'm going to drive ten miles an hour.

"Brooks, we'll be fine."

I nod once and climb on the bike, kick up the stand. Jules swings her leg over and settles in behind me, the way she always did, but she keeps a few inches between us and doesn't seem to know what to do with her hands.

"Hold on to me, Jules."

"But—"

"It's fine. You have to hold on to me."

Tentatively, and with shaky fingers, she wraps her arms around me and holds my stomach. Her breasts press against my back, and holy fucking shit, it's like coming home for the first time in decades.

It's like taking your first breath after coming up out of the water when you've almost drowned.

After starting the engine, I press my hand over hers.

"Hold on," I remind her.

"I will," she says.

When I look back at her, her blue eyes are big, and her cheeks are flushed. I know I'm not the only one feeling all this emotion.

As I take off, she yelps and then laughs with joy behind me, her hands clenching against my abs, and I can't help but smile.

Jules always loved the bike.

I can see her in the side mirror, smiling, her face tilted up at the sun as she enjoys the wind blowing through her hair.

Christ, she's beautiful.

That hasn't changed.

If anything, she's gotten more gorgeous with time. She's not the girl I once knew anymore. She's all woman, with more curves than before. More shadows in her eyes.

I slow as I pull into town, and to my absolute surprise, Jules tips her face forward and rests her cheek on the center of my back.

It makes my chest ache.

Yet, at the same time, I'm not ready to let it go.

So instead of taking her home, I drive through the residential areas of town, and she doesn't say a word. Her grip on me has loosened a bit since we're not going as fast.

When I go to take a turn, I reach back and lay my hand on her thigh, keeping her in place. Dammit, that feels good. She scoots a little closer to me when we come out of the turn, and I let go of her.

Because this isn't real.

I'm giving her a ride home, and that's it.

Setting my jaw, I drive behind the restaurant and cut the engine. Jules hops off the bike, and I follow. She starts to fumble with the strap of the helmet, but I step up to her, brush her fingers away, and unfasten it myself.

Her baby blues watch me.

"Have you ridden much over the years?" The question surprises me. I don't really want to know if she was wrapped around some other asshole the way she just was with me.

"Not since the last time you took me," she admits. "I think I missed it."

I'm relieved. I have no right to be, but I am.

"Come on," I say, gesturing to the stairs. "Let's go up."

"What? Why are you coming upstairs?" She takes half a step back from me, and that has me narrowing my eyes.

"To see the receipts and to make arrangements for your car."

Could she bring those to me at the garage? Sure. But I want to see her place. I shouldn't, and I'll hate myself for it later, but I can't help myself.

"I probably have stuff lying about."

"No, you don't. I know you. Let's go."

Jules hates clutter. There's no way her place is messy. And even if it is, I don't give a fuck.

"Thanks for the stairs," she says as she leads me up them. "It helped a lot."

"Don't know what you're talking about."

She huffs out a laugh, making the side of my mouth tick up.

"Sure, okay. Well, thanks anyway."

She unlocks the door, and I notice she has two deadbolts. Not one. Our town might have its fair share of crime, but it doesn't usually warrant that kind of security.

What are you afraid of, Wildfire?

But I immediately forget about the locks when I get a look at her apartment.

Oh, fuck no.

The walls are bare to the studs. No insulation or drywall. The electrical and plumbing are exposed. She has a little area sectioned off for a kitchen, but it only has a portable fridge and a microwave. No sink.

She has a bed and a nightstand on one side of the room. A single chair with a coffee table by the window.

It's stuffy up here. The floor is made of wood, but not the kind of hardwood most people use in homes.

This isn't an apartment.

This is a goddamn storage attic, and it is not good enough for my girl.

She's not your girl.

"I have a folder with all of the receipts," she says, pulling my attention away from the fact that I hate with all of my fucking soul that this is where she lives.

Not my problem. She's not my problem.

She opens a drawer on a short, two-drawer filing cabinet and pulls out the folder, then walks back over to me, and we move over to the window so that I can see better.

71

It's fucking dark up here, and it's the middle of the day.

It's also hot, and Jules opens the windows, letting a breeze blow through. It had to be sweltering up here in the heart of summer.

And there's no way this will work in the winter. She'll freeze to death.

Not my problem, I remind myself as I start thumbing through the invoices in the folder.

"It doesn't take four hours to change out brakes," I mutter, shaking my head. "And he totally upcharged you for the pads. Asshole."

The more I see, the angrier I get.

Because it's clear without a shadow of a doubt that Barry fucked Juliet over, time and again. She should have paid a fifth of what he charged her.

"Can I keep these?" I ask her.

"Oh, sure. No problem." She pushes her hair behind her ear. "Uh, just let me know how much the tow costs, and I'll pay for it. Unless you want me to call right now, and I can just give them my card number?"

"I've got it." I shake my head and walk away from her. If I keep standing two feet from her gorgeous body, I'll do something stupid like kiss her.

Jesus, I want to kiss her.

"The tow won't cost you anything. I'll take a look at it this evening."

"Oh, there's no rush—"

I spin and pin her in my glare. "Why didn't you bring it to me?"

She swallows hard, then frowns down at the floor.

"Look at me, Wildfire."

She raises her gaze, and heat fills her eyes. Frustration. Embarrassment.

And I feel like an asshole.

"Because you made it *very* clear to me that I'm not welcome at your shop. More than once. At the engagement party, I believe the words were *I don't exist for you.* You don't want me in your way, and I understand that. I respect it. So do you think that I'd bring my piece-of-shit car to you? Of course not."

"Jesus." I rub my hand down my face in frustration. "I'll figure your car out."

"I appreciate that." Her voice is quiet again, and we're both standing here, unsure, awkward. It's the fucking worst because Jules and I never used to be uncomfortable around each other. She was my person. And now she's a stranger.

"Why do you live up here, Juliet?"

"So you're just going to completely humiliate me today." She fists her hands and shakes her head. "Fine. I live up here because I invested every dime I had into this building and my restaurant. Because I needed something just for me. It's mine, and I own it outright. *Mine,* Brooks, and I refuse to be embarrassed by it. No one can take it away from me. So if I have to live up here and deal with crazy temperature swings, and join the gym to take showers, and do my laundry at the laundromat two miles away that I have to walk to when my car is out of commission, and sleep in the restaurant when it's so fucking hot outside that it's two hundred degrees up here, I don't care. I'll gladly do all of that and more without a complaint because it's a million times better than anything I've had before this."

She swallows hard, like she didn't mean to say that much, and my heart is lodged in my throat.

What the fuck does she mean?

"Jules—"

She shakes her head, and I work to gentle my tone.

"Jules," I try again. "There are other places for you to live. Hell, I have—"

"No," she says, interrupting me. "I don't need you to fix this for me."

"Don't be so fucking stubborn. You shouldn't be living up here. Baby, it's—"

"I'm not your baby. Not anymore. And I know exactly what this is, and I won't be ashamed. I'll fix it up. I can learn to finish walls and put in a decent sink. This isn't for you to deal with, Brooks."

My hands are in fists, and my breath is coming fast. I don't want her here. But she's right, she's not *mine*. I can't make her go with me.

"I have to get back to work. Dinner's about to start, and we get busy at this time. My crew needs me. Thanks for the ride home."

She won't look me in the face again, and I want to crush her to me, demand she tell me *everything* that happened, and take her home with me where she'll have everything she needs.

She's not my problem.

It's getting harder to believe that. Harder to walk away. To stay away.

Blinking quickly, as if she's about to cry, she whispers, "Please, Brooks. Just go, okay?"

"I need your number so I can call you about the car."

I tug my phone out of my jeans and pass it to her, and she texts herself, then passes it back to me.

"I'll be in touch."

She bites her lip and nods, and I leave her alone in that attic that isn't good enough for her.

As soon as I arrive at my house, I call the tow truck to retrieve the car and deliver it to my garage, then I text Beck and Bridger. I'd call Blake, too, but he's at the hospital today.

> Me: I need some help with something. Are you free?

I pace my kitchen and tip my head to the side to crack my neck. Agitation builds in me as my phone pings with a response.

> Bridger: I'm off today, just doing some yard work. What do you need?

Then a message from Beck comes in.

> Beckett: Just finished at the barn. What's up, B?

I grin and text them back.

> Me: It seems Barry's been ripping off Jules. Took her for thousands. We're going to teach him a lesson.

> Bridger: Uh, Brooks, I don't want you to go to jail.

> Me: No jail.

> Beckett: I'll pick you both up in twenty.

That gives me time to study the rest of the invoices and make notes.

Barry owes her a fuckton of money. And he's going to pay her every dime.

When Beck pulls into the driveway, Bridger's already with him, and I climb into the back seat.

"You don't get to kill him," Bridger says. He's not joking. There's nothing funny about this. "You'd break your niece's heart if you got sent to prison."

"As much as I'd like to, I'm just going to remind him that his piece-of-shit actions have consequences," I reply.

"Skyla mentioned that Jules made a comment about her car at book club," Beckett says.

"Why didn't you tell me?"

Both of my brothers send me a look.

"Because none of us is allowed to speak about her to you," Bridger reminds me. "So we just keep everything we know to ourselves."

"What else do you fucking know?" Yeah, I sound like

a broody asshole, but I don't care. They know things about my wildfire and haven't told me?

What the fuck?

"Not much," Beck admits with a shrug. "Skyla doesn't tell other people's secrets. She just mentioned the car thing to me."

"Dani doesn't say much either." Bridger shakes his head. "The girls lock it down. They're loyal to each other."

I actually love that. I love that the girls trust each other and are not only best friends but also family. And I can admit that I like the fact that Jules is being welcomed into that friend group. Something tells me that she needs it, and I've been an asshole to resent it. But dammit, seeing her all the time is torture.

And an addiction.

Fuck.

We're quiet until Beckett pulls into the parking lot and cuts the engine.

"What's the plan?" Beck asks before we get out of the vehicle.

"I came with receipts." I hold up the folder. "I think I'll be extra nice."

"Shit. Someone's gonna call the cops," Bridge mutters, making me grin. "We don't have Chase Wild at our back in Silver Springs, Brooks. We don't know the cops here."

"I know Tucker's brother, Easton," I counter. "But trust me. We won't need the cops."

Probably.

The three of us walk into the garage. Barry works

77

alone. He says it's because he does better by himself, but it's really because no one will work for him. He's an asshole, he underpays, and he's a complete piece-of-shit human.

The fact that my wildfire was anywhere near him makes my blood boil.

Barry looks our way and scowls. "What the fuck do you want?"

"I just need to ask some questions." I slap the folder on the counter, and Barry opens it, scans the top page, and then his face goes red.

"That little bitch."

"Uh-oh," Beck breathes behind me.

"What did you just call her?"

"Listen, I don't know what she told you—"

"She didn't have to tell me anything. I found her stranded at the side of the road this afternoon after she *left here* with a car that should have been fixed. Instead, that engine looks like you've done nothing but make sure she'll be back in here so you can suck more money out of her."

"So what?"

"Fucking hell," Bridger scoffs. "You're a stupid piece of shit. You know that, right?"

"If she doesn't like how I do business, she doesn't have to come to me. Maybe she just likes me. She flirts with me constantly."

And that's all it takes to have my fist connecting with his face and dropping him to the floor.

"I'll have you charged with assault," he yells out at me, but I shake my head.

"No, you won't. Because I'm quite sure that Juliet isn't the only customer you've fucked over. I'd bet the IRS would love a phone call. I bet the Better Business Bureau would enjoy a conversation. Maybe I'll call Alex at the newspaper. I can ruin your business, you piece of shit."

"No one would believe you."

That makes Beckett laugh, and Beck rarely laughs.

"Are you that clueless?" Beck asks him. "*Everyone* would believe us. You have the shittiest reputation in the area. People won't even work for you."

"So if you don't want to lose what little business you have left, you'll refund all of her money."

His face goes white.

"I can't do that."

"I don't give a flying fuck what you can do. You're going to refund every cent to her. I added it up. Looks like that's six thousand, four hundred dollars and twenty-three cents. All of it goes back to her *today*."

"Or what?"

"Or I'll burn this whole place to the motherfucking ground." I push my nose in his face. I'm taller by three inches and outweigh him by fifty pounds of muscle. "Fuck around and find out, you piece of shit."

He doesn't reply.

"And if you try to retaliate, you'll lose everything. You could have just been a decent human being and fixed her car. You could have even upcharged her by fifty bucks here or there. But *thousands*, Barry? Jesus, you're an idiot."

"Fuck you."

"Not my type." I shrug, and we head to the door. "Every penny refunded to her card today. I mean it."

We leave the building, get in Beck's truck, and he pulls away.

"Do you think he'll do it?" Bridger asks.

"Yeah, he'll do it. He knows I'll ruin him if he doesn't."

Chapter Seven

JULIET

Sixteen emails.

Sixteen.

I stare at my laptop, the sip of strawberry lemonade I just had still sitting in my mouth because I hadn't even swallowed yet when I opened the emails, and now I'm just sitting here, frozen, staring in disbelief.

Because that bitch has sent me sixteen emails in the past two days.

The audacity.

Finally, I swallow my drink.

At least she's not texting or calling me, but still. That's a whole lot of emails in two freaking days. And every single one gets more aggressive. When I open the last one, all I can do is laugh. Because she's lost her mind if she thinks she can talk to me like that and still get her way.

WHY WON'T YOU ANSWER ME? I need the fucking money, you stupid whore. Just send me the five grand! He would want me to have it! He gave me anything I wanted, and now you're holding out on me, you selfish, jealous bitch! He never loved you. You were a joke to him. Give me what you owe me!

Without responding, I shut the computer and sigh into my glass of lemonade. I fucking hate her. I wish with all my might that delegating money to her wasn't my responsibility.

Why did you do that to me, Justin? After everything else, you had to add in the fact that I have to pay your mistress until the end of time?

Asshole.

I move to my small dresser and pull out some clothes for today. I don't have much that isn't dirty since I haven't been able to go to the laundromat. I also have towels, aprons, and other linens from downstairs that I need to wash. I've heard that there's a laundry service run by a really nice woman named Abbi Wild. I wonder if I could hire her until my car is fixed?

In fact, I pick up the phone and call her. She owns a cleaning service in addition to the laundry services for businesses, and I'll happily carve out the funds to pay her to help me.

"This is Abbi," she answers.

"Hi, Abbi, my name is Juliet. I own Sage & Citrus here in town."

"Oh, I *love* your restaurant," she says, and has a smile in her voice. "We eat there at least twice a month. How can I help you?"

"I'm so happy to hear that you like it, thank you. Hey, my car has broken down, so I can't get to the laundromat for both my personal and professional laundry. I was hoping—"

"Say no more. I'm happy to help. If you bag everything up for me, I'll have one of my employees pick it up from you this morning. I can give you a two-day turnaround, if that's okay?"

Holy shit, it feels like a weight has just been lifted, and I sigh in relief. "You have no idea how much I appreciate this, Abbi."

"Oh, it's my pleasure. It sucks when you feel stranded, even in a small town."

"And just to clarify, you're okay with washing my personal clothes?"

"Honey, that's no problem. Happy to do it. I'll even do it myself. Don't even worry about it."

"Thank you so much."

"You got it. Happy to help."

I end the call, and with a smile, I get dressed, put on my makeup, tie my hair up in a bun, then gather up my clothes to take downstairs.

Today is looking up.

We're past the lunch rush, and we're sitting in that quiet lull before dinner, when we have a couple of people in the restaurant, but it's slow enough that we can get some cleanup and restocks done before the next wave of hungry customers.

Christy just went home for the day, and now I have Tandy and Hazel with me. The girls are chatting about the concerts they want to attend this year, and I'm trying to decide how many eggs I need to order from Beckett. The bell over the door chimes, and when I glance up, I freeze.

Because for the first time ever, Brooks Blackwell is walking into my restaurant.

He glances around and then pins me with that intense hazel gaze as he strides toward me. Seeing him is always a punch to the gut. He's so tall, so broad and muscular. And maybe the worst part is, I know what he can do with that body.

Or what he used to be able to do.

I'm sure it's only gotten better.

Don't think about that.

"Hey," he says as he reaches the counter.

"Hello. Are you hungry?"

His eyes rake down my body. Then he takes a deep breath and shakes his head.

Okay, that might have hurt my ego just a bit.

"I was across the street and thought I'd pop by to give you an update on your car."

"Great. Is it dead?"

Brooks's lips tip up in the slightest grin, but then his eyebrows pull together in a frown.

"No, but it's going to take me a while to figure it all out and clean it up. He made a goddamn mess of it."

"Yeah." With a sigh, I cross my arms over my chest

and lean my hip against the counter. "Brooks, it doesn't have to be a priority. I'm fine. I walk almost everywhere anyway, and I found Abbi Wild to help me out with laundry."

He scowls at that. "Just come to my place to do your laundry."

"I don't need to. Abbi's got it. I mostly eat down here, so I don't need groceries. As pathetic as it sounds, I really don't have anywhere to go. So the car isn't a rush job."

His jaw muscles tic, and he looks pissed.

"Would you rather I told you I need it by tomorrow?"

"I'd rather you weren't so stubborn and would just do your goddamn laundry at my place."

"I don't need to." I sound like a jerk. I'm snapping at him, and he's doing me a favor, but dammit, he's so grouchy with me, makes it no secret that he doesn't want me around, and now he wants to have me at his house?

No. Because it would be too easy to take him up on that. I don't need him to save me and then rub my nose in it later.

"Fine." He shakes his head, and without another word, he turns and walks away, storming out the door. I let out the breath I wasn't even aware I was holding.

"Wow," Tandy says, fanning herself. "All of the Blackwell men are sexy, but Brooks is next level."

"And he looks at you like he wants to fuck you on this counter," Hazel adds, and I choke on my own spit.

"No, he doesn't."

"Yeah, he does," Tandy joins in. "Or on the floor, or against the wall ..."

"Stop." I laugh and shoo them back to work. "Trust me, he does *not* want to do any of that."

"She's blind," Tandy says to Hazel. I simply shake my head and get back to work, figuring out how many eggs I need before calling Beckett to place an order.

I don't honestly know what Brooks wants from me, but it's not sex.

Actually, he probably wishes I'd move away. But I'm not going to.

I've just come out of the walk-in refrigerator when I see a woman scowling at my staff.

"How many times do I have to tell you *no dairy*?" a woman yells at Tandy, whose eyes are huge, and I notice her hands are shaking.

"Hey, how can I help?" I ask as I walk over. My restaurant is set up for customers to place their orders at the counter, and when the food is ready, we deliver it to the tables. That way, they can customize anything they want, and if they want to watch us assemble their meal, they can do so. I know that many people with stomach sensitivities prefer to keep an eye on how their food is prepared.

"Are you the owner?" the customer demands as Tandy steps to the side, chewing her lower lip. I rest my hand on her shoulder and give her a nod before turning back to the customer.

"I am the owner, yes. Was something wrong with your meal?"

The woman narrows her eyes at me. She's tall and

willowy thin, with perfect nails and makeup and a designer handbag slung across her body. She's beautiful.

And I can see that she's about to be a bitch.

"This idiot who works for you doesn't seem to understand what it means when I tell her *no dairy*. She's made this same salad for me three times, and every time she brings it to me, it's wrong."

I frown down at her salad. "I don't see any dairy there."

She scoffs and shoves it forward, almost making it spill over the side and onto the floor. "Are you fucking kidding me? What do you call that?"

She points her red-tipped nail at the center of the lettuce. I look from the bowl to her and raise an eyebrow.

"I call that a hard-boiled egg."

"Exactly."

"I told her—" Tandy begins, but the bitch in front of me cuts her off.

"You told me what? That you didn't do it wrong? Because you clearly did, you stupid little—"

"Stop." The hard crack of my voice has her taking a step back. "Number one, you won't abuse my staff. Not today or any other day. Number two, eggs are *not* dairy. They're poultry."

"You're stupid if you truly believe that," she says. "Why are they in the fucking dairy section of the store?"

"Because the store keeps them cold to make them last longer, but they're *not* dairy. Google it. In the meantime, if you don't like eggs, we won't add them to your salad. But you won't call my staff, or myself, stupid for knowing our jobs."

"You're wrong." She crosses her arms over her chest.

"You can go now."

Her jaw drops. "I'm not leaving until you make me the salad the way I want it."

"Yeah, you are. You're done."

"I would *never* be treated this way in LA."

"Then go back to LA. Now, are you taking this with you or not?"

"Are you hearing impaired, you stupid redneck?"

I glance at Tandy, who's staring in shock. "Call the police."

"Are you fucking *crazy*?" The customer is screeching now, and everyone in the restaurant has stopped what they're doing to watch us.

"You have five seconds to get the fuck out of my building before I have you arrested for trespassing."

Her lip curls in a sneer before she turns and stomps away, and once she's gone, the place erupts in applause.

"You go with your badass self," Billie says, a grab-and-go salad in her hand as she steps up to the counter. "What a bitch. I hope she doesn't go over to the bookstore."

I rub a shaky hand over my forehead. Now that the adrenaline is wearing off, I feel unsteady.

"I hate people," Tandy says with a deep sigh. "Thanks for having my back, Jules. I knew that eggs aren't dairy."

"Everyone knows that." Billie rolls her eyes. "I want a brownie, too. I'm eating this salad, which is delicious by the way, but I need something sweet to go with it."

"You got it, Bug." I wink at her and ring her up.

"Did you pick up the new book club read?" she asks me. "It's *War* by Brittanée Nicole, and it's *so good.*"

"I did pick it up, and I started it last night," I reply with a grin. "Daddy War might be my new favorite hero."

"He's *so* hot," Billie agrees. "Okay, gotta run back. See you later!"

After Billie leaves, we get swamped, and for the next several hours, the three of us bustle about, taking and filling orders, running them to tables, then cleaning tables between customers. It's a chaotic evening, but eventually, it's time to close. Once everything is cleaned and put away, Tandy and Hazel leave for the night.

I stay in the kitchen, making dough to bake in the morning. I mix up more brownie batter and decide to try the scone recipe that Jackie sent me.

Finally, at around ten, with everything ready for the morning, I turn off the lights and toss my apron in the laundry basket before walking out the front door and locking it.

I check the lock three times before I walk away and head down the main street in town.

I take two walks every day. One first thing in the morning and the other before bed. I've done that for years. It was the only time I truly had to myself, and it's a routine that I keep.

When I reach Brooks's garage, I notice that the lights are still on inside, and music is playing.

He's probably staying late because of my car, and that makes me feel guilty. I don't want him working overtime because of me. I also feel like shit because I snapped at

89

him, not just today, but the other day when he gave me a ride on the bike and came up to the apartment.

I told him at the time that I refused to be ashamed, but the truth is, I *was* ashamed. It's embarrassing that I live in an attic. I can call it an apartment all day long, but that doesn't make it more than it is. I didn't want Brooks to see it, at least not until I've had the opportunity to fix it up more.

So I got defensive and snapped at him.

And he really is doing me a favor by helping me with the car. I shudder to think how much it's going to cost me in the end, but at least I'll have it back.

Without overthinking it, I walk back to the restaurant, let myself in, and head to the kitchen, where I make Brooks a steak fajita with chips and guacamole. It's his favorite thing.

At least, it was *his favorite thing.*

I hope he still likes this kind of food.

After putting it all in a brown bag with handles, I shut the kitchen down again, check the lock three times, and walk back to the garage.

The lights are still on, and the music still plays.

Am I stupid to bring him dinner as a thank-you? What if he's not working on my car at all? Maybe an emergency came in, and I'm being silly.

Maybe he'll just glare at me the way he always does and send me packing.

That's the most likely scenario.

I don't even know why I'm here. However, I know that standing up for myself and Tandy made me feel more confident. Stronger. It made me feel like my old self again, and I like it. If I'm strong enough to put that woman in her place, I can offer Brooks dinner as a thank-you for his help.

So I square my shoulders and try the door, which is unlocked.

And when I walk inside, I almost trip over my own feet.

Because Brooks is shirtless, all those impressive muscles on display and flexing as he leans over an engine —my engine—twisting a wrench. The music is so loud that he didn't hear me come in, so I can observe him quietly.

Good God, his ass in those jeans.

Every inch of this man is pure perfection. Narrow waist and broad back with muscles that look like they're carved from marble. I wish he'd turn around so I can see his abs, but then he'd see me, and I wouldn't get to ogle him anymore.

I also wish I could just walk over to him and kiss him, right between the shoulder blades. Once upon a time, I had free access to touch him any way I liked.

Fuck, I miss him.

He's right here, and I miss him so much that every muscle in my body aches with it. Tears fill my eyes, and one falls down my cheek, but I don't brush it away because I don't want to wipe away the spell of this moment.

This man, *my* man, oblivious to me watching him, wanting him, yearning for him. I stopped doing this years ago, simply for self-preservation.

But right now, I can admit that every cell in my body wants him.

And I can never have him.

Suddenly, his whole body tenses, and I school my face because he knows I'm here.

He doesn't turn all the way around. He glances over his shoulder, sees me, and then curses. I can't hear him over the loud music, but I can see the word *fuck* leave his gorgeous lips.

And that sets me into action.

I hurry over and set the bag of food on his table, and then turn to scurry out the door, but suddenly the music stops. Just as I reach for the doorknob, his voice stops me in my tracks.

"Wildfire."

Chapter Eight

BROOKS

Maybe if I play the music loud enough, it'll drown out all thoughts of my wildfire. Because she consumes me, and it pisses me the fuck off. All I've thought about is how damn perfect it felt to have her pressed against my back on the bike. I hate that she lives in that attic, but I love that she stood up to me and told me that she wasn't ashamed.

Even though I could see the embarrassment in her eyes, and I don't want her to feel that way.

Christ, why do I have this *need* to help her? To protect her? She's a stranger to me, yet I want her.

And the more I dig into her car, the more pissed I get. Barry sabotaged every component of this car, making sure it would break down over and over again. I've never seen such a fucking mess, and I've been at this job for a long time. I'm so pissed, I had to take my shirt off because I was sweating.

I want to get Barry in a room and beat the ever-loving fuck out of the piece of shit.

I need to ask Jules to check her card and make sure she got her money back, or else I'll be paying him another visit, and I won't stop at a punch to the jaw.

Nirvana is blaring through the speakers. Old Man Hanson used to play this and other old rock music on repeat, and I never stopped because I like it.

I turn it up a notch because I'm still thinking about Jules, and then every hair on my body stands on end.

She's here.

Without standing up straight, I glance over my shoulder, and sure enough, there she is, staring at me with glassy eyes, wearing a black T-shirt and shorts, holding a bag of what I assume is food.

"Fuck," I mutter before I cut the music off and reach for the rag to wipe my hands. When I turn around, she's already set the bag down and is making a break for the door. "Wildfire."

She stops, but she doesn't turn around, and I slowly walk toward her.

I don't like having her in my garage. She looks too beautiful. Too perfect. Too *right*, here in my space. It reminds me of having her here with me when we were teenagers. She'd keep me company while I worked.

It's late, dark outside, and no one is around.

It's just us.

Fuck.

"I'm sorry," she blurts, and wrings her hands together at her waist as she turns to me. She won't look me in the face. "I was taking my evening walk—"

She walks in the evening, too?

"—and I saw that your lights were on and heard the

music. I had just closed the kitchen, so I ran back to make you dinner because if you're still here, you might not have eaten, and I had some beef fajitas, and you used to like those. I don't know if you still do, but it's all in the bag, along with some chips and stuff. I feel bad that I've snapped at you. You don't deserve that. Anyway, sorry that I interrupted—"

Unable to stop myself, I close the gap between us, frame her face in my hands, and press my lips to hers, kissing her for the first time in fifteen years, and my entire being stutters to a stop as I breathe her in.

She doesn't move at first, as taken aback as I am, and then with a little moan, she melts into me. Her hands go to my sides, and her lips part, inviting my tongue in.

God, she tastes good.

Sinking into her, I back her up until her hips meet my countertop. Her fingertips brush up and down my bare back, up my sides, over my stomach, and I can't stop myself from wanting her, here and now.

I hate myself for it, but I *need* her.

Every bit of her.

I tug her shirt up out of her shorts, and she immediately lifts her arms, giving me consent to remove her clothes. That's all I need to know that she wants this as much as I do.

"Jesus, Wildfire," I mutter against her lips as I unfasten her bra, and it falls down her arms. Cupping her breasts, I tip my forehead against hers, and when my thumbs brush over her already hard nipples, my cock strains against my jeans. "Tell me to stop now. If you don't want me inside you, you need to say so, Juliet."

"Don't stop." Her voice is breathy and full of need, full of lust, and it's exactly what I need to hear.

And I'm suddenly as angry as I am turned on.

Because I've needed her for *fifteen motherfucking years*. And I hate her for it.

I hate her, and I can't walk away from her.

I can't look at her face, in her sweet blue eyes, so I twirl her around and plant her hands on the edge of the counter, making her bend over at the waist.

"Hold on," I say, my voice hard and gruff. "Don't you fucking let go."

She nods, but I pinch her nipple, making her gasp.

"Words, Juliet."

"I won't let go."

I bite her shoulder as I circle behind her, unfasten her shorts, and let them fall around her ankles. She's left standing there in nothing but little yellow panties. She's panting, her face is flushed, her hair is a mess from my fingers. I didn't even realize I'd messed it up.

"Fuck," I mutter as I squat behind her and hook my fingers in her panties, pulling them down her legs, exposing her gorgeous ass and pussy to me. "You're more beautiful than I remember, and I didn't think that was possible."

She whimpers, and her head falls forward when I drag a finger through her already sopping slit.

"I'm not going to think about how many men have been here since me. Because if I think about it, I'll fucking kill someone."

"Brooks—"

I push two fingers inside her, making her gasp and

rock forward. She's tight, so fucking tight. Her walls squeeze the hell out of my fingers, making my already hard cock strain. Pulling them out, I lean in and swipe my tongue from her clit to her entrance and back again, and she cants her hips back, seeking more.

"You want my tongue inside this pretty pussy, Jules?"

"Yes. Please."

"I like it when you ask for it." I fuck her with my tongue and my fingers, driving her out of her mind. She's falling apart, screaming, when I push my thumb against her hard clit and make her come so hard, I'm quite sure she can't remember her own fucking name.

But she sure knows mine because she's screaming it right now.

"Brooks! Holy fucking shit."

"That's right. It's me, Wildfire." Standing, I keep one hand on her cunt and unfasten my jeans with the other. "You're so fucking gorgeous, it almost pisses me off."

I notch my weeping cock at her entrance and push inside her, bottoming out, making us both groan.

"Mine," I whisper as I pull back and then slam back in, hard and unyielding. I'm not in any way making love to this woman. I'm fucking her. I'm reminding her who belongs here. And then a tiny patch of ink on her left side, over her rib cage, catches my eye and my hips stop moving as my thumb brushes over it.

She's gone perfectly still.

I narrow my eyes and lean closer, and in perfect writing, it says, *his wildfire*. There's the outline of a flame at the very end.

It's simple.

It's covered when she's clothed.

And it's for me.

"You marked yourself for me."

She doesn't reply, and I've never been harder in my goddamn life. I start to move again, more punishing than before. Because I'm *so fucking angry.*

I slap her ass, then grip onto her side. My hand covers the ink as if I can soak it into myself. When her pussy ripples around me as her climax works through her again, she pulls me with her, and I come inside her.

Fuck, I just came inside her.

But I can't bring myself to be sorry.

When I pull out, I tug her panties up, keeping my cum exactly where it belongs. She's panting, still leaning on the counter, and I know it's because I haven't given her permission to move.

Such a good wildfire.

One of the things that I loved about Juliet was how submissive she was to me. I'm dominant by nature, and she always followed my directions *perfectly.*

It seems that hasn't changed.

"You can get dressed."

She immediately moves into action, pulls up her shorts, then reaches for her bra and shirt as I tuck myself away, wondering what in the hell I'm supposed to do now.

I fucked up.

Yet I'm not sorry. Because for the first time in fifteen years, I feel alive.

Not one word comes from her beautiful mouth as

she finishes dressing, and then without a word to me, she sets off for the door.

"Jules."

She doesn't look back. She doesn't acknowledge me at all.

She simply leaves.

"Fuck!"

I stomp my feet, pacing back and forth, until I finally close up the garage, grab the food, and go home. The house is dark and silent as I walk through to the kitchen and set the bag down. I can still smell her on me. I can feel her soft skin, see that tattoo.

She made me dinner because she felt guilty and grateful, and she brought it to me.

And what did I do?

"I fucked her six ways to Sunday." I shake my head and pull the contents out of the bag, and my stomach growls. I haven't eaten since lunch, and it might be almost midnight, but I'm not about to waste my wildfire's food.

I eat every delicious bite, toss the packaging, and then go to my bathroom and take a shower.

I should *not* have fucked her.

But I couldn't help myself. And she didn't say no.

I'm full of self-loathing when I step out of the shower and dry off. Because she might not have said no, but I didn't handle it with any kind of finesse. And that makes me an asshole.

I want to know about the tattoo.

His wildfire.

How long has she had it?

Is she okay after what I just did to her?

I have her number, but I don't want to just text her. I don't think she'd take a call from me. So I pull on some clean workout shorts and a T-shirt, then grab my keys and drive over to her place. She's just approaching the stairs when I pull up, and she bites her lower lip, frowns, and then climbs the steps, ignoring me.

You can't ignore me, baby.

Without a word, I follow her upstairs. She unlocks both deadbolts, opens the door, and doesn't bother to try to shut it in my face. I walk in behind her, close the door, and then we're standing in her stuffy attic. Her back is to me, her hands on her hips.

"Ten years," she says, finally breaking the silence. "I got the tattoo ten years ago."

Five years after we broke up.

My already shattered heart cracks again.

"I assume that's what you want to know," she says as she turns to look at me. Her arms wrap around her middle, like she's protecting herself from me.

"I was curious, yeah."

She nibbles that lower lip.

"The food was great."

Her eyes fill with tears.

"Fuck."

Without asking permission, I close the gap between us, tug her against my chest, and wrap my arms around her.

"I hate how much you hate me," she mutters against me. "I hate it so much. I don't know how to change it. I don't know what to say to anyone. I feel so fucking *alone*."

Just when I'm about to tell her that I don't hate her, she shakes her head and backs out of my arms, wipes her face, and turns her back to me once more.

"I'm glad you liked the food."

She's back to that stiff politeness.

"Jules—"

"I needed those orgasms," she admits with the shrug of one shoulder. "I know it's nothing personal, but it was a good trade for the food. Won't happen again, though, because I won't fuck another man who hates me. Learned that lesson."

I want to fucking *roar*.

What does she mean by that?

"I need you to go now."

"I'd like to talk to you."

Juliet shakes her head and sighs so deeply, it's as though she's exhausted down to her soul.

"I don't want to talk. I need you to go, Brooks."

I stay rooted where I am, watching her. If I really hated her, I wouldn't be here. I wouldn't give a flying fuck about her feelings.

I *do* care.

"You being here hurts me."

Those whispered words are all I need to make me leave.

The truth is, we won't ever be together again. She's not mine. I'm an idiot for not being able to control myself and keep my cock under control.

I'll fix her car, and then I'll wash my hands of Juliet forever.

This has to end.

Chapter Nine

JULIET

For the first time since I opened my restaurant, I don't want to work today.

I'm lying on my back, staring at the ceiling of my attic apartment. To be fair, it's not a ceiling. It's bare wood beams, and not the fancy kind. I'm naked because even though it's no longer hotter than Satan's ass outside, it's still stuffy and warm up here, and I don't have the energy to turn on the fan.

I don't want to leave my bed.

Which means I *have* to leave my bed. I've been here before, years ago, and if I let myself stay here, I won't get up for days.

But do I have to go to work?

I quickly do a mental tally of who I have coming in to work today. I have a full staff, and the new hires are even working out just fine. Technically, they should be okay without me. Christy and Hazel can lead things just fine, and James, one of the new hires, comes in at eleven.

They don't need me.

So without overthinking it, I shoot Christy a text.

> Me: Good morning! Hey, I won't be in today. The dough for today's bread is in the fridge and ready to go. Are you okay handling things with Hazel and James? You can always call me if you need me.

I cringe when I see the time. It's just past five in the morning, so I don't expect a quick response from her. To my surprise, less than five minutes later, she replies.

> Christy: No problem! You deserve a day off. I hope it's for something fun and not because you're sick. We'll be fine. Should I call Erica in for the dinner shift?

I grin. Christy is damn good at her job. I should promote her to manager and start delegating some things. Now that the restaurant continues to get busier and more popular, it's becoming increasingly difficult to manage everything myself.

> Me: Laurie should be coming in at three for the dinner shift, but this is only her fourth day, so if you need more help, call Erica.

> Christy: Laurie's great! We should be fine. Thanks, Jules. I'll head over in a bit to get started on the bread.

Me: I appreciate it!

I let out a sigh of relief and toss my phone onto the bed. I feel a little guilty that I don't want to work. I love my restaurant. I worked damn hard for it, and I'm grateful that I have it.

But I haven't had a true day off in longer than I can remember.

Maybe Jackie's right. Perhaps I should schedule a day off every week to avoid burnout.

I can admit, though, that my funk has nothing to do with the restaurant and everything to do with a certain auto mechanic.

It's been a week since he fucked me in his garage. I haven't seen him since. It's like we've gone back to the way it was when I first moved back to town, and we're avoiding each other. He did text me two days ago to let me know that my car would take a few more days, but otherwise, there hasn't been any communication.

And I didn't expect more from him.

The sex was off-the-charts amazing because it's Brooks, and the sex was always fantastic with us. He was my first. Hell, I was *his* first. We were always good together. But it surprised the hell out of me when he kissed me, then bent me over that bench. Fuck, I wanted him. I didn't say no. I didn't push him away. Because being close to Brooks like that? Well, there's nothing better in the world, and I've been craving him for most of my adult life.

Like I said, the sex itself was great.

But there was no ... *emotion.* And that's what I

needed, if I'm being honest with myself. I needed him to kiss me tenderly, to hug me to him, and say soft words.

And that's something that Brooks is no longer willing or able to give me. I can't do one without the other.

Not with Brooks.

So I don't regret putting my foot down when he came here later that night and telling him that he didn't get to do that again.

But then I remember how it felt when he covered my tattoo with his hand and pounded into me harder, so *maybe* I could let him do it again.

I blow out a breath, frustrated with myself.

"Go on your walk, Jules. Get fresh air, then take your book somewhere that isn't in this building and relax for the day."

Actually, that sounds nice.

I don't want to have to come back here at all, so I grab a bigger handbag to sling across my body and slide my book inside, along with all of the essentials. Once I'm dressed, I lock the door, checking it three times, and descend the stairs. I pop into the restaurant to grab some breakfast and a snack for later, stowing those in my bag, too, before I head off.

It's good that I made myself get up and out of that stuffy apartment.

It's cooler today, so I'm in jeans and a sweatshirt, and I take my time on my walk. I don't have to rush to get back to start work.

I can meander. Soak everything in.

I always avoid the street I grew up on, and I do that

again today. I don't want to see that house. Some of my worst memories live there, and I don't want to relive them on a daily basis. Hell, I don't want to remember them at all.

But I do walk in front of the big house that I love. Someone has been fixing it up. There are hanging baskets of flowers that give it some color. I can tell that the porch has been repaired recently.

I never manage to see the owners outside, but that's okay. I probably don't want to know who lives there.

Just as I'm past the house and about to turn the corner, my phone pings with a text from Harper.

> Harper: Good morning! Any chance you have cinnamon rolls at the restaurant this morning? I'm just leaving the hospital, and they sound so good.

I laugh and call my friend. She answers on the first ring.

"Give me the good news," she says.

"Unfortunately, no cinnamon rolls today. Sorry, friend."

"Well, damn. This baby is craving them."

I smile and then decide I probably *could* go back and make her some.

"You know, I'm not working today, but I can go in and make you a pan, if you want."

"What? Oh, absolutely *not*. Are you sick? Are you okay?"

"I'm ... not sick."

She's quiet for a second. "But you're not okay?"

I blow out a breath of frustration. "I'm ... I don't know, Harper. It's just been one of those weeks."

"Where are you? I'm coming to get you. Ava will meet us at my house, and we'll eat something delicious and talk."

Holy shit, that sounds amazing.

"Harper, you're just getting off work, and you need to rest."

"Do you go to sleep the second you get off work? Of course not. I'll be up for a few hours at least. Seriously, come hang with me for a while since you're not working today."

"If you're sure."

"Oh, I'm sure. Where are you?"

I look up and give her the cross streets, and she assures me she'll be here in less than ten minutes.

It takes her seven to pull up to the curb, and I climb in the passenger seat.

"Ava's on her way."

"Does she have today off, too?"

"She doesn't usually go in to work until later because she likes to do Pilates in the morning." Harper shudders. "That sounds horrible to me."

I smirk because it doesn't sound fun to me, either.

Not that I've ever *done* Pilates.

Harper pulls into her garage just as Ava pulls in behind us, and we all climb out of the cars. Harper gestures for us to follow her inside through the garage door.

She has a nice mudroom area where we kick off our

shoes, and when we walk into the kitchen, Blake is there, leaning against the counter, drinking his coffee. He's in scrubs, so it looks like he's about to go to work.

And he looks so much like Brooks, it almost breaks my heart all over again.

"Good morning, ladies," he says, but he only has eyes for his girl.

"They're about to get disgusting," Ava says, taking my hand and pulling me through the kitchen and to a nearby living room. "Hi and goodbye, Blake."

"Hey, Blake," I say with a little wave as Ava pulls me past them.

Blake smirks, sets his coffee down, and I catch a glimpse of him pulling Harper into his arms just as we turn the corner and they're out of sight.

"It's good that they're in love," I tell Ava as I sit on the sofa and pull my feet up under me. "They're having a baby. They're getting married. These are all beautiful things."

"I agree, but I don't want to watch them *make* the baby."

I snort and set my bag at my feet. Harper joins us, her lips shiny and a little swollen, and the bun that her hair was in is gone.

Looks like Blake had his hands in her hair.

That's adorable.

"Okay, I have breakfast burritos that I premade in my air fryer. Don't worry, Jules, they're gluten-free. I haven't had gluten in this house in a long time."

"Thank you." I don't know what I did to find these

friends, but I'm grateful. I haven't had girlfriends in ... I don't even remember.

Justin did a good job of isolating me from just about everyone.

"Jules gave me the short version: that you took the day off, you're not sick, but you're not great either." Ava's eyes soften as she smiles at me. "We're in the cone of silence here. You can tell us anything."

I eye Harper, and she nods with encouragement. "Blake isn't here. So if this is about Brooks, I'm not his soon-to-be sister-in-law, I'm *your* friend."

I blow out a breath and stand to pace.

"I really love your house. It's so spacious and nice."

There's no reaction, and when I turn to look at my friends, they're both just staring at me.

"I fucked Brooks. Or he fucked *me*, and then it was weird, and I ran out and told him never again, but he still has my car, and I hate that he hates me, and I miss him, and I just want to pull the covers over my head and die."

Ava's smile is as wide as the Grand Canyon.

Harper starts to slow clap.

"Why are you happy? Did you not just hear what I said?"

"Oh yeah, we heard," Ava says, nodding. "You fucked Brooks, and it's about damn time. Was it good? Where were you? We need details."

"Details," Harper echoes.

So I tell them. I start from the beginning, seeing his lights on, taking him dinner, and everything that happened until he left my apartment that night.

"You've been struggling with this for a *week*?" Ava demands. "Why weren't we your first phone call?"

"Because ... I don't know, you guys, I'm not good at being a friend."

The air fryer dings, and Harper holds up a finger.

"Stop right there. Let's go to the kitchen."

We file in, and Harper sets the burritos on plates, and they smell so freaking good. I don't even know how much I've eaten in the past week, since I've been so up in my head.

"You're a good friend, Juliet," Ava says after taking a bite.

"I'm so out of practice," I admit with a sigh. "I used to have friends, especially in college. But Justin made sure that *he* was my only friend and isolated me from everyone."

"Wait, who's Justin?" Harper asks, and I share a look with Ava.

"My late husband."

Harper's burrito drops onto her plate with a *plop*, and she stares at me with wide eyes.

"*What?*"

"He was your *husband*?" Ava demands.

"It's a whole thing." I sigh and roll my shoulders, trying to get the kinks out. "A long-ass story."

"I'm wide awake and here for it," Harper states. "Spill it. Tell us everything."

"Tell us *everything*," Ava echoes. "And no leaving stuff out this time. You told me about your history with Brooks from before, but you didn't say that Justin was your *husband*."

"This is a whole lot of drama."

"Great. Tell it." Harper rolls her hand in a *move-along* gesture.

And an hour later, when we're back in the living room, and I'm exhausted and crying, and we're all just staring at each other, Ava says, "Fuck."

"Yeah, fuck."

"But you're having sex," Harper says.

"No, we *had* sex. Once. And it was just fucking. Actually, now that I think about it, it was hate fucking. Because the man can't stand me."

And that's what makes me the saddest of all.

"I call bullshit." Ava shakes her head. "If a man hates you that much, he doesn't fuck you. No matter how good it is."

"Agreed." Harper nods. "He may be angry, and he might not *want* to want you, but he does, Jules."

"He destroyed me once," I admit softly. "I can't do it again."

"Who said anything about destroying?" Ava demands. "Unless it's him destroying your vajayjay. Because I've met the man, and Holy Baby Jesus, he looks like he'd be fun in bed."

"He's fun everywhere," I admit with a smug grin, but then I shake my head. "But I haven't even heard from him this week, except to tell me my car isn't ready yet."

"You told him to leave," Harper points out. "So he left, Jules."

Well, shit.

She's right.

"I was embarrassed, and I didn't want him in my apartment." The last word is whispered.

"What's wrong with your apartment?" Ava tilts her head to the side as she frowns at me.

"It's just an attic, really. And I know that I shouldn't be embarrassed by it, but I am, and it makes me uncomfortable when he's up there."

"Honey, you need to have this entire conversation with *Brooks*," Harper says. "You should tell him about that piece-of-shit Justin."

"You did the right thing there," Ava says.

"He'll be so mad."

"Yeah, he will," Harper agrees. "Because that asshole fucked everything up for you, and that makes me so mad and sad all at the same time. But he deserves to know how it all went down."

"Wait." Ava holds up her hand. "Jules, have you only ever had sex with Brooks and Justin?"

I bite my lip and nod.

"Wow. That's ... intense."

"Yeah." I sigh and notice that Harper's eyes have gotten heavy. "You have to sleep. You worked all night, and you're pregnant."

"I guess it is my bedtime." Harper yawns. "Did we help you feel better?"

"It helps to talk it out, and I think you're right. At some point, I have to talk to the man, but he's so broody and angry, and I hate that."

"Maybe he wouldn't be so broody if he knew what you told us today," Ava points out. "Something to think about."

113

Ava drops me off in front of the restaurant. It's not quite noon—I was with my new best friends for a long time—and I said that I didn't want to just lie around in bed all day.

I still don't.

But I don't have my car. So I walk down to the city park right in the center of town and find a bench in the shade, pull my book out of my bag, and settle in to read for the afternoon.

There's a nice breeze today, and the sun came out, so it's pleasantly warm.

Before long, I'm lying in the grass, my sweatshirt under me as a pillow, and my eyes are heavy as I try to read my book.

I should go home and take a nap.

But it's so lovely out here. I lean back and close my eyes for just a minute.

"Jules? Are you okay? Christ, what happened?"

I blink my eyes open and frown up at Brooks, who's scowling down at me.

"What?" I sit up and realize that I'm still in the park.

I fell asleep.

"Are you okay? You scared the shit out of me."

"A girl can't take a nap in the park?" I rub my hands down my face. I'm totally disoriented and have no idea how long I've been asleep. It could have been ten minutes or five hours. It could be ten years in the future, or I could be late for school for all I know.

This is why I don't take naps.

"By yourself? Fuck no."

I sigh. I don't want to look at him.

So I don't.

"I'm fine, Brooks. I was reading and fell asleep." I check the time. "It wasn't even thirty minutes."

"You shouldn't let your guard down like that."

Now I do look up at him. His hands are on his hips, and he's so broody. So ... *handsome.*

Why does he have to be so damn handsome?

"I haven't let my guard down in fifteen years. I think thirty minutes in this little park, in the middle of the day, is fine." *Shit, I've said too much.* "Thanks, though. I'll head home."

"No, stay and read. I just had to make sure you're okay, since it looked like you were passed out on the grass."

"Why?" I stand and brush off my clothes, then face him. "Why do you care?"

"Jules, I do care if you're safe."

I smirk at that and turn away.

"I'm safe, Brooks."

"You're so fucking infuriating!"

I spin around and gape at him. "*I* am?"

"Yes. You."

Not wanting to have a screaming match in this public park, I get close to him, glaring up at him.

"You don't want me, remember? You told me to stay away, to avoid you at all costs. I'm doing that. You don't get to have it both ways, Brooks. I wasn't bothering you by taking a little nap here in this park. I was just trying to take a day off and relax. But obviously, that offends you."

"Stop it." He lowers his head so his lips are next to my ear, and a shiver rolls through me. "I was fucking worried about you, and I won't apologize for that. I don't know how to handle you, Wildfire."

"You don't handle me." I shake my head and pull away. "We're strangers. Is my car ready?"

"A couple more days."

"Jesus, I'm going to be so fucking broke." I swallow hard and then shrug. "Oh well. Thanks for waking me up."

I turn to leave, but he calls my name.

I don't stop.

I wake up to the sound of running water.

Not like it's coming out of a faucet.

Like it's rushing down a ravine in the middle of the woods.

Sitting straight up in bed, I cock my head, trying to decide where it's coming from. Is it raining?

No. It's *inside*.

"Shit." I turn on the lamp beside me and stare in horror as a river of water flows down from where a pipe has burst in the middle of my attic and is rushing all over the floor, through the floorboards, and likely into my restaurant below.

I don't know what to do.

I have no idea where the water valve is located to shut off the water to the building.

I step out of bed and fall on my ass because of the wet floor, and all I can do is sit here, in the middle of this mess, and cry.

Then the power goes out, and I'm in the dark.

"Fuck my life," I mutter as I pull myself back onto the bed and reach for my phone.

I guess I'll call the fire department.

Twenty minutes later, there's a knock on my door, and I slosh through the room, in my wet clothes, to open it, letting about a foot of water out to fall down the staircase, and find Bridger staring down at me.

"Hi, Bridge."

"I hear you have a water problem."

"I've heard the same rumor." I'm on the verge of having a nervous breakdown. I'm shaking, and my heart is pounding.

"Do you have shoes on?"

"I can't find them." A tear slips out of my eye. "I think they floated out when I opened the door. I have my purse and my phone."

"Then that's all you need. Let's get you out of here."

"Oh, I can show you—"

"No, Jules. I'm evacuating you now. I don't need you getting electrocuted."

I blanch at that and let him guide me downstairs to

where two big fire trucks sit, along with five other fire-fighters.

"Sorry to bring you out in the middle of the night," I say to them.

"This is our whole job," one of them reminds me with a wink.

"Let's get power and water shut off to the whole building," Bridger calls out, clearly in fire chief mode.

It's kind of hot.

Let's be honest, all the Blackwells are hot.

I don't have anywhere to go, so I step out of the way and wait, clutching my purse to my chest as I watch the men scatter, calling things out to each other, working together to get the water stopped and the electricity shut off.

Thirty minutes later, Bridger crosses to me, his hand-some face grim, and my stomach explodes with nerves.

"I have good news and bad news, Jules."

Swallowing hard, I nod. "Okay."

"Which do you want first?"

"The bad news?" It's said like a question, because honestly, I don't think I want any bad news at all.

"You have a *lot* of water here. Both the upstairs and downstairs have sustained significant water damage."

"It couldn't have even been running for a full hour."

"A lot of water can run in that amount of time, especially at the rate it was flowing out of that pipe. I'm sorry, Jules. I really am. You will need to call a water restoration company tomorrow. They'll come in and remove the rest of the water, then set up fans to dry it as much as possible. Then you can assess what's salvageable."

"Are you telling me that I can't open for business in the morning?"

Bridger scowls and takes my shoulders in his hands. "Yeah, that's what I'm telling you. It's a mess in there. I'm so sorry."

I want to lean my forehead on him for support, but of course I don't.

You have got to be kidding me.

"What's the good news?" I ask him.

"I found your shoes." He gestures to the ground next to him. "They're a little damp, but they're fine."

I let out a huff of a laugh and slide my feet inside, sick of standing on the asphalt of this alley in my bare feet. I scrunch my nose up when I slosh around.

"Do you have somewhere to go tonight?"

No.

"Sure. Can I go in there to grab some things first?"

"The electricity is off and won't be turned back on until all the water is gone. It's safe, but it's a mess. And slick in some places, so you'll need to be careful."

"But it won't kill me."

"No."

"Thanks." The others have gotten in the trucks. One has already pulled away, and the other is waiting for the chief. "You can go. I've got this."

"You sure you have somewhere to go? You can crash at my place for the rest of the night if you want and come back here in the daylight."

I shake my head. "Nah, I'm okay. Thanks, though. Tell Dani hi for me."

He turns to walk away but then looks back at me. "We missed you, Jules."

Oh God, don't make me cry.

"I missed you, too."

Chapter Ten

BROOKS

"We took her to Vegas for the weekend," Gabe says as he crosses to his tool chest to grab a drill. "She'd never been before."

Gabe is my cousin on my dad's side, and he's been working for me for a while now. We've always gotten along well, and he does excellent work. He's in a relationship with Dani's sister, Alex, and a man named Adam who I've met a few times.

The three of them are making it work, and I'm happy for him.

"I don't think Alex has traveled much," I reply as I close the hood on Juliet's car.

It's finally finished. I can't procrastinate giving it back to her any longer. I could have had it done a few days ago, but this is my only tie to the woman I can't stop thinking about. The one I want more than I'm willing to admit or am happy about.

The woman who has haunted me for fifteen motherfucking years.

Once I give it to her, there won't be any reason to talk to her.

And that pisses me off.

The door of the garage opens, and Birdie skips inside. It's late, almost quitting time. With the change of seasons, it's getting dark outside earlier.

The sun has already gone down, and it's raining.

Fall is here.

"Hi, Uncle Brooks," Birdie calls out as Bridger walks in behind her.

"What are you guys up to?" I ask as I squat, and Birdie walks right into my arms so I can lift her.

"I had to have a checkup at the doctor," she tells me. "And then I wanted to see you."

I raise an eyebrow. "You did?"

"Yeah. Are you going to teach me how to fix cars?"

I chuckle and glance at my brother, who's wandered over to chat with Gabe.

"Sure. I'll teach you. But you'll get your hands dirty."

She scrunches up her nose and then shrugs. "I guess that's okay. I'm sad, Uncle Brooks."

Birdie pushes that little lower lip out in a pout, and I do the same, mirroring her.

"Why?"

"Because my restaurant is closed."

Unease niggles its way into my stomach. "Did they close early today?"

Birdie shakes her head, and Bridger walks my way.

"No, there was a flood," Birdie says, and my eyes immediately move to my brother.

"What?"

"Yeah, poor Jules," Bridger says with a sigh. "Middle of the night the other night, one of the pipes in her attic burst, flooded the whole damn building before we could get it shut off."

"What the fu—" I glance at my baby girl, cutting off the swear word. "Why didn't anyone tell me?"

"Is it your favorite, too?" Birdie asks, patting my cheek, as if consoling me.

"Something like that." I set the little girl on her feet. "Gabe, I have to go."

"I'll lock up," he calls back with a wave.

"I don't think she's staying there," Bridger says as he and Birdie walk out with me. "She said she had somewhere to stay."

I stop next to my truck and turn to him. "Where?"

"She didn't say."

"Her parents are dead, no siblings, not many friends. Where the hell do you think she had to go, Bridge?"

He shifts on his feet. "I offered my place, but she insisted—"

"Yeah, because she's a stubborn little thing." I shake my head and climb into the cab of my truck, wave at Birdie, and pull out of my lot.

I have a feeling that my wildfire has been staying in that attic, *with water damage*, because she's too fucking stubborn to ask for help.

I'm going to spank her perfect ass.

After I take her home with me, where she belongs.

It takes seconds to get down the street. It's fully dark now and still raining. When I pull into a parking space in front of the restaurant, I see that the lights are on inside.

There's a note taped to the door.

Dear Customers,

We are closed due to plumbing issues. We are working on this matter and will reopen ASAP. Don't worry, this is temporary!

Thank you for your patience,

Juliet

I don't see anyone inside. Big fans are blowing, and the chairs are on top of the tables.

I can see from here that the floor is ruined. All that original hardwood bubbled up and will need to be ripped out and replaced.

Fuck, baby. I'm so sorry.

Circling to the alley, I climb her stairs and knock on the door of her apartment. I'm impatient to get to her.

I need to see her and make sure she's okay.

When she opens the door, humid air hits me, and I'm so damn ... *pissed.*

"Are you staying up here?" I ask as I muscle my way inside. The floor is still squishy under my feet. My eyes scan the area, and I see the water line on the walls, as well as the clothes she has hanging from the wire she strung to dry them out.

"Of course I am," she says. "I live here."

"No, Wildfire." I turn to her and can't keep my hands to myself. I frame her face, and she doesn't pull away. Christ, she looks exhausted. She has bruises under her eyes from the lack of sleep, her hair is a mess, and I'd swear that she's lost weight in the few days since I last saw her. "I'm taking you home with me."

"Brooks—"

I lean into her and *almost* rest my forehead against hers.

"Let me help you. You shouldn't be staying up here, Juliet. It's too wet, and you could get mold. It's not safe. It's definitely not comfortable. Come home with me."

She bites her lower lip, and I can see that she wants to cry, but she swallows the tears down.

She's going to refuse me.

"Please, baby." I tug her into me, wrap my arms around her, and hug her close. "I can't stand the thought of you here."

She takes a deep, ragged breath, and her arms circle around me, and I feel like I can breathe.

"I would love to get out of here for the night." Her voice is small, and I don't have to be told twice.

"Grab what you need."

She hurries to retrieve her handbag and phone, then opens a drawer to pull out some clothes that look as if they have escaped the water, and tosses them into a grocery bag.

A fucking grocery bag.

I take the bag from her, and we leave the apartment. She locks the door, but then I notice that she moves back to the door three times to check the locks.

That's different.

I lead her down the stairs and around to the front of the building where I'm parked.

"Do you want to turn off the lights in there?" I ask her.

"No, it's okay. I'm too tired, Brooks."

I'm going to punch everyone who knew about this but didn't tell me. Even my brother.

"Come on then." I open the door of the truck, and she climbs in. When she's settled in the seat, I put the seat belt on her, then kiss her smooth cheek.

She stiffens but doesn't pull away.

I've been such a dick to her that she can't stand me touching her.

I should punch myself.

As I drive through town, I glance over and see that she's resting her head on the window. Her eyes are closed, and her hands are in fists in her lap. As I get closer to the house, her hands soften, and she relaxes.

She's fallen asleep on the two-minute drive from her place to mine.

My girl is wrecked. And I haven't been there to help her.

And goddammit, that stops now because no matter what happened between us in the past, she's here now, and I can't stay away.

I can't continue to live without her.

I pull into my driveway and cut the engine by the back door, in front of the garage. She doesn't stir.

"Hey, Jules, we're here. Baby, I'm going to come around and get you, okay?"

She wrinkles her brow but doesn't fully wake up, and it breaks my heart.

Christ, she's destroying me here.

Pushing out of the truck, I circle the hood and gently open her door, catching her when she would lean out. I unfasten her seat belt, then lift her into my arms and kiss the top of her head as I close the truck door with my foot and carry her to the back door, which I never lock.

I get her inside and decide that putting her in my bed, where I want her, would only piss her off when she wakes up, so I take her to the only guest room I have. Birdie has stayed in here a few times, but otherwise, this room is mostly unused.

Thankfully, the bedding is clean, so I lay her on top of the blankets. Jules snuggles right down into the pillow, hugging it to her. I've never wanted to be a pillow so bad in my life.

Striding away from her, I go out to the truck to get her things and bring them inside. I lock the back door—I now have something to lose in here—and set her things on the dresser in the room she's in.

She's dressed in red sweat shorts and a black tank top, and I assume those are her pajamas, so she'll be comfortable.

Which is good because if I had to strip her down and put her in one of my shirts, I might not survive it. I was inside her over a week ago, and I've thought of nothing else since. I handled it so fucking poorly that all I did was piss her off and push her away.

Which, a few months ago, I would have said is exactly what I wanted.

But now that I've had my hands on her, there's no way I can let her go. I don't simply want her.

I *need* her.

And I'll prove to her that I'm not a complete asshole. There's a lot to learn when it comes to my wildfire. She

KRISTEN PROBY

wasn't wrong the other day when she said we're strangers.

We are.

But that's about to change.

Turning around, I grab a blanket from the closet and cover her with it. Then I leave the room altogether because every cell in my body is screaming at me to get in that bed with her. To snuggle up to her, hold her against me, and comfort her. To *be with her.*

Doing that without her consent would be a dick move. She tensed up when I simply kissed her cheek. I don't think she'd welcome my entire body wrapped around her while she sleeps.

Leaving her here alone, however, is out of the question, so I walk out to the kitchen and grab a chair, then return to the room and sit in it, right next to the bed. I'll respect her space, but I'm not leaving her side.

Not ever again.

"Brooks?"

Someone is nudging my leg. When I open my eyes, I see Juliet's hand touching my shin where I've rested my feet on the bed, and she's looking at me with a frown on her beautiful face.

My neck is killing me, and my lower back is *not* happy, but she's touching me, so I refuse to move.

"You don't have to stay in here."

Her voice is a raspy whisper here in the dark. I check the time and see that it's still the middle of the night. We fell asleep early, so I shouldn't be surprised that she woke up.

"I'm fine right here," I reply softly.

"You can't be comfortable."

"That doesn't matter. I want to be near you."

She lies back on the pillow, watching me in the moonlight. My leg is cold where her hand just was.

"Come here." She pats the bed beside her. "You should lie down."

"I can't."

"Why?"

I sit forward, pulling my legs off the bed, and rub my hands down my face.

"Because if I lie down next to you, I'll want to hold you, and—"

"Brooks. Get your butt over here."

I watch her for a moment, but her gaze doesn't falter. I stand and then lower myself next to her, keeping at least a foot between us. Jules wiggles onto her side to face me.

"Thanks for letting me come here tonight."

"If I'd known what happened, I would have brought you here much sooner."

She nibbles her lower lip, and I can't resist reaching out to tug that lip free with my thumb. This is where she was always supposed to be. With me, in this house.

And now she's here, lying on this bed with me, and it feels completely surreal. Nothing's ever felt so right, yet unbelievable at the same time.

"Do you want to tell me what happened?" I ask her.

"I woke up in the middle of the night to the sound of rushing water. Scared the hell out of me. The pipe in the attic burst, and it ran for so long that it destroyed the floors, both upstairs and downstairs. It's a mess. I called the fire department because I didn't know what to do, and Bridger came. Got the water and electric shut off."

"So you've been living there for several days without water or power?"

"Just water. We got the power back on the next day after the water experts came in and drained most of it so I wouldn't get electrocuted from walking across the floor."

I growl. There's no holding it in. The mere thought has me pulled tight in agitation.

And she must sense it because she reaches over and takes my hand, as if she does it every day, and it immediately soothes me.

"It's going to be a couple of weeks of repairs." She swallows hard. "And it's so expensive. I didn't want to dip into the money Justin left me, but—"

"Whoa." I tighten my hand in hers, frowning at her. Her eyes go wide, as if she just realized what she said. "Back up, Wildfire. What money?"

Her eyes close, and she buries her face in the pillow, letting out a little moan.

"Hey, it's okay." Hearing his name makes me a little unhinged, but I stay calm as I nudge her back so I can see her face. "Talk to me. I'm going to be real with you right now. I *need* to be able to move forward with you because being without you is nothing but pure hell. I suspect that we can't do that until you fill in the past fifteen years for me. We need to put it behind us, Jules."

"You're going to be so mad," she whispers.

"Maybe." I won't lie to her and deny it. "But we need to be honest. I can wait if you're tired and want to go back to sleep."

She shakes her head and rubs her free hand under her nose.

"I'd like to sit up, though." She pushes up and leans her back against the headboard, then draws her legs up to her chest, as if she's protecting herself. "How much do you want to know?"

"Every-fucking-thing."

"Jesus." She drops her forehead to her knees, and I sit up to face her, waiting patiently for her to gather her thoughts. "I think we're both going to be mad."

"Then we'll be angry together." I reach for her hand again, and she lets her legs fall, her eyes pinned to her linked fingers. "You can tell me just about anything. I'm not going anywhere."

"Of course not. You live here."

Her lips twitch, and I smile at her.

Those gorgeous blue eyes widen and fill with unshed tears.

"I think that's the first time you've smiled at me in ... *God*." She shakes her head and looks away, pulling herself together. "Okay, so I'm going to talk, and you can ask questions as you have them because it's a lot."

"Sounds fair."

She licks her lips, and I hold up a finger. "Hold that thought. I'm going to grab us some waters. Do you want a snack?"

"Just the water is good."

I lean forward and kiss her cheek, then climb from the bed and rush to the kitchen, snag the bottles from the fridge, then return to her, sit on the mattress, and pass her the drink.

She watches me as she takes a sip from the bottle, then clears her throat.

"He was *just* my friend back then," she begins. "I never lied to you about that. He was my roommate, and he was ... nice. Charming, I guess. All of us got along, and I thought he was a harmless, normal guy."

I nod because I know this. I never suspected that she was fucking around on me with him. She wouldn't have done that.

"That second year we lived in the house together, my senior year, it was the anniversary of my dad's death, and I was having a hard time that day. You were at work, and my mom wasn't answering the phone, and I felt lonely. Just a shit day, you know?"

I nod, and she takes a drink and keeps talking.

"Justin came home from class and asked me why I looked so blue, and I told him. And that's when the suicide threats started."

"Fuck."

She nods. "Yep. He saw the weakness, the thing that would get my attention, and he used it for the next thirteen years."

My heart stops, and I stare at her. "*What*?"

"Are you sure you want to know this?"

"No." I shake my head, but she takes my hand. *Fuck*, she had to deal with that piece of shit for thirteen years? I finally shrug a shoulder. "Okay, go ahead."

"Any time he thought I wasn't paying him enough attention, he'd threaten to kill himself. He did it often, and as you know, that's why I'd go back to Seattle when I was visiting here, or get off the phone with you. It wasn't just you, either. He hated it when I talked to my mom or any of my friends. He'd find a way to manipulate the situation and make me feel sorry for him. I didn't see it at the time. I truly thought he meant what he was threatening. That he was suicidal, and after finding my dad, I just ... I couldn't risk it."

"Christ."

"I'm going to skim over some things because otherwise, we'll be here all night. The gist of it is, he played the role of supportive bestie really well. After you and I broke up, he was Mr. Dependable. Ate ice cream with me, consoled me, told me how stupid you were."

She gives me a half smile, and I huff out a laugh.

"He played the part. For five years, he was *just* my friend. We weren't always roommates, but he lived close by. Then he got cancer."

My eyebrows climb at that.

"And he told me that his dying wish was for me to marry him."

No. Absolutely fucking not.

I stand and pace the bedroom, needing to punch something. I can't sit still.

If the next words out of her perfect mouth are to tell me that she married another fucking man, I might lose my goddamn mind.

"I told you," she says with tears in her voice. "You don't want to know this, Brooks."

"*Fuck.*" I push my hands through my hair and then stare at her. "Finish it."

"Brooks—"

"Just say it."

"Come back here." Her voice is so shaky, and she's so upset, I couldn't resist her if I wanted to. So I climb back on the bed and take her hand again. "He said that he'd been given one year to live, and he wanted to spend that year with me. He manipulated me into marrying him."

"You fucking *married* that prick?"

She nods, pressing her lips together.

"Then he miraculously went into remission."

"Jesus Christ. Did you not go to his appointments with him?"

"Oh, I did. But Justin was wealthy, and he could pay a doctor to say whatever he wanted. So for the next eight-ish years, whenever I told him that I wanted to separate, he'd either *attempt* to kill himself, or his cancer was back."

"That motherfucker."

"We had separate bedrooms."

My eyes fly to hers in surprise. "Why?"

"Because he was so sick, and he said he needed to rest. Which worked well for me because sex with Justin—" She shakes her head, and I feel nauseous. "Just, no. And that's all I'll say about that. He was controlling. He was manipulative. And honestly, I think I was a prize for him. It's not that he was so head over heels in love with me that he couldn't live without me. He just decided at some point that he wanted me, and figured out a way to make it happen, and decided that he'd *won*. He never said that, but that's my gut feeling."

"Is he why you react the way you do to being startled?"

Her eyes close again. "Yeah. He liked to scare me. He did it all the time, and then he'd laugh and laugh. He was cruel. He isolated me from everyone. By the time he died, my mom was gone, but I never really talked to her much anyway. My old roommates stopped checking in to see if I wanted to get together. I was his *thing*. For the most part, he left me alone. I couldn't tell you the last time he touched me. Not just sexually. When he was my *bestie*, as he called himself, we'd hug or he'd touch my arm, that sort of thing. But later, no. He didn't touch me at all."

She swallows, and I can tell that we're nearing the end of the story.

"How did he die, baby?"

Jules blows out a breath and tips her head back against the headboard.

"We were in a car accident."

Every muscle in my body tightens, and I can't stand it anymore. I pull her into my arms and hug her so close, I'm surprised she can still breathe.

"Hey, I'm okay."

"Fuck. *Fuck*."

Her fingers comb through my hair, and she rubs her hand up and down my back.

"I'm right here, Brooks."

I pull back enough to cup her chin and lay my lips over hers. "Are you telling me I almost lost you?"

"No, I was barely hurt," she says, and the knot in my stomach loosens just a bit. "I'm okay."

Letting out a shaky breath, I relax my hold on her so she can continue with her story.

"We'd been arguing because I wanted to *finally* leave him, and he was throwing a fit, talking about how his chemo was about to start again, and how could I abandon him, blah blah blah. He wasn't watching the road, and there was a curve, and he went into the ditch. A tree smashed his side of the car. By the time we got to a hospital, he was brain dead."

Her eyes find mine, and they look so haunted. So fucking tired.

"They asked me if he was an organ donor, and if I wanted to donate his organs to save someone else, and I was so confused. This was the same hospital system where he received cancer treatment, so they had his medical records. I said, '*How can you donate organs from a cancer patient?*'"

I shake my head. Fuck, I know where this is going.

"And they told me that he didn't have cancer. He was as healthy as could be. He'd *never* had cancer, Brooks."

"Jesus." I plant my lips in her hair and hug her to me. "What did you do?"

"I told them to take everything they needed from him and then pull the plug."

She shifts in my lap and cups my cheek.

"That was two years ago. After he died, I found *meticulous* notes that he'd taken about how he'd manipulated me. How he broke us up, kept me close, did all he could to make me marry him. But that's not all I found, Brooks."

I frown down at her. "What else is there?"

She blows out a breath. "Jesus, I've never said this out loud to anyone."

"I'm not just anyone," I remind her.

"He must have had fifty mistresses in the time we were together," she whispers, and my blood heats with more anger. "That's why he insisted on separate rooms, so he could come in and out of the house without me noticing. He wasn't fucking me, which is fine, but he *was* fucking. When his estate was settled, it was discovered that he had left a huge sum of money in a trust for one of those women. I don't care. I don't want his money. But he made me the executor of her trust."

I frown down at her. "Wait. That piece-of-shit motherfucker made it so that you have to be in constant contact with his side piece?"

"Pretty much." She nods and then huffs out a laugh. "She gets automatic payments, but she burns through the money so fast that she always tries to get more from me."

That must be who called her that morning, asking for money.

"Jesus, he fucked you over."

"I think that's the shittiest part. I mean, he left me with everything else. I sold the huge house we lived in and used the money to buy my building and start my restaurant. The rest of the money I don't want, so it just sits in an account. I won't touch it. Although with all the water damage, I might have to dip into it to fix my place up."

Jesus, I feel like shit. All those years, she dealt with an abusive piece of garbage, and I didn't know.

"I never should have let you go." I press my forehead to hers. "I should have stood my ground and fought for you. I shouldn't have walked away."

"I understand why you did," she insists. "Brooks, I was a shitty girlfriend that last year. I was absent. You were way more patient than you should have been."

I'm shaking my head, but she finally straddles my lap and frames my face in her sweet hands.

"Listen to me. We can *shoulda woulda coulda* the whole situation for days, but it doesn't change anything. The past is the past. It happened, and thank God it's over. *Thank God* it's over."

She wraps her arms around my neck and hugs me close, and I hug her back.

I want to burn down those fifteen years.

I want to resurrect that asshole and kill him all over again.

More than anything, I wish I could go back and do everything differently.

But I can't. All I can do is build something new with her now.

"I'm sorry," she whispers into my neck. "I'm sorry I moved home. I know you don't want me here, and I should have gone anywhere else, but I really missed it here."

"It's your home." She shifts in my arms, and I brush

her blond curls back from her face, then run my fingertips down her soft cheek.

Christ, now that I've touched her again, I can't seem to stop.

"This is your home, Wildfire. You have as much of a right to be here as I do."

"I really don't," she whispers. "But I haven't fit in anywhere in so long, and I really missed the mountains, and—"

"Hey. You don't have to justify anything to me. You don't owe me anything."

"I think I'm a really bad person," she says with a voice so small, it shatters my already broken heart. "And that's why all of these horrible things keep happening to me."

"No, you're not. You're a beautiful person. That's why he was able to control and manipulate you. I'm the shitty one because I'd like to skin him alive, then set the rest of him on fire. I would relish his screams of terror. *That's* a bad person, Jules."

"You're not bad." She wiggles closer to me, and I soak in the feel of her cuddled up against my chest. "You're protective. Even when you hate me."

We sit in silence for a moment as I drag my fingers up and down her arm.

"I don't hate you," I murmur. "It's not possible for me to hate you. And I think that's what pissed me off the most. Because I wanted to hate you, Juliet."

"I know."

Chapter Eleven

JULIET

The smell of bacon pulls me out of a deep, dreamless sleep. Sitting up, I rub my hands over my face and look around. Daylight spills in through the curtains on the window, and Brooks is gone.

He's making breakfast.

I have no idea where the bathroom is in this house. I hardly remember him carrying me in here last night. I was so freaking exhausted. Not only physically but also emotionally.

I still am, if I'm being honest.

I pad out of the open door and find a bathroom just across the hall. There's a new toothbrush sitting by the sink, and I use it after doing my business, washing my hands, and splashing some water on my face.

Then I let my nose lead me out to the kitchen, where Brooks stands with his back to me, pulling bacon out of a pan.

"Good morning," he says without turning around.

"A couple of things. First, I have *some* celiac-safe things in the kitchen because of Birdie. Her dishes are pink."

He opens the cupboard to show me, and it melts my heart.

"I'm using the one pan I bought for her that has never touched gluten. I'll get more."

"Oh, you don't have to—"

"I'll get more," he says again, and points with the tongs to a stool in front of the island. "Sit. Do you want orange juice?"

"Are you kidding me? I need coffee."

He smirks and then stops to examine me. "How are you, Wildfire?"

"Tired. I slept hard, but I could drift right off again." My yawn is wide and not a little embarrassing, and Brooks crosses to the fridge, where he pulls out a jug of juice and fills a pink glass, then hands it to me. "Drink this. I'm going to send you back to bed after breakfast."

I take a sip and narrow my eyes at him.

Brooks is naturally bossy. He always has been. I'm sure being the oldest of five kids has something to do with it, but mostly, he's just a dominant man.

Especially when it comes to sex.

My thighs clench at that thought. *I love following his orders when he fucks me.*

Not that we're doing that. I just crashed here last night, nothing more.

"You're really overthinking something over there." He shakes his head at me.

Our conversation in the middle of the night seems to have changed things. I can feel the shift. He's no longer looking at me like he wishes I'd disappear. He *smiles* at me. The tenderness that was always there before is back, but with the added benefit of many years of adulthood.

Thank God he doesn't hate me anymore.

"It's just a lot to take in. I feel like I've been over-thinking for *years*." And now that things are calmer with this man, I can breathe again.

My stomach isn't in knots.

That alone makes me want to cry like a freaking baby.

"You know, I didn't take you for a queen-sized bed kind of man."

Brooks smirks at that and then plates our food with bacon, eggs, fruit, and some yogurt. He passes me a pink plate.

I love that he has safe dishes for his niece.

"We didn't stay in my room," he says. "It's the guest room."

"Oh." I nod and stuff some eggs in my mouth, trying to keep my face clear.

He didn't want me in his room.

That's okay. He didn't have to bring me here at all, and it felt good to be in a cooler room without the mildewy smell that's permeating my apartment.

"I didn't want to take you in there without your consent, Wildfire. Not because I didn't want you there."

I narrow my eyes at him. "Why are you suddenly reading my mind?"

His lips tip up in a half smile. "We may be starting over from scratch with each other, but I do still know parts of you."

Starting over.

Is that what we're doing?

Is that what I want to do?

I nibble my food and watch him move about the kitchen. He's eating, but he's also cleaning up after himself as he chews, and I love watching his broad shoulders move in his white T-shirt. He has some new tattoos on his left arm that weren't there when we were younger. I'm still so damn attracted to him.

Maybe more now than ever before, and I wouldn't have thought that was possible.

If there's a way for Brooks and me to start over, to put the past behind us and move forward ... yeah. I'd love to try that.

But it also makes me so nervous because if it doesn't work again, it could destroy me. I'll have to keep my walls up for a while. Protect myself until I can trust that things between us could work out.

"I don't even know where we are," I realize out loud, frowning. "I think I fell asleep in the truck as soon as you pulled out of your parking spot."

"You did," he confirms. "We can walk outside when you're done eating so you can get your bearings. We're in town."

Nodding, I glance around. "It's a great house, Brooks. How long have you lived here?"

His fork pauses midway between his plate and his mouth. "A long time."

I take a bite of bacon, and he picks up the conversation.

"Are you planning to live in your apartment long term?" he asks.

"I don't know. Probably not, but it'll work for a while, once I get it fixed. It's going to take more work now." Sighing, I push aside my mostly empty plate. I was hungrier than I thought. "I should get back to the restaurant and figure out how I'm going to tear out the floor, and all of the million other things that I need to do."

"Come here." Brooks holds his hand out for mine, and without hesitating, I slide my hand into his, linking our fingers, and just like last night, it feels like coming home. "Let me give you a quick tour around here. The house isn't huge. One story, four bedrooms, two bathrooms."

He leads me back down the hallway, past the guest room and bath, and points out the other rooms.

"I use one room for a small home gym, and the other is my office. This at the end is the primary suite."

He leads me inside, and I can't help but smile. This is *so* Brooks. Decorated in browns and oranges, it's masculine. And it smells like him.

Like leather and whiskey and a little motor oil.

His bathroom has recently been remodeled, just like the kitchen. The vanity and double sinks gleam, there's a soaking tub in the corner, and the standing shower looks *heavenly.*

"I have to say, I have bathroom envy."

He smirks, and without thinking about it, he brings my hand up to his lips and kisses my knuckles.

"The laundry is off the kitchen in a mudroom."

"Nice."

He leads me back out through the living room, where a brown leather couch and recliner sit in front of a massive television, and we walk right out the front door.

When I see what's across the street, my jaw drops.

"Holy shit, Brooks. You live across from the big house." I'm staring at my dream home, and it honestly brings tears to my eyes. "This is a good spot."

"Yeah." His own voice is rough. "It's walkable, but you won't have to do that. Come on."

He leads me down the stairs of the porch and around to the garage, where my car is parked out front.

"How—"

"Gabe dropped it off for you this morning. I finished it up last night before I came to your place. The keys are in it."

Oh man, the cost of these repairs on top of the cost of renovating my restaurant is going to kill me.

I have no choice but to use Justin's money.

"Thank God, I can drive again. Thank you. How much do I owe you?"

"You don't owe me anything, Wildfire."

I turn and frown up at him. "It doesn't cost you *nothing* to repair vehicles, Brooks Blackwell. I'm happy to pay you."

"Have you checked your credit card? The idiot who shall not be named should have refunded all of your money."

I blink up at him, then pull my phone out of my pocket and check the app.

Sure enough, more than six thousand dollars was credited last week.

"Holy shit."

"You shouldn't have been treated that way. You have your money back, and I don't want a dime of it."

"But—"

"Christ, you'd argue with a turnip." He frames my face and bends down to slide his lips over mine, brushing gently back and forth and making my skin tingle as he effectively shuts me up. *Fuck, he always was a grade A kisser.* "Come on, you're going back to bed."

"I really should go home—"

"Your home smells like mildew, is likely to get mold, and you're fucking exhausted, Jules. And while you're always fucking gorgeous, you have bruises under your eyes. You need to get some more sleep."

We walk back inside through the back door, and I catch sight of the laundry room before he leads me through to the kitchen.

"See? You're not even arguing with me."

"I *am* tired. But I have so much to do." Tears fill my eyes, and I know it's because of the exhaustion and feeling overwhelmed. "I can't take the day off."

"This is why you need to go back to bed." He picks me up bridal style and walks right past the guest room and into his bedroom. "And I really love the thought of you in *my* bed, Wildfire."

If we're being honest, I love that thought too. But this feels like a slippery slope. I don't want to get too used to it.

"I can use the guest room."

"Are you uncomfortable in my room?"

I bite my lip as I think it over. "No."

146

"Then you'll sleep in here." He sets me on my feet, then opens the covers for me. "Slide in there, pretty girl."

I can't help but smirk as I slip between the sheets, and he covers me up. My eyes are still *so heavy*.

"Why am I so tired?"

"You've had a lot going on," he says, brushing his fingers through my hair. That only makes me sleepier, and before I know it, I've drifted off again.

Chapter Twelve

BROOKS

I am *damn* tempted to climb into my bed with her, strip us both naked, and fuck her until neither of us can breathe.

But she's exhausted, and I have shit to do.

I press my lips to her forehead and walk out of the bedroom. I called my brothers this morning, and they're going to meet me at Sage & Citrus in fifteen minutes. I don't even feel guilty when I find the keys to the restaurant in her purse and lock up behind me before walking out to my truck.

Before leaving, I shoot Jules a text.

> Me: Whenever you wake up, there are coffee pods in the kitchen and cream in the fridge. I'll be at your restaurant all day today, pulling out the old floor.

With that done, I call Dani.

"Hey, you just caught me before I go in to volunteer in Birdie's class. What's up?"

WHERE YOU BELONG

Dani used to teach kindergarten, but after having the baby, she decided to take a few years off to be at home with the kids. She volunteers in Birdie's class once a week, and Birdie *loves* it.

"I need your help," I tell her.

"Of course, anything you need."

I fucking love my family.

For the next ten minutes, I brief Dani on what I need her to help with, then I walk up to the front of the restaurant, unlock it, and enter.

Minutes later, my brothers all walk in after me.

"God, this is horrible." Blake scowls. "We should probably all wear masks. I have some in the car."

"Of course, you do." Bridger shakes his head.

"Fuck you, I'm a doctor." Blake flips Bridger off, then marches back out to get the masks.

"I brought saws," Beckett announces. "A bunch of other tools, too."

I don't say a word until Blake comes back inside. Then I stand in front of my three younger brothers, cross my arms over my chest, and sigh.

"Uh-oh," Beckett says. "He's gonna blow."

"I want to punch the fuck out of Bridger."

Bridge just smiles, the fucker. "For what? Saving Juliet's ass the other night? You're welcome."

"For not *telling me*. I should have been your first phone call."

"Respectfully, that's bullshit," Blake says, shaking his head. "You've said for years that we should never mention her."

"*Keep her name out of your fucking mouth* were your

exact words, I believe," Beckett adds.

"You'll punch me if I talk about her, and you'll punch me if I don't," Bridge says. "So which is it, Brooks?"

I drag my hands down my face and turn away from them. They're right. Hell, Jules is right, too.

I can't have it both ways.

I can't expect to know anything if I won't talk about her, and now I know that I can't stay away from her.

"We talked last night." I turn around to find them all staring at me in surprise. "A long talk. The kind that clears up a lot of shit."

"Are you saying that you and Jules are back together?" Blake asks.

"She's asleep in my bed right now because I *refuse* to let her stay upstairs. We're going to try to get to know each other again. Start over." I shrug, then glance around at the restaurant. "I probably made some rash decisions when I was young and stupid, and she's been through hell and back. It's time to move the fuck on."

"Amen." Bridger pats me on the shoulder. "Now, let's get this floor out of here. I called the city, and a dumpster will be dropped off for us later this morning."

"Excellent. Let's get started."

It's not an easy process. Real wood that's been soaked and then dried and warped isn't easy to manipulate. We're all in masks, sawing, pulling, and hauling all morning.

Around lunchtime, Billie opens the door, but when she starts to step inside, Connor stops her. He steps around her, his brows pulled together in concern.

"What happened here?"

"Flood," I tell him.

"Wait." Billie holds up a hand and eyes her husband. "You know, it's really hard to have a conversation with my brothers when you won't let me *near* my brothers."

"I won't let you in *here*," Connor counters. "That's different entirely."

"I'm pregnant, not a freaking invalid." She shakes her head. "Anyway, Brooks, if you guys are helping Jules, does that mean that you two aren't enemies anymore?"

I scowl at my baby sister. "We weren't enemies."

"Bullshit," Bridger says, making it sound like a sneeze in his hand, and I reach over and clip the back of his head with my hand. "Ouch. Fucker."

"We're working on it," I reply simply, and Billie hops up and down on the balls of her feet with excitement.

"Thank *God*. It was so hard not to be extra warm and fuzzy with her because I love her, Brooks. And I want her at book club meetings, and all of the things."

"I felt guilty as fuck for eating in here," Blake agrees. "And the food is awesome. My woman craves it every day, and if my pregnant fiancée wants to eat here, she'll eat here. Still feel guilty for it, though."

"I love you guys." I sigh. "And I appreciate the loyalty. I don't want you to feel any sort of way about being friends with her. I shouldn't have expected that."

"I mean, she *did* leave," Beckett reminds me. "There's history there. But, if you're okay, then we're okay."

"Where is she now?" Connor asks.

"At my place, sleeping."

Billie's eyebrows climb into her hairline. "WHAT? Jesus, you work fast, big brother."

"She's exhausted." My voice is as dry as sandpaper. "And her apartment is shit. I don't want her living there."

"Like while this is happening or *ever*?" Billie asks, that grin still firmly on her face. "Because I vote for ever. Who's with me?"

The guys chuckle at our little sister. Connor reaches over to drag his finger down her cheek.

"You're the sweetest thing, Bumble."

"One day at a time," I say, shaking my head. "First things first. This place needs a lot of repairs, and she's on a budget."

I don't want her using a fucking dime of that asshole's money. Not if I can help it.

"I'll make some calls," Connor says simply, pulling his phone out of his pocket. "Angel, you need to get out of here. I don't want you breathing this in. I'm going to stay and help."

"You're going to stay?" That surprises me. Connor's a billionaire. He doesn't do demo day. He hires people for that. The man owns hundreds of hotels and resorts all over the world.

"Am I not welcome?" he asks, lifting an eyebrow.

"You're welcome wherever we are." I shrug a shoulder. "Be my guest. The more, the merrier."

"I'm so happy," Billie says as Connor backs her out of the doorway. "I just want them to be happy."

"Freaking hormones make all the women in this family cry," Beck mutters. "Between Dani *just* having a baby earlier this year, and now the rest of the girls being pregnant, it's nothing but tears around here."

"It's not forever," Blake reminds him. "Just a few more months."

"Until someone else gets pregnant again," Bridger says.

I can picture my wildfire pregnant with my baby. I've been able to picture that for years. Maybe we have a second chance for that. We're not too old yet.

I don't even know if she wants babies.

I don't even know if she wants me.

"I have a crew on the way," Connor says as he walks back inside. "They'll remove everything that's ruined and start replacing it with new materials. Does she want it to stay the same as it was, or does she want to take this opportunity to change anything up?"

I blink at him. "Connor, I can't pay you—"

"Fuck that," he says, shaking his head. "You're my family. Jules is important to all of you, and we love this restaurant. So let's get it back up and running and worry about the rest another time. Like never."

Have I mentioned how much I love my family?

"We'll have to ask her what she wants to do as far as materials go," I reply. "I expect her to come in here this afternoon."

"Good. We can get the rest of this emptied out. How's the upstairs?"

"Worse than this, but we'll need her permission to go up there. She was living up there, and her personal things are there."

Connor nods, and Blake's face transforms into a scowl.

"Wait. She doesn't know that we've been in here all morning, ripping up her floor?"

"No, but it's not like she'd stop me. This floor has to go."

"Jesus, she could call the cops and have us arrested for trespassing."

"She's not going to do that." I shake my head at my brother. "Don't be stupid."

Beckett's eyes shift to the doorway and narrow. "Ask her yourself."

I turn around to smile at my girl, but she's scowling.

"What the hell is going on in here?"

Chapter Thirteen

JULIET

> Brooks: Whenever you wake up, there are coffee pods in the kitchen and cream in the fridge. I'll be at your restaurant all day today, pulling out the old floor.

I stare at my phone in disbelief.

Brooks is at my restaurant. Without me.

Shaking my head, I sit up and take a deep breath, and just like that, I can smell him. I fell asleep with him surrounding me, his scent anyway, and I love being here among his things.

God, I missed him.

Years ago, when I got the tattoo on my side, I told myself that was the end of it. The closure I needed. I needed to put my relationship with Brooks and the future I'd planned to have with him to rest. Because he wouldn't respond to any of my messages, and I really had to move on for my own mental health.

But now, here I am. In his house, in his *bed*. And I

think we might have something resembling hope happening between us for the first time in so many years. The spark of something new that I'm so fucking scared to trust but also want with everything in my body.

His eyes softened. He smiled at me. He *held me.* God, it felt so amazing.

Except now he's at my restaurant without me.

So I need to set him straight.

I pad into the guest room and slip on some clean clothes, then sweep my hair up in a knot. I forgo the coffee, and once I've grabbed my purse and keys, I walk out to my car.

It feels so damn good to have my car back.

And it runs like a dream as I drive into the downtown area and park it behind my restaurant. When I drove past, I saw a huge truck setting a dumpster in the parking spaces in front of it.

I didn't order a dumpster. I didn't have the foresight to even *think* about a dumpster.

I was still stuck on *what the fuck am I going to do?*

I mean, a huge part of me is grateful that I didn't have to make that call myself, but the other part wants to know who the hell decided to do this without me.

Actually, I know who.

Brooks.

My controlling, protective man.

Wait, is he *my* man? Ugh, I don't know.

I stomp down the block and see that the front door stands open, and all four Blackwell men are inside, talking.

And what a sight to behold. The Blackwell brothers should come with a fucking health warning.

May Cause Vaginas to Spontaneously Combust.

"Ask her yourself," Beckett says, staring at me, and the other three sets of eyes turn to me.

"What the hell is going on in here?" I ask, stepping inside, but I'm careful where I set my feet because most of the floor has already been torn apart. It's a freaking war zone in here.

"Did you get my text?" Brooks asks me.

"Yeah, but it wasn't very informative. First of all, how did you get in here?"

"I grabbed your keys," he says with a nonchalant shrug.

"Fuck," Blake says, rubbing his hand over the back of his neck. He looks ... *guilty.*

"You stole my keys, came in here, and the four of you decided to start ripping my floor apart?"

"You needed to rip it apart anyway, you said it yourself," Brooks says, the scowl I've come to know all too well back on his handsome face. "And I won't have you doing it alone."

I blink at him. "You won't *have me* doing it?"

"You're so dead," Bridger mutters. "Idiot."

"We're *helping*, Wildfire."

"I didn't ask for help."

Now Brooks's face falls, and I feel like an asshole.

"Okay." I take a deep breath and wrinkle my nose.

"You should be wearing a mask in here," Blake says, offering me one.

I take it, covering my nose but not hooking it to my

ears, and then push my hand into Brooks's, and he immediately links his fingers with mine, giving them a squeeze.

"Can I talk to you alone for a moment?" I ask him.

"I want coffee," Bridger says, making a break for the door. "Let's go harass Millie."

"Good plan," Beck agrees, and Blake follows them.

"Why are you pissed?" Brooks asks after they're gone.

"Because this is *my* business," I reply and squeeze his fingers. "It's not that I don't appreciate your help, but I should have been here to make the decisions."

"It's literally just pulling out a destroyed floor. I didn't make any other decisions for you."

"Okay. If this were the garage, and I told you to go to sleep while I went to your building and started giving orders on how to clean it up, you'd be cool with that?"

"You're pretty good at giving orders, so probably."

I narrow my eyes at him, and his shoulders droop.

"I get it. I didn't mean to piss you off. I was trying to take this off your plate."

"And I really do appreciate it. Because I admit, this is so fucking overwhelming, and I like having you here to help me figure it out, but I should be here with you. Your brothers came."

He frowns. "Of course, they did. I asked them to."

His family is so fucking amazing. Brooks hit the jackpot when he was born a Blackwell.

"So what's your plan?"

He lets out a breath and looks around the room. "Right now, it was to finish emptying out the rest of the flooring, and then see what you want to do from there."

"That's the right answer."

He lowers his mask, and his lips twitch, and then he lowers them to mine, but doesn't kiss me. He hovers just an inch away.

"Were you really mad at me, Wildfire?"

"Maybe not." I boost up on my toes and close the distance between us, and he lets out a low groan as the kiss intensifies, our bodies pressed together. I plunge my fingers in his thick, dark hair, and he covers my ass with his big hands.

He's sweaty, but I don't care.

I'd happily stay here, just like this, all freaking day.

But then he pulls back and brushes my hair behind my ear.

"We just finally got to a place where we're not both angry with each other. Let's try to stay there," he says softly.

"I like that idea."

Suddenly, there's a knock on the doorframe, and when I turn, I find Connor Gallagher walking into my building. He's in jeans and a long-sleeved black T-shirt, the sleeves pulled up on his forearms. He walks over to us, pushing his glasses up the bridge of his nose.

"Hi, Jules," he says, shaking my hand. I've met Billie's husband several times, and he's always been nothing but kind to me. His Irish accent is also incredibly swoony. "I'm sorry about this mess."

"Yeah, me too. Unfortunately, I can't make your wrap for you today."

Whenever Connor stops by to see his wife at her bookshop, he always swings in here for lunch.

His lips tip up in a half smile. "I figured. Actually, I

159

was here earlier before you got here. I have a team ready to come in and clean out the rest of the damage, and then start repairing everything right away."

I stare at him in shock. "What?"

"If you'd like it to look exactly the same as before, they can do that, or they can switch up anything that you'd like."

Brooks drags his hand down my spine, and I have to lean into his side because I might fall over.

"I'm sorry, I think my brain is coffee-deprived. Connor, that's very generous, but I can't afford—"

"I didn't ask you to pay me," he says simply.

Frowning, I nibble my lower lip. "Actually, I *could* afford it," I finally admit. "I just didn't want to touch the money that my asshole of a late husband left me."

"Money isn't personal." Connor shrugs. "It doesn't care if it sits untouched in an account, or if you spend it all in one go. It's *not* the arsehole who mistreated you, Jules. But it's your choice. If you'd rather not use that money, I'll front it."

"I can't ask you to do that and not pay you back."

"Do you want a silent partner?" he counters, and I recoil as if he hit me.

"No offense, but no. I don't."

Connor's smile spreads over his face. "I can't blame you. I wouldn't either. You're a smart businesswoman. Here's the thing, Jules: my wife, whom I'm completely in love and obsessed with, adores you and this restaurant. She wants to make sure you succeed. Her family"—he gestures to Brooks—"who is now *my* family, cares about you, and we take care of our own. You don't have to deal with any of this by yourself."

I will not cry in front of these men.

Brooks kisses the top of my head, and I take a shuddering breath.

"I haven't asked for or accepted help from anyone in a *very* long time," I admit quietly. "I'm not sure I know how."

"Maybe this is a good time to start," Brooks murmurs.

Meeting Connor's gaze, I nod but reach out to lay my hand on his arm.

Brooks growls low in his throat, but I ignore him.

"I will gratefully accept your help," I tell him. "But I would like for us to come to an agreement for how I can return the favor. Somehow, free chicken wraps for life doesn't feel like it'll cut it."

Connor smirks. "We'll talk about it later. The first order of business is to get this cleaned up and restored so you can open your doors again."

"I know my staff would love that, too," I agree.

"Then let's make it happen."

Chapter Fourteen

BROOKS

It's been a long fucking day.
Long.
Fucking.
Day.

And I'm ready to call it, take my wildfire home, and lose myself in her for the rest of the night. The fact that I even get to do that is still completely foreign to me.

I'm so fucking proud of her.

She didn't leave and let *the guys* handle the heavy lifting today. No, my girl put on a mask, some gloves, and worked her gorgeous ass off right next to the rest of us. And when the floor was all gone, she jumped in to sweep and make decisions. She consulted with Connor and his construction foreman, devising a plan.

She fucking blew my mind.

But now everyone has cleared out. My brothers have gone home to their women, and Connor has collected Bee from across the street and taken her home as well.

The crew is gone.

Now it's time for me to do the same with Jules.

"Let's hang it up for tonight," I say as I come up behind her and wrap my arms around her chest, hugging her to me. "I need to feed you, and we should get some rest."

I lower my mouth to her ear. She's so fucking short, I have to almost bend in half.

Worth it.

"After I sink inside you for about twelve hours."

Jules huffs out a laugh and turns in my arms.

"All of that sounds like fun, but there's something else I want first."

I raise an eyebrow. "Name it."

"I'd like a ride on your bike over to Silver Springs so we can get ice cream at Sundae's."

"That's what you want?"

Jules grins and nods, and I can't help but kiss her forehead.

"Let's do it, then. I'll meet you at my place."

I wait for Jules to lock the door, watching as she checks the lock three times, and walk her to her car. Once she's on her way, I follow her in my truck.

She's waiting by the back door when I pull into the driveway.

"I'll give you a key," I tell her as I unlock the door.

"Oh, you don't have to. I probably won't be here that long."

Those words coming out of her mouth are like a kick to the jaw.

163

You're not going anywhere, Wildfire.

"It will be a while before the crew can get up to the apartment, Jules. You're here, with me, for the foreseeable future."

She bites her lip and steps inside, and I cup her chin, making her look up at me.

"Unless you don't want to be here. I won't make you do anything you don't want to."

"It's not that. I don't want to take advantage of you. I don't want to give you another reason to resent me later—"

"Whoa." Cupping her face, I frown down at her. "I'm an asshole, but I'm not a complete monster. We're figuring our shit out. I couldn't resent you for being here with me, when that's exactly what I want. I don't *want* you anywhere else. And if I didn't want you here, I'd tell you so."

"Yeah." She gives me a soft smile. "You definitely would. Thank you. I can sleep in the guest room—"

"We're going to clear this whole fucking thing up right here, right now."

Lifting her, I carry her to the kitchen and set her on the countertop so I'm eye to eye with her. Leaning my hands on either side of her hips, I cage her in.

"I want you in my room and in *my* bed for as long as you want to be here. Does that spell it out for you?"

"Yeah. It's just ..." She nibbles her lip.

"What, baby?"

"I don't know if I can trust this."

I frown down at her. "Trust what, exactly?"

"This." She swallows hard and looks down at my

chest. "That you'll still feel this way in a few days. That it's not just happening because we've been sort of forced together here and there, and you've let your guard down, but when you remember everything that happened, you won't hate me again, and make me leave, and—"

I rest my lips over hers, kissing her softly, nibbling those perfect lips. And when I pull back, I tip my forehead to hers.

"I. Don't. Hate you." I drag my fingertips down her soft cheek, to her neck, and hold her there. Hold her gaze. "I never hated you. I was hurt and angry, but we already said that we're going to let the past stay behind us and work on something new."

"Yeah," she whispers. "Still scares me. Aren't you scared?"

"Fucking terrified." Her eyes soften with my admission, and it sets me at ease, too. "But I want you more than I'm scared of it."

"Okay." She nods, then leans in and rests her forehead on my chest. "One day at a time. Can I use your super beautiful shower?"

"You can use whatever you want." I kiss the top of her head and help her off the counter, then lead her down the hallway.

This afternoon, Jules went up to the apartment and packed up the rest of what she could salvage from the flood, and I brought it back here. She finds what she wants to change into and gathers it into her arms.

"You should have everything you need in there," I tell her, gesturing to the bathroom.

"I'll be ready to go in about twenty," she replies.

With a nod, I back out of the bedroom. I'll shower down the hall. I would prefer to be in there with her, but once we start, I won't want to let her go any time soon, and my girl wants ice cream for dinner.

She can have anything she damn well wants.

And when I'm inside her again, it's not going to be a quick, angry fuck in my garage.

Not that there's not a time and place for that, and I look forward to it happening again, when she doesn't run out on me after.

This time, it'll be in my bed, where I can fucking devour her.

Thirty minutes later, I'm pulling the bike out of the garage. I pass the helmet I bought for Jules to her, and her eyes go big.

"This fits me."

Suddenly, as I'm tying the chin strap, her eyes narrow and go sapphire blue.

"Wait." Her hands cover mine, stopping my movements. "Who the fuck did you buy this woman-sized helmet for? I don't want to wear something that you bought for someone else, Brooks—"

"Stop." I hold the chin guard of the helmet and make her look me in the eyes. She's glaring at me, and fuck if it doesn't make me hard.

There's my wildfire.

"Number one, I've never had another woman on my bike. Not once, Juliet."

Those eyes widen, her jaw goes slack, and I keep talking.

"Two, I bought this for *you* last week."

"B-before you knew I'd be staying here."

"Yeah. After I had you on the back, I knew I needed something for you." At the time, I considered it to be a weak moment because I wanted to hang on to my anger.

"Three, and I want you to listen really carefully to this one."

She bites her lower lip, watching me with those wide eyes.

"We aren't talking about the past and who we might or might not have been with. Was I celibate? No. I wasn't. I won't lie to you about that. But that's not now, and it doesn't matter. Fifteen years is almost a lifetime, baby. But I'll tell you this: you're mine now. No one touches you but me."

"Yeah, well, same goes." She narrows her eyes again.

"I think I like you jealous. Makes me hard as hell." I kiss her nose and finish tying the strap, then we get settled on the bike.

I push off from the house and turn onto the street. Jules wraps those arms around me, holding on.

When we hit the long stretch of highway, the wind blowing around us, and the sun just starting to set, I reach back and hook my hand under her thigh, tugging her closer to me. I want to feel the heat of her pussy against my ass, her tits on my back, and fuck if I just don't love having her pressed against me again.

The ride into Silver Springs takes less than thirty minutes, and I pull up in front of Sundae's, an ice cream place that's been here since long before I was born.

Jules and I used to come here every weekend. It was our thing.

KRISTEN PROBY

She swings her leg over and steps off the bike, and I follow, helping her with the helmet. Moments later, we're walking into the scent of sugar and waffle cones.

"It always smells so good in here," Jules says with a happy sigh as we step up to the counter. This place offers about ten flavors that remain constant, then rotates a half dozen seasonal flavors as well.

"Hi, welcome in. What can I getcha?" the young woman behind the counter asks.

"I'd like two scoops of huckleberry in a dish," Jules says. "Please."

"You bet." The girl looks up at me expectantly.

"I'm going to try that apple pie a la mode. Two scoops, also in a dish."

Once I've paid, we find a table and I have a seat next to her, rather than across.

Just like before.

"Mmm, so good," Jules says, closing her eyes, and my dick twitches.

I'm going to make her make that noise later with my face between her legs.

"How are your parents?" she asks before scooping a bite of purple ice cream into her mouth. "I haven't seen them much since I've been back."

"They're doing well. They retired a few years back and moved to Florida because of Mom's arthritis, but they had serious FOMO and moved back last year."

Jules frowns. "Your mom has bad arthritis?"

"Yeah, but she does okay. Blake keeps an eye on her."

"I still can't believe that Blake's a doctor." She grins and turns so she's facing me. "It makes me happy that

168

everyone is doing so well. Billie's bookstore is my favorite place in town."

I raise an eyebrow. "Even over your restaurant?"

"Yep. Favorite place by far. I always loved to read, you know that."

"Sure, but your restaurant is fucking amazing."

That has her blinking up at me, and then she leans over and kisses my shoulder.

"Thank you for saying that. I had a vision for it, you know? I knew what I wanted the vibe to be for so many years, so seeing it come to life was exciting. I love that people like Birdie can eat there without worrying about getting sick."

"What made you decide to start a clean kitchen?" I ask her as I finish my ice cream and toss the paper cup in a nearby can.

"I have sensitivities," she says. "No official diagnosis, but it wouldn't surprise me if I have celiac, like Birdie. It started right after college, and just got worse with time. It helped to cut out the gluten, but sometimes something would set me off."

She looks like she wants to say more, but presses her lips together.

"You can tell me anything."

"But it has to do with *before*, and we're not talking about that."

"Go ahead."

Jules wrinkles her nose. "He would basically gaslight me whenever I had a stomach flare and tell me that no pain I was in could compare to what he was going through with the chemo. Piece of shit. He wasn't even *on* chemo."

"I'd like to punch him." My voice is perfectly calm, but my blood simmers. "Repeatedly."

"Same. Anyway, I did a lot of research over the years, because there are few things worse than having severe stomach pain and not being able to eat. And I thought it would be good to put all that knowledge to use."

"Smart girl," I murmur and lean over to kiss her head. "Birdie loves it."

"Birdie is the best. What a little sweetheart. She just spreads joy and glitter everywhere she goes."

I can't help but laugh at that because she's absolutely right. "She's the princess of the family, that's for sure."

"How's she doing with having to share with a new baby brother? And the other new babies on the way?" she asks.

"So far, she's been great. She loves having the baby around. Birdie's not one to get very jealous. She doesn't need to. We all shower her with affection and attention."

She smiles softly. "That's sweet."

"Do you want kids?" I feel my eyes go wide because I didn't mean to blurt that out.

"I mean, we just started seeing each other again about six minutes ago, so probably not right now." Her lips twitch, and then she barks out a laugh. "Your face."

I narrow my eyes at her, and she snorts. She's fucking adorable.

"You know, I'm not sure," she says and wipes a tear from the corner of her eye. "I kind of decided that wasn't in the cards for me a long time ago."

"What about now?"

"I'm not as young as I used to be."

Reaching over to tuck her hair behind her ear, I shake my head. "We're not old either."

"I'd consider it," she says at last. "Under the right circumstances. What about you?"

"I'd consider it," I echo and wipe a little drip of ice cream from the corner of her mouth, then lick it off my thumb. "Under the right circumstances."

We're finished and about to leave when the door opens, and Tucker Hendrix walks in, followed by his sister, Ava.

"Hey!" Ava makes a beeline for Jules and hugs her tight. "I was going to call you later and ask if you need help at the restaurant, but I can see that you already have help."

Ava turns to me with a knowing smile.

"I do have help," Jules agrees. "But thanks for thinking of me. And who is this?"

"I'm Tucker," the other man says, holding out his hand. "Ava's oldest brother."

"The famous oldest brother," Jules says, and I take her hand out of his, thread our fingers, and glare at my friend, who just smirks.

Asshat.

"I decided to harass Tuck tonight," Ava says. "It's my little sister duty to check on him and make sure he's taking his vitamins. You know, because he's old."

"We're the same age," I remind her, and Tucker smirks.

"And I'm *their* age," Jules says with a laugh. "So go easy on the old people talk."

Ava shakes her head. "No way, you don't look a day over twenty-five."

"I already knew I liked you, but now you're my favorite," Jules tells her.

"She just misses me," Tucker says and ruffles Ava's hair, which earns him a glare. "I'm her favorite brother."

"Sure you are, because you're buying me ice cream." Ava smooths her hair out and then turns back to Jules. "I'll call you later."

Then she leans in and whisper-shouts, "And I want details."

"No." I shake my head, and with Juliet's hand in mine, we walk back outside and get settled on the bike. All the way back to the house, her hands move up and down my chest and stomach, and then she plants them on the gas tank. With a smirk, I grab them and plant them back on my stomach.

I can feel her laughing behind me.

Gonna have to teach you a little lesson, Wildfire.

She leans into the turns with me, as naturally as if she'd been on this bike with me for twenty years, and then I park in the garage, and we put the helmets away and go inside.

Before she has the chance to do much of anything at all, I swing her onto my shoulder and march back toward the bedroom, making her gasp in surprise.

"What the hell?" She giggles and smacks my butt, and I return the favor by swatting her perfect globe of an ass, making her yelp. "Brooks!"

"You're mine tonight." I carry her into the bedroom and drop her onto the bed, and she pushes her hair out of her face. "You think you can touch me on my bike like that, get me so fucking hard I ache, and that I won't fuck you the second we get home?"

She bites her plump lower lip in excitement, watching me.

"Clothes off. Now." My voice is deeper, harder, and her eyes glass over, just the way I want them to.

My wildfire has a gorgeous submissive side.

"I won't tell you twice."

That sets her into motion, pulling her shirt over her head, then lying down to shimmy out of the jeans she wore for the bike. When she's only in blue panties, I lift an eyebrow and cross my arms, rub my fingertip over my bottom lip, waiting.

"It all comes off."

"I want you naked, too," she says before swallowing hard.

I don't reply. I simply stand here, over her, watching. Her nipples pucker. Her legs scissor. Her breath hitches, and her pulse jumps in her throat.

She's so fucking gorgeous.

Finally, her fingers hook into the sides of her panties, and she works them down her hips, down her legs. Before she can fling them aside, I take them and press them to my nose, inhaling deeply.

"*Fucking delicious,*" I growl, then set them aside. "Those are mine now."

"I might need them."

"You don't." I reach over my shoulder and yank my shirt over my head and let it fall to the floor.

Juliet's gaze takes me in greedily. I fucking *love* the

way this woman looks at me, as if I'm the hottest thing she's ever seen in her life.

I unbuckle my belt and yank it through the loops of my jeans with a snap, then let it fall with a clatter to the floor.

"Do you like what you see, baby?"

"Hell yeah, I do. God, you just got ... *better*, Brooks, and I didn't think that was possible."

Christ, she's good for my ego.

With a smirk, I let my jeans fall and peel down my boxer briefs. I take her ankle in my hand and lift it to my mouth as I crawl onto the bed. I pepper kisses on her soft skin, over the ankle bone, down to the arch of her foot, and she grins.

My girl is ticklish.

"I am going to consume every amazing inch of you." I nibble my way up her calf to the inside of her knee and lick her there, grinning against her skin when she gasps. "I'm going to pound you so hard that you'll be begging me to stop."

"Never." She shakes her head and reaches for me, but I back out of range. "I want to touch you."

"You will. Be patient, little wildfire."

My hand glides up the outside of her thigh to her hip, then around to her mound, where my thumb brushes over her clit, making her gasp.

"Oh God."

"He's not here, beautiful. Just you and me. It'll be *my* name you scream when you come. And you're going to come a lot tonight."

"Yay me." Her voice is weak and thready, like she's already barely hanging on by a thread. "*Please.*"

She wants more. She needs my thumb to press harder. She wants my mouth.

My cock.

And she'll get them.

When I decide she's ready for them.

"My greedy little girl. What are you begging me for, Jules?"

"You."

I lift an eyebrow. "You can do better than that."

"I want you to ... *ah, that's so good.*" My thumb is still ghosting over that hard little nub. Her hips lift, seeking more, and her cheeks have darkened. She's fucking beautiful. "Just a little harder."

I pull away entirely, and she groans in frustration.

"Tell me what you're begging me for."

"Your mouth. Your fingers." She swallows hard and drops her head on the bed. "Your cock."

"Which one?"

"All of them."

With a grin, I press a wet kiss right next to her pussy, where her leg meets her core, and her hips lift again.

"There's no need to hurry. You're going to get everything you want, baby. But I'm going to take my time this go around. No fast fucks against the bench in my garage."

"*Brooks.*"

My hand glides up her stomach, and I pinch her nipple, making her flinch and then groan.

"Yes. More of that."

"I'm sorry, are you under the impression that you're in charge here, Juliet?" I shake my head slowly and move to the other nipple, giving it the same attention. "Because you're not. I am. And you'll get what I give you."

"You got even bossier."

"You have no fucking idea just how bossy I can be, baby. But you're about to learn."

Chapter Fifteen

JULIET

He's trying to kill me.

Death by vagina. It's honestly not a bad way to go, but I want him to touch me, and he's holding back.

His eyes, however, are on fire, and he's watching me like he wants to do unspeakable, dirty, depraved things to me, and I'm *so* here for it.

That fast, angry fuck in the garage? It was hot. It confused me, and I ran from it, but in the heat of the moment, holy hell.

But I have a feeling it's going to pale in comparison to what he's going to do to me tonight.

"You're thinking too much," he mutters and pinches my nipple again, making me squirm. The pain subsides into an ache that makes me want to beg for more.

"Just about you," I reply, and that earns me a smile. *I love it when he smiles at me.*

"That's a good answer." He nips at my shoulder, and

then over to my collarbone. "Jesus, you're beautiful, baby."

"I'm not as—"

"Don't compare yourself to before," he says, shaking his head as he kisses my cheek. "We were kids then. *Nothing* is the same about us. Physically, emotionally. It's all different. Not better or worse, just different. And I can't fucking *wait* to rediscover every inch. To learn what makes you gasp and writhe and come undone."

His fingers ghost up my inner thigh, and I whimper.

"What makes that hot as fuck little noise come out of your perfect mouth."

God, his words are so filthy, so damn everything.

"One thing that hasn't changed," he continues as he kisses and licks his way up my throat to my ear. "This pussy was made for me. Fuck, you're so wet, baby."

I arch up into his hand, and cup his face as he moves over to kiss me, his tongue slips between my lips and slides over mine, making me groan as his fingertips brush over my clit, making electricity burst through me.

"Brooks," I moan against his lips.

"Yes, baby." *Fuck*, his fingers are magical.

"I need you."

His eyes find mine. He moves over me, nudges his way between my legs, resting his thick, heavy cock against my sopping-wet slit. Bracing his weight on his elbows, he brushes my hair away from my face.

"Where?"

I reach between us, but he captures my wrist, kisses my palm, and holds my hand over my head.

"Where do you need me, Wildfire?"

Wildfire. God, I love that name, and I missed him calling me that. It makes me feel bolder. Stronger.

"Inside me. I need you inside me, okay? Please."

"I'm going to fuck you without a condom."

"Great. Fine. Just *do it.*"

He growls, pulls his hips back, and lines the head of his cock against my entrance. We both watch as he pushes his crown inside me, and I bite my lip.

He's so ... *big.* The first time we had sex, I thought he was going to split me in two. This isn't going to be any different, and I'm so ready, so turned on.

"I need you to breathe for me." He brushes his lips over mine again and his free hand pushes into my hair, softly combing my curls. "Take a breath, Jules."

I do, and his eyes soften.

"You're so fucking beautiful."

His whispered words bring tears to my eyes. I can't help it. This is the first time we've been like *this* in so long, and I didn't think I'd ever have him like this again.

It's everything.

"No tears." He rubs his nose against my own as he sinks another inch inside me, and we both moan. "Fuck, you're so goddamn tight."

I lift my hips, taking more of him, and he grits his teeth.

"Jules."

"I'm right here."

"I need to pound into you, but I don't want to hurt you."

With a happy sigh, I drag my hands up and down his back. *This is my man.* I always loved how intense and

179

rough Brooks gets. "Hurt me, handsome. Fuck me until I'm bruised and sore and I can't walk tomorrow."

His face hardens, his eyes darken, sending a thrill through me, and with his forehead on mine, he starts to move, pushing the rest of the way inside me, pausing there, and then pulling out again.

Before I can form a thought, he slams back inside, balls deep, and I cry out. My back bows off the bed, and *holy shit, I want more.*

"Is that what you want, greedy girl?"

"Yes!"

He repeats the motion, pulls out and then slams back in, grinding his pubis against my clit and making me cry out again. *Holy shit.*

"Take it, baby," he growls against my neck. "Take all of this big fucking cock."

"Oh God."

He's moving faster now. He finds a hard, punishing rhythm that makes my breath catch and sets my body on *fire.*

I can't get enough.

It'll never be enough.

"Brooks—"

"That's right. Say my fucking name. Who's fucking this gorgeous pussy right now?"

"*Brooks.*" The word is broken, choked out through ragged breaths, and it makes him growl and move faster. Harder.

He lifts on his knees, spreads me wider, and presses his thumb to my clit as he continues to pound into me mercilessly, his eyes pinned to where we're joined together.

"Oh God!" I clamp around him, my walls shuddering, on the verge of a blinding climax.

"Did I say you can come?" His voice is demanding, hard.

I shake my head, unable to form words.

"Hold on, Wildfire. Don't you *dare* fucking come."

"I c-can't hold back—"

Suddenly, he pulls out all the way, leaving me empty, my pussy contracting, searching for him, and I cry out.

"What the fuck!"

"*I* say when you can come." He shakes his head, breathing hard. "I own your orgasms. Don't fucking forget who's in charge here, Juliet."

"Brooks, please. Please, don't do that." I reach for him and rise up onto his lap. I wrap my arms around his neck, bury my face there, and tremble. "Please."

He lifts me off the bed, and my back hits the wall seconds before he plunges back inside me and starts to pound into me again.

"Oh yes."

"I love it when you fucking beg," he growls against my lips. "It drives me out of my fucking mind. This pussy hugs me so goddamn perfectly. *Fuck.*"

My legs wrap around his waist, and I hold on for dear life as he fucks me ruthlessly. The climax builds again, and he bites the top of my shoulder, hard enough to break skin, but I don't care.

I need to come.

"Please." I sound so ... *needy.*

"Come on my cock, Juliet." His words are hard and dark, and I couldn't defy him if I wanted to.

Which I don't.

The hands holding my ass in the air tighten almost painfully, and I gasp as I fall over the edge into euphoria. He continues to fuck me through it, rocking into me so perfectly. Wave after wave of electricity rolls through me until he groans against me, and I can feel his cock swell. Then he's coming, too.

"Goddamn it," he growls, pulsing inside me, filling me up. He jerks and shudders, and then murmurs, "Hold on to me."

I hug myself around him, and he walks us into the bathroom, where he sets me on the cold marble counter-top, making me shriek and then giggle.

"That's cold."

"Sorry." He nibbles my lips. "I have to clean you up."

He wets a cloth with warm water and gets to work wiping me down, and he does the same to himself, but his eyes never leave my body.

What I was going to say earlier is true.

The last time he saw me naked, aside from in his garage when everything happened so fast, I was twenty. I was smaller, firmer, and a whole lot younger.

But from the fire burning in his gaze, I'd say he doesn't mind at all.

He tosses the cloth in a hamper and pulls me back into his arms, lifting me off the counter.

"I can walk, you know."

"Yeah, but why should you when I can carry you?" He presses his lips to my temple and lowers me into the bed, then joins me, pulling me against him. "I have a question."

"Okay." I wiggle into his side and lay my head on his chest. When we were kids, we never really got to enjoy this part of sex. We both lived at home, so sharing a bed was out of the question.

"What's the scar from?"

I frown up at him. "Scar?"

"The one on your stomach."

I blink and then remember. "Oh, I had my appendix out about six years ago. That sucked, let me tell you. Zero out of five stars, do not recommend."

I had to recover alone because Justin claimed he had to spend all day, every day at the hospital for treatment. It was horrible, but I told him I understood because *cancer treatment*.

"Hmm." He wraps his arm around my shoulders, holding me close, and kisses my forehead. My eyes are so heavy with fatigue.

"I can't believe I'm so tired. I slept really late today."

"You worked hard this afternoon," he reminds me. "And I might have just worked you hard again."

With a smile, I nuzzle my nose against his warm skin. "Not complaining."

"I was rough with you."

"You know I like it."

My eyes are so heavy, and I can feel him relax beneath me. He has to be tired, too.

More than anything, I'm relieved.

Brooks isn't mad at me anymore.

It's been a whole week of living at Brooks's house, sleeping in his bed, fucking like rabbits, and it feels *so good* I won't want to leave when my place is fixed up. Now that the construction crew is doing their thing, Brooks has gone back to work at the garage, and I spend my days at the restaurant, mostly in the way.

I can't help it. I'm a control freak when it comes to my place.

"Jules," Anderson, the head of construction, says as he approaches me. I have no idea what the man's first name is. He always just goes by Anderson.

"Yes?"

"I'm going to say this in the nicest way possible. You need to get the hell out of my way."

My jaw drops. "This is *my place.*"

"For right now, it's *my* project, and you're in the way. We have a plan. I won't deviate from it, and if I have questions, I'll call you."

"But aren't you planning to start demoing the upstairs today?"

"I was, but that's been pushed back to tomorrow. You should go, and I'll let you know if I need anything."

"Do you talk this way to Connor?" I lift my chin, and Anderson smirks.

"Of course I do. Not that he spends much time on-site with me."

I sigh and look around. The walls had to be stripped down, and new drywall was hung, then painted. That's what they've been working on. I don't even have a new floor yet.

"Fine. I'll go. I'll be across the street at the bookstore if—"

"Great. Go." He flips his hand, as if shooing me away. "Have fun."

"Hey. I'm starting to think you don't want me around."

Anderson rolls his eyes. "What gave you that idea?"

With a smirk, I walk out, check for traffic, and cross the street to Billie's Books. I need to pick up the next book club read, and I can always curl up with my new paperback for a while.

It's raining today, and that actually sounds nice.

So I push into the store and am happy to see that Dani and all of her sisters are here, too. Charlie is the youngest, and from what I hear, she's a damn good, highly sought-after wedding planner. Alex is Dani's twin, and a reporter for the newspaper. Darby, the oldest sister, is even here, and I haven't seen her since high school.

We were friends back then, but lost track of each other.

She looks *amazing.*

"Hi, guys," I say with a smile as I walk toward the back of the store, where the checkout counter is, and all the women are gathered. "It's a Lexington sister party."

"Oh my gosh, Jules," Darby says and gives me a side hug. "Shit, I haven't seen you in ages."

"I was just thinking the same thing about you. Are you home? Are you visiting? What's up with you?"

"She's just visiting." Charlie sticks her lower lip out with a pout.

"Stop." Darby chuckles and shakes her head at her baby sister. "I'm visiting *for now*, but after this next term, I'll be back up here, looking for an internship job to finish my degree."

"Oh my God, that's awesome. What are you in school for?" I ask.

"I'm in veterinary school," she says. "Down in Colorado. And I like it down there, but I'm ready to come home."

"Thank God, we miss you," Billie adds with a wink. "Are you going to be here long enough for book club?"

"I'm here until next Tuesday."

"Then that's a yes," Alex says. "Because book club is on Saturday. Right? Am I mixing up my days?"

"Saturday is right," Billie confirms. "And we're reading a Mafia romance. *Be With Me* by Gabrielle Sands."

"Oh, hook me up, sister." I wink at her, already excited to dig in.

Mafia romance is my jam these days.

"I'm down for that," Darby says. "Reading something other than an animal anatomy book sounds fabulous."

The next thing I know, Ava and Harper come striding into the store, and it turns into a spontaneous hour-long party of chatting and talking about books.

Millie even comes over from the coffee shop next

door, takes our orders for some caffeine, then joins us. She's married to Holden Lexington, the oldest sibling and only boy in the family, and I can tell that she's excited to have Darby home, too.

It feels so good to have *friends*. To be home in a familiar community, and I don't have to do my best to avoid Brooks anymore, worried that he'll be somewhere, glaring at me.

I don't feel like I have to hide or be ashamed.

I can just be me, and for the first time in a long, long time, I feel like I belong. I didn't realize just how much my heart needed this until now.

"I have to say, you look fantastic," Darby says as we drift away from the larger group. "And I heard a rumor that you and Brooks are back together."

I press my lips together, but I can't stop the smile that spreads. "Yeah. We're back together."

"Good. You were always meant for each other, Jules. Anyone with eyes in their head could see it, even when we were in high school. I'm glad it's working out."

"So far, so good. How about you? Any men in your life?"

Darby smirks and shakes her head. "Nah. I'm way too busy with school, and I'm not really interested anyway."

"Women, then?" I lift an eyebrow, and she laughs.

"No, no relationships *at all*. I'm as straight as can be, but men take work, and I have to put in enough of that in every other aspect of my life. I don't see a relationship fitting into that any time soon. And that's okay, you know?"

"For sure. I think it's awesome that you decided to go back to school. Have you always wanted to be a vet?"

I sip my iced coffee, compliments of Millie, and Darby shakes her head. "I didn't know *what* I wanted for a long time. Mostly, for the majority of my life, I was just surviving, you know?"

I nod slowly. Darby's childhood was *horrific*. I don't know the details, just that their father was an abusive piece of shit. And I hate that so much.

"But now you can thrive," I say with a smile. "And I know how that is. I had a rough time in my teenage years, and then I found my way into a marriage that wasn't healthy or happy. We can thrive in our thirties, girl."

"Hell yes, we can." She holds her coffee up to cheers with mine. "If you hear of a ranch around here needing an intern, let me know. I'd rather not work for my brother. I love him, but no."

"Did I just hear the magic word of *ranch*?" Ava asks, drifting our way.

"Yes, I'm going to need a job in the spring," Darby says. "I'll be finishing up my large animal vet degree. Do you have a ranch?"

"My family does," Ava replies, tapping her lips with her finger. "I'll ask Tucker if he could use some help next year. He's my oldest brother and runs the Hendrix Ranch now that my dad has retired."

"Good for him," I say with a nod. "He has *hi, I'm a hot-as-hell cowboy* written all over him."

"Ew." Ava wrinkles her nose. "No, he doesn't."

I turn to Darby. "He's hot. Around our age, tall, dark, and handsome."

"He could look like a toad for all I care. I need a job."

"I mean, it can't hurt to look at a sexy cowboy while you work," I reply, shrugging one shoulder.

"Who the fuck are you talking about, Wildfire?"

I jump, my stomach climbs into my throat, and Ava breaks out in laughter.

"You startled me."

I turn to find Brooks's sizzling gaze on me, his eyes narrowed, his jaw tight. "Who. Are you. Talking about?"

"Tucker," Ava says helpfully. "We were talking about your friend Tucker. Who your girlfriend thinks is hot."

Ava is a shit stirrer.

"Look, I can observe that a person is attractive without it meaning anything or threatening you—"

Brooks cuts me off by wrapping his hand around the back of my neck and covering my mouth with his. I can hear everyone around us whoop and clap their hands, and my face heats.

How can he turn me on so much with just a single kiss?

"You were saying?" he growls against my lips.

"I have no idea."

His lips twitch into a smile. "Good. Hello, ladies."

"I'm just so happy," Bee says, wiping tears from her cheeks. "I want you two together so bad. Don't mind me, it's just the hormones."

Brooks chuckles and reaches out to brush his hand down Billie's hair. "Don't cry, Bee."

"I can't help it."

My phone buzzes in my pocket, and when I pull it out, my face falls.

Unknown Number: Send me ten grand. Today.

Brooks is looking over my shoulder, and I'm not trying to keep the words out of his line of vision.

"Dammit," I mutter.

"Let's go, Wildfire. You can take care of that at home."

I nod, and then make the rounds, giving hugs and saying goodbye. And with the book club book, along with three others, tucked under my arm, I set off with my man.

"Did you leave work early?" I ask him as he takes my hand and links our fingers.

"I want to spend time with you."

Excitement bubbles up in my chest. "Good. I was kicked out of my place earlier. Apparently, I'm in the way."

"You're not in *my* way," he says and kisses the top of my head. "Let me show you just how *not* in my way you are."

"That sounds like a really good idea."

Chapter Sixteen

BROOKS

I fucking *hate* the way the fire left her eyes when she got that goddamn text at the bookstore. My wildfire was having fun, laughing with her friends, and then the text came through, and her gorgeous face dropped.

I wanted to smash that phone to pieces for giving her even a *moment* of pain.

After pulling into the driveway behind Jules, we walk in through the back door, and she kicks off her shoes, sighs, and grabs a bottle of water out of the fridge.

"It was fun to see the girls at the bookstore," she says as she twists off the cap and takes a sip. "Darby looks fantastic. I haven't seen her since high school."

I cross to her, set her bottle on the counter, then tip her chin up and cover her lips with mine, kissing her thoroughly.

"What was that for?" she asks, her breath coming faster when I pull back.

"It's been too long since I kissed you."

Jules smirks. "Yeah. Like twenty minutes."

Her phone pings with another text, and when she pulls it out of her pocket, it's another message like the last one.

> Unknown Number: Are you listening?
> Send the fucking money!

"That's enough of that bullshit," I growl, and Jules bites her lip.

"She's not supposed to be contacting me on my phone at all. Email only. She knows that."

"Then ignore it."

She sighs and nods. "I will. I usually do. Actually, from what I understand, I'm not supposed to approve *any* extra money for her. As a trustee, that's the whole job, according to Google. But *fuck*, I hate being the trustee."

Another text comes through, full of shitty, angry emoji, so I take the phone, turn it off, and toss it on the counter.

"We're going to consult with an attorney, baby. There's no reason in this world that you should be in charge of that shit. Not to mention, she's abusive, and I won't have it."

"I'll change my number, too," she murmurs and hops up on the counter, reaching for me. I move close and cage her in, breathing in her flowery scent. "Let's not think about that anymore."

"Good idea." *Fuck*, I love having free access to her again. My hands glide up her thighs and around to her ass, squeezing. She bites that plump lip, and her blue eyes go wide with lust. "I want to take you for a ride."

"It's raining," she reminds me, and her eyes lower to my lips.

Yeah, baby, I want to kiss you, too.

"Not on the bike." I chuckle and nibble her lips, making her sigh.

Her brow furrows. "I mean, we just had sex this morning, but okay."

I laugh out loud and bury my face in her neck. "I always want to fuck you, but that's not what I'm talking about either."

She sighs softly as I pull back and smile down at her, brushing her curls behind her ear.

"Wanna know what I hate?"

I lift an eyebrow. "Tell me."

"That I missed the *whole summer* with you and the bike." She sticks that lower lip out, and I nip at it. "Why couldn't we have kissed and made up six months ago?"

My smile falls, and I glide my thumb over that delicious lip.

"Because I wasn't ready for you six months ago."

"I know," she whispers. "I wasn't, either. I'm just pouting. We'll have a few more bike days before the snow flies. Where are we going today?"

"Just away for a while. Let's get away, baby. Just you and me."

Twenty minutes later, we're in my truck, driving on the highway out toward Bitterroot Lake. It's a huge lake that you can drive all the way around, but it takes a couple of hours.

Jules and I always loved this drive. And there's a spot we haven't been to in far too long.

As I drive out on the highway, I glance over to find my girl watching me, her lips tipped up in a soft smile, her curls hanging around her gorgeous face.

"What are you thinking?" I ask her.

"I want to be in your lap. Right now."

I frown and then look out the windshield.

"Like *right* now?"

"Yeah." I hear the seat belt click, and my gaze whips back to hers.

"Fasten your seat belt, Juliet."

"Nope." She shakes her head, and suddenly, she's crawling over the center console and into my lap, sitting sideways so her back is against the door. She wraps her arms around my neck and kisses my chin so sweetly, it makes my chest ache. "This is way better."

"Baby, I don't want you to get hurt."

"I'm not getting hurt. Because you'd never let that happen." She pushes her fingers into my hair, and *damn,* that feels good.

Keeping my eyes on the road, sure that there are no dangers anywhere around us, I lean in to kiss her forehead.

"I love having you on me like this."

"It's my favorite place to be," she admits with a whisper right next to my ear. "And if I've learned anything, it's that I need to be where I'm happiest. Always. No more wasting time."

She cuddles into me, and when I turn off the highway, onto the lake road, I breathe a little easier. It's still paved, and I'll take it at a decent speed, but not like the highway.

"I'd prefer you were buckled in."

Her head comes up, and she frowns. "If you're scared, I'll move."

"Just stay still." I kiss her head, her temple, and cuddle her close again. I want her on me as much as possible. Christ, I love to touch her. There's no better feeling than having Jules in my arms, right where she's supposed to be.

Thirty minutes later, Jules is breathing softly, sleeping in my arms as I pull off onto the dirt road that takes us back to the pretty clearing by the river that we discovered in high school. We used to come out here on the weekends and all summer to swim, fish, and camp.

We lost our virginity out here to each other, all those years ago in the back seat of my old truck. I don't have the truck anymore, but our spot is still here.

And when I pull in, I'm relieved to see that it seems to be quiet. It's off the beaten path, so I didn't think it would be crowded with tourists.

Not to mention, it's raining, giving us an extra layer of privacy.

I cut the engine and wrap my arms around my girl, hugging her close.

"Are we there?" she asks softly, not opening her eyes.

"We're there," I confirm, watching as her eyelashes flutter. She looks around, her cheeks flush, and tears fill her pretty eyes. "Hey, no crying."

"It's our spot," she whispers and then buries her face

in my neck once more, pulling in a ragged breath. "It's our favorite spot."

"Yeah." My voice is rough as my hands glide up and down her slim back. "It's okay, baby. I hate it when you cry."

She sniffles, then pulls back to look out the windshield. "There's no one here."

"It's not summer, and it's raining." I shrug a shoulder. "Makes sense that it's pretty deserted today."

"I don't want to swim in that cold water."

With a grin, I brush my knuckles down her soft cheek. "Me neither. But we could take a walk. The rain has slowed down."

She nods, and I help her maneuver so we can climb out of the cab of the truck. With her fingers linked with mine, we set off for the bank of the river.

"I used to *love* it out here." She tips her head back to take a deep breath of the clean air. "The sound of the water always drowned out the bad thoughts."

"What kind of bad thoughts?" I ask.

But I know.

She never kept them a secret.

"About my dad," she murmurs. She's watching the water run, and I kick a rock out of her way. "I always held so much guilt."

"I know." Lifting her hand, I press my lips to her knuckles. "But it wasn't your fault, you know."

"I understand that now," she replies. "But when you're only twelve, and you come home from school to find your dad hanging in the garage, well ... it felt like my fault. I took the long way walking home from school that day, and I thought if I'd gotten there sooner, I could have stopped him. Or called for help sooner."

"That's not true, either."

"No." She shakes her head and lets out another sigh. "He'd been there for some time."

I pull my hand from hers, then loop my arm around her shoulders, tugging her into me.

I didn't know Jules then. I mean, we went to the same school, so I knew who she was, but we weren't friends yet. She told me about it through the years we were together, and I know that finding her father is something that she never got over.

I mean, how could *anyone* get over that? You don't. You carry it with you forever.

It's really the root of what eventually caused us to break up, because if she hadn't been so paranoid, if that son of a bitch hadn't known that it was her trigger, he never could have manipulated his way into breaking us up.

"Remember, in the summer, when we'd bring some of the younger kids out here to swim?"

I grin down at her as I let the memories flood me, and they don't break my fucking heart. "They loved it."

"Billie learned to swim in that spot over there." She points at the area where the river calms, and there's a shallow pond. "We did the back float for hours."

"My siblings all loved you to death."

Her smile turns melancholy. "Yeah, I loved them, too."

We're quiet as we keep going, taking in the sounds of

the birds. A little family of deer comes out of the trees and walks down to the water to have a drink.

They watch us, but they don't run away.

The rain starts up again, and we turn back to head to the truck. The sky opens up, dumping on us in cold sheets, and we start to run, laughing.

I open the back door of the truck and help her in before I join her and close it behind us. For a long minute, we listen to the water beat down on the roof.

"Montana weather, am I right?" she says with a chuckle, and when she turns her face up to look at me, I can't help myself.

I cup her face and lean into her, brushing my lips over hers, and she whimpers, throws one leg over my lap, and straddles me.

Her pussy grinds over me through her leggings, and my hands drift under her sweatshirt, tugging it up.

Jules pulls back long enough to shed that layer, and I unfasten her bra, and she lets that fall, too.

"You're so fucking gorgeous," I growl as I lean in to nip and lick her already tight nipples. She bows back, holding my shoulders as I consume her. The storm rages around us, and it's like we're in our own little cocoon.

It's fucking perfect.

"You're so good at that," she breathes, circling her hips over my straining cock.

"Can't get enough of you," I mutter against her skin. My hands are all over her warm skin, up and down her back, then up in her hair. I want to touch her everywhere at once. "I'm never letting you go. Not ever."

"Not going anywhere." She shakes her head and

moans when I tweak a nipple *hard*. "God, you always make it hurt so good."

"Lift up, baby."

Without a moment of hesitation, she rises on her knees. I rip her leggings, then push her panties to the side and sink a finger inside her wet heat.

"You're so fucking *soaked* for me."

Her breathing is ragged as she starts to ride my finger, her pussy squeezing me, begging for more. I press my thumb to her hard bundle of nerves, and she moans.

"God, Brooks."

"You like that, baby?"

"Hell yes, I like that. But I need more."

I add a second finger, and she shudders around me. Her pussy is quivering, and I know she won't last much longer.

Which is fine because I'll just make her come again on my cock.

"*God*, you have thick fingers."

"All the better to finger fuck you with in the back seat of my truck."

She huffs out a chuckle and starts to bear down on me, her body tensing as she's just on the precipice of coming.

"Chase that orgasm, baby. Fuck my hand and come all over it. You're so fucking amazing. I can't get enough of you."

"Ah, shit." Her eyes clench shut, but I grab her throat with my free hand.

"Eyes on me."

Biting her lip, she opens those baby blues. Her jaw drops, and she starts to come apart.

"That's it. Fuck, you're so perfect when you fall apart like this."

"*Brooks.*"

"Goddamn, you're tight. So fucking tight, your pussy's sucking my fingers like crazy."

"Oh God." She leans in, rests her forehead on my shoulder, and rides the wave of the orgasm. I pull my hand free and lick my fingers clean before unbuckling my belt and opening my jeans.

"Take my cock out."

She shivers at the sound of my voice and immediately does as I say. She reaches into my boxer briefs and pushes them down, unleashing my pulsing, hard dick.

"I want you to ride me, baby." I kiss the middle of her sternum, right between her breasts as she sinks down over me, making us both groan, and then I'm pushing up into her. I can't stop myself.

With my hands on her hips, I guide her up and down on my shaft. She leans in again and rests her forehead against mine.

"How does it get better every time?" she whispers against my lips.

"Because it's us." My hands knead the globes of her ass, and she clenches around me even tighter, strangling my cock. "Keep doing that, and you'll make me come."

"I think that's the point." She nibbles my lips, and I pull her down harder, slamming her down on me. "Yes, *fuck.* Harder, babe."

The thing is, Jules and I always loved rough sex.

Rough and hard and fast. And thank fuck that hasn't changed.

I reach back and drag my finger over the tight muscle of her asshole, making her gasp and that perfect pussy tighten even more.

"I'll have you here," I growl against her lips. I don't know if it's a warning or a promise. "I'm going to own this perfect body."

"You already do." She starts to shatter over me. "Please let me come. *Please.*"

"That's my good girl." I thrust up hard, and she squeezes me so tightly with her own climax, there's no way I don't follow her over. "Goddamn, Jules."

"*Yes.*" She's holding me with all her might. "Yes, yes, yes, yes."

I come apart, emptying myself inside her. "Christ Jesus."

"He's not here," she says with a sigh as she collapses against me, hugging me close, her sweet face in my neck. "But holy shit, I might have seen heaven just now."

I chuckle and kiss her forehead, pushing her sweaty hair off her face.

"This spot is still magic," I growl into her ear. "We'll be coming here often."

"It's a date."

Chapter Seventeen

JULIET

My morning walks haven't changed since I've been staying at Brooks's house. I need the jaunt through town to start my day with my head on straight, no matter what the weather is. It's my mental health time.

Thankfully, the rain has moved out, and the fall air is crisp and perfect. I'm in a red hoodie that I stole from Brooks this morning, and feel quite smug about it. He saw me in it before I left the house, and he smirked, fisted the collar, and pulled me in for a hot, deep kiss.

The kind of kiss that only Brooks can deliver.

The kind that makes my toes curl and my ovaries do the cha-cha.

God bless him.

I snort and walk down to the sidewalk, staring ahead at the big house across the street. God, I love that red roof. Those black shutters. And that deep front porch is perfect for a porch swing. It's so crazy that Brooks lives right here, where we daydreamed so many times about that big house on the corner, how we'd fill it with kids and make it our forever home.

Shaking away the melancholy—because frankly, I have *nothing* to complain about right now because I have my man back, and he's *everything*—I set off for my usual walk through town. The sun is rising later and later as we firmly move into fall, and I kind of love it. The mornings are quiet, with not many people out and about, and I can soak in Bitterroot Valley. I walk through downtown and notice that Jackie's already in her kitchen, so I knock on the window and give her a wave.

She smiles widely and waves back, and then I continue down to my own restaurant.

I don't go inside, but peering through the glass, I can see that Anderson has accomplished a lot over the past couple of days. The walls are up and painted, and it looks like the flooring has arrived, and the boxes are sitting in the middle of the room to acclimate.

According to my contractor, I should be able to open my doors in two weeks, and I hope he's right because I miss being in there, feeding people.

I took Connor's advice because it had been playing in my head over and over again since that day he offered to help me.

Money isn't personal.

The money didn't treat me like shit. Justin did that all on his own. And because I endured *years* of being married to that prick, I inherited the fortune from my late husband. It's mine to do with as I please. Every cent is in my name. Except for the money he left to *her*, but that's not relevant to anything else.

I have millions in my name, and I've been stubborn about using it.

I'm not going to be stubborn anymore.

My staff have been off work for two weeks, and I need them to come back to me when I reopen. If I couldn't pay them, they'd have to get new jobs, and I'd be stuck. So I've been paying them their regular salaries while they've been off. Every single one of them has offered to help me in any way that I might need, which made me feel good.

Christy, Tandy, and Erica check in with me almost every day.

So, I've used the money to pay my staff, and rather than accept Connor's financial help, I've paid for the repairs myself. I am, however, accepting his help when it comes to the construction crew and any other business advice he might want to send my way. Who am I to say no to a *ridiculously* successful billionaire? People pay a lot of money for that kind of advice.

I quickly go around to the back of the building and climb the metal stairs to the apartment above. Pushing inside, I take a quick look around. It's empty now. Anything I could salvage—which wasn't much—was taken to Brooks's house, and the rest was hauled away in the massive dumpster. It's dried out, and Anderson treated all of the raw, exposed wood with something to prevent mold.

And now that I take a good look around, I realize that I was so freaking bullheaded to think that I could live up here without remodeling it and making it a true apartment. Once the restaurant is finished, Anderson will get started up here, and I guess I'll be moving in after it's finished.

The thought of that is *horrible*. I love living with Brooks in his little house, which offers a view of my dream home and the mountains. I love sleeping beside him at night, wrapped up in his strong arms. It's where I was supposed to be all along, but we haven't discussed the future or what will happen when the renovations are complete.

With a sigh, I shut and lock the door behind me, check it three times, and then get back to my usual route. The sky is starting to cloud up, hiding the sun away and making the air cooler. When I approach Brooks's house, he's waiting for me on the porch, with two mugs of steaming coffee in his hands.

"How did you know I'd be back now and ready for coffee?"

He smirks as he holds a mug out for me, then leans in to kiss me.

"You're nothing if not a creature of habit, Wildfire." He sits on the top step of the porch, and I join him, quietly sipping our morning coffee.

His garage is closed today, and we've been spending Sundays together lately. It's quickly becoming my favorite day of the week.

"Darby came to book club last night," I tell him, filling the silence. "She sure has changed a lot since high school."

"She's changed a lot since she went to Colorado for vet school," he rumbles, watching as a delivery truck drives by. "She seems lighter. Happier. Quicker to smile."

"I agree. She was laughing with Ava and me last night and having a blast. I'm glad she's moving back to town when she's finished with school. She also said that she's going to start joining us for book club via FaceTime."

I grin and wave at a woman who walks past with her golden retriever.

"What are you reading next?" he asks me, reaching over to hook my hair behind my ear and then brushing his thumb down my cheek.

"It's an A.L. Jackson book. *At the Edge of Surrender.* Romantic suspense. It should be good. I love her books."

My man nods, and I nibble my lip as I continue to stare at the house across the street.

"This is going to sound crazy."

He glances down at me and lifts an eyebrow. "I doubt it."

"I kind of want to march over there and ask the owners if I can have a look around. It's killing me, Brooks. I *so* want to see the inside. Do you think they'd have me arrested for being a creep?"

He searches my gaze, not even cracking half of a smile at my creepy comment, and then the next thing I know, he stands, sets our mugs aside, and offers me his hand.

Sliding my palm against his, I'm confused as hell as he leads me down the sidewalk, across the street, and up the walk to the big front porch.

"Uh, I mean, we don't have to do this *now* ..."

Brooks pulls some keys out of his pocket, unlocks the front door, and pushes it open, then steps back.

"You want to have a look? Go have a look, Juliet."

My mouth goes slack as I frown, and my feet are

rooted to this spot as I stare up at this amazing man I'm already so in love with, it makes my chest ache.

"What?" My voice is nothing but a whisper. He lifts his free hand and brushes his thumb over my lower lip.

"Go ahead, baby."

I glance inside and then back up at him.

"Brooks, why do you have a key to this house?"

He doesn't answer. He just pulls me by the hand over the threshold, closes the door behind us, and starts turning on the lights.

The air is a little musty, like no one has lived here in a long time, but it's clean. The original hardwood floors need to be sanded and refinished. There's a gorgeous staircase straight ahead that leads up to the second floor.

Brooks guides me past what looks like a little study, then a living room—these old houses weren't open floor plans—and then into a kitchen that has my eyes bugging out.

Not because it's gorgeous and new.

No, this kitchen has avocado-green appliances from the 1970s and faded orange wallpaper. I can see the outline of where pictures hung on the walls. The cabinets are dark brown. The floor is yellow laminate.

It needs to be gutted.

"Brooks—"

"It's my house. *Our* house, really," he says, his voice soft but still echoing a bit in the empty room. "It came on the market a few years ago, and I couldn't stand the thought of someone else buying it. You always loved it."

Holy fucking shit.

My heartbeat speeds up, my breaths quicken.

Holy.

Fucking.

Shit.

"Brooks—"

"I've thought about selling it," he admits with a shrug as he looks around. "Buying a hundred-year-old house is a *lot*. And I'm not just talking financially. It needs a lot of work, so before you and I ... well, I thought about selling it."

The tears roll unchecked down my cheeks.

"You bought me a whole house."

"Two of them." He turns and looks me in the eyes now and leans back against the old Formica countertop, his hands on the counter at his hips.

"What do you mean?"

He glances toward the front of the house and lifts his chin, gesturing to his home across the street.

"You asked me how long I've lived over there." He clears his throat, pushes his hand through his hair, and I can see that he's nervous.

Brooks is *never* nervous.

So I cross to him and take his hand in mine, lift it to my lips.

"I've lived there for fifteen years," he says quietly, and my gaze whips up to his. "Every house I've ever bought was done with you in mind."

I wrinkle my forehead, doing the math. "But fifteen years—"

"Yeah, baby. That last day, when the asshole manipulated you into going back to Seattle?"

I can't force any words over the huge lump that's

formed in my throat, so I just nod. That was the worst day of my life.

"I was going to propose to you that day."

The world shifts beneath my feet, and I start to shake my head as pure anguish fills me. The pain is unlike anything I've ever felt before.

"I'd already bought the house," he continues. His voice is so rough. Full of so much raw emotion. "It was a fixer-upper, but I planned to have it ready by the time you finished school for good and moved home."

"Brooks." My voice breaks on his name, and he scoops me against him, clinging to me almost desperately. "Fuck."

"I was going to surprise you and take you to the house. I had flowers and balloons all over the place, thanks to the help of my mom and the rest of the family. Then we were going to have a little party at the ranch," he says, peppering the top of my head with kisses.

No.

God, that's all I've ever wanted.

"You begged me to stay." I'm crying against his chest, unable to hold in the sobs, grieving what we both lost. "You told me that you needed me, and I was too blinded, too fucking overwhelmed—"

"Hey, shh."

"No, you *should* hate me." I step out of his arms and walk across the room to the wide windows that look out over the backyard. There's a concrete patio out there, where I would put a pergola and furniture and *God.* "You should still hate me, Brooks. Shit, *I* hate me."

"No, stop it." His hand grips my upper arm, and he

turns me to him, then cups my face. "I'm so fucking over being angry, Jules. It consumed me for more than a decade. Besides, we were both at fault for how things went down."

My face crumples again, and I close my eyes.

"I have you back with me, and I'm not going to feed into the anger or the frustration anymore. I'm just not. It was eating me alive. For whatever reason, it just wasn't the right time for us, baby."

"I'm so sorry."

"Hey." He tips my chin up and makes me look him in the eyes. I absolutely *hate* seeing the tears in his beautiful hazel eyes. "I am *not* telling you this to make you hurt, Wildfire. I don't want you to hurt any more than you already have."

"It's fucking agony," I reply, my lips quivering as every muscle in my body shakes with rage and despair. "I could have been your wife for all of these years. We could have had babies, and an amazing family, and—"

"No more." He shakes his head and leans in to rest his forehead to mine. He has to lean down so far, it would be laughable if I weren't losing my mind with regret and sadness. "We can still have those things, baby."

"We lost so much time."

"And we have plenty ahead of us." He wipes his thumbs under my eyes, clearing away the tears. "We need to stop dwelling on what we lost and focus on the fact that we found each other again, and this is just the beginning of an amazing life together."

His voice holds so much conviction.

"You need to understand that I'm never letting you

go again, Juliet. *Never.* You're mine. If you want to live in the house that I bought for you fifteen years ago, that's great with me. If you want me to gut and renovate this one for you, perfect. Let's do it. I don't care where we live as long as we're there *together*, sleeping in our bed, with you in my arms. Because I've already endured this life without you, and I refuse to spend another minute in that fucking purgatory."

"I'm not going anywhere," I promise him, wrapping my arms around his neck. He easily lifts me into his arms, and I wrap my legs around his waist before he deposits me on the countertop. "I don't care where we live, either. I just need to be with you because you're the love of my life, Brooks. You're the only one who makes sense, the only person I need."

"Jesus, I needed to hear you say that." He buries his face in my neck, and I push my fingers into his thick, dark hair. "I love you, baby. It's always been you. Hell, I'd marry you today."

I smirk at that, letting the love pouring from him fill my heart and smooth out all of the rough edges.

He's holding me so tenderly, it's a balm to my bruised heart. I don't know how long we stay like this. It could be minutes or an hour, but finally, he moves back just a little and wipes the last of my tears away.

"Do you want to see the rest of the house?" he murmurs, still caressing me, soothing me.

"Please. Give me a tour."

I hop down, and with his hand holding mine tightly, as if he's worried I might slip away—spoiler alert: never happening—he leads me through the rest of the first floor, showing me a laundry room, a guest bedroom, the living room, and then leads me to the study.

"I thought this would make a nice library for you. Install built-in bookcases, a cozy chair and table. It wouldn't be as grand as Billie's because Connor's a fancy fuck, but it could work."

I'm blinking up at him in surprise. "I think I just fell in love with you."

Brooks barks out a laugh. "It took me mentioning a library to do that?"

"I mean, it didn't hurt. You'd be okay with me taking over a whole room?"

"The whole house is *yours*, Juliet. Do whatever the fuck you want."

"You would have to live here, too, you know."

"I have what I want." He kisses the top of my head and leads me to the staircase. "I have you. Let's go up. The second floor needs more work than the first does."

"Is that even possible?"

He winces. "Yeah, it's possible. Old house, remember? If this is too much of a project for you, and you'd rather we sold both houses and bought something newer—"

"Do I look like a woman who's afraid of a DIY project, Mr. Blackwell?"

"No, you lived in an attic. Remember?" His voice is growly, and he narrows his eyes at me. "A fucking attic, Juliet."

"Hey, it served the purpose."

"Yeah, the purpose of punishing yourself."

We reach the top of the stairs, and I turn to him, my mouth dropping in surprise. "I wasn't—"

"Yeah, you were." His mouth is set in grim lines as he watches me. "We both know it, Wildfire."

I swallow hard. *Is* that what I was doing? Maybe, without realizing it.

"Okay, there are four bedrooms up here," he says, and starts pointing them out. "One bathroom for the three smaller bedrooms to share. The primary bedroom has an en suite."

I follow him through, poking my head into all of the rooms.

"They're pretty small," I murmur quietly, taking it all in. It's true, the bedrooms *are* small. "But they'd be fine for kids' rooms. Or an office. What about your home gym?"

"I have a garage out back," he says with a shrug. "And I usually go to the firehouse to work out anyway. Bridger has given all of us access to the gym there. I don't need a room in the house for that. We could share an office here, since we both have offices at our businesses."

I'm nodding, feeling excitement bubble up in my stomach as I start to see it all in my head.

"I want to see the primary."

"Right this way." He gestures to the open door, and I walk past him, soaking up his warmth. This bedroom is at least twice the size of the others on this floor.

"I suspect that a previous owner opened a wall to another smaller room to make this bigger," he says, as if he can read my mind. He's leaning on the doorjamb as I walk around. His arms are folded, showing off his *incredible* biceps. "My eyes are up here, Wildfire."

I smirk, then chuckle as I look around. "I like it. I'd paint it something soft, like a yellow or green. Pretty curtains on the windows. A rug in the middle of the floor, after said floors get refinished. It would be really pretty."

"The bathroom's through there." He points at another doorway, and I step over and then freeze.

The ceiling has caved in over the clawfoot tub.

"Water damage," he says behind me, taking my shoulders in his hands. "The leak has been fixed, but the bathroom needs to be gutted."

"I see that. Fucking water damage is the bane of my existence."

He wraps his arms around me from behind and lowers his lips to my ear. "What do you think? You don't have to know today. This house isn't going anywhere."

I bite my lip, afraid to hope and trust that this could be real.

But he's right here, behind me, holding me tight, and it *is* real.

"I love the house across the street." I turn and loop my arms around his middle. "It's a great house."

"You're right. It *is* a great house." He kisses my forehead. "What's going on in that gorgeous brain of yours?"

I work my lip through my teeth as I ponder this. "I'll be perfectly happy living across the street while we fix this one up. It's so handy that we're *right there.* And then, later, we can decide if we want to keep it and rent it out or sell it. But I think I want to keep it. Because I'm greedy as fuck, Brooks."

His lips spread into a smile as he takes my face in his hands and lowers his lips to mine.

"This sounds like an excellent plan. And I love that you're saying *we* so much. It sounds fucking amazing."

"Yeah, I like it, too. And Brooks?"

"Yes, baby?"

"That kitchen is the first thing to go."

Chapter Eighteen

BROOKS

I haven't felt this light, this *optimistic* in ... ever? Maybe not ever. Juliet knows everything now, all the secrets I've carried around all these years, and we're working our way through it. Everything that happened in the house just about ripped my heart out, but we're okay.

We're going to renovate our house together, and I'll make sure it's exactly what she wants. Hell, she could turn it into a bed-and-breakfast, and I'd go along with it.

We left through the back door, so we could check out the three-car garage, a little vegetable garden that hasn't been tended to in years, and a shed, and now we're circling around the side of the house toward the street just as a car pulls into my driveway.

"Who's visiting?" Jules asks, frowning.

"I believe that's Dani." I kiss her cheek as we cross the street, and Birdie comes bounding out of the back seat of the SUV.

"Hi, Uncle Brooks!" She runs to me and leaps into my arms. "We're here."

"I see that, peanut. Do you remember our friend Juliet?"

"When are you opening your restaurant back up?" Birdie asks Jules, who smiles softly at my little niece.

"As soon as possible. I miss it, too. The construction people tell me about two weeks."

"That's so *far away*," Birdie says, acting like her life is over.

Dani and Darby join us, both with their arms full.

"Hey, guys," Jules says. "What in the world are you doing?"

"Operation *make-the-kitchen-safe-for-Jules* is officially here," Dani says with a smile. "We're replacing everything today. I have plenty more in the car. Brooks, do you mind being the muscle?"

"I never mind being the muscle." I flex one arm, and Dani and Darby roll their eyes. Jules bites her lip, which was what I intended.

Birdie climbs across me to hang from my biceps.

"We went shopping," Birdie announces. "Because you have tummy stuff like me."

Jules blinks rapidly, keeping tears at bay. "You didn't have to—"

"Yeah, Wildfire, we did. Come on, guys, let's go inside."

I set Birdie down and open the back of the SUV, pull out a large tote full of what looks like dishes and cutlery, and follow the girls inside.

"We'll donate everything that's already here," Darby

217

says, looking around with her hands on her hips. "There's a new women's shelter looking for donations."

I nod in agreement, but Jules is shaking her head.

"I've been just fine," Jules insists. "I've been eating here without an issue. This isn't necessary."

"Yeah, you've been fine getting by with the few things that I have on hand, and that's not good enough. I want you to be able to relax and feel safe here. Eat whatever you want from whatever surface, dish, or pan you want without worrying. As of today, this and any other kitchen you and I have is a *clean kitchen.*"

Dani and Darby share a smile as I pull Jules in for a hug.

"You live here," I remind her softly. "This is your home, baby."

"And here just a few hours ago, I was trying to figure out how I was going to come to grips with the fact that I had to move back into the attic."

I pull back and narrow my eyes at her, cover her throat with my hand, and lean in to whisper in her ear.

"You're going to get spanked later for even *thinking* that, Wildfire."

She pulls in a sharp breath, then licks her lips as I pull away.

"I kind of love this whole situation. They're mushy, but not disgusting about it like you and Bridger are," Darby tells Dani, as if we're not standing right here. They've already started pulling my old stuff out of cabinets, filling totes with it, and I take the full ones and put them in Dani's car.

"No touching the old stuff," Dani tells Jules when

my girl reaches for the pots and pans. "I want to be sure that you don't have a reaction. No getting sick on my watch, friend."

"Flares suck ass," Birdie announces from the dining room table, where she's set up with her iPad and a snack. She nods knowingly, like she's forty.

"*Birdie*," Dani says, her pretty blue eyes wide with surprise. "You don't say that word. I don't know where she gets this language. I don't swear. Ever."

"Have you heard your husband talk?" I ask her. "He has a filthy mouth."

"I'm not wrong, though," Birdie replies with a shrug. *This kid is hilarious.*

"Where's the baby?" Jules asks as she starts to unpack the new pots and pans and sets them by the sink to wash. Then she starts to unpack a brand-new toaster.

"He's with Holden and Millie," Darby answers. "Holden is *obsessed* with the little ones. It's a bit ... *alarming.*"

"He's always been good with kids," Dani reminds her sister. "Okay, I think that's the last of the old. Time to sterilize."

The four of us spend an hour with bleach and sponges, wiping down every cabinet, every drawer, even the fridge and oven. The microwave. Dani tosses a special tablet into the dishwasher and runs it on the sanitize cycle.

Then we all work together to put the new stuff away, after giving it a good wash in the sink.

"You're a lifesaver," I say to Dani as I pull her in for a hug. The Lexingtons are like siblings to me. All of them.

Having these girls here to help me ensure that my wildfire is safe means the world.

"Now we can eat here and not have bad tummies," Birdie says to Jules.

"That's exciting," Jules agrees. "You let me know what kinds of things you want on the menu when I'm ready to reopen Sage & Citrus, and I'll make sure I have those for you, okay?"

"Anything I want?" Birdie asks with wide eyes.

"Pretty much anything," Jules confirms.

"Mac and cheese," Birdie replies immediately. "I miss that the most."

"Psh. I can totally do that for you. I can do that *today*. Do you guys want to come over later for dinner?"

And just like that, my heart has exploded outside of my chest. Because my woman, the one person I've wanted to have here with me from the beginning, just invited my family over for dinner. To our home.

Our. Home.

Dani grins, and Birdie nods.

"We'd love that. Bridger gets off work around three. What can I bring?"

"Just yourselves," Jules says and hugs Birdie back when the little girl wraps her arms around Juliet's waist. "I'll make ... hmm ... how about fried chicken with mac and cheese and some salad?"

"I can bring baked beans," Darby offers. "Alex has Mom's recipe box, and there's a really good beans recipe in there."

"I'm down for that. And tell all of the others, too.

Everyone is welcome," Jules replies. "How does all of that sound, Miss Birdie?"

"Can we have it *now*?" Birdie asks, making us laugh.

"If you want, you can stay and help me cook." Jules raises her brows at Dani in a silent *is that okay* look.

"Can I, Mom?" Birdie asks Dani.

"I don't mind if you stay," Dani says, kissing Birdie's head. "We'll be back later this afternoon, after your dad is off work."

We walk Darby and Dani out, and then when we're alone with Birdie, who's happy at the table with her tablet again, Jules turns to me, nibbling her lip, looking uncertain.

"What's up, Wildfire?"

"I should have asked you before I blurted out an invitation to have your family for dinner."

I pull her in for a hug. Christ, I can't stop hugging her. "You don't have to ever ask permission for anything. This is your home, remember? Do whatever you want. But for what it's worth, I love that you asked them to come for dinner."

"You do?"

"Sure. I'm close to my family, baby. Having them here is never a hardship. Birdie is, behind you, my favorite person in the world."

"I don't know, I think she ranks above me. She's awesome."

I laugh and kiss the top of her head, breathing in her flowers. "Make me a grocery list, and I'll go get whatever you need."

"Oh, I don't mind going. There will be certain gluten-free—"

"I've got this," I tell her. "Trust me."

Her eyes soften, and she smiles up at me. "Thank you."

I wake up with a start, not sure what might have pulled me out of sleep, but definitely aware that I'm alone.

And I should never wake up in the middle of the night alone. Not now that I have Juliet in my bed.

The sheets are cool, telling me she's been gone for a while. It's just before four, and I want her here with me, so I climb out of bed and tug on some sweats to go searching for her.

She's not in the living room or the kitchen. Just when I'm about to panic, I glance out the front window and see my wildfire bundled up in my old red hoodie, sitting on the top step of the porch. She has her arms wrapped around her knees, just staring out into the night.

Stepping outside, I shiver a little. It's cold, but I don't give a shit. I need to make sure my girl is okay.

Jules glances over her shoulder and smiles softly at me as I sit next to her and tug her against me. She immediately melts into my side, nuzzles my shoulder, and wraps her arms around me.

"I wanted to let you sleep," she whispers.

"I don't like waking up without you," I tell her, kissing the top of her head. "What's wrong?"

"Nothing at all is wrong. Everything in my world is pretty much perfect."

I grin and tip her chin up so I can kiss her. "Good. Just couldn't sleep, then?"

"My brain is moving a mile a minute," she confesses with a sigh and then looks away again. "That's our house, Brooks."

"Yeah, baby. It's our house."

"I have so many ideas already. I don't know if you're ready for this because I basically want to take everything in there down to the studs and start over."

"It pretty much has to be that way. Did you see it?"

Jules chuckles and nods. "Yeah, I saw it. It's amazing. It's better than I ever imagined when we were kids. We'll make it really special."

"You can have anything you want."

"I'm using the money." Her voice is quiet, and before I can argue, she keeps talking. "He owes us so much more than he could ever pay. He took time. He took *you* from me, and now he's going to pay for it in the only way possible. I'm not afraid of using that money anymore. Connor's right, it's not personal."

"Sounds personal," I mumble.

"It's not any better to be stubborn and let a fortune rot in an account where it doesn't do any good to anyone. I'm going to use it for my business, first and foremost. Because he always said I couldn't do it. That it wouldn't work. Well, it's fucking working. And then, I'll use it for some of the work on the house. It's *mine*, Brooks."

"I don't love the idea of anything that came from that piece of shit making its way into our home, Juliet."

She sighs and gives it some thought. "It's going to be expensive to make it all happen, and we can do it without loans. It'll be all ours."

"We'll talk about it some more. I'm not exactly poor, you know."

She laughs and reaches up to brush her fingers down my cheek. "No, you're not. You have a kick-ass business, and I'm so damn proud of you. If you just want me to use that money for the restaurant, I will. I understand."

"We'll discuss it," I say again and kiss her nose.

She's quiet again, snuggled up in my arms, taking in the night.

"Remember earlier when you said you'd marry me today?"

My heart stills. My whole body seems to pause.

"I remember."

"Okay."

I pull back and take her face in my hands, staring down into the most gorgeous blue eyes reflecting the moonlight. "Okay what, Wildfire?"

"Okay to marrying me. Today."

Now the blood rushes through my ears, and my heart's beating in overdrive. My skin is hot, oblivious to the cool night air around us.

"You want to get married today?"

She nods and smiles up at me. "Yeah. Can you take the morning off work so we can go to the courthouse?"

"Baby, I own the business, so yeah, I can take the day off. But I need to make sure that this is what you *really* want. Not because of the house, or because of all of the emotions of the past couple of months—"

"No, I *want* to be your wife, Brooks. It's all I ever wanted. If I'd only known—" She shakes her head sadly. "Well, like you said, we can't dwell on that. I don't want to waste another day. Another *minute*. I want to be Juliet Blackwell today."

Well, that's a punch to the gut.

"They're not open quite yet." I smile softly and ghost my fingertips over her jawline. "A quick visit to the justice of the peace isn't the wedding you deserve, Juliet."

"I don't honestly *care* about the hoopla. Don't get me wrong, I plan to be very loud and obnoxious about announcing to anyone who will listen that I finally got you to marry me."

I snort, but she keeps talking.

"And we can have that party with close friends and family, which means it won't be a *small* party at all."

"Not in the least."

"But I want it to be today. I don't want to wait months to plan something. I'll hire Charlie Lexington to plan our reception."

I take a long, deep breath and nudge her lips up to meet my own. "I love you so much, Wildfire."

"I love you, too."

I stand and pick her up, then walk us inside and back to the bedroom, where I set her gently on the side of the bed and then cross to the dresser and pull a black velvet box out from under my socks.

When I turn around, her eyes widen, pinned to the box in my hands, and I move slowly back to her, then kneel in front of her. Her hands are clenched tightly together in her lap, and she's chewing so hard on that bottom lip that I'm surprised she's not bleeding.

I pull the ring that I've held on to for all these years out of the box, then set the box aside and reach for her hand.

"I've held on to this for you. It was always supposed to be yours."

Tears spill down onto her cheeks as she stares at the small diamond ring.

"I would buy you something bigger now—"

"I want this one," she says, shaking her head, and I can't help but smile and lean in to kiss her cheek, then down to her neck and breathe her in.

"You're the sweetest thing, Wildfire. God, I fucking love you."

"I love you, too. Do I get to wear that now?"

I chuckle and pull back to do this right. "I have to ask a question first. Will you—"

"Yes."

"—please do me the honor—"

"Absolutely."

"—of marrying me—"

"Without question."

"—and being my wife?"

"A million times yes. Yes, yes, yes." She sticks her shaking hand out, and I slip the ring on her finger. It fits perfectly. I bring her hand up to my lips and press a kiss there, and then she's in my arms, laughing and crying and holding on so tight, she might strangle me.

I don't mind.

"We can do it today?" she asks.

"We can be waiting when they open," I confirm as I shift us onto the bed and roll us so she's beneath me. "Now, since we have several hours to kill before I can make you my wife, I'm going to fuck you like I hate you, then make sweet love to you."

"Oh, that's the best news I've ever heard."

Chapter Nineteen

JULIET

"They're taking forever to open." I'm sitting in the front seat of Brooks's truck, my knee bouncing with nerves and my eyes pinned to the door of the courthouse, which is still locked. We're parked right out front, waiting. I'm *not* patient.

We were the first ones here.

"They still have ten minutes before they open." Brooks is as calm as can be next to me, and I turn to look at him.

He's in a crisp white button-down, the sleeves rolled up on his forearms, showing off muscles and veins and *damn*. Don't even get me started on the gray slacks that show off that hard ass to perfection.

"Keep looking at me like that, Wildfire, and I'll fuck you right here for all the goddamn world to see."

I press my lips together and feel my cheeks heat at his gravelly voice. We never went back to sleep because he was too busy fucking me senseless for the rest of the night.

No regrets.

"I'm still sore from earlier," I inform him, and watch as he smirks, his eyes full of mirth and joy and ... *lust.* "I'll be walking funny on our wedding day. Are you proud of yourself?"

"Fuck yes, I'm proud of myself. Tell me, Juliet. Am I still dripping out of you?"

I can't even look him in the eyes now, and he chuckles as he reaches over and brushes the back of his knuckles over my white dress, right where he knows my nipple is, making it pucker.

"I'd better still be running down your thighs. I'll be making you my wife with my cum all over that pretty soft skin."

"*Brooks.*" His mouth is filthy, and I freaking *love it.*

He grins and leans over to me.

"The next time I'm inside you, you'll be my wife."

Okay, that sends a shot of electricity right up my spine, and I reach for his hand, gripping it hard and lacing our fingers.

"You like the idea of that."

"Yeah." My voice isn't altogether steady. "I do like that."

"Me too, baby." As he kisses the back of my hand, someone unlocks the door of the courthouse, and we turn to face each other. "Are you sure about this?"

"Never been more positive about anything in my life." A grin spreads over my face. I put on a full face of makeup today, and I'm wearing a pretty white dress that I've had for a while but never worn before today.

I'm *so* ready to marry this man.

"Then let's go. Wait for me."

He pushes out of the truck and circles around to open my door, and then, before I know it, we have a marriage license and are standing before a judge.

"Congratulations," he says, smiling at Brooks. *They must know each other.* "When we get to the vows, do you want to go with the traditional ones, or do you want to speak your own?"

"We'll speak our own," I answer, and Brooks winks at me, making me melt.

"Sounds good. Dearly beloved ..."

There are only two people here, the janitor and a cop who was walking by. Those are our witnesses, and frankly, that's fine by me.

I can't take my eyes off the man who's holding my hands, staring down into my eyes with so much promise and tenderness, it makes my breath catch.

"I do," he says.

"I do," I echo.

"Go ahead with your vows," the judge says, nodding at me first.

"Thank you for waiting for me," I begin, and Brooks brings his hand up, brushing a tear off my cheek. "I know it took us a long time to get here, but I like to think that it was always destined to happen this way. I vow to stand by your side, no matter what kind of insanity comes our way. I will love you, honor you, always make sure that you are my priority, and take care of you when we're old and gray and sitting in the porch swing I'm going to ask you to install at our house."

His lips twitch, and his eyes fill, making my chest swell.

"I will respect you and *listen to you*. I will be your constant, your home base, and your safe place for as long as we both shall live."

Brooks takes a deep breath, then answers with vows of his own.

"They say that you should never refer to the person you love as what completes you because you should come to them as a whole person already. But that's bullsh—" He glances at the judge. "Crap. Because *you* complete me, Juliet, and for fifteen years, I walked around with a huge chunk of myself missing. You are the only thing I need. I look in your eyes, and I see our future so perfectly; our babies in your arms, our kids running around that backyard. School pictures and anniversaries and weekends away together. Graduations, weddings. And, one day, us swinging on our porch. It sounds so simple, but nothing could be more valuable or more exciting to me."

I sniff and brush away a tear, and he continues.

"I vow to be the man who deserves you. Who wakes up every day with a mission to make sure you're so well loved, respected, and taken care of that you never regret this day. Not for one minute. I promise to give you a life that keeps you guessing, that keeps you walking funny—"

I snort in surprise.

"And makes you the happiest woman on earth, for as long as we both shall live."

"By the power vested in me by the state of Montana,

I now pronounce you man and wife. You may kiss your bride."

Brooks growls—freaking *growls*—then bends me backward and crushes his lips to mine, kissing me more passionately than he ever has before.

And that's saying a lot.

When we leave the courthouse, we stand on the sidewalk, staring at each other.

"Hi, Mr. Blackwell."

"Hello, Mrs. Blackwell."

I press my lips together and then do a little happy dance, making him chuckle.

"We need to get you a ring," I inform him, brushing over his ring finger.

"We'll go there next," he says and brings me to him for a hug. My ear is pressed to his chest, and I can hear the wild thumping of his heart. "Fuck, we did it, Wildfire."

"We *totally* did it. Oh, *and* we got married."

He laughs and kisses my head. "Let's walk down to the jeweler."

"And I need coffee," I inform him. "I was too nervous to drink it earlier."

"There was no reason to be nervous, baby."

He takes my hand and leads me around the corner to where Millie's coffee shop is, and when we walk inside, Millie glances over and smiles.

"Hey, you two. What are you up to?"

"WE GOT MARRIED!" I'm jumping up and down as I scream it, showing her my hand, and then she's screaming too, and runs around the counter to hug us both. "You're the first person we've told."

"I won't say anything." She mimes zipping her lips. "Did you go to the courthouse?"

"Yeah, I didn't want to wait."

"Nothing wrong with a courthouse wedding," she says with a wink. "That's what Holden and I did, too. Aw, I'm *so fucking happy* for you two."

"Thank you. I'm happy for us too." I do another happy dance and then sigh happily. "I need coffee."

"You came to the right place."

We both order our drinks, and I'm chatting with Millie when I notice that Brooks is typing away on his phone. He's probably telling his guys that he's not coming in today.

Am I sorry?

Fuck no.

Armed with our drinks and more hugs from Mill, we make our way down the block to the jeweler, where Brooks claims he has to try on every damn ring they have because he's going to wear it forever, and it has to be just right. He tries them all on three times, and more than an hour later, Brooks has a cool-looking black ring on his finger, and I have a shiny new gold band to go with my engagement ring.

I might get a little extra emotional when I look at our hands together.

We got married.

He's mine. I get to keep him forever.

"I'm starving," I inform him as we walk down the block. I frown because I could swear I just saw Harper dash out of Paula's Poseys, but then I shrug it off. I'm not kidding when I say that I'm *so hungry*. "Let's go home and eat some leftovers."

"I actually have a plan," he replies and opens the door of his truck for me.

"What plan?" I ask when he climbs behind the wheel. "And does it involve food, or is it just more sex?"

"First of all, never refer to what we do as *just more sex*." He narrows his eyes at me and leans over to brush his lips over the shell of my ear, sending a shiver through me. "Because what we do, baby, is way more than that."

"Okay."

He checks his phone, then pushes it into his pocket.

"If you need to go to work—"

"Absolutely fucking not. Second of all, you need to trust me."

"Of *course* I trust you, but I'm going to starve to death if you don't feed me."

"Were you always this dramatic? Or is that a new thing you've developed since becoming a wife?"

I huff out a laugh. "Seriously, though."

"Trust me, Wildfire."

He pulls out of the parking spot and heads out of town, and I frown over at him because he's not even going the speed limit.

"I'm not telling you where we're going."

"Are we going to our spot by the river so we can consummate this marriage?"

"Tempting, but no. Unfortunately, I can't mess you up like I want to. Well, not until later. Later, all bets are off and I'm going to fucking *wreck you*."

I press my legs together, trying to ease the ache between them. "Can't wait."

As we head farther out of town, a bad feeling starts to set up residence in my gut.

"Brooks."

"Yes, baby."

"Do *not* tell me that you're taking me to the ranch."

He's quiet, so I turn to him and poke his shoulder.

"Ouch. Domestic violence already?"

"Tell me we're *not* going to the ranch for a party."

"I can't tell you that because although I didn't specifically say in my vows that I wouldn't lie, it was implied."

"Is it just the siblings and the kids? Because if that's the case, it's okay."

He frowns over at me. "What are you worried about, Wildfire?"

"I've barely seen your parents since I've been back. Just briefly at Blake's engagement party."

"Okay. My parents always loved you."

"Sure, before I was the bitch who broke their baby boy's heart."

Suddenly, Brooks pulls the truck over to the side of the road, jumps out, and strides around to me. He opens the door, unfastens my seat belt, and turns me to face him. His hands cup the sides of my neck.

"You will *never* refer to my wife as a bitch ever again. Do you understand me?"

Holy fucking shit.

"It's an expression, Brooks—"

"One that I won't tolerate. You're *mine.* I love you so much that I would burn this fucking world to the

235

ground for you. So you won't speak about yourself that way again."

"Br—"

"Say you understand."

I rub my hand up and down his chest. "I understand."

"Good." He leans in to nibble my lips. "It's going to be great, baby. I promise, I wouldn't take you into a situation that could hurt you. Never."

With a nod, I offer him a smile. "Okay. Maybe the hunger was making me act unreasonably."

With a snort, he bites my lower lip, then gets me back into the seat belt. Within a few seconds, we're back on the road.

"So it's a party."

"I'm not telling you anything more." He shoots me a grin. "Love you. Mean it."

"You're a weirdo."

Shaking my head, I can't help but reach for his hand as he pulls onto the ranch road, and a couple of minutes later, we pull up to the old farmhouse that Brooks grew up in. I spent so much time at this house back in the day.

"Beckett and Skyla live here now," he says as we just sit for a minute and let the memories come. "Mom and Dad have a place in town. Not too far from us, actually."

"There are about twenty million cars here."

"Or, you know, twenty." He smirks and climbs out and then comes to fetch me again. "Let's go, Bride."

"You're getting such a kick out of this."

"Fuck yes, I am."

With his arm wrapped around me, Brooks leads me

around the house to where there's a tent set up with tables, food, flowers, balloons, and music. There's even a table full of desserts.

And every person that we love is here, including Jackie, all of the Lexingtons, the Wild family, most of whom I haven't seen in a long time, all of Brooks's family, and even Ava and Tucker are here.

It's a *party*.

"How did you do this?" I ask Brooks. No one has noticed we're here yet.

"I called my mom while you were in the shower." His lips twitch into a smug smile. "And she put everyone to work. Charlie and Connor made calls. Everyone scurried. Happy wedding day, Wildfire."

"Oh my God! They're here!" Billie is the first to notice us, and then we're engulfed by hugs and chatter. Everyone wants to see my ring, and I can't even count the number of times someone says, "It's about time."

I couldn't agree more.

"Oh, my sweet girl," Brooks's mom, Becca, says with a kind smile as she wraps me in a hug. "I just couldn't be happier for the two of you."

"Are you sure?" The question is a whisper, and has her backing up to frown at me. "Are you sure this is okay? I hurt him so bad before, and then I made him marry me without any of his family there, and he's your oldest son. I'm sure you would have wanted to be there, but I was selfish, and—"

"It's *your* day," she says, cutting me off. "And it should be exactly how you want it. That's the only thing that matters. Yes, you hurt him, but honey, you were both so painfully young. I'm so happy that you found each other again. This is where you belong, you know. With all of us to love you."

"Welp, looks like I'll just be crying all day today."

Becca laughs with me and then hugs me again. "You're such a gorgeous bride. Let me see your ring."

I proudly hold it up to her, and she sighs. "He kept it for you."

"You saw this ring? Before?"

"That was *my* ring, once upon a time."

My jaw drops. "No."

Her brow furrows. "I hope that's okay."

"No. Yes. Oh shit, *of course* it's okay. I love it so much. I just can't believe ... you know what? Never mind. I love that I have your ring. I'm surprised you gave it to Brooks since you're still married and everything."

She snorts out a laugh. "Well, for our tenth anniversary, Brandon upgraded my ring for me, and Brooks asked if he could have the original when he decided to propose to you."

"That's sweet."

"What's sweet?" Brooks wraps his arm around me and kisses the top of my head. "Mom, you're monopolizing my wife."

"Well, we can't have that." Becca winks at me. "Let's get together soon, Jules."

"I'd love that."

She walks away, and I turn to look up at my husband.

"Not as bad as you thought, is it?"

"Not bad at all."

"Every single one of those desserts is safe for you, by

the way." He kisses my nose. "And all of the food is brunch food, since a certain someone couldn't wait until the afternoon to get married."

"Good. I like brunch food. And I'm starving to death, remember?"

"Then let's feed you, Wildfire."

Chapter Twenty

BROOKS

"T hat was fun." Taking Juliet's hand in mine, I help her out of my truck and onto the concrete of the driveway. She's carrying her sandals in her free hand, walking barefoot. "I don't remember the last time I was at a party for like ten hours."

I smirk and lift her hand to my mouth. Everyone spent *all day* at the ranch, laughing, eating, and just being together. Some people came and went, but it was a steady stream of celebrations all day.

"And not one of them was mad at you," I remind her, and she smiles softly.

"No, no one was mad. It was really nice."

Rather than lead her into the house, I pick her up in my arms and carry her across the street. I can see the candles flickering in the window upstairs.

"What are we doing?" She curls her arms around my neck and kisses my cheek.

"Going home."

"It's back there."

"We're headed to *this* home," I inform her and walk up the steps of the porch, then open the door that was left unlocked, per my request. "I want to spend our wedding night in our forever home."

"You're a softie," she murmurs and nuzzles her nose against my neck, making my cock twitch. "And I kind of love it."

I head straight for the stairs and climb them easily, then move into what will be our bedroom, and turn so she can take everything in.

"Oh God." Setting her on her feet, Jules looks up at me with wide eyes and swallows hard. "*Brooks.*"

A king-sized wrought-iron bed has been set up with pretty white linens and fluffy pillows. Flameless candles flicker all around, dozens of them, lit and sending bouncing light against the walls and ceiling. It smells like roses from all the petals spread on the floor, and when I hit a button on my phone, music starts to play out of a speaker in the corner.

"It'll do," I say with a nod, and my wife lets out a surprised chuckle.

"This is *gorgeous.*"

"I agree." She catches me looking at her and shakes her head. "You're the most beautiful woman I've ever seen, Wildfire."

She turns into my arms, pushes her hands up my chest, then starts to unfasten the buttons of my shirt, one by one, setting my skin on fire.

"It wasn't a traditional wedding day," she begins softly. "But it was everything I ever wanted. So much better than *traditional*."

"I'm glad you had a good day." I brush her blond curls behind her ear, then let my fingertips drift down her neck to her collarbone, and my lips twitch when goose bumps break out over her delicate skin.

With my shirt undone, she pushes it over my shoulders, and I let it fall to the floor, allowing her to take the lead.

The dynamic will change soon, but I'll let her have this control for now.

"My husband is sexy as fuck." She glides those little fingers down my abs, to my belt buckle, and when my pants are unfastened, I step out of my shoes and then the pants, casting them off to join the shirt on the floor.

"What now, beautiful?"

She starts to lower to her knees, but I shake my head and lift her in my arms.

"Not on this floor," I tell her with a growl. "No splinters in your perfect knees, Wildfire."

"But—"

"I didn't say you couldn't suck my cock," I remind her as I join her on the bed, which is actually really cozy, and help her out of her dress. She's not wearing a bra, and when she's left in lacy white panties, I growl, not willing to wait any longer to get my hands on her.

"I like pretty underwear." She shrugs. "But I like it better when you get me out of it."

"Oh, I'm going to fuck you with this on," I inform

her, tracing the edges of the lace with my fingertip, making her squirm. "It's too pretty to rip off you."

Urging her onto her back, I kiss the ball of her shoulder, then drag my lips over to her neck. She sighs as my fingers find her nipple and give it a good tug. All day, I envisioned bringing my girl back here and fucking her, hard and rough, the way we usually like it, the way she *begs for it*, but tonight feels more tender.

Less chaotic.

I want to savor every inch of her, every moan and sigh.

"Grab the headboard, baby."

She blinks up at me, but does what she's told, reaching up over her head to hold on to the black iron headboard.

"How did you get all of this up here?"

"I can't reveal all of my secrets." I nibble her jawline, then bite her lower lip before licking over it and sinking into her, kissing her deeply and glorying in the groan that comes from deep in her chest.

When her fingers dive into my hair, I pull away.

"Brooks."

"Hold. The. Headboard." I bite her chin. "I won't tell you again."

"I want to touch you."

Smiling softly, I nibble her thumb and then her wrist before placing her hand above her head, around the wrung once more.

"You'll touch me. I promise. For right now, I want to explore my wife's stellar body, and I want you to keep your hands up there."

"Bossy," she whispers, but her eyes are full of humor as I go back to kissing her deeply, my hands taking a tour of her perfect-as-fuck curves. She squirms when my fingers drift up the inside of her thigh, making me grin.

"I fucking love how responsive you are when I touch you. I'll bet you're already wet for me, aren't you?" I nibble my way down her breastbone to her belly button and draw a circle around it with my tongue before nudging my shoulders between her legs and spreading her open. "Just what I thought. Your pretty pussy has soaked these panties."

"Not a surprise," she murmurs. "Can I touch you now?"

"Not yet."

Her skin is warm and fucking irresistible, and I press wet kisses over her inner thigh, then up to her core, and grin when she gasps.

"What made you this wet, baby? Was it the thought of your husband fucking you hard and fast?"

She whimpers and bites her lower lip. "It's the way you touch me. Look at me. Hell, all you have to do is breathe in my vicinity and I'm a faucet."

I huff out a breath against her pussy, and she moans.

"You like that."

"You know I like it."

Out of the corner of my eye, I see her hand leave the headboard.

"Juliet." My hard voice has her gripping it once more, obviously frustrated.

"It's *my* wedding night too, you know."

With a chuckle, I pull the crotch of her panties to the side, tugging them tight over her clit, making her gasp.

"Oh, I know it is. *Wife.*"

Fuck, this woman is my wife.

I lower my face and lap at her, from her entrance to her clit, and her back bows beautifully off the bed, pushing her tits into the air, those nipples begging for my fingers. She cries out when I pinch one hard and then move to the next.

"You're going to come on my face, make a mess out of me, and *then* you can touch me." My finger slides through her soaked lips, then pushes inside her, making her groan. "So tight. Fuck, you're perfect."

"Brooks," she moans, shifting her hips. "*Please.*"

I'm so fucking hard that I'm humping the bed. Christ, I had her several times this morning, and I'm already starved for her. All I wanted all damn day was to whisk her away somewhere so I could pound into her, reminding her that she's *mine.* But there was no time to sneak away. Our family and friends didn't want to let us out of their sight.

Another finger joins the first, and I move the lace aside so I can wrap my lips around her hard bundle of nerves, making her cry out. God, she tastes like pure fucking sin, and she sounds even better, with all of those soft little whimpers coming out of her lips.

"Yes! Holy shit, that's so good. Just like that."

Her voice is so rough, so full of lust and need, it only fuels my own. I'm finger fucking the hell out of her, rubbing against her G-spot and making her legs shake next to my ears.

It's the most beautiful thing I've ever seen.

"Come on my face, Wildfire." I suck hard, and she cries out as the climax moves through her. Her back bows again, her feet dig into my back, and I lap up every delicious fucking drop. "That's my girl. That's my good fucking girl."

She's mewling, moaning as she comes down from the climax, and when I move over her, caging her between my elbows, she finally lets go of the rungs above her head and wraps them around my back and down to my ass, pulling me against her. My cock is nestled against her slit, sliding back and forth lazily, as if it's *not* pounding and raging, wanting to fuck her into oblivion.

"So fucking wet," I growl against her mouth. "And all mine."

"All yours," she agrees, tipping her hips up in invitation. "*Please.*"

"Please what?"

"I need you inside me."

With my mouth covering hers, I pull my hips back, then push inside her perfect pussy. I go slow, so damn slow that we just hold each other's gaze, soaking the other in.

And when I bottom out, she clenches around me, making me growl against her lips.

"I love you," I whisper, then pull out until the tip is still inside, and slam back in, making us both moan. The pace is punishing now, no more holding back. I have to fuck her, claim her, ruin her for anyone else.

Because there will never *be* anyone else.

"Mine," I growl again and grip her chin in my hand, holding her gaze as my hips thrust hard and fast.

"God, yes. So damn good," she says. "*Fuck.*"

"Now you need to come on my cock, Wildfire." I bite that lower lip. "Fucking strangle me, baby."

I don't have to tell her twice because she's *right there.* Her jaw drops, and her whole body clenches as her pussy grips onto me so tight, it makes my eyes cross.

"Goddamn, you're perfect."

I couldn't hold back if I tried. I come violently, splashing inside her until we're both a panting, sweaty, blissed-out mess.

Still inside her, I roll us to our sides so I'm not crushing her.

"Are you okay?" I murmur, brushing her soft hair off her cheek.

"Pretty sure no one's ever been better than I am right now." She cups my face and leans forward to lightly kiss my lips.

We lie like this for a long time, quietly talking. Hands exploring. Until we fall into a deep sleep.

"Brooks."

I shift in the bed, tugging her closer to me. "Go to sleep."

"I need you to wake up."

"No. Sleep."

She chuckles and kisses my chest, but doesn't nuzzle in to go back to sleep. "We have to go back to the other house."

I crack an eye open. The sun is still down, and some of the candles' batteries have died.

But my woman is in my arms, so everything is perfect.

"I'm happy here," I tell her.

"I need to use the bathroom," she whispers. "And I think I heard something scamper above us in the attic."

"It's not a ghost."

She snorts. "I think it's a squirrel or something."

"It'll go to sleep if we do."

"*Get up.*"

I sigh deeply and drag my hand down my face. "Fine."

"Come on. If we hurry, we don't even have to get dressed. We can just scurry over there, and no one will see us."

I lift an eyebrow and pull her to me. "No. No one sees you naked but me. Ever."

"Well, then, come on."

I drag on my slacks—no underwear—and she just loops the sheet from the bed around her like a toga, and we leave the bedroom, headed for the front door. I hear the noise above us, too. It's probably squirrels or maybe a raccoon.

I won't suggest bats. No need to scare her.

A few seconds later, we make it inside the other house, and Jules makes a beeline for the bathroom.

I open the fridge for a bottle of water and grin when

I see that someone dropped off some food for us. It was probably my mom.

When I get back to the bedroom, Jules is already in bed. Dressed in one of my T-shirts, she's waiting for me to join her.

"Come snuggle." She holds her hand out for mine, and I get naked once more, then climb between the sheets and scoop her to me. "That's better."

"I have to go back to work later today," I whisper against her hair as my lips drift back and forth.

"I know. I should, too."

"Maybe in a couple of months, we can carve out some time for a honeymoon. Where do you want to go?"

She pulls back just a bit to look up at me. I'll never get over how her blue eyes shine in the moonlight.

"Frankly, I'd love to take some time off together and stay *here*. Work on the house, spend time at the river, and have all the sex in the universe."

"That's a whole lot of sex."

"You're up for the challenge."

I smirk and nudge her nose with mine. "You bet your ass I am. We can always take a trip later, if you want."

"Where would you like to go?" she asks. Her fingertip drifts over my jawline, and it makes me a little drunk. "If you could go anywhere?"

"I'd love to take you somewhere tropical. Snorkel, swim, hike, and play. Not have to worry about the weather."

"I changed my mind. Let's do that."

With a chuckle, I pull her in for a deep kiss. "We'll make it happen, baby. Now, get some sleep."

"Okay." She yawns and curls up around me, as if we've been doing this all of our lives. As if the past fifteen years never happened, and she's been here the whole time. And for the first time in all of those years, I don't have a pit in my stomach. I feel complete, like my missing piece is finally here.

Because she is.

And it's the best feeling ever.

Chapter Twenty-One

JULIET

"The thing is, he has an incredible dick." Tandy's voice carries loudly in the restaurant today because it's still empty. I have my crew here helping me get ready for our reopening in just two days. Tandy's across the dining room, mopping the brand-new floor in the corner so we can bring new tables and chairs in here first thing tomorrow. "Like, we're talking a huge, make tears roll down my face, cry for my mother cock that I can't seem to give up."

Is it TMI? For sure. But poor Tandy has been in an on-again, off-again relationship with some guy named Matt for a couple of months now, and it seems right now is an off season.

She's definitely feeling some kind of way about it.

"Should she be talking to a therapist about this?" Christy asks in a low voice, making me snort. She's emptying the dishwasher in the next room, but she can hear Tandy, loud and clear.

"I get it," Erica joins in as she scrubs out the cooler that will hold the grab-and-go meals. "Anthony was *packing*. But despite his impressive dick, he *was* a dick. And sometimes it's not worth trying to mend a relationship with someone who isn't nice to you, Tandy. I've been telling you this for *weeks*."

I kind of love that my staff are friends outside of work. They have a fun camaraderie that always makes me smile.

I had the rest of the staff here earlier, the newer hires, and they helped with a ton of stuff, but now it's just the four of us, making sure everything is sterilized and ready for the food that'll be delivered tomorrow, and then I can roll up my sleeves and get back to work baking and cooking.

I'm so freaking excited.

"I get it," Tandy says with a sigh, her shoulders dropping. "I just wish I could keep the bottom half of him and send his attitude packing."

"Someone else with a talented dick will come along who isn't a class A jerk," Christy calls out. "You're too good to settle, Tan. No way."

"I hope you're right," Tandy says as she mops in our direction. "This floor is so pretty, Jules. I love the pattern of it."

I grin as I gaze out at the room. It's a white oak in a herringbone pattern that really is stunning. The tables and chairs will be black, and I'll change the linens out with the seasons. Since it's fall, I'll cover the tables in cream cloths with orange and yellow napkins.

"I have your T-shirts," I inform the girls. "Five each,

and they're *so* pretty. I got new aprons with the logo, too."

"Everything is gorgeous, Jules," Christy gushes. "I love the new signage out front, too. You really went all out and took this place from amazing to unbelievable."

"The vibe is the same, but I wanted to brighten it up, since I was starting from scratch and could change everything. The new logo is fun, and I think it looks great on the new shirts and aprons. They're green, by the way."

"Like lime green or Christmas green?" Erica asks.

"Sage green," I reply with a chuckle. "I'll grab them for you before you go."

"Okay, I'm going to address the giant elephant in the room that no one else is brave enough to talk about," Tandy says as she sets the mop in the bucket and then comes to stand at the counter. "Tell us about Brooks. You told us that you got married, but we need some details because just before the flood, you two were *not* in a let's-get-hitched kind of place, my friend."

"I know." I sigh and drop my used rag with the others in a trash bag. "I admit, once we decided, it happened fast."

I tell them about the house, and how Brooks and I were together many years ago.

"So you rekindled the feelings that were simmering from years ago," Erica says with a sigh, clearly finding the whole situation romantic.

"I mean, Brooks is hot," Tandy adds. "And I'm sure the man has talents that none of us will ever discover now."

"You definitely will *not* discover my man's talents," I

agree with a snort. "He's ... *everything.* It's honestly as simple as that. And now, he's mine."

"See, *that's* the goal," Tandy says, pointing at me. "That look that you have on your face right now, the one that says that you can't live without him."

"Oh, I *can* live without him," I reply. "I did for a long-ass time. But it's a miserable existence, and I don't ever want to do it again."

"Okay, that's the most beautiful thing I've ever heard." Christy wipes a tear from the corner of her eye. "And I'm so damn happy for you. You deserve every minute of happiness. You just look like a weight has been lifted off your shoulders. This whole mess here at the restaurant was a *lot*, and you're so calm and serene."

"Love does that." Erica nods. "Makes all the bad stuff seem less ... *bad.*"

She's exactly right.

When this started, it felt catastrophic. I didn't think I'd get through it in one piece. And here we are, just a few weeks later, and everything is so much better than I ever dared even hope for.

"Hey, guys," Ava says with a wave as she comes charging through the door. "Holy shit, it's *gorgeous* in here."

Harper is right behind her, and then to my utter surprise, all the other girls file in, too. Billie, Skyla, and Dani, along with Dani's sisters.

It's a whole girl gang.

My girl gang.

"Tell me I can get my salad soon," Harper says, looking desperate. "Come on, you're about to be my sister-in-law. Hell, you *are*, since Blake already put a ring on my finger. Help a sister out."

Sisters.

I don't just have friends.

I have sisters.

Holy shit.

"I reopen the day after tomorrow, and I'll have your salad. But I could probably make one for you tomorrow night. All of the food is being delivered in the morning."

"I can wait for opening day." Harper grins. "I'm so excited for you, friend."

"We all are," Dani adds. "And since you and Brooks got married so fast and we didn't have time to have a party, we're having one now. Tonight."

"That's our cue to head out." Christy winks. "Come on, ladies. Let's get out of the way so the boss lady can party."

"Have fun," Tandy says with a wave, and when they're gone, I turn back to my gang.

"I'm not exactly dressed for a party."

"It's super casual," Darby replies. "We're all going to Billie's mansion, so we can drool over her library, eat all of the amazing food that Cassie's made for us, and those of us *not* knocked up can drink a bunch of liquor."

"I'm *so* down for that. Let me just text Brooks so he knows not to expect me."

I pull my phone out of my back pocket and shoot my man a message.

> Me: Hey, babe! I'm headed to Billie's with the girls for a post-wedding girls' night. Won't be home until later.

"I wish I had some goodies to bring with me," I tell the girls while the three little dots hop on the screen, signaling that Brooks is replying. "But there isn't a morsel of food in this place."

"Trust me." Billie shakes her head. "Cassie has been cooking up a storm at the house. I told her we wanted snack foods. Appetizers. Desserts. And everything is safe for you, I promise. She sanitized the whole kitchen before she started and is using new tools."

I blink at my gorgeous sister-in-law. Billie's in Dior today, because of course she is. But it's casual Dior.

If there is such a thing.

"You didn't have to do that. It's expensive."

"Hi, she married a billionaire," Alex says helpfully. "That's just a normal Friday afternoon for them."

I snort and check my phone.

> Husband: I heard, and I'm glad. Billie planned a bunch of stuff. Have fun. Call when you're ready to come home, and I'll come get you.

> Me: Okay, sounds good. Love you!

"Let's go party, girls."

"I haven't read this one," Alex says, plucking a paperback off one of Billie's shelves. This is my first time here, and now I understand what Brooks meant when he said that my library won't be as fancy as this.

No one's library is as fancy as this.

Unless you're Belle, and your boyfriend is a beast.

Because *holy shit*, this is something to behold.

It's a two-story library with floor-to-ceiling shelves and the amazing rolling ladder that every girl dreams of. The whole room is painted in robin's egg blue, with a wallpapered ceiling in all different colors.

"This is dreamy," I announce as I stand in the middle of the room, just looking around. I notice that some of the shelves are still bare. "You have room to grow with new books."

"I know, I love that," Billie says with a grin. "I spend a lot of time in here."

"I would, too," Darby agrees.

Have I mentioned that I love that Darby's home?

"I thought you had to go back to Colorado," I say to my friend, but she grins.

"I delayed by a couple of days. I had the extra time, so I stayed. I leave the day after your opening, so I can stop in and try all of the amazing food I've been hearing about."

"Oh, that makes me happy. I'm going to pretend that you're staying just for me."

"Who's read *Sinful King* by Natalie Kane?" Skyla asks, waving the book in the air. "Because this sounds good. A Mafia romance set in Vegas where the mmc owns a sex club and the heroine is plus-sized? Hell yes."

"Oh, it's *so good*," Billie says. "I read it. They play with Shabari ropes. You need it in your life."

"Do you have it in the store?" I ask her.

"Sure do." Billie grins, and the next thing I know, she's hugging me close and sniffling in my ear. "Is it real? Are you seriously my sister now? It's not a dream, right?"

"Aw, bug." I drag my hand over her hair and kiss her cheek. "It's not a dream at all. But do you know what *does* feel surreal? This library."

"I know." She sniffs again but doesn't let go. "It's so fancy. And you can come over and we can hang out in here and read and talk and have wine after the baby comes."

"I'd love to do all of that."

"I want in on that action." Dani raises her hand.

"You need more chairs in here," Harper adds. "Oh! And maybe some little bassinets for us to put the babies while we read."

"No way, the men can keep the babies." Skyla shakes her head. "Library time is for peace and quiet."

I chuckle as we leave the gorgeous library and head back out to the kitchen, where Cassie, who happens to not only be Billie and Connor's personal chef but also works for Alex and her guys, is just setting up what looks like an amazing spread of food.

"You're just in time," Cassie says with a wide smile. "This end of the island is charcuterie. Cheeses, meats, nuts, and fruit. There are some delicious local jams that I found that pair well with the cheese and these amazing gluten-free crackers that I made."

"Wait." I hold up a hand. "*You made them?*"

"Yep." She nods.

"Would you want to make them for my restaurant? Or share the recipe?"

Cassie grins. "Oh girl, we will talk. Over here, we have nachos, cheeseburger rolls, and veggies accompanied by a variety of different dips. And finally, on this end, I have a couple of different green salads with both oil-based and creamy dressings to choose from."

"Holy shit, this is a *lot* of food," Charlie says as she walks in the room, the last to arrive. "And I am *here for it.*"

"Save room for dessert," Cassie says with a wink. "I have ice cream sundaes on tap, and since we're celebrating, the calories don't count."

"I want to marry Cassie," Charlie announces, making us all laugh.

With heaping plates and refilled drinks, we make our way into a grand living room that features floor-to-ceiling windows, showcasing a stunning view of the sun setting behind the mountains.

"Holy shit, it's pretty here," I say as I take a seat and dig into my cheese and huckleberry-jalapeño jam, which is now my favorite thing in the universe.

Right behind sex with Brooks.

"My billionaire chose well when he found this

house," Billie agrees. "Okay, so now that you know that Brooks bought that big house, talk to me."

"What big house?" Skyla asks. "You have to recap for those of us who didn't grow up here and are new to this whole situation."

"Are Brooks and I the *situation*?" I ask the room, and everyone nods in confirmation, making me snort. "Good to know."

"We know that you dated and then you ... *didn't*." Dani winces at that. "But I didn't know the house story."

"What's the damn house story?" Darby demands.

"Okay, so there's this house in town," I begin. "It sits on a corner lot. It's pretty big, with a red roof and black shutters."

"Yep, I know that place," Charlie says, and the others murmur agreement.

"Well, when we were kids, Brooks and I used to daydream about owning it and having a family there. We made a lot of plans back then, to be honest." I shrug and pop a grape into my mouth. "Anyway, Brooks told me that it came up for sale a few years ago, and he bought it because he couldn't stand the thought of someone else buying our dream house."

"Damn, the grumpy mechanic is a big ole softie," Harper says, and Ava steals a cracker off her plate. "There's an entire kitchen full of food, you know."

"Don't be stingy," Ava says, crunching on the cracker, and then turns to me. "Are you guys going to move in there?"

"Well, it's empty right now because it needs to be gutted and pretty much completely redone," I reply. "So we're going to do that together. Make it exactly what we want in our forever home. He even has plans for my own little library in there."

"Everyone has a library but me," Charlie says with a pout. "That's so dumb."

"Not *everyone*," Dani reminds her. "I don't. There's no room in our house, with all the kids' stuff everywhere."

"We'll help with the house," Ava says with a shrug, as if it's no big deal at all. But it's a huge deal to me. "My brothers and I can come help tear stuff out, and they're handy with construction stuff. Comes from being raised on a ranch."

"I'm sure you won't have any trouble getting lots of extra hands," Harper adds. "I, however, will not be helping unless you want it to fall apart."

I smirk and take a drink of my margarita.

Damn good.

"I don't think we'll turn down any help. Thank you."

"All of the Blackwells are now happily spoken for," Darby says, tilting her head to the side, looking at all of us. "It's so crazy. I grew up with all of them, and now they're all married and having kids."

"We're old. *This* is what we're talking about?" Charlie wrinkles her nose. "We should be talking about sex and ... stuff."

"I'm seeing a new guy," Ava announces. "So far, the sex isn't bad. I'd like him to maybe pull my hair a little more than he does, but I think he's trainable."

"Who is this guy, and why haven't you told me about him?" Harper demands.

"We've all been a little busy," Ava replies. "And it's only been a few dates."

"And sex," I add.

"I mean, yeah. The sex, too. His name is Chad Kincaid."

"He's an attorney in Silver Springs," I say, surprising everyone.

"How do you know him?" Ava asks.

"I hired him to help me with some stuff regarding my late husband. He's handsome. Seems nice. Very professional."

"You can say it," Ava says. "He's stuffy."

I laugh. "Maybe a little, but you could do so much worse."

"We'll see. Now, let's talk about all your sex lives."

"My husband would *not* be okay with me discussing that," Skyla replies with a giggle. "Although I might enjoy the punishment for it."

"*Now* we're talking," Alex says, shimmying her shoulders. "What kind of punishment? Spanking? Edging? A little light knife play?"

"WHAT?" we all exclaim, making Alex double over in laughter.

"Come on, we all read the books."

"If you tell me that you let those two men *cut you*," Darby says, her voice tight and with no humor *at all*, and Alex swallows hard.

"No, sissy. It was just a joke. I swear, they'd never do that."

Darby takes a deep, shaky breath. "If anyone ever cuts any of you, I'll kill them myself."

She downs the rest of her drink, then walks into the kitchen for a refill.

That's definitely a hot button for my friend.

"Beckett enjoys some edging for sure." Skyla changes the subject.

"Is that a Blackwell trait?" I ask, tilting my head to the side.

"You all *do* realize that you're talking about my brothers." Billie wrinkles her nose. "Right? My *brothers.*"

"Does Connor edge you?" I ask, and this time, Skyla shifts in her chair.

"Oh, *all the time.*"

"Obviously not often enough."

We all whip our heads over to where Connor's leaning on the wall, his arms folded, listening unabashedly with a sexy-as-hell smirk on his face.

He looks like he should be on the cover of GQ.

Wait. I think he *has been* on the cover of *GQ.*

"This is a girls' party," Billie reminds her husband, who just pushes his glasses up his nose, then crosses over to her.

"I'm checking to see if you needed anything, Bumble."

"So freaking sweet," Dani whispers to me, and I nod in agreement.

"No, we're all happily fed, thank you very much."

He frames her face in his hands and leans in to kiss her. "More than all the stars in the sky."

Billie's face softens into goo, and it's the most adorable thing ever.

"*Why* is there a man in this room right now?" Harper demands, glaring at Connor.

"It's *my* house, you know."

"Not tonight, it isn't," Skyla says with a laugh. "Go on now. We're discussing things that you don't need to be privy to."

"I'll be edging you later tonight, Angel," he says to Billie, before his hands dive into the pockets of his slacks and he walks away.

"Damn," Ava whispers, fanning her face with her hand. "Where can I get one of those? Is there a store, or a website or something?"

"I'm afraid he's one of a kind," Billie says with a sweet smile. "Now, let's go find that ice cream."

The phone rings in my ear as I wait for Brooks to pick up on the other end of the line, and I hiccup.

I might have had one too many margaritas.

No regrets.

"Hey, Wildfire. Are you ready to come home?"

"Yeah. I need a ride. It's really far to town, and I can't even walk down the driveway."

He chuckles, and I can hear him walking. "I'll be there in fifteen minutes. Did you have fun?"

"So much fun. Holy shit, babe, you weren't kidding about Billie's library. It's something out of a Disney movie."

"I know. Sorry, wife, I'm not a billionaire."

I snort and shake my head even though he can't see me. "Well, you'd better start fixing more cars. Just kidding. I already have ideas for my own library in our house. It's going to be *adorble.*"

"You mean adorable."

"That's what I said. Are you on your way yet? I need orgasms. We've been talking about sex for a while, and I'm gonna need some. Okay?"

"Christ, I'm getting in the truck now, and I'll be there in twelve minutes."

"Make it ten."

Chapter Twenty-Two

BROOKS

"I'll be in later to help," I inform my wife. We're both leaving the house for the day. Her restaurant reopens tomorrow, and she's buried with work today. I want to help, to do the heavy lifting. I know a crew will be there all day with her, but that's not good enough.

Okay, fine. I just want to be with her.

"If you can't get away, it's fine," she reminds me, and waits for me to lock the door before walking with me to the truck. I'll drop her off on my way to the garage. "I have a ton of help."

"And you'll have me. How are you feeling this morning, Wildfire?"

I glance over as I turn the corner and see her wince. She was adorably hammered when I picked her up last night, and the sex was fucking *fun*. By the time we lay down to go to sleep, she was mostly sober, exhausted, and it was well past midnight.

"A little hung over, but I've had worse. Wait, no, I haven't."

I snort at that, and she smiles.

"I took something, and I'll hydrate all day. It's fine."

Bringing her hand up to my lips, I press kisses over her knuckles. "I'm just glad you had fun."

"I did." She's looking at her phone, and her hand tenses in mine. "Well, fuck."

"What's wrong?"

"*She* emailed me. Again. This is the sixth time this week."

"We have an appointment with Chad next week," I remind her, and she nods, nibbling her lower lip. "Ignore her, and we'll figure it out."

"She's going crazy because I changed my number," she murmurs as she closes out of the email. "And frankly, I don't care."

"Good girl." I pull up to her restaurant, and before she can climb out of the truck, I lean over, cup her chin, and brush my lips over hers. "Drink lots of water."

"Yes, sir."

My cock fucking twitches.

"I love your smart mouth." I bite that lower lip, making her grin, and then she's off. She waves at me before unlocking her front door, and once I see that she's safely inside, turning on lights, I pull away and drive down to the garage.

Gabe's already here, which isn't unusual. He prefers to work earlier in the day so he can get home earlier with his family. These hours work for me, too. I don't care if he comes here in the middle of the night, as long as the work gets done.

Mitch pulls in just as I do and looks like his grumpy-ass self.

"My wife isn't feeling well today." He shakes his head. "So if she calls and needs me—"

"You'll go home to her." I clap him on the shoulder. "It's no problem, Mitch."

"I'm sick of her being sick." He sighs. "For *her* sake. It's horrible watching her ... well, it's horrible. I'd gladly switch places with her."

I can't even imagine. Mitch's wife was diagnosed about six months ago with breast cancer and has been fighting her way through treatment. The prognosis is good, but getting well is a battle that I don't wish on anyone.

"If she needs you, just go home, buddy. Gabe and I can handle this."

"What am I, chopped liver?"

I glance over in surprise as Jake Wild saunters in, wearing jeans and a T-shirt, a smug smirk on his face.

"I'm here for a few days, thought I'd come in and log some hours, if you need the help."

"I think we *always* need the help," Gabe calls out from under the hood of a Chevy.

"You're not between semesters, are you?" Jake goes to college in Bozeman.

"I wish. No, just didn't have classes for a few days this week, thought I'd come home. Get some decent food, see the horses, tinker in an engine."

"Tinker away, kid." I laugh and nudge his shoulder with mine. Jake's a tall guy. "How's the girlfriend?"

"Fucking gorgeous, man." He wiggles his eyebrows. "Now, what do you need me to do?"

The morning moves fairly smoothly. Not many interruptions, the music's playing, the guys and I are quiet, doing our own thing.

The perfect morning at the shop.

Then just before lunch, Mitch's phone rings, and when I glance over, his eyes meet mine, and I know.

He needs to go.

I can't hear what he's saying into the phone, but he hangs his head and rubs his hand over the back of his neck.

When he hangs up, he crosses over to me.

"Go," I tell him before he can say anything.

"I'm in the middle of this oil change, and then I have—"

"I know what you have." I signal for Jake to join us. "Show Jake the oil change, and he'll finish it up, and then we'll figure out the rest."

"I'm sorry, Brooks—"

"She's your *wife*," I remind him, and he swallows hard. "Go take care of her."

"I've got this," Jake says, his usual playful smirk long gone. "No problem, man. Glad to help."

Mitch nods, then gestures for Jake to follow him so he can get the kid—who isn't so much a kid anymore—caught up on what he's doing.

And that's just the start of the shit show that today ends up being.

The motor failed in my air compressor, and I have to wait a day for the repairman to come take care of it.

It took me *three times* longer than it should have to access a goddamn fuel filter in a Suburban and ate up more than two hours of my time.

I had three *emergencies* brought in, and by emergencies, I mean the owner practically begged me to get their job done next, no matter the cost.

Yeah, that's not going to happen.

It's just a colossal dumpster fire of a day, and when I have two minutes to check the time, my frustration level is at a ten when I see that it's well past six in the evening. Gabe and Jake are long gone for the day, and I'm here alone.

I was never able to get away and help my wife with her restaurant. I still have several hours of work to do here tonight.

Picking up my phone, I notice that I missed a few texts from her.

> Wildfire: I hope you're having a good day! All is well over here, just miss you.

Fuck, she's sweet.

> Wildfire: Things are going faster than I expected. Should be done by around six. Want me to bring you dinner?

Shit, that was an hour ago. I wash my hands and am about to start typing a response when the door opens, and my girl walks in, holding a bag of food, very much like that night a few weeks ago.

Fuck, I want her.

Her eyes scan the garage, and then she smiles when she sees me.

"You've always loved John Mellencamp," she says, pointing up, as if the speaker is just above her head. "I brought you dinner. I made some—"

"Put the bag down, Juliet."

Her blue eyes widen, and she licks her lower lip as she walks to the counter and sets the bag of food—that smells fucking *incredible*—aside.

"Take your clothes off."

Her eyebrows climb in surprise.

"You want me to—"

"I won't tell you twice."

I'm wound the fuck up. Seeing her here, with all of those blond curls gathered in a bun on her head, in little denim shorts and a blue T-shirt that matches her eyes, has my blood simmering. She's *so fucking beautiful,* and she's all fucking mine.

Jules tilts her head to the side as I finish drying my hands, and she reaches for the hem of her shirt, tugs it over her head, and tosses it onto the clean counter.

I lean back on the car I've been working on, cross my arms over my chest, and watch.

She starts to walk toward me, but I shake my head, and she stops.

"I didn't say you could do that."

Her pupils blow wide. Juliet *loves* it when I dominate her. When I'm in control. She responds to me so beautifully, so fucking *perfectly*, it's all I can do to stand here and not lift her against the wall and pound into her until neither of us knows our own name.

"You're—"

"Take off your fucking clothes, wife."

She fights the smile that wants to spread over her pillowy lips, unfastens her shorts, and lets them fall, stepping out of them and setting them with her shirt.

When her hands fall to her sides, I brush my finger over my lower lip and wait.

"Do you need me to finish the job for you, Wildfire?"

She swallows thickly, so fucking turned on her panties have to be soaked for me. Reaching behind her back, she unfastens her bra, and when she's left in her pretty pink panties, I push off the vehicle and slowly walk to her, like I'm an animal stalking its prey.

"Brooks." It's a whisper and makes my already hard-as-fuck cock ache.

"Yes?"

"Are you okay?"

Taking her face in my hands, I lean down to brush my lips over hers and breathe her in.

"I am now. I'm going to fuck you, right here, just like last time." Her little gasp and the way her nipples are rock hard tell me that she doesn't hate that idea. "I'm going to feast on this pretty pussy."

My hand glides down her stomach, under her panties, and when I cup her and feel how sopping wet she is for me, I groan.

"Fuck, Wildfire."

"You're the sexiest man," she says with a sigh, her

hands diving into my hair as I slide a finger inside her. "You can do whatever you want to me. I'm yours."

"Fuck yes, you are."

I turn her away from me.

"Hands on the counter."

She follows directions so damn well, and pushes her ass out, inviting everything that I'm about to give her.

Hooking my fingers under the elastic at her hips, I lower the pink panties, help her step out of them, and then stuff them in my pocket.

"These are mine now."

"Stop stealing—"

I smack her perfect peach of an ass, making her gasp as I squat behind her. Her pussy is fucking dripping, her juices running down her inner thighs, and I lick her soft skin.

"Fucking delicious. Widen your legs."

She follows the order, and I spread her open with my thumbs.

"Goddamn, this pussy is perfect." I lick her, from clit to ass to clit, and her head falls forward as she moans, pushing back against my face, and I fucking *love it*. I press my thumb against her clit and my tongue inside her, and she starts to shake, her thighs quivering, making my blood run even hotter.

"Oh God," she moans. "Brooks, I'm gonna come. Oh, fucking hell."

My thumb makes a little circle over her hard nub, and her walls tighten as I fuck her with my tongue, and when she comes, I lap those juices up, feasting on what's mine.

"Good girl." I bite her ass and then smooth it over with a kiss as I stand behind her, unfastening my belt and then my jeans, and unleash my cock. "It was a shit day until you walked in here, looking like sex on a goddamn stick."

"I look awful." I slap my cock on her ass, and she whimpers.

"You're so fucking beautiful." With my hand fisted around the base, I rub the crown through her sopping-wet slit. "So fucking *everything*. You make everything better."

"Please." She pushes back against me. "Please, baby."

"What do you need? Use your words."

"You. Inside me. Ple—*fuck*."

I push all the way in, my hips hitting her ass, and I pause here, reveling in how perfectly she fits me. I lean over, press my forehead against her shoulder, then bite her there.

"God, yes," she whispers. "I'm bringing dinner every day."

I grin against her shoulder blade, and then I can't hold back anymore. Gripping her hips, I start to pound in and out of her. I'm not gentle. I'm not tender.

I'm fucking *feral*.

She reaches back for me, and I spank her ass, making it pink.

"I didn't say you could touch me."

"*Brooks*."

"Grab the fucking counter, or you don't get to come again."

She sighs, my sassy little wildfire, but does as she's told, and I reward her with my thumb over her asshole.

"*Fuuuuck*," she moans.

"I haven't taken you here yet," I murmur as I watch that little hole pucker under my thumb. "But I will."

She tightens around me, making me almost lose control.

"Oh, you like that, you greedy girl." I smack her other ass cheek, and she looks over her shoulder at me. Her eyes are wide and glassy with lust and need. Her lower lip is swollen from biting it. "You're the most beautiful woman I've ever seen."

Her eyes soften, and her pussy squeezes around me, and then her jaw drops. I can see it written all over her gorgeous face.

"Come for me, baby. Make a fucking mess out of my cock. God, you were made for me—"

She cries out, her body convulsing as she succumbs to the climax, and fuck if she doesn't milk my own out of me.

I come inside her, and then pull out, fist my cock, and come on her back.

Marking her.

Fucking mine.

We're panting, sweaty, and my girl is a complete, glorious mess.

I fucking love it.

"Stay." I kiss her shoulder, then cross to the bathroom to wet a towel. I wipe myself off, tuck myself away, and then, with a fresh towel, I cross back to her and get to work cleaning up my mess. When I've finished, I help her back into her clothes, sans panties, then tug her to me, tuck her under my chin, and hold her tight. "*This* is how it was supposed to go before. No running away from me. No being angry."

"We've come a long way." She presses her sweet lips to my chest and tips her chin up to smile at me. "Better?"

"I'm fine, baby."

"What's wrong? You're on edge. Did something happen?"

Yeah, my girl knows me.

"It was just a shitty day. One thing after another. And I couldn't get away to come over and help you get ready for tomorrow."

"I'm fine." She rubs a circle over my heart. "We got everything finished and ready to go. I even managed to prep a bunch of stuff, and I'm ready to bake at five in the morning."

"Fuck, that's early."

She smiles and nuzzles into me again. "Sometimes if I'm not able to prep the dough the day before, I have to go in at three."

"You won't go in alone at that time of the night."

She frowns up at me. "It's perfectly safe."

"I said what I said."

"You're bossy."

"You knew that when you married me." I kiss her forehead and then her nose. "Did you bring enough food for two?"

"Yeah, I thought I'd eat with you. Do you still have a lot of work to do?"

I sigh and reach for the bag, pull out two to-go containers, and take a deep breath.

"Yeah, I have to stay for a while yet. Is this pasta?"

"Yes, but it's better when it's warm."

I laugh and open one, put a fork in it, and pass it to my girl before grabbing my own.

"I'll eat cold pasta any time if it means I get to fuck you into oblivion first."

Her cheeks heat at that.

"You're fucking adorable, Jules. You know that, right?"

"I'm *not* adorable. I'm a mess. I can't believe you—"

She shakes her head, and I narrow my eyes at her.

"Finish that thought."

"No."

With raised eyebrows, I set my food aside, take her chin in my fingers, and make her look at me.

"*Yes.*"

She sighs. "I can't believe you went down on me. I worked all day. I haven't had a shower, Brooks."

Leaning in, I brush my lips over hers, then along her jaw and to her ear. "I don't care, Juliet. You could run a marathon and roll in mud, and I'd still eat you like a man starving for his next meal."

"That's ... *gross.*"

"Never." I nip her earlobe. "Now, eat."

Chapter Twenty-Three

JULIET

S o here's the thing that no one tells you when all your dreams come true: *It's fucking scary as shit.*

Sure, I was a nervous wreck the first day that I opened this restaurant, not quite a year ago. I had high hopes, but no real expectations because I only had myself to disappoint. No family. No friends. Even the one employee I'd managed to snatch up—Christy—was a stranger to me, and if I failed, it wasn't a big deal.

But everything is so different now.

So different.

In every single way.

I have a lot of damn expectations now because I know what I can do. I've already made this place something that my customers love and come back to. I've made it a safe place for people like me with food sensitivities. But bigger than that—*scarier than that*—is that I have a whole tribe that I'm terrified to disappoint. My girl gang. My new besties.

My husband.

I have a husband, the one man I've loved for so long. I don't remember what it felt like to *not* love him, even when I was married to someone else and tried so hard to pretend that I'd moved on. It's always been Brooks. And I absolutely do *not* want to disappoint him.

I just pulled the last of the daily fresh bread out of the oven to cool. I have morning pastries and breakfast sandwiches ready to go in the display cases, and once my girls get here, they'll start prepping for lunch and dinner.

Christy is the first one to walk through the door with a spring in her step, wearing her new Sage & Citrus shirt and a pair of black shorts. Even though it's fall, we get warm in here, with the ovens and cooktop.

"Hey, pretty boss lady," she says with a grin. "Happy first official day back."

"You didn't have to come in for another thirty minutes."

"I know." She shrugs a shoulder and steps back into the office to stow her handbag away before joining me again, tying a new black apron around her waist. "But I knew you'd be here, probably nervous as hell, and I wanted to come in and mellow you out."

I let out a deep breath and smile ruefully. "You're right. I'm freaking out."

"Of course, I'm right. I know you, girl. You have *zero* things to worry about," she assures me. "It's gorgeous in here. I loved it before, but you've managed to make it even more incredible. The new menu is going to *slay*. In fact, can I try one of those huckleberry muffins?"

"Help yourself. I made double what I normally do,

with the optimism that I might be extra busy today and sell out."

Christy takes a bite and then leans dramatically on the counter, making me grin.

"Holy fucking shit. *This* is gluten-free?"

"And dairy-free," I confirm with a knowing smile. Those muffins are *the bomb.* "But leave a few for the customers, okay?"

"I make no promises." Her eyes move to the front of the restaurant and widen a little, making me turn to look as well, and *can't believe my eyes.*

"Is that a *line*?" I ask her, staring at the group standing in front of the still locked door, all chatting and laughing, some looking at their phones. "Holy shit, Christy."

"I think that optimism has paid off," Christy says, nudging my shoulder. "Tandy and Hazel will be here in ten minutes. We can handle it until then if you want to go ahead and open."

"Are you sure? Do I have enough food? Why am I suddenly so nervous?"

"We'll sell food until it's gone, and then they'll have to wait for lunch. No need to be nervous. You're badass. Let's do this, Jules."

With a smile on my face to cover the nerves, I walk to the door and unlock it, swing it open, and announce, "Come on in, everyone!"

With my back propping the door open, I greet the twenty or so people as they walk in. When I glance up, I see Brooks waiting in line, and it makes my heart swell so big, I'm surprised my chest can still hold it.

"Well, hey there, handsome." I grin as he cups my face in his big hands and lowers his mouth to mine. "You came."

"Where else would I be, Wildfire? I'm so fucking proud of you." He kisses me deeply before walking into the restaurant.

I'm so fucking proud of you.

God, I don't remember the last time I heard those words from anyone. I didn't know until now how badly I needed them.

I follow him inside, hurrying behind the counter to start filling orders. Tandy and Hazel arrive, and we are off and running.

Brooks orders a breakfast sandwich and a half dozen muffins to take back to the garage to share, and when I pass all the food to him without charging him, he scowls at me like I'm nuts.

"What's wrong?"

"I need to pay for my food, Juliet."

Christy smirks as she whizzes by, filling an order.

"No, babe. You can have the food. You're married to the owner."

"Fuck that. My woman is open for business, and I'm paying for it."

I ring him up, and then my jaw drops when he adds a hundred-dollar tip to his order.

"Brooks—"

"Happy reopening, Wildfire. I'll be back for lunch." With a wink, he steps out of line, and I blink back tears as the next person steps up to place their order.

It's like this all morning—a constant stream of

customers. Some of them are tourists, but the vast majority are friends, people I care about and who care about me, all showing up for me.

I'm proud of myself for keeping my emotions in check. I'm just so *happy*. My cheeks hurt from all the smiles, but I don't mind at all.

"I always love the smell of it in here in the morning." Ava takes a deep breath. "Coffee and sugar with a little bacon. Gotta love it. I'll have all those things, by the way. So proud of you, friend."

"It's been a *very* good morning, and I didn't even do any advertising."

"You don't need to," she says with a wink. "You're a staple in this town. I'll be by later to check on you. Harper's coming after work for her salad. She'll probably take two, knowing her."

"I have plenty for her, no worries there."

When I glance in the case and I see that all the breakfast options are gone, I'm stunned.

"I'm getting all the lunch pastries out since it's almost eleven," Hazel says as she slides a tray into the case. "And do you mind if we call Erica and the others in, too? It feels like an all-hands-on-deck kind of day."

"Erica and James come in at one for the dinner shift, but go ahead and call Laurie in, if she's available."

With a nod, Hazel bustles off. We have a slight lull in the crowd, since we're in that between time, and we all hustle to get lunch ready to go.

Connor strides in, looking every inch the billionaire in his expensive suit, and he smiles as he looks around my space.

"Well done, Juliet."

Holy shit, I won't make it through this day without crying.

"You have every element that goes into a successful restaurant here. It couldn't be better."

"Okay, stop feeding my ego, Mr. Gallagher."

Connor laughs and shakes his head. "That isn't something I do. You've done well. Now, I need lunch for my wife and me. She wanted me to tell you that she'll be in here before the end of the day, but she just got a shipment in and is buried under a pile of Lucy Score books."

I laugh and start ringing him up as he tells me what he wants. But when it's time to show him his total, I zero it out and shake my head when he opens his wallet.

"It's on the house today, Connor."

"Maybe you *do* need a few lessons in making money. Giving away your product for free isn't the way to do that."

I smirk and cross my arms over my chest. "Oh, I know that. And I'll be happy to charge you the next time you come in. But you were a huge help to me, and I'm grateful. So lunch is on me."

He winks at me behind those hot black-rimmed glasses, then moves to stand to the side. "Thank you."

"You're welcome."

Taking a deep breath, I glance over and am pleased to see that the girls have loaded the cold case with lunch pastries and sandwiches. And then my eyebrows climb when I shift my gaze and see my husband walk through the door for the second time today, carrying a bouquet of red and pink roses.

"What are you doing?" I grin and accept the flowers when he offers them to me. They're already in a vase, and they smell like heaven.

"I came to get lunch, but I also wanted to bring you these. Is it sanitary to have them in here?"

He looks so proud of himself, I can't resist leaning over to kiss him.

"I'll set them right here by the cash register." I lean in to smell one of the velvety blooms and then turn back to my man. "What would you like to order?"

He ends up buying four sandwiches for his crew, and all I can do is grin because my man not only supports this career of mine, but he is feeding into it in ways that I never knew I needed.

Brooks is the best thing to ever happen to me.

"Two hours left," Christy whispers in my ear. She looks pretty disheveled compared to how she did this morning, and we both have food all over our aprons and shirts, but we're still moving.

Hazel and Tandy refused to leave when their shifts were over, which was awesome because lunch was busier than breakfast, and we had to prep for dinner. Laurie and James are killing it, running out orders to tables, clearing and wiping them when people leave, and making sure that everything is running smoothly.

This place has never, not even in the very beginning, been this busy.

It's amazing and horrifying, all at once.

I have to order more food first thing in the morning. I won't make it through the week if this continues. And I'll have to hire more staff.

None of these things are bad problems to have.

Just as I plate a slice of lasagna and add a side of steamed broccoli, ready to take it to a table, I hear voices that I recognize.

"I came for my mac and cheese, Jules!"

"I've got this," Tandy says, taking the lasagna order from my hands. "Go see your family."

With a frown, I turn, and then I can't move.

I can't breathe.

Because it's not just sweet Birdie with Dani and Bridger.

It's the *entire* Blackwell family.

Beck and Skyla. Billie, who has tears in her eyes, with Connor. Blake and Harper, and even their parents.

Brooks holds Birdie high in his arms, and he winks at me.

"Surprise," Becca says, holding her arms out to hug me. "We all had to come in for dinner."

"Oh my God, the lasagna smells so good," Bridger says, before he leans in to kiss my cheek. "Way to kick ass, sis-in-law."

I'm passed around. That's the only way to describe it. Handed from one Blackwell brother to the next for hugs and congratulations.

Then the girls close in, and we have a group hug, and if a human heart could heal in the matter of mere moments, that's what just happened to mine.

"So freaking awesome," Harper says before kissing my cheek. "It's *beautiful* in here."

"We're all just so proud of you," Skyla adds.

And then they all get in line to order, talking happily about what they want to eat, but Brooks's dad, Brandon, pulls me to the side and wraps his arm around my shoulders.

"You've done so well here, sweet girl."

I made it all freaking day without giving in to the tears, and now this amazing man is going to make them spill over. I don't have parents here today. My mom's been gone for several years, and Dad chose to leave—permanently—when I was twelve. I like to think that they'd be proud of me today. That my dad would have some words of wisdom and a supportive hug.

I haven't had a father in my life in a *really* long time.

And now I have Brandon.

"I know it wasn't easy," he continues and hugs me into his side, both of us watching this family as they joke and laugh together. Brooks glances our way, checking on me, but doesn't walk over to us. He helps Birdie order her dinner. "But you turned something pretty damn shitty into this amazing place. It's even better because it's safe for you and our Birdie."

"I'm so honored that you all came," I tell him softly, and give in to the urge to rest my head on his shoulder. He kisses the top of my head, and the first tear spirals down my cheek. "So many of you came by throughout the day, I certainly didn't expect everyone to come back for dinner. And this is the *third time* Brooks has been in today."

"You're our family, Jules. You're ours, so this is what we do. What we'll always do. And my son is so damn in love with you, it borders on inappropriate. Blink twice if you need me to help you escape."

I laugh and shake my head. "No, I don't ever plan to let your son go, especially now that I finally have him in my life again. I don't know how I survived as long as I did without him."

He sighs and gives me one last squeeze. "Timing can be a bitch. Now, what do you recommend I have for dinner? I'm starving."

When the whole family has their food, and they're all seated at tables they slid together in the middle of the room, Christy pushes a plate of lasagna in my own hands and smiles.

"Go join your family. You haven't sat down once all day."

"Neither have you," I remind her.

"You paid me for *weeks* so I wouldn't have to panic or find another job. We're happy to do this for you. Go celebrate with your family, Jules."

Well, shit. I have the best team ever.

Brooks is already sliding the chair out next to him, gesturing for me to sit, and I do. Birdie's across from me, *devouring* her cheesy pasta with chicken on the side, and she grins at me.

"This is the best *ever*, Auntie Jules."

Auntie Jules.

Christ, my heart.

"Good. I'll always keep it on the menu for you, sweetheart."

I'm happy to silently eat, soaking up the conversation around me. Skyla, Billie, and Harper are talking about pregnancy, while Beckett bounces little Bryce on his knee, giving Dani and Bridger a break to eat without entertaining an infant.

Brooks finishes his salmon with potatoes and salad, then rests his arm over the back of my chair, gently rubbing my shoulder.

"It seemed like it was a good day in here," Billie says with a knowing smile. "Every time I looked out the shop windows, people were coming and going."

"We were *swamped*." I sigh and push my half-eaten lasagna away, but Brooks starts working on the leftovers, making me smile. "I'm going to be here late tonight making pastries for tomorrow, but that's not a bad problem to have."

"You need to hire more bakers," Connor says with a frown. "And other staff, too."

"I know. I didn't need more help before. I'd just hired Laurie and James not long before the flood happened, and I felt we were fully staffed. I know that things will calm down a bit after a week or so, once the dust settles, but I definitely need more help with the baking and food prep. I can't do it all by myself anymore."

I grin up at Brooks.

"Besides, we have a house to renovate, and I don't want to miss any of it."

"What's wrong with your house?" Dani asks, and then her mouth forms an O. "Right, *that* house."

"I want to help with demolition," Beckett says. "It's a good way to get out some aggression."

"What are you feeling aggressive about?" Skyla asks him, lifting an eyebrow.

"Never about you, Irish." He kisses her forehead, making us grin.

With less than an hour until closing, the restaurant is finally starting to slow down, and my crew has begun cleaning up.

No matter what my people say, I can't sit out here while they work. I'm just not built that way.

"Thank you all, so much, for coming in. Not just now, but all day today. You made me feel like, well—"

"Part of the family?" Becca asks with a smile. "Good. You *are* part of our family."

I lick my lips, and Brooks kisses my temple.

"Thank you. I see that my people are cleaning up, and I can't let them do that without me, so I'm going to excuse myself and get back to work, but the break was nice. Thanks, you guys."

I stand and grin when Birdie blows me a kiss. Brooks is already standing next to me, and he pulls me in for a big hug.

"So fucking proud of you, Wildfire. I'll be back later."

"You don't have—"

"I'll be back later." He winks, and I go back to work. It's going to be a late night for me, but I won't complain.

This is what I've always wanted.

The business.

The family.

The marriage.

I won't ever complain, not for a minute.

Chapter Twenty-Four

BROOKS

My girl is dead on her feet.

She didn't even hear me come through the front door, which I don't like because she should always be aware of who comes and goes from this restaurant. However, given it was an eighteen-hour day for her, I'll give her a pass.

She's covering a tray of something with plastic and carries it to the big fridge in the back. When I walk around the corner to watch her, she's leaning on the closed fridge, her eyes shut.

Christ, she'd fall asleep right there if I let her.

Actually, she might already be asleep.

"Let's go home, baby."

My voice is soft, so I don't scare the shit out of her, and she opens her eyes and smiles over at me.

It looks like even that much movement is strenuous for her.

"Home sounds great." She sighs and walks right into

my arms, buries her face in my chest and leans into me. "It was such a good day."

"I know I said it about a dozen times today, but I'm so proud of you, Wildfire. You were the talk of the town today."

She doesn't fight me when I lift her into my arms.

"It's past midnight." I kiss her forehead once, and it feels so good that I do it again. "Tell me that you got everything prepped so you don't have to come in here in four hours."

"I'll come in at six and start baking," she replies with a yawn. "You have to put me down so I can shut everything off and lock the door."

I don't like it, but I do as she says, and follow her around as she turns off lights, checks the stove and ovens, then tosses her apron in a hamper and grabs her handbag.

She checks the lock three times before she turns to climb into my truck.

Once I've pulled onto the road to head home, I take her hand. "Why do you always check the locks three times, Juliet?"

She squeezes my hand, and I hear her sigh next to me. "Because Justin used to sneak into my room to fuck with me. He'd hide in there, and when I came in, he'd do the jump-scare thing. Startle me. He loved to do that when I was in the shower, too, and one time I fell and hit my head. Knocked me out. I woke up a few minutes later, still in the bottom of the running shower, and Justin was laughing his ass off in the kitchen. It's a wonder I didn't drown."

My hand tightens on the wheel, and anger pulses through me.

Motherfucking asshole.

"It got to where I not only made sure that I locked the door, but I got to be a bit OCD about it, checking over and over again. Now it's just a habit to check three times."

"Fuck, I'm sorry."

"Yeah, well, that wasn't the worst of it." She says it so casually, as if it's so *normal*, it makes my teeth clench. "Between the control he had on every dime I spent, basically isolating me from everyone, and well. It doesn't matter now. What an asshole. I'm glad I had them pull the plug, but I'll deny it if you ever tell anyone I said that."

"I'd like to resurrect him and skin him alive."

I feel her gaze on me as I pull into our driveway.

"And I don't give a fuck who you tell that I said that. I'll say it to anyone who asks. That motherfucker deserved far more pain than he got."

Here in the dark quiet of my truck, Jules lifts my hand to her cheek and smiles softly.

"I'm so great now, Brooks. I'm not scared or sad. I have an incredibly full life, with *two* houses that my insanely hot husband bought for me, a business that's thriving, and friends and family who make me feel like they've been mine forever. It doesn't get any better than this. So we don't need to be angry with him anymore. He's gone, and he can't hurt me."

"You're incredible, you know that? Come on, let's get you into bed."

"I need a shower," she says as she opens her door.

"What are you doing?" I can hear the amusement in my voice when she frowns over at me. "You *never* open your own door, Wildfire. Not if I'm around."

"Yeah, yeah, chivalry and all that." She rolls her eyes, but I lift an eyebrow, and she lets out a chuckle. "Well, get a move on, husband, I'm tired."

"You're *so* going to pay for that," I mutter as I get out and walk around to help her out of the truck.

Jules heads straight back to the bedroom, shedding out of her clothes on the way, leaving a trail behind her, which I happily collect and toss into the hamper when I get to the bedroom and see her gorgeous naked ass stride into the bathroom.

The shower comes on as I strip out of my own clothes. Although I've already had a shower, there's no way in hell that I won't go in there with her right now.

My girl is in there. Naked. Wet. Perfect.

I need to get my hands on her.

"Baby, I'm coming in there. I don't want to startle you."

I open the glass door and find her smiling at me.

"You don't always have to—"

"Yeah, I do." I grab the loofah out of her hands and take over, gently washing her perfect body. Her pink nipples pucker, and she bites that lip.

"I'm so exhausted, you would think that I wouldn't even *think* about sex," she says quietly, dragging her fingertip over the ridges of my stomach.

"But?"

"But here you are, so damn hot, with a dick that dreams are made of and—"

Not giving her the chance to say anything else, I drop the loofah and plant my hands on her thighs, lifting her. She wraps her legs around my waist as I push her up against the tile and kiss her sweet lips.

"You want my cock, Wildfire?" I growl against her lips and rub my hard dick through her wet slit, making her grin.

"Always." She wiggles her hips. "I *always* want you. Even when I'm so tired, that I can't keep my eyes open."

"That's my girl." I grin against her lips and then push the crown inside her, and her pretty blue eyes widen. "Talk to me, baby."

"It's ... *fuck*, it's just so damn good." She starts to close her eyes, but I slip a hand up and wrap it around her throat, not squeezing off her air, just holding her.

"Eyes always on me, Juliet."

I slide in the rest of the way, my pubic bone grinding on her clit, making her squeeze me like a goddamn vise, and we both groan.

"You fill me up in every single way."

Resting my forehead against hers, I start to move. Not fast and wild like we usually are, not hard enough to leave a bruise.

This is tender.

This is *love.*

"You're so damn *tight*," I breathe, and feel tingles run down my spine. "Baby, I need you to come for me."

Her pussy flutters around my dick, and every muscle in her body tightens.

"That's it. Fuck, you're so gorgeous when you come. Whose pussy is this, Juliet?"

"Yours."

"Say it again."

"I'm *yours*, Brooks. Oh God!" She shatters in my arms, so perfectly that I'm helpless to do anything but follow her over, grinding into her until my cum is dripping out of her and down my legs.

It's fucking amazing.

"Bed," she murmurs, resting her head on my shoulder. "Must sleep."

"Let me clean you up real quick, baby. Can you stand for me?"

"Maybe."

I grin and gingerly lower her to her feet. She wobbles a bit, but she leans a hand on the tile, and I quickly wash us, then grab the spray handle down to rinse us.

Once we're both dry, I carry my sweet wife to bed and tuck us in. She wraps herself around me, lays her head on my chest, and sighs.

"Thank you for the best day, Brooks."

"You did all of the work. Besides, you deserve to be this happy every day, my love. Go to sleep."

"I have to wake up by five."

"I'll wake you."

"Why am I so nervous?" Jules asks a week later as we park in front of Chad Kincaid's office in Silver Springs. "I mean, we're just getting information. I'm not on trial for murder or anything."

"It's okay," I reply and kiss the back of her hand. "Once we start getting answers, the nerves will fade. Let's go see what the man has to say."

She nods and waits for me to walk around and open her door. With our hands linked, we walk into the attorney's office and are quickly escorted back to his private office.

"It's nice to meet you in person." Chad shakes Juliet's hand first, and then my own. "Can I get you some coffee or anything at all to drink?"

"Whiskey might be good," Jules mutters, but then shakes her head. "No, thank you."

"Please, have a seat." Chad gestures to the two brown leather chairs in front of his desk, and Jules and I each take one as he lowers himself into his desk chair. "Let me just summarize the situation, so I make sure that we're all on the same page."

Jules nods. "Yes, sounds good."

"Your late husband, who passed almost three years ago, left his entire estate to you upon his death, except for a trust in the amount of two million dollars with a woman named"—he checks his notes—"Nadine Smith as the beneficiary. The trust lists you as the trustee, or the person appointed to oversee the funds for Nadine."

"Yes."

"Was Nadine a relative?" he asks.

"She was his mistress."

Chad pauses. His eyes come up to meet mine and then go back to her. "Your late husband put a trust in motion that made *you* pay his mistress for as long as one of you is living?"

"Yes. Lovely, isn't it?"

He glances at me. "And Brooks is your new husband."

"Yes, he is. We just got married a couple of weeks ago."

"I reached out to the attorney in Washington, and he didn't reply. So I called his office, and the office no longer exists. I assume the practice went out of business, but he still has an email address."

Jules frowns next to me. "It's impossible that the practice is out of business. It was a generational practice. His grandfather opened it fifty years ago."

"How do you know this?" Chad asks before I can.

"Because Daniel was Justin's best friend. He handled all of Justin's legal stuff."

Chad frowns and rubs his hand over his chin, thinking as he stares over Juliet's shoulder.

"I've requested the trust paperwork from the state," he says. "That can take a few weeks, depending on how backed up they are. In the meantime, I'm going to also make a few calls and see what I can find out about this Daniel guy. Something isn't right with this situation."

"Thank fuck I'm not the only one who thinks so," I grumble.

Chad smiles at me. "If I were you, I'd be tearing the world apart right now."

"If this doesn't work out with you, that's my next plan."

Jules rolls her eyes, but Chad nods. "Let's see what we can come up with. I assume this isn't urgent since you've been paying her for more than two years."

"No, there's no rush. I just don't want her to contact me anymore."

"Tell me more about that," Chad says. "How often does she contact you?"

"Literally every day. Sometimes multiple times a day. I told her that she wasn't allowed to call or text, only email, but she doesn't respect that. I finally changed my number, and that only pissed her off, and my email blew up."

"What is she contacting you *for*?" Chad asks, clearly confused.

"More money."

The attorney that I'm quickly coming to respect shakes his head. "That's not how this works, Jules. She gets a set amount of money, period. It's not a negotiation, so I'm not sure why she's contacting you for more. Have you allocated more to her in the past?"

Jules nibbles on her lower lip. "In the beginning, yes. Because I didn't know any better. Daniel wasn't speaking to me, so I didn't really have anyone to ask questions. But when it got worse and worse and more abusive, I googled the protocol."

Chad sighs and holds up a hand. "You used Google for legal advice?"

"I didn't know what to do. But I read that as the trustee, I'm not supposed to just hand out money whenever the beneficiary asks for it, so I told her that she'd get her monthly stipend and that's it."

"How much does she get?" Chad asks.

"Fifteen thousand a month."

Fucking hell.

"But she blows through it fast and always asks for more."

"You're going to block her on everything. I'm going to file a restraining order. That's bullshit. I'll do some digging, and we'll meet back here in thirty days. You can withdraw yourself as a trustee. You don't *have* to be in charge of that money, Jules."

My wife's lower lip quivers, and then she swallows hard. "Really? Because I was told that I didn't have a choice."

"Christ." I push my hand through my hair, feeling so fucking helpless.

"You have a choice," Chad says gently. "We're going to figure this out. By the end of the year, this will all be behind you."

"That sounds *amazing.* Thank you so much."

She's quiet as we head back to Bitterroot Valley, and when I pull into our driveway, she pushes the door open and hops out before I can tell her to wait for me.

"Fucking asshole," she mutters. She's good and pissed off now. "Motherfucking, cheating, microscopic-dicked piece of shit."

I wonder how she really feels about him.

"Is there a hammer in there?" she asks, pointing at the big house across the street.

"No, but I have a few in the garage."

"Great. I need a big one."

"Uh, baby, I can't let you hurt yourself."

"I can swing a goddamn hammer, and I need to destroy something right now, so please get it for me."

With a nod, I stride into the garage and grab two sledgehammers.

Looks like demo is starting early.

"Come on, Wildfire."

With a tool in each hand, I set off across the street, and Jules is right beside me. Anger rolls off her in waves, rivaling my own.

"My brothers are coming in a bit to help tear some of this out," I tell her.

"Fine. There's plenty here they can demolish, but I get to start."

I unlock the door, and she takes a hammer, hardly flinching at the weight of it, marches right through to the kitchen, and starts fucking swinging.

This is amazing as fuck.

"I hate him!" The hammer crashes through the cabinets. "I hope he's rotting in hell. I hope every single second is fucking *terror* for him."

She rears back and swings again.

Remind me never to piss off my wife.

Jules takes another swing, making the cabinet door fly open. She swings at that, too, and it goes flying across the room.

"Baby, you need some gloves and eye prote—"

"Don't fucking tell me what I need." She rounds on me, her blue eyes fierce as she strips off her shirt and flings it aside. She's now clad only in a bra from the waist up as

301

she takes another swing. "I'll tell you what I fucking need. I need to beat the shit out of something."

Smash.

Crash.

"You're doing that," I reply and grin when she spins to glare at me. "Well, you are. But Wildfire, if my brothers see you like this, I'm going to have to kill them because they'll be looking at what's mine."

"It's a bra, Brooks. The same as a bikini. Are you going to turn into a controlling asshole who tries to tell me what I can and cannot wear? Is *that* who I married? *Again?*"

"Enough." All humor fleeing the premises, I tug the hammer out of her hand and toss it aside, then frame her face and make her look up at me. "First of all, compare me to that piece of shit *ever* again, and I'll spank your ass until it's so red, you won't sit for a fucking week."

She swallows, and tears fill her pretty blue eyes.

"Second, *this* bra is not the same as a bikini. It's sheer, sweetheart. I can see your gorgeous-as-fuck nipples. So no, you *can't* wear this around anyone but me. Not to mention, it's not safe to be this undressed while wood is splintering all over the fucking place."

All the fight leaves her body, and she leans into me, taking a shuddering breath. It just about breaks my heart.

"I am so mad."

My hands roam up and down her back, and I kiss the top of her head.

"I know. You *should* be mad, Jules. You were lied to and manipulated, and it's so fucking unfair. You didn't deserve that."

We stand here for another minute, and then I hear the front door open.

"Hello?" Beckett calls out.

"In the kitchen," I yell back. Jules hurries to pull her top over her head and then wipes her cheeks dry. "Are you okay, baby?"

"Yeah." She sniffs and then smiles at Beck as he walks into the kitchen. He pauses, glances around, and then narrows his eyes at me.

"What the fuck did you do?" he demands.

"Gave her a hammer," I reply. "And if you even *hint* at the idea that I would have hurt her in any way, I'll tear your stomach out through your fucking belly button."

"Wow, that's descriptive," Bridger says as he also walks in. "You guys okay?"

"We're fine," Jules says. "We're not fighting. Honest. I'm going to let you guys handle this and head to the restaurant. They've been filling in for me this morning."

"You can just go home, Jules."

She shakes her head. "Nah. Staying busy is a good idea today. Have fun, boys."

Jules crosses to me and boosts up on her toes, offering me her lips, which I immediately cover with my own.

"Call me if you need me," I whisper. "I love you."

"Love you, too." She pats my chest, then she's gone. I can hear her talking to someone at the door, and then it closes, and Blake walks in.

Everyone's here.

"Why does Jules look ... unhinged?" Blake asks with a scowl. "Is she feeling okay?"

"We're dealing with some stuff from her past," I reply with a sigh, wondering how much to tell them. The prick she was married to isn't my story to tell, but these three are my brothers, my best friends. "You know she was married?"

They all nod.

"The girls told us," Bridger replies.

"He pulled some shady shit, and we had a meeting with an attorney this morning. Pissed us both off, and she needed to let off a little steam." I spread my arms, gesturing to the impressive mess my wildfire made. "I don't know if it helped, but she got to destroy some stuff."

"That sucks," Beckett says. "Let us know if you need anything."

"I think it's just going to take a little time and more patience than I normally have."

"Are you kidding?" Blake smirks, shaking his head. "You're the man who waited *fifteen years* for her. You have more patience than anyone I know."

"You know what I mean."

"It's going well, though?" Bridger asks me. "Other than what you had to deal with this morning, things are good?"

"Better than I thought they could be."

They grin at me, and I roll my eyes.

"Come on, assholes. I want to get this whole kitchen torn out today."

"We can do more than that," Blake says, looking around. "Jesus, people actually thought this wallpaper was a good idea?"

"How are we going to strip it off?" Bridger asks.

"We're not. I don't trust the electrical system since it hasn't been updated in about sixty years. We're going to eventually take the whole house down to the studs and start over."

"Fun." Bridger grins and hefts the sledgehammer he brought with him. "Let's tear some shit apart."

Chapter Twenty-Five

JULIET

"These crackers are *everything*," I say as I pop another one into my mouth, and Cassie grins across from me. I asked the personal chef to pop by today with some for the restaurant and to chat with me about a possible working relationship. "I think I'll put together some cheese and cracker trays for the grab-and-go section."

"That's a great idea," Cassie says. "I can bring you a fresh batch of crackers twice a week. Would that be enough?"

"I think so, for now anyway. We can adjust as we go, if that works for you."

"Of course." She makes a note in her phone. "What else can I help with?"

I take a sip of water and wave at Ava, who's just walked into Sage & Citrus to grab something for lunch. Her order is already bagged up and ready to go.

"Hi, friend," Ava says. "I won't interrupt. See you at book club tomorrow night?"

"I'll be there," I reply with a nod.

"Cool. Hi, Cassie."

"Hey, Ava."

My friend smiles, and then she's off, and I turn back to Cassie.

"Book club?" she asks.

"Spicy Girls Book Club," I reply with a nod. "Do you like romance novels?"

"Are you kidding? I listen to them all day long while I'm working. I'm obsessed with Connor Crais's voice. I know he's a happily married man, or so I've heard, but I totally have a crush on his voice skills."

I snort at that. "Hey, we all have our crushes. If you're a reader, you should join the book club. Right now, we're reading *Play Along* by Liz Tomforde."

"Oh, that's awesome! I just finished that one last week. Samantha Brentmoor's voice is just *so* smooth and sexy. And Jacob Morgan? Yeah, I'm down for this book club. I'll swing by the bookstore after I leave here."

"This is so exciting." I do a little shimmy in my seat. "You'll love it. I should listen to books while I bake early in the morning."

"You really should. It makes the time go fast. Okay, what else do you need?"

"Right. Back to work." I laugh. "I'd actually like to hire a second baker. As of right now, I'm the only one prepping the night before and then coming in super early to bake all of the pastries and breads. I used to be able to handle it, but I didn't really have a life outside of this place before, so it didn't bother me. Plus, we're getting busier, and it's higher volume. I just can't do it alone."

Cassie's nodding slowly, her eyes narrowed as she thinks.

"I can't take on any more than what I currently have, but I have a good friend who just moved to Silver Springs and is a pastry chef. His name is Noah, and he's really good. I don't think he's working anywhere else yet."

"But does he want early hours?"

"I think that's the nature of the beast when it comes to being a pastry chef."

I nod in agreement. "And what about gluten-free recipes? Do you think he'd be cool with that?"

"Only one way to find out." Cassie pulls her phone out of her purse, taps the screen, and then puts it on speaker and sets it on the table between us.

"Hey, pretty girl," a deep male voice says.

"Hey, I have you on speakerphone. I'm chatting with my new friend Juliet, who happens to own Sage & Citrus in Bitterroot Valley."

"I've been in there," he says. "It's fucking good. Hey, Juliet."

"Hi, you can call me Jules. I hear you're a pastry chef."

"Aw, Cass is singing my praises again? How sweet."

I laugh and see that Cassie's blushing. "How do you feel about baking gluten-free? And are you looking for a job?"

"I might be looking for a job if it's the right fit. Gluten-free is just another challenge. As long as it's not sugar-free, I can work with that."

"I have no issue with sugar," I assure him. "But mine is a clean kitchen, making it safe for those struggling with celiac and gluten allergies. Would you be interested in popping by to chat?"

"You know what, I'm headed that way this afternoon, and would be happy to come in. Thanks for thinking of me, Cassie."

"Sure, I hope it works out."

"See you later, Jules."

He hangs up, and I sit back, watching Cassie.

"Are you two ...?"

She shakes her head. "No. Definitely not. I've been seeing someone else for a couple of years now. But I *am* warning you, Noah is hot. Like super attractive."

I smirk at that. "Have you seen my husband?"

"Oh, I'm not suggesting that you'd be interested. Mostly, I'm warning you because of your staff. They may never get anything done. They'll just stand around and watch Noah."

Shaking with laughter, I shrug a shoulder. "I guess we'll see if he even wants the job."

I need to go on record and say that Cassie wasn't wrong. Noah is *damn* attractive. He's not as tall as Brooks, but he's over six feet, with dark blond hair, a chiseled jawline covered in two days' or so worth of scruff, and a killer smile.

All my girls have heart eyes as they watch us walk into the kitchen.

"I really like your place," he says, crossing his arms over his chest, showing off muscular biceps through his long-sleeved T-shirt, as he looks around. "What do you need help with, exactly?"

I spend the next twenty minutes explaining my vision. That I need help with the breads and pastries for each morning. That he'd be welcome to try new recipes, as long as everything stays gluten-free. He gives his ideas, and we brainstorm, bouncing ideas off each other. He's easy to talk to, and he has some amazing creative thoughts.

He's nodding, standing right next to me, when I hear, "Who the fuck are you?"

Noah and I turn around, and I find Brooks standing six feet away, glaring at us.

"Noah." Noah reaches out to shake Brooks's hand, but my husband doesn't even look at it.

"Brooks, this is Noah, *hopefully* my new pastry chef, so I don't have to come here in the middle of the night anymore. Don't be a jerk and ruin this for me."

Noah laughs, and Brooks narrows his eyes.

Finally, he shakes Noah's hand, although I can see that it's reluctantly.

"I'm her husband," Brooks eventually says.

"Noted. For what it's worth, I have my eye on another pretty blonde from Bitterroot Valley," he says with a smile. "And I'm not an asshole."

"Glad to hear it."

"Okay, now that we've got all of the testosterone out of the way, what can I do for you, *husband?*"

"I came to grab lunch. Christy said you were back here."

"Yeah, we were just wrapping up."

"I'll head out," Noah says. "Let me do some research and some thinking, and I'll get back to you in the next day or so. Does that work for you, Jules?"

"That's Mrs. Blackwell to you," Brooks growls, and I can't help but laugh.

"Yes, that's fine with me. Thanks for considering it. I promise my husband won't be a bully every time you see him."

"Yes, he will," Brooks replies.

"It's all good." Noah shakes my hand, and then he leaves, and I turn to frown at my man.

"*Brooks.*"

"What?"

"You can't be rude to people."

"Says who?"

"Says me."

His hands drift from my waist to my ass, and he pulls me against him. "Wildfire, I'm secure enough in my sexuality to objectively say that that man is attractive, and he was standing way too close to you."

"Noah's attractive?" I blink innocently, and Brooks growls again. "I didn't notice. Anyway, he seems nice. He was recommended to me by Cassie, your *sister's* personal chef. And I really need the help, babe. I'm *tired.* I don't want to work every single day anymore even though I love it here, and I'm proud of it. But I want to see more of you and spend time with you."

"Okay, that I can live with." He lowers his head and

nibbles my lips. "If he ever gets handsy, you tell me, and I'll remove them from his body."

"Have you been reading some of my Mafia books?"

He smirks and kisses me once more. "I have to grab the sandwiches I ordered on my way back here and get to work. I'll probably be at the garage a little late today."

"Well, I'm going to head home soon, since my crew seems to have it handled here. I'd like to do a little cleaning and then read. Book club is tomorrow night, and I have a couple of hours left in the book."

"You *should* go home and relax, baby."

He nuzzles my nose, then pulls away. I wish he could go home with me, and we could cuddle up for the afternoon. I'd love it if he would read to me, the way he used to when we were young.

But my man has a busy garage to run.

Christy has his bag ready for him, and he kisses my cheek before he heads back to work.

"I'm out of here," I tell Christy. "Call me if you need me."

"We won't. The craziness has died down a bit, and we have a handle on things. But don't worry, I'll call if anything weird happens."

I nod, take off my apron, and toss it in the hamper. Then I grab my handbag and sling it across my body and set off for the house.

Brooks dropped me off this morning, so I get to walk home. I admit, although I try to take a walk at least once a day, I haven't been as diligent about it since I married Brooks.

I don't feel like I need an escape from anything.

It's cold enough outside that I zip up my hoodie and take in a breath of crisp air. It's been raining, and I hear we're supposed to get a thunderstorm this afternoon, which actually sounds so nice.

I love storms.

I always have.

I know that some people are terrified of them, and I can respect that. But I want to get home in time to open all the windows, light my favorite candle—which also smells like rain—and get cozy with a book before it starts to storm.

That sounds like heaven right now.

The walk home is quick, and the first thing that I do is put a load of laundry into the machine in the mudroom. It's *so nice* to live with a washer and dryer again. Then I quickly clean the primary bathroom and change the sheets on the bed before walking into the kitchen. I set my candle in the middle of the island and light it, then open all the windows in the living room and kitchen.

Yeah, it's chilly outside, but I'll throw a blanket around me. Problem solved.

I've just sat in my new favorite spot, the corner of the couch by the windows, with a paperback copy of *Play Along*, a hot mug of tea, and a cozy blanket, when the thunder booms off in the distance, making me sigh happily.

It's a little late in the season for thunderstorms in Montana. Typically, it would just rain. Or snow. Thunderstorms mostly happen in the spring and summer, but I'm not complaining a bit.

I tip my head against the back of the couch and sigh happily. I feel like this is the first time I've taken a moment to relax since I reopened the restaurant almost two weeks ago. Just as I thought it would, the dust is starting to settle, and we're not bombarded with customers the way we were that first day back.

However, we *are* still busy. We've managed to keep a steady stream of hungry people flooding in each day, and that makes me happy.

I'm also thrilled that I have enough staff that I can take the occasional afternoon—or full day—off. Everyone needs that.

I can hear the rain start outside, and I glance over to the window to watch the droplets fall out of the sky. Thunder rolls in the distance, and the rain picks up, falling in *sheets*.

And suddenly, I can't keep the horrible memories at bay.

"You're such a fucking whiner!"

"Justin, just watch the road."

I despise riding with him on a good day, but today is rainy, and this road is twisty. I don't know why he insisted that I come with him to the beach. He hates it there. Lately, he hates me.

"Don't fucking tell me what to do." He shakes his head and jerks on the wheel. I swear he does it just to scare me.

"Look, I think a separation is for the best. You don't even like me anymore, J. We live in the same house, but that's it. You're in remission. You're in a good place and you don't need me."

"You have no idea what you're talking about."

My stomach clenches. Justin talked me into marrying him eight years ago because he told me he had terminal cancer, would only live for less than a year, and he wanted to spend that year with me.

Yeah, I have issues with telling people no. Clearly. Because I married him, but then his cancer miraculously got better. The medical issues come and go, but there's no threat of him dying anytime soon.

As horrible as it sounds, I didn't sign up for this. Don't get me wrong, I'm so incredibly happy he's going to live a long life, but I don't want to be the one to spend it with him.

Being married to Justin hasn't been a walk in the park. Gone is the man who I was best friends with for so long, and in his place is a mean, horrible bully I don't even recognize.

"You've been in remission for a while," I remind him, trying to keep my voice calm. *"I think it's time for me to move on, Justin."*

"Look, I was going to wait until we were at the beach to tell you this, but the cancer is back, Jules."

Fuck.

"I start chemo again next week."

"Where is it this time?"

He slides a look over at me. "Are you implying that I'm lying to you?"

"No, you've had several different types of cancer, and I'm asking what kind it is this time."

He rubs his hand over his mouth, as if he's agitated. "It's pancreatic."

I frown. I've done a lot of research on this over the

315

years. Justin never lets me go to the hospital with him for treatments because he says he doesn't want me to see him like that, but I've done a lot of searching around online, reading medical journals.

"What stage is it?" I ask.

"Four."

I shake my head. "Justin, you had stage four pancreatic cancer when we got married. I don't—"

"Are you calling me a fucking LIAR?" He screams it, bangs his fist on the steering wheel, just as we're about to go through a turn, but his hand slips, and he doesn't turn in time. The car fishtails, and I scream as we careen straight toward a tree, hitting it so hard that the airbags deploy, and I'm stunned as I try to breathe and look around, the silence deafening.

"Justin?"

I glance over and feel my heart stop. He's leaning forward, and blood is flowing down his face.

Frantically, I search for my phone, which had been in my hand, but I dropped it during the crash. The rain is pelting down in sheets around us, so ear-piercing now in direct contrast to just seconds ago.

And the ringing in my ears is suddenly all I can hear.

I find my phone and manage to call emergency services, but I can't hear whoever is on the other end of the line, so I just scream for help and hope they can trace the call.

My neck hurts, and my shoulder is screaming.

And when I look to my left, it looks like Justin is dead.

"Hold on," I say, my voice shaky as fuck as I reach over and feel his neck. I think I can feel a pulse.

Suddenly, someone opens my door, and then it's a flurry of chaos, first responders getting us out of the vehicle and into ambulances.

Voices.

Questions that I can't answer.

Finally, after what feels like days, although it's only been a couple of hours, I'm led into Justin's room. He's already in a room? How long have we been here?

Everything is a blur.

And through his window, I can see the rain still coming down.

"You need to say goodbye, Jules."

My eyes move to the kind doctor standing next to me. Her arm is around my shoulders. I feel cold. I hate the smell in here.

"But before you do that," she continues, "do you know if your husband is an organ donor?"

Something about that doesn't feel right.

"Uh, why would you want a cancer patient's organs?" I ask her, frowning in confusion. "Can they even donate?"

The doctor shakes her head in confusion. "Jules, Justin doesn't have cancer."

"Yes, he does. He gets treatment at this hospital. Check his records."

"I looked through all his medical records. He had his tonsils out here as a child, and a broken arm when he was sixteen, but I assure you, your husband was a very healthy man before the accident."

I stare at her. Swallow. My jaw drops, but no sound comes out.

"There was never *any cancer?"*

317

She shakes her head slowly. "No."

I look back at the man lying in the bed. He's completely still, his face swollen and broken. They had to shave his head because of the injuries there. His hands are on top of the covers. Tubes are breathing for him. I know he's brain-dead and is never going to wake up.

There was never any cancer.

He tricked me into marrying him, just so he could treat me like shit for EIGHT MOTHERFUCKING YEARS.

"Jules—"

"Can I give consent for organ donation if he isn't able to?"

"Yes, you can do that."

"Take everything." I don't look away from him. I speak to her while keeping my eyes pinned to this piece of garbage in this bed. "Take whatever you need. Organs, eyes, skin. Take it all. His life should bring some good to someone."

"Are you sure? That doesn't leave—"

"I'm sure." I swallow hard, feeling hollow.

He lied about everything.

He was never going to kill himself.

He was never sick.

I lost everything because of him.

"Does he have parents or siblings?" she asks. "Anyone else who would want to come and say goodbye?"

"No." He has no one. Just me. And he wasn't going to have me for much longer. "I'll sign whatever you need me to sign."

She nods at someone who's standing outside the room, and they bustle in, showing me where to sign the forms.

"The sooner we're able to har—retrieve the donation—"

"You can take him after I have just one minute alone with him."

She nods and offers me a sympathetic smile. "Take your time, Jules."

I cross over and bend so my mouth is near his ear.

"I hope you can hear me, wherever you are. I never loved you the way you wanted me to. You stole everything from me. I thought you were my friend, but it turns out you were nothing. I hope you burn in hell."

With that, I stand and walk out of the room.

Chapter Twenty-Six

BROOKS

All I can think about is the fact that my wife is at home, doing normal everyday things, and I can't be there with her because I'm at work.

Yeah, I'm a sap. But fuck, I lived without Juliet for fifteen years, and now that I have her back, nothing is better than being with her, even if it's just to watch her read, or if we're cleaning the house together.

Normal shit is sexy on my girl.

I love that she's taking the rest of the day off for herself. Jules is as dedicated to her business as I am to mine, and she puts in long fucking hours. Her work ethic is one of the things that I've grown to respect and appreciate the most.

But today, she's at home, and I'm stuck at work. Normally, I look forward to being at the garage with the guys, but not today.

"Why are you glaring at that manifold?" Gabe asks me.

"I'm going home."

His eyebrows climb in surprise. "Are you okay?"

"Fine. I just need to go home. There's nothing here that can't wait for tomorrow."

"I've got things here," Gabe agrees. "I'll see you later. Let me know if you need anything."

I nod, wash my hands, and then check the time. It's late afternoon now and rainy outside. The perfect time to strip my wife down and bury myself inside her.

With that goal in mind, I drive home. The storm is a doozy, with thunder and lightning and a shit ton of rain, so I drive slower than normal.

When I walk through the back door, I take a deep breath and grin. I missed Juliet's candles. She used to burn this same one all the time when we were younger, and it seems that hasn't changed. It smells ... clean. I have no idea what it's called, but it's so her.

The washer and dryer are both running in the mudroom as I kick off my boots, and with a grin, I walk through and see the lit candle on the island. The house is quiet, except for the sound of the rain and the storm outside because she's opened all the windows. It's chilly, but it smells and sounds fucking awesome.

And then I spot her.

My girl is on the couch, wrapped in a blanket. She's not reading. Her book lies next to her, unopened. She's watching the rain, her hands wringing in her lap.

And when I narrow my eyes on her face, I can see that she's pale. Her eyes are glassy, as if she's caught in a memory.

Or a nightmare.

"Baby," I whisper, not wanting to startle her. But she doesn't respond to me.

Fuck. What am I supposed to do? If I scare her, she'll freak out.

"Jules," I say just a little louder, and this time, she blinks, then looks over at me, and presses her lips together in a grim line. "What's wrong, my love?"

I cross to her and squat down on my haunches, reaching up to brush a tear from under her eye. Her lower lip quivers, but she swallows hard and shrugs a shoulder.

"Just memories, I guess."

"Of?"

She shakes her head, and her gorgeous blue eyes meet mine. "Just bad shit that you don't want to know about. Trust me. It's the rain. The car accident happened in the rain."

Well, shit.

"You wanna know what sucks the most?" Another tear falls as she asks me the question, and I nod in response.

"Yeah, Wildfire. I wanna know."

"I love storms. You know that."

I nod again and brush her soft hair back from her face. "I know you do."

"But now he's ruined it for me. I was going to sit here and enjoy the storm and read my book, and all I could do was remember that horrible day, and—"

"Okay, take a breath for me, baby." I cup her sweet face in my hands. "Deep breath in for me."

She takes that breath and slowly lets it out.

"We're not letting him ruin one more thing for you. Never again. So come on." I take her hand and pull her to her feet, then kiss her pillowy lips, sinking into her. She whimpers, leaning into me, as if she's soaking in my strength.

"I'm so glad you came home early."

I grin against her lips and pull away.

"Me, too. Now, let's grab your candle and go out back on the patio."

With her hand in mine, I lead us to the kitchen, where I carefully pick up her candle. She opens the door for us, and we walk out to the covered patio in the backyard. The rain is still coming down *hard*, pelting the metal roof above us as thunder booms between flashes of lightning.

"What are we doing?" she asks with a small smile. The color is already coming back to her cheeks.

After setting the candle on a little side table, I pull her to me for a big hug and kiss the top of her head.

"I'm going to fuck you out here in the rain."

She looks up at me, her chin resting on my chest, and grins. "Oh really? Is this what you came home for?"

"Not necessarily." My fingers ghost down her jawline. "I came home to be with you, no matter what that looks like. But I'll be fucking *damned* if every time it rains, you're thrust back into nightmares. No way. Now, be my good girl and take all your clothes off."

"It's not exactly hot outside today, Brooks."

I lift an eyebrow, and her lips twist to hide a smile.

"I mean, yes, sir."

Christ, that's hot.

323

She starts to undress, and I flip on the outdoor gas fireplace, which springs to life. It'll keep us warm enough for what I have planned.

When I turn around, she's wiggling out of her pants and stands before me gloriously bare, her nipples already tight and begging for my mouth.

"I bet you're wet already, aren't you?"

"I don't know, maybe you should check for yourself."

She bites her lip, and I narrow my eyes as I cross to her and slide my hand down her stomach and to her center.

"You're fucking soaked."

"I mean, you said the words, *I'm going to fuck you*, and that's all it takes."

I chuckle and bring my wet fingers to her lips, painting her own arousal over them before sliding them into her mouth, and she immediately closes her lips and sucks.

My cock strains against my jeans, but I don't strip down and sink inside her the way I want to.

I need to take it slow.

But before I can move on to what's next, she surprises me by wrapping her hands around my wrist and pulling my hand away, then lowering to her knees, her eyes pinned to mine.

Lightning flashes and then thunder booms around us, and her hands go to my pants.

"Jules—"

"Can we please start here?" she asks. "I know you're in charge, but *please*?"

Christ, I couldn't deny her anything, ever.

"If my girl wants to suck my cock, who am I to say no?"

She licks her lips and opens my jeans, then reaches inside my boxer briefs and takes out my already hard dick.

Juliet doesn't hesitate. Her lips immediately wrap around the crown, and she licks the drop of precum out of the slit, making me groan.

"Eyes on me," I murmur as I sink my hands into her hair and fist them there. "Do you want me to fuck your throat, Wildfire?"

She hums, her eyes smile, and *Christ Jesus*, I'm turned on.

"You want me to take control, baby?"

She nods, and that's all the confirmation I need.

"If it gets to be too much, tap my leg."

She hollows her cheeks and sucks a little harder, narrowing her eyes at me.

"I'm serious, Juliet. Tap out if it's too much."

She rolls her eyes.

"I am going to fuck the sass right out of you."

My perfect wife wiggles with excitement, and I push into her mouth, hitting the back of her throat and making her gag.

"Relax your throat muscles, baby." I pull back, so she has just the crown, and then I push in again. I massage her jaw, encouraging her to relax, and soon, we find the perfect rhythm. Her throat opens beautifully, and I start to fuck her harder, making tears form in her eyes and spill over the sides.

But she clenches onto my ass, pulling me into her, and after gripping her curls again, I guide her up and down on my shaft.

"That's my girl. Fuck, your mouth is perfect. There is nothing better than pushing my dick down that tight little throat of yours."

She gags a little, but then recovers, and I keep going, thrusting into her until the tingling starts in my spine, and then I pull out.

"No!"

"I'm not coming in your mouth." I shake my head and pull her up from her knees as she wipes the spit off her chin. "I'm coming in your pussy, after you've made a fucking mess of my fingers first."

I sit in one of the chairs, then tug her over me, and before she can sink down onto my cock, I push two fingers deep inside her wet cunt and grin when they clench around me.

"God, your pussy's tight."

"It's so good." She rests her forehead against mine, riding my fingers. "God, you always hit the right spot. I can't stay like this. I'll lose my balance."

"Yes, you can."

She shakes her head, but I press my thumb to her clit, and it's my hands keeping her up as she shudders over me, coming so hard around my fingers, it's a wonder they don't break.

"Look at you. Christ, you're the most beautiful thing. You're dripping down my hand, baby."

She shudders again, and before she collapses on me, I pull my hand out, then line my cock up against her entrance and push up inside her, making us both groan.

"Fuuuuck, you take me so well," I growl against her lips. "So fucking perfect."

"Brooks."

"That's right. I'm the one inside you, baby." I take her face in one hand and kiss her softly as the other guides her up and down. "I want you to hear what I'm about to say to you."

"I'm listening," she whispers against my lips.

"A man's job is to calm storms, not create them. Do you hear me?"

Tears fill her eyes, and she nods, watching me.

"I'm the calm in every fucking storm. Me. If you're having a bad day, or a bad minute, or whatever, you let me help you. Because this—"

I surge up inside her, and she gasps.

"—is us. Do you hear the rain?"

"Yeah, I hear it."

"This is what you think about when it rains, Wildfire."

"How did I survive without you?" Her voice is broken as she collapses against me, her face in my neck. Her hips are still rocking. I'm buried so deep inside her, I don't know where I end and she begins. "How, Brooks?"

"It doesn't matter. The point is, we *did* survive, and we're here now."

"Thank fuck."

I plant my hands on her ass and lift her, then guide her back down again, and she gasps.

"Now, I want you to come all over this dick, baby."

She starts to move faster, harder, and when she leans back, I pull one of her nipples into my mouth, sucking hard.

"God, yes," she groans. "Shit, I'm gonna—"

"Do it." My voice is so hard now, and it only makes her clench around me harder. "Fucking come for me, Juliet. Right the fuck now."

Her orgasm rolls through her, pulls me with her, and we tumble over the edge together, gasping for breath, heaving, sweaty.

And when we start to come down the other side, I grip her chin in my fingers and pull her lips to mine.

"I love you, Wildfire."

"I love you, too."

Chapter Twenty-Seven

JULIET

When I glance at my phone after finishing with dinner prep, I notice that I missed another call from Chad. The attorney has called me twice this week, and I've missed them both. Whenever I call him back, he's in meetings, so we're playing a massive game of phone tag.

I assume that if it were an emergency, he'd say so in his voicemail, but I'm curious about what he has to tell me.

With a sigh, I tap on his number, and his receptionist, Rose, answers.

"This is Kincaid and Leonard, attorneys at law, Rose speaking."

"Hi, Rose, this is Juliet Blackwell. I missed another of Chad's calls."

"Boy, you two are having a hard time tracking each other down, aren't you? Well, it seems you're out of luck again because he's left for the day. He's in court for the rest of the afternoon."

"Of course, he is," I reply with a chuckle. "I'll try back tomorrow."

"Sounds good. He'll be in his office all day tomorrow."

"Thanks, Rose."

After hanging up, I take a deep breath and let it out slowly. I'm tired, but in a good way. I met Noah here at five this morning to get him acquainted with the kitchen and to discuss ideas for what to put in the case this week. I'm *so* happy that he took the job, and he's excited to get started, taking over the bread and sweet side of the menu. I'll handle it two days a week on his days off, which will be a huge weight taken off my shoulders.

I've decided to start going into the restaurant from midmorning through the afternoon to prep for lunch and dinner, and handle all the business side of things. I've also hired two more waitstaff, and I'm finally at a place where, with Christy as my new manager, I feel like Sage & Citrus is a well-oiled machine.

It makes me beyond happy.

"Okay, you guys are all prepped for dinner," I tell Tandy, who's building a salad for Harper. My friend will swing by for it on her way home from work. I wondered if, as she progressed through her pregnancy, she'd start craving other things, but she's still stuck like glue to this salad. "I also got all of the food put away from the shipment that came in, so there shouldn't be any issues, but you have my number if you need me."

"We won't need you," Erica says as she bustles by. "We're professionals now."

I laugh and nod in agreement. "You're the best. I

have such an amazing team. None of you can ever leave me."

"If Noah's here every morning," Tandy says, "you couldn't make me leave if you tried."

"No flirting with my pastry chef," I tell her, narrowing my eyes. "I mean it."

"Dammit," Tandy grumbles. "She's no fun at all."

I gather my things and leave the restaurant, walking toward home. Brooks should be home by about five, and I promised him that we'd have steak fajitas for dinner. I already have the meat in a marinade in the fridge.

I *love* cooking for my husband.

In fact, just thinking that thought makes me grin. I know it might sound like a cliché, the little woman cooking for her man, but I enjoy it. Food is my love language, and the fact that Brooks likes what I cook is just a huge bonus. My favorite part, though, is cleaning up together afterward—doing dishes, talking about our day, and making out in the kitchen.

Okay, making out with Brooks anywhere is my favorite thing. The man can *kiss*. And don't even get me started on the sex in the rain last week.

Holy shit, that's going to be a core memory for the rest of my life.

Once I'm home, I make sure that I have everything for dinner, just in case I have to make a last-minute run to the store, but all of the ingredients are here. I have a couple of hours before Brooks is due home, and I glance across the street, smiling at our house just across the street.

I want to go look around.

I haven't really spent any time over there by myself. I want to wander through and daydream a little. So I grab a tape measure out of the drawer, toss on a light zip-up hoodie and my sneakers, and set off across the street with my phone in my hand.

I'm not going to lie. I was hoping we'd find a secret room with a bunch of old stuff hidden inside. I mean, that could still happen. Brooks and the guys have been tearing everything apart as they have time, but it's not easy, and they have to be careful because the house is so old. We don't know what kind of stuff could be hidden in the walls. I don't want anyone breathing in something they shouldn't.

We're into November, and the days are getting *much* shorter, which means that it's already headed toward dusk, but I have about an hour of light left, which is just the right amount of time.

Brooks put a new lock on the front door with a keypad, so after I entered the code, I pushed inside and closed the door behind me, not locking it.

"Wow." My voice echoes through the house. All of the walls down here are pretty much down to the studs. I can see through to the kitchen, which really doesn't look like a kitchen anymore.

In fact, we could do literally *anything* down here. I wonder if we could open up the living room to the kitchen and create an open-concept space? I'd still want my library separate, though.

I plant my hands on my hips and gaze around, pondering it.

"Maybe these are load-bearing walls, though," I say

out loud. "And we can't take them down to make it open. I'll have to ask Brooks."

Walking into the kitchen, I feel my eyebrows climb in surprise.

"It's so big in here." The dark cabinets and wallpaper made it seem so small, but now that it's empty, I can see that it's much more spacious than I thought. Immediately, I open the Notes app on my phone and take some measurements.

I want an island in the middle the size of California, *without* a sink in it. I want all that counter space for baking. And I need the sink to be under the window, so I can stare out into the backyard while I do dishes.

There's enough room for a nice-sized butler's pantry, so I put that on the list. Then I open Pinterest to create a new vision board for the kitchen and pantry, pinning some ideas for that.

"I really need to consult with Ava. She'd have some great ideas in here."

My new best friend is an interior decorator and is actually working with Billie and Connor on the new condos up at the ski resort. Those condos are *super* expensive, and the uber rich expect them to be gorgeous inside. That's where Ava comes in. I haven't been up to see her handiwork yet, but I know she's killing it.

She'll help me with decorating this house.

Brooks said we have about four thousand square feet to work with in here, and that seems like a lot of space. There are two guest bedrooms on the first floor, but without sheetrock, I can't really make heads or tails of them, so I'll wait to daydream in there until I'm with my husband.

One of those rooms will be our office. The other will be a guest room. I don't know who might come stay with us, but it's nice to have the extra space, just in case.

I step outside and take in the backyard. I'll absolutely put a covered pergola over the concrete patio, similar to the one we have at the other house. I also want a water fountain.

No fish, though. I'd probably kill them.

With a smirk, I go back inside and head up the stairs, which have been reinforced. Probably a good idea.

My phone pings with a text from Brooks.

> Brooks: Hi, beautiful. Running about thirty minutes behind here. I'll call you when I'm on my way home.

When I reach the top of the steps, I fire off a response.

> Me: No worries at all, but thanks for letting me know. I'll see you soon! xo

In addition to it being later in the day, the clouds are low and heavy today, so it seems darker upstairs. They haven't started tearing out walls up here yet.

Starting in the primary suite and bathroom, I grin when I see the bed that Brooks and I spent our wedding night on. The linens, candles, and rose petals have all been cleared away, but the bed remains. The bathroom is still a hot mess.

I'll be glad to get all of the destruction out of here

and start brand new. Opening the app again, I start a board for primary suites and pin some ideas for bathrooms and closets. I don't need a huge closet like Billie. I am not a fashionista, and that's just fine with me, but we'll want something functional and nice.

Finally, I walk down the hall and spend some time in each of the smaller bedrooms.

Pulling my lip through my teeth, I ignore the creaking down below.

"It's an old house, Jules. They settle. They make a lot of noise."

It sounds like something falls downstairs, and I jump, but then cover my heart and try to slow my heartbeat.

"Just a loose board," I mutter, doing my best to believe it. "This is *our* house. Nothing can hurt us in here."

It's cold up here, and I tug my sweatshirt tight around me as I stride across the hall to the next bedroom and walk a slow circle, taking everything in. The walls are baby pink.

"This might have been someone's nursery."

The idea is a pang in the chest.

I want to have babies with Brooks. I always did. He'd be such an amazing dad, and I know we're in our late thirties now, but there's still time if we get started right away.

"We just got married," I remind myself as I walk over to run my hand down the white molding around the small closet. "He might not want babies yet."

But since we don't use protection when we have sex, and I am *not* on birth control, we'd better figure out what we want. Although if we didn't want kids, I think we would be more concerned about preventing pregnancy.

"This was someone's baby's room," I murmur and smile before walking farther down the hall, past another bathroom that needs to be gutted, to the last bedroom.

It's bigger than the other two and has tacks in the wall that no one ever bothered to remove.

"Probably a teenager who had posters on the wall."

I glance out the window, which looks out to the backyard, and then turn to look around the room again.

Something feels *off*.

"Why does this room feel smaller than it should?"

Frowning, I pace back and forth, then glance outside again.

The window is only about a foot away from the interior wall perpendicular to it. However, when I look outside, I can see that the wall should be about six feet away, as the outside extends much farther.

But there's no door.

I knock around on the wall, and then feel when I hit a solid spot.

That's not a wall.

"I need a hammer."

I push my phone into my back pocket and hurry downstairs to where I saw one leaning against the wall by the back door, then head back upstairs with it.

These walls are coming down anyway. There's no reason I can't start now.

I take a swing where the solid spot was, and the drywall starts to fall away. It's brittle. I cover my mouth and nose with my sweatshirt, but soon I'm too hot from all of the swinging, so I shed the sweatshirt, and then grin.

Because I just found a freaking *door*.

"This is what I'm TALKING ABOUT!" I yell as I dance in a circle. "A secret door! I'm absolutely not waiting around for Brooks. I need to know what's back there."

I have to chip away at more of the drywall, but soon, I'm able to shimmy the door open, and when I grab my phone out of my pocket and turn the flashlight on, I see a stairway that goes up.

"There's an *attic*?"

I frown and poke my head around the corner so I can shine the light up to see where it leads.

Sure enough, there's an attic up there, and it looks like it's full.

"Sold. Going up."

But there are a lot of cobwebs. I'm refusing to call them spiderwebs. I'm in denial that there could be a whole family of big-ass spiders up there.

No. Just no.

Gingerly, I climb the stairs. They're not … great. But they're holding me as I climb, and when I get eye level with the floor, my eyes widen and I let out a low whistle.

"Holy fucking jackpot, Batman."

There are trunks, stacks of newspapers, old toys, and a stroller that looks like it held a baby a hundred years ago.

I climb the rest of the way and pick up a newspaper, and once I clear about an inch of dust away, I see the date.

August 7, 1964.

But then, in the back corner, are more newspapers, and once I make my way around a ton of stuff, I see that they are dated twenty years prior to that, announcing the end of the Second World War.

"Crazy," I whisper, shaking my head. "This is a fucking treasure trove."

I'm giddy at the thought of opening all the boxes, the trunks, and the bags. Obviously, I can't do all of that tonight. It's starting to get dark, and I need to go home and take a shower before I cook dinner.

Checking the time on my phone, I see that Brooks should be headed home soon, too.

It's time to set this all aside for another day, but man, it's *cool.* I direct the light to the other side of the attic. It must span the entire house, and every square inch is full of stuff, with just little paths here and there for walking. I'm standing on old two-by-fours, and as I start to make my way back to the stairs, the wood beams give out beneath me.

"Ahhh!"

I scream as I fall through the floor. Pain shoots up my leg, the crash is almost deafening, and I lose my phone. But I don't fall all the way through.

My hips catch on something, with my legs hanging down through the ceiling below me. I cough because of all the dust and God-knows-what that just got kicked up. My heart pounds, I have tears in my eyes, and my leg is on *fire.*

My phone rings, and it's Brooks's ringtone, but it sounds far away.

With my heart in my throat, I search around me. "Come on, I need you to come help me."

I sound out of my mind. My voice is shrill and full of panic.

"WHERE IS MY PHONE??"

It rings again, and I'm able to look down between my legs and see my phone, face up, on the floor below.

"No." Tears spring to my eyes. "Oh shit, I'm in trouble. I'm in so much trouble."

Did I tell Brooks I was here?

I think back on our texts. No. I didn't. I just told him I'd see him soon.

Oh God.

I can feel blood running down my left leg, and I can even hear it dripping on the hardwood below. The ache in that leg has its own heartbeat. It fucking *hurts*.

"I hope that blood doesn't hit my phone."

My laughter at that thought sounds hysterical.

I'm stuck here, hanging half in, half out of an attic that no one even knew existed. It's getting dark, and *no one knows where I am*. And I'm worried about blood messing up my phone.

I'm so fucked.

Chapter Twenty-Eight
BROOKS

"Honey, I'm home!" I grin as I walk through the kitchen. I expected to see Jules in here, starting dinner, just because she said she was making my favorite tonight, but she must be in the shower or something. She didn't answer my call on the way home, but I didn't think too much of it.

Although she never called me back, either.

Frowning, I saunter down the hallway to our bedroom, then through to our bathroom.

No Jules.

"Jules?" I call out as I pull my phone out of my pocket and dial her number again. It rings and rings, then goes to voicemail.

After checking the backyard and confirming she's not here, I call the restaurant.

"Sage & Citrus, this is Christy."

"Hey, it's Brooks. Is Jules still there?"

"Oh no, she left a couple of hours ago."

"If she calls, or pops in there, will you please tell her I'm looking for her?"

"Of course. Hey, maybe she stopped at the bookstore. Sometimes she gets caught chatting in there."

Okay, my heart calms down with that reminder. "Good thought, I'll call there. Thanks, Christy."

After hanging up, I call my sister, who answers on the third ring.

"Hi, biggest brother, what's up?"

"Are you at the bookstore?"

"Yep." She pops the P at the end of the word.

"Is Jules there?"

"No, I haven't seen her."

What in the actual fuck?

"Is everything okay?" Billie asks, her voice turning more serious.

"I don't know. I can't find her, and she's not answering my calls or texts. She's not at home and not at the restaurant. If she's not with you, where could she be?"

"The grocery store? The post office? A doctor's appointment?"

"Okay, you've made your point, but she was going to meet me here. At home. Something's not right, Bee."

"Take a deep breath. I'll try calling her too."

"I'm calling the brothers."

I hang up and call each of my brothers, but every single one of them says they haven't seen or heard from her either.

When I hang up with my parents with the same result, I want to throw my phone across the room.

Because panic is starting to set in. Where. *The fuck.* Is my wife?

"Fuck!"

Something is wrong. Jules doesn't disappear like this. She always has her phone on her or returns my call fairly quickly.

There's a knock on my front door, but before I can open it, Billie comes striding through with Beckett and Skyla on her heels.

"We're all coming to help," Beck says. "How long has she been missing?"

"We don't know—" Billie begins, but I cut her off.

"She left the restaurant a couple of hours ago. I was supposed to meet her here."

Bridger and Dani file in, and then Harper and Blake behind them. Blake's still in scrubs, and he's scowling.

"Where the fuck is she?" he demands.

"We don't know yet," Billie replies.

"Maybe she went for one of her walks and forgot her phone?" Skyla asks.

"Her phone isn't here," I reply.

"But it's not impossible," Bridger adds. "I'll make some calls."

He steps out of the room, and all I can do is stare at the people I love so much.

"I don't know what to do." I rub my chest, over where my heart thumps in overtime. "Fuck, I don't know what to do."

"She's fine," Billie insists. "She's just not hearing her phone. Maybe she really did have to run to the store."

"She'd be back my now," I growl. "I'm going to tear this town apart."

"No need," Bridge says, shaking his head. "I just spoke with Chase Wild. He's getting some eyes out there, in case she's taking that walk."

"I'm texting Christy," Billie adds. "Just asked her to check the upstairs of the restaurant."

Harper flips on my lights, since the sun has gone down and it's getting dark.

"She could be hurt," I mutter, my hands moving in and out of fists, as I pace back and forth in the living room. "What if her car went off the road?"

"Her car is in the driveway," Blake reminds me. "I'll call the hospital and see if anyone with her description is in the ER."

He walks away to make that call.

When my own phone rings, I blink at Chase's name and answer it. "Please tell me you found her."

"I'm sorry, no. I'm checking in to see if she came home."

"No, not yet. Can I file a missing person's report?"

"Not until it's been twenty-four hours." His voice is grim. "But I have our guys looking for her unofficially while they're out on patrol. Tell me what you know."

I run it down for him, feeling the frustration swell as I go through it all over again, my family listening in.

"Let's keep each other posted," Chase says. "I'm sure she's fine. We just have to find her."

I hang up, and our gazes fly to the front door when it opens, and Millie and Holden walk in.

Fuck.

343

"We drove all over town just now," Holden says grimly. "We didn't see her."

"I'm going out of my motherfucking *mind*."

"I get it." Holden claps me on the shoulder, and I know he does.

Millie was missing once, trapped in a deep hole on his property, and we all rallied together to find her, riding our horses over a hundred thousand acres. Holden was as out of his mind as I am now.

"Who has Birdie and Bryce?" I ask Dani.

"Your parents. They're on standby, and want to be updated, but we didn't want the kids here when everyone's afraid."

I nod and let out a breath.

Come on, Wildfire. Where the fuck are you?

I'm going to spank her ass until it glows for scaring me like this.

The door opens again, and Connor strides in, followed by Miller and Simon, his security team.

It's a full fucking house.

"Any word?" Connor asks me as he presses a kiss to his wife's forehead.

"No."

"If you give me Juliet's cell number, I can track her location," Simon says, pulling his laptop out of a bag I didn't notice him carrying. "As long as it's on, I can see where she is."

Thank fuck.

He boots up the computer, and I stand behind him as I give him her number.

"It takes just a minute," he murmurs.

I push my hands through my hair and look up at the ceiling, but then Miller, who's looking over Simon's shoulder, says, "Has anyone checked the house across the street?"

Not bothering to answer or even look at anyone else, I take off at a sprint, through the door and across the street.

She'd better be okay.

Chapter Twenty-Nine

JULIET

It's so fucking cold in here.

I'm shivering, and my teeth are chattering. My legs both went numb long ago. I don't have any idea how long I've been suspended up here, but it got dark a while ago, and let me just tell you right now, it's scary as fuck in a secret attic after dark.

The noises are the worst. The skittering. The creaking. At one point, I thought I heard voices, but it turned out to just be me talking to myself.

I might be going crazy.

Or going into shock.

Maybe this is what hypothermia feels like because I'm *so damn cold*.

Every once in a while, my phone will ping with a text, or Brooks's ringtone will start to play because he's trying to call me, and it makes me cry because I know he has to be worried. If the roles were reversed, I'd be terrified and tearing the world apart to find him.

He'll find me.

Eventually.

Will I still be alive when he does? I mean, I know that sounds dramatic, but no one knows the attic exists, and I didn't tell anyone that I was coming over to the house.

So stupid.

For about the tenth time, I try to wiggle my way back up, but the piece of wood that cut the hell out of my leg is still embedded in the skin, and when I try to work it back up, it hurts all over again.

Not to mention, I'm so cold that I'm numb in half of my body, and my arms don't want to work.

The dark is the worst. If it were light outside, it would still suck, but it wouldn't be this scary. This *creepy.*

That's an understatement.

"This is terrifying."

Something skitters over the floor behind me, and I gasp, then let out a whimper.

"Go away," I say, but my voice is scratchy because for the first hour or so, I screamed my ass off.

No one came.

My phone rings, and when I look down between my legs to the floor below, I see that it's Chad returning my call.

"Sorry, Chad. I'm a little hung up."

I giggle at the thought. I've officially lost my marbles. And when something moves next to me, I scream, flailing my arms, hoping that I knock whatever the hell it is across the room.

"I want out of here!" I yell and try to drag myself out

of this hole once more, gritting my teeth when the wood drags through my flesh. "Fuck, that hurts."

I'm tired. I kind of want to sleep since I'm so cold. My eyes are so heavy, and my body is tingly. I can't feel my lips anymore.

And my fingertips feel funny.

Suddenly, something crashes somewhere in the house, and then I hear Brooks scream out, "JULIET! JULIET!"

Oh God, he's here.

"Help!" I try to yell, but it comes out as a croak. "Help!"

I clear my throat and try again.

"HELP! UPSTAIRS!"

Footsteps thunder below me. More than just Brooks is here.

"Help!" I cry out again, tears running down my face now. "Please help."

"Jules?"

I'm looking down between my legs, and I can feel when someone runs into the room. I'm over the pink bedroom. Suddenly, I can see the glow of a flashlight, and then it's shining up into my eyes.

"Ah!"

"Baby! Fuck, how did you get up there? You're bleeding!"

I'm hyperventilating again. Sobbing. "Stairs. Back bedroom."

He runs away, taking the light with him, but then more people are below me with more flashlights.

"We're all here, Jules." That's Blake's voice. "We've

got you, pretty girl. Take a deep breath for me. I see the blood. Where are you hurt, gorgeous?"

"Leg." I swallow hard. "Hips hurt. So cold."

"You're cold?" he asks. God, his voice is so calm.

"Yeah. T-shirt." My voice sounds weird to my own ears.

"Fuck, we need blankets," he calls out to someone.

I'm shaking again, and then I hear Brooks behind me. I didn't hear him come up the stairs.

"For fuck's sake, Wildfire." He doesn't sound mad. He sounds like he can't believe what he's seeing.

"I'm s-s-sorry. I just wanted to look, and—"

"You can tell me later," he says gently. "I have to walk carefully. It won't do us any good if we both fall through. Are you okay? Talk to me, baby."

"Please don't fall." I can't see him. I want to see him *so bad*. "Brooks, don't you dare fall. I will be so fucking mad if you hurt yourself. It's not safe up here. Just pass me some blankets and come back for me when it's light out tomorrow morning."

Oh God, please don't leave me here all night.

"You're delirious," he says. "If you think I'll leave you here like this, you're hurt worse than—"

"Brooks." My voice cracks. "Please hold me. Can't you just hold me?"

"I'm coming. Talk to me, baby. How badly are you hurt?"

"So cold. I'm so c-cold."

He shines his light over to me. "You're only in a T-shirt? Shit, it must be under forty degrees in here."

"So cold." My voice is smaller. "Please get me."

349

"Holy fucking shit." That's Beckett behind me, at the top of the attic stairs. "We shouldn't all be walking on that. We're too big, Brooks."

"I'm taking it slow," Brooks tells him.

"We'll go get ladders," Bridger says. "And see if we can pull her through from below."

"My leg," I call out. "I'm cut, and the wood is still inside me."

"*Baby*," Brooks says, his voice full of anguish.

"Ladders," Bridger says again, and I hear them clomping back down the stairs.

"I'm going to be here a while," I whisper.

"I'm with you." His voice is getting closer, like he's not up on his feet, but maybe … *crawling?* "I'm making my way over to you, Juliet."

"I'm really tired," I reply.

"Don't you dare fall asleep."

"We have blankets down here," Blake calls up. "I'm bringing them up to you guys."

"You have to be careful," Brooks yells back, but someone's already on the stairs. "Just throw it over."

"Shit, that's a long throw for a blanket," Blake says grimly.

I can't see anything, but they must make it work, because suddenly, Brooks says, "Okay, baby, I'm going to toss this your way. I'm not too far from you, but I can't put it around you myself."

"Okay." I manage to get my fingers to work to scoop the clean blanket around me, and I shiver. "Legs are numb."

Suddenly, someone must have set up some kind of light in the room below because the attic is illuminated and cast in shadows from a bright light below.

I twist so I can see Brooks, and his face is ... *devastated* as he takes me in.

"God, baby, I want to scoop you up and get you the fuck out of here."

He's closer than I thought, and I stretch out, hoping he can hold my hand.

Brooks tries, but he's about three inches too far away.

"I need you." My lips tremble as I start to cry. "I need you to touch me."

"I know, baby. The guys have to get a look at you from below so we can figure out how we're going to get you out of here."

There are flashing lights coming from outside, and my eyes widen.

"Bridger called in the fire trucks?"

"Probably an ambulance and some cops, too. Chase Wild's been helping us find you. We made the girls stay outside, and they're *not* happy about it."

"I don't want the pregnant girls in here," I reply, shaking my head. "Brooks?"

"Yes, my love."

"Can we have babies?" I press my lips together and look back to see his face. "I want babies. And we're not getting younger, and I just—"

"You want to talk about this *now*?"

"I've been thinking about it a lot." My voice is a whisper.

"Wildfire, I'll give you all the babies you want. Absolutely, let's have a dozen kids, but we have to get you out of here first."

I bite my lip, and then I hear a commotion below me.

"Okay, Jules, we have ladders down here," Bridger says. "Beckett and I are going to be next to your legs and hips, trying to see how we can get you down. I hope these aren't your favorite jeans because they're torn to shit."

"I can live without them. Thank you," I call down to them.

But someone tries to move my injured leg, and it makes me cry out as pain lances through me.

"I'm going to dismember whoever just hurt my wife," Brooks bellows. "Be careful down there!"

"They can't help it," I say while tears track down my cheeks. "It's deep, Brooks. It's really bad."

"Hey. Wildfire, you look at me. It's going to be okay. Do you hear me?"

"What if it's not okay?"

"That's not an option. Guys? How does it look down there?"

"We're going to get a saw to get this wood that's in her leg. Her hips are hung up on the two-by-fours on either side of her, which have not given out."

"See? I have birthing hips. Saved my life. Or a broken leg," I say, trying to lighten the mood, but Brooks's face is mutinous.

"It's not safe to pull her up into the attic," he growls at his brothers.

"We can cut the wood around her hips and help her down," Bridger says, his voice perfectly calm. "We'll run the electrical across the street from your house, like we did for this light. I had guys from the fire station bring our extra-long cords over."

"You guys didn't have to do all of this."

"Uh, Jules?" Bridger says. "You're my sister. You're part of our family and community. Of *course*, we're going to do whatever we need to do to get you out of here as safely as possible. You're going to be okay, and we're not going to injure you any more than you already are. Blake's still down here with all kinds of medical junk to help, too."

"As soon as they get the wood separated from the ceiling," Blake calls up, "I'm going to have to remove it and cover the wounds so you don't bleed anymore. We'll treat you for any infection at the hospital. Are you bleeding anywhere else?"

I swallow. "Before they went numb, my hands were bleeding from catching myself in the fall."

Brooks growls next to me, and I try to offer him an encouraging smile.

"We need to warm her up better," Blake says. "She's still too cold."

"If this goes as planned, we'll have her out of here in less than thirty minutes," Bridger tells him.

"I'm so scared," I whisper. Brooks is still inching along, and he's finally close enough to take my hand in his. He brings it up to his lips, careful not to hurt the scrapes on my palm.

"Blake," I say loud enough for him to hear.

"Right here, gorgeous."

I swallow hard, and Brooks squeezes my fingers. It's

warming up, and it feels good even though my palm aches.

Blake was always a flirt. I kind of love that we have a doctor in the family.

"This is going to hurt, isn't it?"

Chapter Thirty

BROOKS

"Yeah, pretty girl, I'm not going to lie to you, this is going to hurt. Actually, I can work on getting an IV going and put some pain meds in it. I can also get warm fluids going. That'll help warm you up. I'm going to run out to the ambulance, and I'll be right back."

"He's smart," Jules says as she glances over at me. *Fuck*, her eyes are still so scared. They were glassy when I first got up here, with cold and shock and fear. All of that is still there, but with me here next to her, she's calming down a bit.

I hate that she's in this filth. It's so fucking dirty up here. I saw a squirrel run across the other side, and there's definitely some feces up here.

I do *not* want her anywhere near this mess.

"Blake will get you set up," I assure her. "Baby, we're going to burn this house down. We're not going to live here. At the very least, I'll sell it as-is."

"You're taking my house away?" Her beautiful blue

eyes fill with tears again, and it's almost my undoing. "No. Please, Brooks, it'll be okay."

"Baby, it's so much work, and it *hurt you.*"

"It's not the house's fault."

"I'm back," Blake calls out. "Beck and Bridge are getting what they need to cut you out of there, so that gives us time to make sure you're not in pain, sweet girl. Unfortunately, I have to put the IV in your foot."

"Jesus Christ," I mutter as Jules scowls.

"In my *foot?*"

"I can't reach your arms," he reminds her. "It'll be a quick poke, and then it'll be over. You have great veins here."

She grins, and then giggles. "Stop tickling my foot."

"Keep flirting with my wife, and see where it gets you."

I can practically hear him roll his eyes. "I'm *touching* her foot," he says. "That's involved in placing an IV. Okay, quick poke."

"That's what *he* said," she whispers, making me smile.

At least she still has her sense of humor.

She winces, but then her face calms.

"That was easy," Blake says. "I'm going to pass the bag of fluid to you because they need to be up high. Can you reach down to grab it?"

"I think so." She catches her tongue between her teeth and reaches down, and then she has the bag in her hand. "Got it. Wow, it's warm."

"I can add the medicine down here."

"Oh, that's nice. I feel a little floaty. And my leg doesn't hurt."

"Good. Hey, Brooks?"

"Yeah." I wish I could see him, but I'm not willing to leave her. I need to be up here, by her side.

"She's cut on the outside of her thigh from her knee to almost her hip. I can see where the wood has sliced into her. The bleeding is mostly stopped, but that wood is still sitting pretty deep in her upper thigh. I'm tempted to say we leave it in there and we get it out in the ER."

"Jesus." I pull my hand down my face.

"I want it out, Blake. I don't want to wait for the ER."

"Let's see how things go down here, okay?"

Finally, Bridger and Beckett return with saws and tools, and after an hour of painstaking work, Jules is cut free, and my brothers lower her to the floor.

I back out of the attic slowly, not wanting to be the next victim of this cursed house. Finally, when I'm down with Jules, and she's on the stretcher, I tug her against my chest and kiss the top of her head.

"I love you so much," I growl into her ear. "You were so fucking badass up there."

"Let's get her to the hospital," Blake says. "I can't treat you there, sweetheart, because you're my sister-in-law, but I'll be there."

Jules nods, and Bridger and his team whisk us out of the house, taking her carefully down the stairs that I'm *so* glad we reinforced last week.

"Oh my God!" Harper cries out as we step onto the porch. "Oh, sweetie, are you okay?"

"We love you so much," Skyla says, brushing away tears.

"Jules." Billie's crying, but Jules reaches for her.

"I'm okay, Bug. I'm okay, friends."

"Where is she?" Ava demands as she comes running onto the property. "Where's my girl?"

"Hey." Jules smiles at all of them, and then her pretty blue eyes fill with tears again. "I'll be okay."

"We have to go," Bridger says. "She'll be home soon, and then you all can spoil her."

"Good," Dani says, and they all huddle together as they watch us leave. "We'll come see you as soon as you're home!"

"I love them all so much," Jules whispers.

"We all love you back, Wildfire."

Chapter Thirty-One

JULIET

Brooks was afraid to leave me home alone today while he went to work. In fact, I've been home for two days, and I'm feeling *much* better, but he still didn't want to leave me.

He didn't have to worry.

Because I have people in our house pretty much around the clock, whether he's home or not. Harper and Ava just left after dropping by with breakfast from my restaurant. They stayed for an hour, chatting and eating with me, making sure I was okay before they left to each go to work.

My crew has been incredible. Noah's fine with working on the baking side of things for the foreseeable future even though I assured him I'll be back next week. My staff has basically informed me that they can handle everything for as long as I need them to.

They're sweet, and I appreciate it, but I'll be going back to work as soon as the doctor gives me the okay.

I've just hobbled out of the bathroom—shit, this leg

still hurts like a bitch—when my phone rings with a Face-Time call from Darby.

With a smile, I sit on the couch and accept the call.

"Hey, friend."

"I hear you're causing all kinds of trouble over there," she says with a frown. "Falling through ceilings and having séances and shit."

I snort at that. "No séances but falling through the ceiling is true enough." I reach for my water and take a sip. "That wasn't fun, let me tell you. I assume your sisters filled you in?"

"Yeah, and it scared the shit out of all of us."

"Same, girl. Same. But I'm going to be okay. I need to rest for about a week, and then I'll be able to return to work. My leg took the worst of it. Bad cut up the outside of my thigh, thanks to a jagged piece of rotten wood."

"Yikes." She winces.

"I'll have a gnarly scar, but as long as I don't get an infection, it'll be okay."

"I have a little concoction that I make for scars. I'll send you some. It's just coconut oil and vitamin E and some other stuff, but it really helps."

"Hey, I'll take it." I smile at her. "When do you get to come home for good again?"

"Probably not until the spring," she replies. "But I've applied for several internships, and I'm just waiting to hear if I get hired for any of them. They're all around that area."

"You could work with your brother."

Holden co-owns the biggest cattle ranch in Montana with the Wild family.

"They must have a ton of large animals."

"They do, but I do *not* want to work for my brother. Don't get me wrong, I love him, but he's stubborn, and I'm stubborn, and I want to continue loving him."

I laugh and nod in agreement. "I can see that. Did Ava ever get you info for her brother's ranch?"

"Actually, yes. That's one that I applied for."

"Cool. Well, I'm excited to have you home for good. You must be busting your ass because you look tired."

"I don't sleep a lot," she admits. "And yeah, the work is grueling. But I do love it. I was up all night helping a horse have a baby. It's not the right time of year for that, but here we are."

"That's pretty awesome." My eyes are getting heavy because my pain medicine is kicking in. "I'd better go take a nap."

"You do that, and I'll send you the ointment."

"Thanks, Darby."

"You bet."

After I hang up, I don't even bother going into the bedroom to nap. I just lean my head back on the couch, prop my feet up on the ottoman in front of me, and close my eyes.

"Don't wake her up." That's a whisper shout that makes my lips twitch. "We'll just leave it and go."

"I'm awake." I flutter my eyes open and find Dani

and Skyla trying to sneak to the front door. "What are you guys doing?"

"So sorry," Dani says, turning back to me. "We didn't know you were sleeping, and the door was unlocked, and—"

"It's really okay. Honest." I check the time. "I slept for like two hours. Come on in and chat with me."

"We brought you lunch." Skyla holds up a bag to show me before stowing it in my fridge.

"And books," Dani adds, gesturing to the stack on the ottoman in front of me that I didn't even notice. "Billie just sent a bunch that she thinks you'll enjoy. That one on top? *The Empress* by Michelle Heard? *So good.* Also, it's the next book club book."

"I'll read it next." I eye the cover. It's *pretty.* "We read a lot of Mafia romance. I'm not mad about it."

"I couldn't agree more," Skyla says with a laugh as she sits across from me and crosses her legs. "How do you feel?"

"Tired from the medication. Sore. *Really* fucking sore, but don't tell Brooks because I kind of told a white lie and insisted that I was fine and he should go to work today."

"It's only been a few days," Dani says with a frown. "It's okay for him to stay here and take care of you."

"I can get around just fine."

Dani shakes her head. "I don't think you understand. When we couldn't find you, Brooks was so distraught. I've never seen him like that before. He looked—"

"Like one of the unhinged men from our books," Skyla adds. "It honestly broke my heart."

My poor husband.

"So maybe it's not that he thinks he needs to take care of you physically, as much as he just needs to be with you," Dani finishes. "Just to reassure himself that you're okay. What you both went through is traumatic, my friend."

She's right. It *is* traumatic. I'm still having some nightmares, and every time I do, Brooks wakes up with me and holds me until I calm down.

"Shit, I might have messed up."

"Nah, just text him and tell him you want him here with you after all. It'll make you both feel better."

Biting my lip, I reach for my phone and open our text thread.

> Me: Hey, my love. If you're not too busy at the garage today, would you mind coming home early to be with me? I might have overestimated my willingness to be without you so soon.

I smile and show them both what I said.

"Aw, that's perfect," Skyla says. "Our guys are care-takers. They want to help us."

"You're right," I reply with a nod. "The Blackwell men have always been like that."

"*Always*," Dani confirms. "And they're so good at it."

"I guess I felt guilty keeping him home for another day. I know his business is important, and honestly, I'm okay to be alone."

"But you don't have to be. Brooks is the boss, and

one of the perks is being able to take as much time off as he needs," Dani replies.

I grin over at them. "Can you believe we all married Blackwell men?"

"Best thing I ever did," Skyla says. "I couldn't love anyone more."

But then she pats her slightly rounded belly.

"Well, maybe I could love someone just as much."

"Okay, I have a question," Dani says, looking right at me. "Do you still want to live in that house, after everything that happened?"

I lick my lips and take a deep breath. "Yeah, I do. But Brooks and I discussed it at length yesterday, and rather than trying to do a lot of it ourselves, we're going to hire a construction company to finish the demo, clear out that attic, and rebuild for us. It's not worth someone getting hurt again. We should leave the construction to the professionals."

"That's a *really* good idea," Skyla replies. "And then, once it's all finished and new, the bad memories will be gone."

Nodding, I sip my water again. "We're going to make sure no one can ever use that attic again. Get the rodents out of there, remove the stairway, and close it up. We don't need it."

The girls and I chat for another fifteen minutes or so, and I don't hear back from Brooks, but he's probably bent over an engine right now, and he'll reply when he can.

When my friends leave, I grab that new Mafia book and dig in.

Chapter Thirty-Two

BROOKS

I want to call or text her constantly to check in, but in case she's sleeping, I don't want to disturb her.

I should *not* have come to work today. Jules assured me that she was feeling better and that she's fine on her own, but *I'm not fine*.

I'm not okay at all.

My girl continues to have nightmares, waking up terrified and whimpering, and I hold her, reassuring her that nothing like that will ever happen again. The entire experience is one I wouldn't wish on my worst enemy. I'll never get the sight of her, suspended in that floor and freezing, bleeding, and in pain, out of my head.

It'll haunt me until the day I die.

"Why are you here, boss?" Mitch says as he saunters over my way.

"I own this business," I remind him as I close the hood of an old Camero. "And it's a workday."

"Come on," he says with a sigh. "When things are bad at home, you always tell me that I should go take care of my wife. Same goes. I can see it written all over your face that you'd rather be with her. You're worried about her, and I get it. So go take care of your wife."

I swallow and nod just as a text comes in. Checking my phone, I see that it's from my wildfire.

> Wildfire: Hey, my love. If you're not too busy at the garage today, would you mind coming home early to be with me? I might have overestimated my willingness to be without you so soon.

The rough edges I've been carrying around all day suddenly smooth right out, and I look up at my friend.

"I'm going home."

"Good. Tell her I hope she's feeling better."

Without replying to her text, I simply get in my truck to head home. As I pull into the driveway, I see Dani and Skyla pulling away. They both wave at me, and I wave back before parking and striding into the house.

When I get to the living room, I can't help but stop and just stare at her. She's reading a book, her candle is lit again, and her leg is propped up on the ottoman in front of her. She's been wearing shorts because having anything brush against the wound irritates it even though it's still covered in gauze.

"Hey, baby."

She startles, but then she smiles at me. *She doesn't look like she's about to have a panic attack.*

We're making huge progress.

"Sorry, I was absorbed in this story already. You came home."

I cross to her and brace myself on my hands against the back of the couch on either side of her head, then lean in to kiss her softly.

"You needed me, so of course I came home. I'm going to take a quick shower, and then I'm all yours."

"If my leg wasn't an asshole, I'd join you."

I narrow my eyes at her. "Don't talk about my wife like that. I'll be right back."

She grins, and I kiss her forehead before I stride down to our bedroom to strip out of my clothes and get into a hot shower to get the smell of motor oil off me. When I return to her, she's still reading, and I sit on the couch next to her, pull her against me, and kiss her temple.

"Better?" she asks me.

"So much better. I didn't want to go in this morning in the first place."

She looks up at me and bites her lower lip. "I know. I felt bad, though, keeping you away from work."

"Never feel bad." I drag my knuckles down her cheek and neck. "You're the number one priority, always. I'm happy to be here with you. Have you had a million visitors already? I saw Dani and Skyla leaving."

"Yeah." She sighs happily. "Some of the girls came by to feed me and bring me books. I texted Christy and Noah, and they've both got things handled at work. I even managed to take a nap for a while."

"You've been busy."

She smirks at that. "Right. Busy. I feel guilty for being so *lazy*. But at the same time, it kind of feels good."

"You need the rest so you can heal," I remind her. "How's your pain?"

"Not bad. I took something earlier. That's why I napped for so long. I don't think I'll take the meds after today. Ibuprofen should work fine."

I frown and brush the pad of my thumb over her lower lip. "Use them if you need them. It's only been a couple of days."

She nods and then settles in next to me, nuzzling my chest, and her perfect little hand roams down to push under my shirt so she can touch my stomach.

What is it with women and abs?

"Brooks ..."

I know that voice.

"No."

"Babe, I'm *fine.*"

"I'm not fucking you, Juliet."

She sighs and frowns up at me. She's so fucking adorable, I can't resist kissing the tip of her nose.

"Okay, don't fuck me then. Make love to me. Come on, it's been *days,* and I'm feeling better."

"You're injured. It hurts for you to bend your knee, baby. I refuse to make you hurt any more than you already are."

"It hurts that I can't be intimate with you more than my leg aches," she admits. "You won't hurt me."

"No lying to me." I shake my head. "If it gets worse, you have to tell me."

Her eyes widen and sparkle with lust. "Is that a yes?"

"Why can't I ever say no to you?"

"Because you love me?"

"I don't think that's it."

She grins so big, it lights up the whole room.

"Come on." I stand and take her by the hand, pulling her to her feet. "Let's go to our bed, where we have more space."

"I'll follow you anywhere," she murmurs as she climbs to her feet, and we take it slow, walking to the bedroom. "Wait. Go lock the doors, please. The girls have been just walking in, which is fine if we're *not* making babies in here."

I smirk and leave her where she is, then hurry over to lock both the front and the back doors. Then I return to my wife and lead her the rest of the way to the bedroom.

"Jules, I'm serious. If this hurts too much, just say so. It won't hurt my feelings."

"It might hurt *my* feelings," she replies and pushes her hands under my shirt again. "Please take this off. I like seeing your chest and abs all muscly and hard."

No pressure.

I can never stop going to the gym. I want my girl to always look at me like this.

I shed the shirt and then the lounge pants I pulled on after my shower. I'm already hard as fuck, but that's just my permanent state whenever I'm around this woman.

It's been this way since we were sixteen.

"Do you remember the first time we did this?" I whisper, pushing my fingers into her soft, golden curls and tucking them behind her ear.

"Of course, I do." She leans in to press her lips over my heart. "We were both so nervous."

"It feels like that right now."

369

Her eyes jump to mine, wide and surprised. "Why?"

"Because I don't want to hurt you, and I'm not sure how to navigate this."

Juliet's beautiful face softens, and her hands glide up to frame my face. "You won't hurt me. You would never hurt me. I want you to hold me when I'm not coming out of a nightmare. I can spread my legs without it hurting, babe."

I want that, too. I've been so fucking worried about her, I haven't even thought about sex. I just wanted to make sure she was healing and whole.

But now, her nipples are puckered, and her cheeks are rosy. If my wife needs to come, I'll fucking make her come.

Several times.

"Let's get you naked so I can worship your gorgeous-as-fuck body," I growl against her lips, my hands fisting in the hem of her T-shirt and dragging it up her torso. She raises her arms, and I cast the shirt aside. Then I unfasten her bra, and she lets it fall to the floor. "I love your tits. I always have."

I cup them in my hands and roll the nipples between my fingers, making her sigh and tip her head back, exposing her neck. I can't resist leaning in to nibble her there, and grin when goose bumps break out at the touch of my lips.

"God, that feels good," she whimpers, leaning into me.

My hands glide down her sides to the elastic waist of her shorts, and I nudge them down her legs, careful that they don't brush over her injury. When she's finally naked, I cup her sex and growl against her neck.

"So fucking wet for me, Wildfire."

"Always." She swallows hard when one finger slips through her lips and circles her entrance.

I pull away, making her pout, but I want her on the bed.

"Such a greedy fucking girl," I growl against her mouth before biting her lower lip. "I want you to lie down and get as comfortable as possible. Right in the middle of our bed."

She sits and winces, but then wiggles to the middle and lies down, sighing happily.

"How do you feel?"

"Horny as hell," she replies and crooks her finger at me. "Come here, husband."

Well, that'll make my cock hard, if it wasn't already.

With a grin, I climb onto the bed at her uninjured side, careful not to touch her other leg, and pepper kisses from her lips to her ear.

"You're such a fucking temptress, Wildfire."

She gasps as my hand drifts down her belly to her sopping wet core.

"Do you want my fingers, baby? Or my mouth?"

"Your cock."

"That wasn't one of the options right now." Nibbling the ball of her shoulder, I make my way down to her breasts and lick one nipple before moving over to the other one. "Fingers or mouth, Juliet?"

"Mouth." She pushes her fingers into my hair. "Holy shit, this is the best medicine ever."

I chuckle against her and kiss down to her belly button. She's pushed her legs wide, and I look up to watch her face as I nudge my way between them.

"Where's your pain, baby?"

"I'm okay. I really am. Please don't stop."

Her pussy is swollen and pink and so fucking wet as I lower my face and lap up her sweet juices, sliding my tongue through her lips and up to her clit.

Jules arches her back and moans, her hand still in my hair.

"You taste like a motherfucking dream," I growl against her slit. "Like you're *mine*."

"I *am* yours," she reminds me. "Always. Forever. Fuck, Brooks."

Sliding two fingers inside her, I rub that rough patch that makes her legs shake, but then pull them out and frown up at her.

"Pain?"

"If you stop again—"

"What's your pain level, Juliet?"

She bites her lip. "Maybe a three."

With my eyes on hers, I lower my face once more and wrap my lips around her clit as my fingers slide back inside her, and her jaw drops, watching me as I eat her gorgeous cunt.

"Yes," she whispers, her eyes half closing. "Fuck yes. Jesus, you're good at that."

I crook my fingers, and she moans, and then she's exploding against my lips, falling apart so beautifully, it makes me feral to get inside her.

When her muscles start to relax, I kiss her inner

thighs and then work my way back up to her chest and then her lips, and kiss her deeply, brushing my tongue against hers so she can taste herself.

"Mmm," she breathes against my lips. "Need you inside me, babe."

"I want that too, but baby, I'm so afraid of hurting your leg."

She frames my face and smiles up at me. "You could *never*—"

"You make me lose myself, and all I want to do is pound into you, smack your ass, pull your hair, and remind you exactly who you belong to. I want to *ruin* you."

She licks her lips. "Hell to the yes. You have full consent for that."

"But I can't do it until you're healed. And I'm afraid I'll lose control and hurt you."

"Never." She shakes her head, and her fingertips drift up and down my arms. "You're the calm, remember? You take away the chaos."

God, I couldn't love her more than I do right now.

"Come on." I push myself off the bed, then help her to her feet, pulling her to the bathroom and boosting her up onto the counter.

"Brace your foot here." I show her where to plant her foot on the wall next to me, and she does, then nods. "Good?"

"Good."

Notching the head of my cock against her, I push inside and reach over to brace myself on the mirror while I move gently in and out of her.

373

"Oh God, yes," she moans as she clings to me. "Harder."

"Wild—"

"*Harder*. Please."

I can't say no to her. I move faster, pushing deeper and harder, but am still careful not to jostle her leg, and she watches me with those big blue eyes.

"Is this what you need, Juliet?"

"Yes. God, yes."

She reaches between us and pushes her fingers against her clit, and she clenches around me like a fucking vise.

"Fuck. You're going to make me come, baby. Jesus Christ, look at how well you take this cock."

She's starting to quiver, her hand moves faster, and as she falls over the edge, I tumble with her, groaning as I come inside her, filling her so full that it spills out around my cock.

"Pain?" I can barely talk, I'm breathing so hard, but I have to check in with her.

"What pain?"

I smile and lean in to kiss her forehead.

"I love you. You're so fucking badass."

"I'm so much stronger with you," she says, brushing her fingers down my cheek. "Now, clean us up so we can go back to snuggling."

"Yes, ma'am."

Chapter Thirty-Three

JULIET

"Can we just do this every day? Sex and cuddles? Like why do we have to work? Let's retire now so we can actually enjoy it, you know?" We're back on the couch, and I'm totally clinging to my man, running my hand over his chest.

"I'm down for that," Brooks replies. "I mean, we'll eventually go broke, but we can live on love."

I smirk, and his fingers ghost over the shell of my ear, making me shiver.

"I'm donating the rest of Justin's money."

His eyebrows climb in surprise, but he's quiet, letting me continue.

"You never said anything before about being mad or not wanting to use the money that I inherited for the house, or for our lifestyle, but I could tell that you didn't love the idea."

"I'd rather not use anything that came from him," he admits. He's not angry, but he stiffened up a bit, and I don't like that.

"I've always felt the same way," I reply with a sigh. "I hated using that money. Well, not the money from the sale of the house. I had no problem using that to start my business. To buy the building and get everything going. But the cash? It always gave me the icks. Connor had a good point when he said that money isn't personal, and I was grateful that I had it for the repairs on the building after the flood. I was able to pay my staff, so they didn't have to find other jobs while we were closed."

"Then keep the money, baby."

I press my lips together, watching him. "I'm going to keep one million in an account specifically for the business. In case I have a down year or another catastrophe happens. Things like that."

"For emergencies," he says.

"Yeah. I like the idea of having a cushion. But honestly, I make enough at the restaurant to draw a decent wage for myself. I don't need his money."

"I make good money, too, you know. And we're married, so my money is your money."

"That's just it. We do so well together. Just you and me. I don't want to bring what he left me into our relationship. He doesn't deserve that. He wasn't kind to you. Hell, he wasn't nice to *me*. And he would go absolutely ballistic if he knew that I planned to give the money to a women's shelter for domestic violence victims in Seattle."

I grin up at him.

"One last fuck off to him, then?" Brooks asks.

"It's a perk. But also, that money would just sit because I don't plan to spend it. It should do some good somewhere. I need you to know that I choose *you* and your feelings, what you need, always. You're my priority. Our beautiful life together is my priority."

He's watching me with so much emotion running through those dark eyes, and then he's framing my face and kissing the hell out of me.

"I love you," I tell him.

"I love you, too."

Suddenly, the doorbell rings, and Brooks kisses my forehead before he stands to answer it. I crane my neck around to see who it is, surprised when I see Chad standing there.

"Hi, Brooks," Chad says, and then smiles over at me. "Sorry to interrupt you both at home, but Jules and I have been playing phone tag, and I was in the neighborhood."

"Come in," Brooks says, gesturing him inside. "Have a seat. Do you need anything?"

"No, thanks. How are you feeling, Jules?"

"I'm getting there," I tell him with a smile. "Are you going out with Ava tonight?"

"Yeah, I'm picking her up from work in a bit, but I thought I'd stop here first. I have news."

I lean forward, and Brooks sits next to me, taking my hand.

"You know, it's interesting," I say as a thought occurs to me. "I just realized that I haven't heard from Nadine in a couple of weeks. All of the emails just stopped. I've been so busy with reopening the restaurant, and then the accident and everything going on, that I didn't think about it. The restraining order must have worked."

"That's the thing," Chad says, leaning forward and

frowning. "There hasn't been a restraining order. Jules, did you ever meet this Nadine Smith in person?"

"No. I didn't have a funeral for Justin, and there was never a reason to meet her. Daniel said I didn't have to."

He nods slowly. "But you *did* meet Daniel in person?"

"Sure, of course. Several times throughout the years. He and Justin would drift apart and then come back together, the way some friends do. You know, you get busy with stuff, and don't talk to your friend for a while, and then you're like, 'Hey! We should play golf,' or whatever."

Chad's nodding again.

"What's going on, Chad?" Brooks asks.

"Well, after the state failed to send me any information on a trust set up for Nadine, I called them and was informed that no trust exists. At least, not in the state of Washington."

My mouth drops. "Uh, but—"

"Then I did some digging in the bank account you gave me information on. The one that was set up for this. It's not a trust account either. It's just a regular checking account, but it only has your name on it."

"I don't understand."

"Frankly, it's a fucking mess," Chad says.

"Are you saying that *Nadine* doesn't exist?" Brooks asks.

"She does exist," I counter. "Justin wrote all about her in the journals I found. He was OCD about writing everything down. His manipulation of me, how he got me to marry him, and then the women he screwed around with. Nadine's name was listed."

"Well, she may exist somewhere, and he might have fooled around with her, but he never left her any money as far as I can tell," Chad replies, and all I can do is stare at him. "I suspect that Daniel was committing a *huge* amount of fraud by falsifying the trust, making you sign papers that weren't actually Justin's wishes, and taking you for a ride. He couldn't access Justin's money directly because his name wasn't on any of the accounts, but *you* could. So he made up a false trust and was getting a shit ton of money from you every month."

"I'm going to fucking *ruin* him," Brooks growls next to me.

"He should be arrested," I add. "Jesus, he should be in jail for this."

That man made my life a living fucking hell!

"That's the other thing, Jules." Chad clears his throat and then pulls his hand down his face. "When I started making inquiries about the trust and requested information from him, Daniel must have panicked because just a few days later, he was found dead in his office."

Brooks's arm immediately wraps around me, and I close my eyes.

Shit.

Shit.

"That's why I haven't heard from *Nadine*."

"Yeah." I open my eyes and see Chad nodding. "That's why. It was all a scam, Jules. You were never the trustee for your late husband's mistress. And the fact that

Daniel made you feel that, and live it, is so despicable, I can't even. I'm sorry."

I shake my head and let all of this news soak in.

I don't have to pay Nadine another dime.

Daniel might have been a bigger piece of shit than Justin.

"I hate that he killed himself." I clear my suddenly tight throat. "Because he should have paid for what he did. He should have owned up to it."

"I agree," Chad says, and Brooks squeezes my shoulder.

"But also, this all means that I'm free from that nightmare."

A smile spreads over Chad's face. "You're right. The money in that account is yours. No one is going to abuse or manipulate you again."

"No, they won't," Brooks agrees.

"Chad, if I want to gift the majority of all of the money to a charity, or non-profit, do I need an attorney for that?"

His eyebrows climb into his hairline.

"No, you just need a checkbook or a wire transfer."

I nod, and then Brooks helps me stand, and I cross over to shake Chad's hand.

"Thank you for all of your work. Just send me a bill—"

"Nah, this one was on the house. This might be my most interesting case to date. And I hate that he fucked with you like that. You've been through enough. Just enjoy your life, Jules."

He shakes Brooks's hand, and then he lets himself

out. Brooks and I sit down again, cuddled up together in the silence.

"I don't know what to say," I whisper.

"How do you feel?" he asks.

"Oh, my leg is—"

"No, baby. How's your heart doing?"

I let out a breath and look up at him. "It feels lighter. I hate how Daniel chose to go out. You know that."

"I know. And I'm sorry." He kisses my forehead.

"But it's a relief to know that it's over. It's time to move on, Brooks. With you. I want our family. Our big, loud, crazy family. And I want babies. I want to watch our kids play in our backyard and go camping at the river. I'm where I'm supposed to be, right by your side."

"You're right where you belong, Wildfire. And we're going to have all of that and more."

"I can't wait."

Epilogue

BROOKS

Five Years Later

"They'll be here in thirty minutes," Jules reminds me as she rushes by with Michaela on her hip. The fourteen-month-old is crying because we finally took the binkie away despite the fact that she cries nonstop without it, and we've been up for three nights in a row with her.

We've vowed to stay strong.

God, I want to give her that binkie.

"Come here, baby girl." I hold my hands out, and the baby leans into me, then tucks her face in my neck, still whimpering pitifully. "We took her best friend away."

"She's just good at manipulating you," Jules replies with a smirk. "She was fine until you walked in here. Did you buy the ice?"

"Yeah, I got it and dumped it in the coolers." I kiss

my daughter's head and then lean over to kiss my wife's lips and smell the white chocolate mocha on her breath. "You got a coffee without me?"

"I'm sorry, I'm dead on my feet." She lowers her voice. "I'll make it up to you later."

"Yeah, Wildfire, you freaking will."

"When is Uncle Bridger coming?" Caden, our four-year-old, demands as he runs into the kitchen. "He's bringing a fire truck."

"Uh, buddy, I don't think he is." I frown down at my son as he reaches for a cookie, side-eyeing his mom.

"He said he would," Caden replies with a shrug. "Bryce and I are gonna play on the climbing wall today."

"Oh good, someone will leave here with a broken arm," Jules mutters. "Why don't you play in the sandbox?"

"Because the neighbor's cat poops in it."

Her eyes shoot to mine in horror, and I can't help but laugh.

"I cleaned it out. It's fine. We forgot to cover it over the weekend before we went camping."

"I don't have time to think about poopy sand. I have to get this salad made."

"I thought you brought home a crap ton of food from the restaurant?" My woman's business has grown a ton in the past five years, adding on more staff and another baker, and I couldn't be prouder of her.

"I did, but Harper's pregnant again, and she needs this salad. I forgot to get it from the restaurant earlier."

"You're a really good sister-in-law," I murmur in her ear before I kiss her cheek.

Before I can blink, the house and backyard start to fill up with family. We're hosting a cookout at our big house on the corner, which has been finished for three years now. It took us a while to get it exactly the way we wanted it, but I'd say it's just about perfect.

"What's up, buttercup?" Michaela squeals, her little legs pumping as Blake grins at her over my shoulder. "Come here, gorgeous. Come hang out with me."

"He's such a ladies' man," Harper says, shaking her head. Then her eyes go round when she sees Jules making her salad. "Oh my God, you're my favorite sister-in-law."

"I heard that," Billie says as she swings through, then kisses Michaela's cheek.

I *love* seeing my siblings with my kids. I love being with *their* kids.

Billie has three of them already. It took her a while to get pregnant that first time, and then it seemed she was pregnant every time Connor just looked at her sideways. With Bridger's two, Beckett's daughter, who never stops dancing, and Blake's one with one on the way, we're a full house.

My parents are thrilled with ten grandkids.

Ten grandkids.

I shake my head and then grin and open my arms when Birdie walks into the house and straight to me.

She's still my special girl, even if she is twelve.

"Uncle Brooks?" she whispers, pulling me away from everyone else.

"Yes, peanut?"

"I have a boyfriend."

"I. Will. Kill. Him."

She dissolves into laughter, making me glare at her and cross my arms over my chest. This is an ongoing joke we have running, but someday, she won't be joking.

And then, I really will likely go to jail for homicide.

The kids filter outside to play on the structure my brothers and I built last year, and as I stand on the patio watching them, Jules joins me and slides her hand into mine.

"This was the dream," she says and laughs at Beckett and Skyla's daughter, Ashling, doing pirouettes across the grass as Belle turns cartwheels. "This is what we wanted all along."

I glance around at all of the kids running around. At Birdie sitting at the table, her nose in her phone, and then my siblings with their spouses, and my parents, each with a baby on their hip. They're smiling so big, it makes my chest catch.

And then I gaze down into my wife's gorgeous blue eyes. My soulmate. The one who fits me in every way, and I bend over to kiss the top of her head.

"We did this together," I murmur so only she can hear. "You and me, Wildfire. It was worth waiting for."

"You know, I've been thinking."

I lift an eyebrow as she smiles up at me with fire in her eyes. "What's going on in that gorgeous head of yours?"

"Maybe we should give the kids a baby brother or sister."

Blinking rapidly, I feel the blood leech out of my face.

"Baby, are you—"

"Yeah. Is that okay? Are we too old? Shit, we're gonna be tired forever."

"It's more than okay." I pull her against me and tip her chin up so I can nibble her lips. "We're not *that* old, and we may be tired, but we're damn happy."

"The happiest." She puckers, waiting for me to kiss her again. "Let's go tell the others."

That's the end of the Blackwells in Montana series, but if you'd like to go all the way back to the beginning of the Bitterroot Valley world, you can start with Wild for You here: https://www.kristenprobyauthor.com/wild-for-you

Next, we're going to the Triple Creek Ranch in Safe Haven, the first in a new series. You can check it out here: https://amzn.to/4gkydGd

Turn the page for a preview of Safe Haven:

Safe Haven Preview

RYKER

Chapter One

"That's right, motherfucker! Try that shit again, and I'll pound your ugly face into the boards!"

I laugh at Mac, my enforcer, and shake my head at him. Mac's an animal, which is good, given that it's his whole job to either pick fights or end them.

He's damn good at his job.

"Come on, Cap, we got this," Mac says to me as we skate to the bench. "One more period, and we can win this. We're only down by two."

We're not gonna win this.

It's the last game for us in this season. I know it. Coach knows it. Fuck, even the fans know it.

We've won the last two Stanley Cups in a row, but this year has been a rebuilding year since we lost some players after the last season and recruited some rookies, and frankly, I'm surprised we made it this far into the playoffs.

It was a mediocre season.

And that's okay. Everyone has them. I have no complaints.

But this is the last game for the Seattle Blizzard this year.

"James!" Coach flags me down, and I walk over to him.

"One more period," he says, echoing Mac's words. "Tie us up, at least."

"I'll do my best."

"You *are* the best," he reminds me and slaps me on the back. "Let's do this!"

I was the best.

For fifteen years, I've been known as *the phenom*. The best of the best. The GOAT. Better than Gretzky, having smashed his record for scoring in one season, and total scores in a career, and I've played for five years *less* than that legend.

He's also a friend and mentor of mine.

But am I *still* the best? Fuck no.

I'm thirty-five.

I've been beating my body up my whole goddamn life.

I'm tired.

But for the next twenty minutes on the ice, I'll fake it till I make it. No cringing when my knees feel like they're exploding. There is no pain. There is no messing up.

But shit, it's so much harder now than it was ten years ago. Even *five* years ago.

I do manage to score twice, much to the delight of

the fans and my teammates, but so does the opposing team, and when it's all said and done, we lose, 4–2.

"James!" Dozens of reporters shout my name as I make my way to the locker room, and I stop to give interviews.

"What happened out there, Cap?"

Some of them call me Cap because I've been the captain of the team for ten years. I was recruited by Seattle my rookie year, and I've been lucky enough to stay here my whole career.

Aside from Montana, Seattle is my home.

"Hey, Mike." I swipe my forearm over my sweaty forehead and tip my head down so I can hear the shorter man ask me questions for the camera. The hallway leading to the locker room is loud as hell.

"What happened out there, Cap? Do you think there was anything you could have done to change how this one ended?"

I want to roll my eyes, but I simply shake my head. "You know, our guys really showed up tonight. Spencer had some amazing saves in the goalie box. I don't think we have anything to be ashamed of, and a great foundation for next year."

"So you think you'll still be in Seattle next year, with you being a free agent after this game?" Mike asks, his eyes shrewd.

Fuck you, Mike.

"Only God and my agent know that for sure." I smile at the camera, wink for Willow the way I always have, and turn to leave.

No more interviews tonight.

The locker room is somber, but not as sad as it gets if we lose during the Cup. *That* sucks ass. Tonight, we're disappointed, even though we saw it coming.

But I'm the captain, so it's my job to say a few words to lift their spirits.

"Listen up," I begin, getting everyone's attention. "I'm proud of every single one of you. You all worked hard this season. We knew that there would be a learning curve this year, and there's nothing wrong with that. You played your asses off out there tonight."

"Not hard enough," Mac mutters, and I reach out to pat him on the shoulder.

"You spent more time in the penalty box than on the ice," I remind him with a grin. "No pouting tonight. We made it into the second round of the playoffs, and that's nothing to be ashamed of. Now, we rest for a bit before we get back at it."

For me, that downtime will take place in Montana, with my dad and the animals, breathing in fresh air and listening to nothing but quiet. I need that.

But first, we're going on a trip as a team. The reservations, the plane, *everything* has been on standby to whisk us away whenever we're finished with the season. Whether that was tonight or after the Stanley Cup, we're going somewhere as a team.

Somewhere fucking warm.

With sand, sun, and hopefully plenty of scantily clad women. I haven't gotten laid in far too fucking long.

"But first, Bora-Bora!" Spencer calls out, and I grin at him.

"Damn right. We leave first thing, so don't get so

drunk tonight that you pass out and miss the flight. We won't wait for your stupid ass."

Against a backdrop of snickers and smiles, I walk over to my locker and start to strip down to hit the shower. Now that the adrenaline from the game is over, my knees ache. My back is stiff.

I feel eighty.

As I joke with the guys—always keeping my hockey-star mask on—I get showered and then pull on my suit and tie.

The guys give me shit for always dressing up for game day, but it's habit. It's my image. Ray—or Dad, as I've called him since I was sixteen—always says that you need to show the world who you are.

I'm not a slob. I'm a professional, elite athlete, and I fucking look like it.

Reaching for my phone, I frown when the screen lights up and I see that I've missed ten calls and a shit ton of texts during the game.

Fuck.

Still frowning, I see the calls were from Gideon. Most of the texts, too, except for a couple from Willow. They started coming in when we were still warming up for the game, almost four hours ago.

> Willow: I know you're playing but you need to call me ASAP.

> Willow: Seriously, I'm so sorry, but we need you.

Gideon: I'm getting on a flight home
now. Call me, bro.

My stomach is in knots, dread sitting heavy on my chest, as I immediately dial Gideon's number, but it goes straight to voicemail.

He's in the air. The flight from Washington, DC, to Montana is a long one, but he should be almost there by now.

I dial Willow's number, and she picks up right away.

"Ry!" I hear the tears in her voice, and I have to sit down. My chest aches. My breaths are already coming fast. *Jesus, what is going on at home?* "Oh, Ry, I'm so sorry. I know you're playing—"

"I'm never too busy for you, and you know it, Wills. What's wrong? Breathe for me, and tell me what's going on."

She pauses, and I hear her take a long breath.

"It's Ray." *No.* Goddamn it. "It's not good, Ryker."

"Is he still alive?"

"For now, but you need to get here as soon as you can."

"I'm on my way. I'll be there in three hours."

"Come straight to the hospital, okay? Gideon will be here by then, and I'll tell you everything when you get here."

"Three hours. Deep breaths, honey. We're coming. We'll take care of everything."

"Oh, God." She lets out a choked sob, and I want nothing more than to be able to teleport myself there, to be there for them.

"I'll see you soon."

"Okay. Thanks, Ry."

She hangs up, and I immediately make some calls, arranging for the team private jet to take me home, and then I turn to the guys.

They're already watching me with somber faces.

"How much did you hear?"

"Enough," Mac says. "Go home, Cap. We can postpone Bora-Bora."

"No, you guys go and have fun. You've earned it."

"Keep us posted, yeah?" Spencer says, and I nod as I swallow hard.

Fuck. I need to get home.

"Thanks, guys."

***

I hate hospitals. I've spent my fair share in them after particularly rough injuries on the ice, but mostly I despise them because it was a place like this where I said goodbye to my mom after the last asshole she was with beat her so severely, it killed her.

I always think of her when I have to be in a hospital. I know she would hate that, but I can't help it.

I held her hand in places like this more times than I could count, and one day, she didn't get to go home with me.

"Ry!"

I look up to find Willow rushing down the hallway, her pretty face ravaged from tears, and then she's hugging me, holding on tight as I stare over her shoulder at Gideon, who walks toward us, his face grim. We're both in suits. We look like we're late for a wedding.

"Am I too late?" *God, is that my voice?*

"No," Gideon says, and when Willow eases back, he pulls me in for a hug. "But you need to get in there."

"You two go together," Willow says.

I slip my hand in hers and link our fingers, our palms pressed together. "You come with us."

She nods and holds on to me tight. Willow has been my best friend since I was fifteen. Since she managed to make Gideon and me brothers rather than enemies. We're the Three Amigos.

These two are my best friends. The people I can count on, ride or die, no matter what.

Having Gideon next to me and Willow's hand in mine is the only thing keeping me from losing my shit right now.

We walk into a dim room, where Ray, the only father I've ever known, is lying on the bed. He's hooked up to monitors, and he's sleeping. He's lost all his color. I've never seen him so gray.

"What happened?" I ask, my voice a ragged whisper. *Christ. That's my dad.*

"Stroke," Gideon says. "We'll go over it all later. It doesn't matter now."

No, I suppose it doesn't.

I cross to him and sit in the chair beside the bed, then take his hand in mine and bring the back of it to my lips. Since that day that we stepped foot on the Triple Creek Ranch all those years ago, this man has been bigger than life itself. Strong. Tall. Proud.

But then we lost Mama two years ago, and it was as though Dad died with her.

I hardly recognize the man lying in this bed.

"Hey, Dad," I say, squeezing his hand. To my surprise, his eyes flutter open, and he looks at me, and it's a hit to the solar plexus. *I love him so much.* "If you wanted to get me to come home, you didn't have to be so dramatic about it."

Humor flickers in his eyes, but he doesn't say anything.

"He can't talk," Willow whispers.

"I'm here, too, Dad," Gideon says, joining me, and Dad's gaze shifts to my brother.

None of us are related by blood, but we're linked by something far more important. Years of respect and laughter. Hard work. And the devotion we all had for the love of his life.

Dad's eyes fill with tears. I can tell that he wants to say something, and he's frustrated, but he's also so weak and tired.

"We know," I assure him, and kiss the back of his hand again. Gideon lays his hand on Dad's shoulder and gives it a gentle squeeze.

"We love you, too, Dad," Gideon says.

"Thank you." I swallow the tears down. "Thank you for everything you did for us. For giving us Mom, and the ranch, and Willow. Hell, for giving us a *life.*"

A tear falls from Dad's eye, and Gideon brushes it away.

"Hey," Gideon says, his gruff voice soft. "You go to Mom. We know you've been missing her like crazy."

"Just tell her we love her," I add, my own tears falling from my eyes.

"I love you too," Willow adds, leaning over so he can see her. "So, so much. Please kiss Aunt Deb for me, Uncle Ray."

Christ.

"We've got this," Gideon says.

Dad looks at each of us once more, and then he closes his eyes and sighs, and the machine makes a static, beeping noise, signaling that there is no heartbeat.

Dad's gone.

If you'd like more *Safe Haven*, you can get all the details here: https://amzn.to/4gkydGd

Newsletter Sign Up

I hope you enjoyed reading this story as much as I enjoyed writing it! For upcoming book news, be sure to join my newsletter! I promise I will only send you news-filled mail, and none of the spam. You can sign up here:

https://mailchi.mp/kristenproby.com/newsletter-sign-up

Also by Kristen Proby:

Other Books by Kristen Proby

The Wilds of Montana Series
Wild for You - Remington & Erin
Chasing Wild - Chase & Summer
Wildest Dreams - Ryan & Polly
On the Wild Side - Brady & Abbi
She's a Wild One - Holden & Millie

The Blackwells of Montana
When We Burn - Bridger & Dani
When We Break - Beckett & Skyla
Where We Bloom - Connor & Billie
When You Blush - Blake & Harper
Where You Belong - Brooks & Juliet

Get more information on the series here: https://
www.kristenprobyauthor.com/the-wilds-of-montana

Dance With Me Levi & Starla
You Belong With Me - Archer & Elena
Dream With Me - Kane & Anastasia
Imagine With Me - Shawn & Lexi
Escape With Me - Keegan & Isabella
Flirt With Me - Hunter & Maeve
Take a Chance With Me - Cameron & Maggie

Check out the full series here: https://www.
kristenprobyauthor.com/with-me-in-seattle

The Big Sky Universe

Love Under the Big Sky
Loving Cara
Seducing Lauren
Falling for Jillian
Saving Grace

The Big Sky
Charming Hannah
Kissing Jenna
Waiting for Willa
Soaring With Fallon

Big Sky Royal
Enchanting Sebastian
Enticing Liam
Taunting Callum

Heroes of Big Sky

Honor
Courage
Shelter

Check out the full Big Sky universe here: https://
www.kristenprobyauthor.com/under-the-big-sky

Bayou Magic

Shadows
Spells
Serendipity

Check out the full series here: https://www.
kristenprobyauthor.com/bayou-magic

The Curse of the Blood Moon Series

Hallows End
Cauldrons Call
Salems Song

The Romancing Manhattan Series

All the Way
All it Takes
After All

Check out the full series here: https://www.
kristenprobyauthor.com/romancing-manhattan

The Boudreaux Series

Easy Love
Easy Charm
Easy Melody
Easy Kisses
Easy Magic
Easy Fortune
Easy Nights

Check out the full series here: https://www.
kristenprobyauthor.com/boudreaux

The Fusion Series

Listen to Me
Close to You
Blush for Me
The Beauty of Us
Savor You

Check out the full series here: https://www.
kristenprobyauthor.com/fusion

About the Author

Kristen Proby is a *New York Times*, *USA Today*, and *Wall Street Journal* bestselling author of over ninety published titles. She debuted in 2012, captivating fans with spicy contemporary romance about families and friends with plenty of swoony love. She also writes paranormal romance and suggests you keep the lights on while reading them.

When not under deadline, Kristen enjoys spending time with her husband and their fur babies, riding her bike, relaxing with embroidery, trying her hand at painting, and, of course, enjoying her beautiful home in the mountains of Montana.